BROKEN NUMBERS

The Aleph Null Chronicles: Book Three

A Dark Fantasy Novel

DEAN FRANK LAPPI

"Trith. Circle. Zranh. Raith. Death."

– from **The Black Numbers** *manuscript*

macroscian
books

Cover Design by Dean Frank Lappi
Original artwork by Sandaboy, royalty free and licensed from Dreamstime.com.

ISBN-13: **978-0-9891726-5-3**

Published by **macroscian books**

An imprint of **Dean Frank Lappi Publishing**

Dedication

Mom, I will miss you every day of my life.

1934-2015

To My Editor

A sincere thank you to Erica Anderson — master editor, proofreader and story arc consultant. You made this book better in every way.

Acknowledgements

To Pam, thank you for being such a fantastic beta reader for this book. Your feedback was exceptional.

To my colleagues at Myrddin Publishing, thank you for your excellent feedback on the map and cover.

To Lisa Danforth, thank you for your help in finding continuity issues.

To Wayne, as always, thanks for being an early reader.

To my family, friends and fans who always support my work, you are the best.

Other books by DEAN FRANK LAPPI

BLACK NUMBERS

The Aleph Null Chronicles: Book One (Now Available)

BLOOD NUMBERS

The Aleph Null Chronicles: Book Two (Now Available)

BEYOND NUMBERS

The Aleph Null Chronicles: Book Four (Coming Soon)

Visit **http://www.deanlappi.com** for the latest news and updates on books and news by Dean Frank Lappi

A Note From the Author

The mathematics in this series were intentionally described without going into any mathematical depth because I wanted them to be conceptual, a way to explain magic in a more visually spectacular, less mathematically precise way. I felt the story transcended the math. Secondarily, I imagined most readers were not mathematicians. My apologies to any mathematicians who may read this and be disappointed. I hope the story itself pulls you in and the visual way I describe maths is just as rewarding and enjoyable as it would be had I concentrated on pure mathematical concepts.

Audience

While Broken Numbers is a traditional fantasy novel in most ways, it has adult-oriented themes not suitable for children under the age of 17, including sexuality and scenes of sexual-based violence. Parental review is recommended before letting your child read it.

CONTENTS

Prologue

The Korpor pulled its long claws from the chest of its prey and stared at the red blood dripping from them, each globule hanging thickly for a moment before falling to the ground. It looked down at the human male and closed its nose slits in disgust at the smell emanating from the body covered in filthy black furs. The Korper lifted its head to scan the rocky shoreline of the giant lake that it had been following but didn't see any more humans in the area so it kicked the crude spear from the outstretched hand of the lone hunter and continued making its way along the shore. It soon came upon the trunk of an ancient tree that had washed up onto the rocky beach long ago, its wood as smooth and gray as the Korpor's own face. It leapt over the tree and absently raked its claws along the hard wood as it passed, creating four deep gouges, and landing lightly on the other side, it broke into a run again. As it ran, the Korpor relived the final confrontation with the Aleph Null in the obelisk clearing of the Srithian Wood that had led it to this place now.

> The Korpor watched in disbelief as the Black Robe was stabbed by the Aleph Null's mother and then impaled by the Vringe's sword before stumbling through his mathematical portal and escaping. The Korpor prepared itself to make one final attempt to capture the Aleph Null but before it could move, it heard the distant approach of the colossal creature that oozed rotten pus, and icy fear coursed through its body as it remembered the last time it had faced the creature in battle and barely escaped with its life. There were too many powerful forces surrounding the Aleph Null, and the Korpor accepted that all was lost. So it ran away, something it had only done once before, and made its escape from the obelisk clearing, abandoning the Aleph Null after spending so much effort to finally get its grasp on him.
>
> It quickly retraced its route through the tunnels of the Kulkraken mountains and exited them into a snowstorm that raged down the mountain face. As it stepped into the blowing snow, its connection with the Aleph Null shattered, sending intense pain through every nerve fiber in its body. The Korpor fell to its knees in the deep snow, tilted its head back, and screamed until it could no longer make a sound. When the pain had finally faded, it had desperately tried to reestablish the link to the Aleph Null but there had simply been nothing there.
>
> The Aleph Null no longer existed.
>
> The only explanation was that the Aleph Null had been killed by the giant creature. With a guttural cry of loss, the Korpor realized its only reason for existence was now gone.
>
> The Korpor continued down the mountain until it came to the impossibly tall cliffs. Half way down the chimney shaft it briefly considered retracting its claws and letting itself fall to end its misery, but it slowly made its way down the remainder of

the shaft instead. Once at the bottom, it turned to the west and took off at a run, having no particular destination in mind and not caring.

Just after sunrise on the second day it came to a giant body of water and gazed out across the sun-streaked surface. A light breeze caused the water to ripple, sending thousands of sparks of light in different directions that made the water look alive.

The Korpor came out of its thoughts when its foot landed on a stone that shifted under its weight, making it stumble mid-run. It caught its balance and slowed to a walk and then sat down heavily on the rocky shore. It tilted its head back and closed its huge blue eyes to let the sun warm its face, then lay back on the rocks with a sigh, feeling sleep creeping up on it, sleep that had been tantalizingly close for days but had remained stubbornly out of reach. It felt consciousness slipping away to the soft sounds of waves lapping against the rocky shore.

The Black Robe's dark and menacing voice suddenly boomed in its mind, the third time he had tried to contact the Korpor since the events of the Srithian Wood. Wincing, the Korpor quickly shut down the communication. It hadn't been surprised the Black Robe had survived the Srithian Wood, but it had no desire to speak with him at this time, if ever again.

The Korper wearily stood up and stretched its back, feeling its bones popping as it did. Sleep would not come this day, so it turned and started running along the shoreline again. It traveled like this for almost two more days until it reached the west side of the lake and saw the forbidding presence of the Kuldragg Forest looming on the horizon, a place so immense and dark that not even the Korpor had ever fully explored it. It would make the ideal place to collect its thoughts, a place where even the dark tendrils of the Black Robe's mind could be ignored. The Korpor left the shoreline of the lake and arrived at the edge of the forest just as the sun disappeared behind the trees.

The forest was like a wall of darkness stretching out in both directions as far as it could see. The Korpor tilted its head back to gaze at the almost impossibly tall trees, trees that were black of bark and covered with boils of sap, many of which had burst, causing sticky liquid to slowly ran down the tree trunks, giving off a rotten smell that made the Korpor close its nose slits in disgust.

The Korpor entered the gloom of the Kuldragg forest and soon found itself lost in thought, at home in the darkness and solitude of the forest. For the first time in its long life it did not know what to do next. Its only purpose had been to search for the Aleph Null, something it had done with singular focus for thousands of years, proofing thousands of young women and men but never finding the one that filled it with the orgasmic pleasure that was the true indicator of the Aleph Null. When it had finally found Sid, the pleasure that had coursed through the Korpor had been greater than it had ever imagined, and that pleasure had increased ten fold when it had consummated the Proofing and then Ringed Sid, creating the ultimate physical and psychosexual bond between them. The Korpor had been complete for the first time in its long life.

Consumed by its thoughts, the impact of something heavy slamming into its back caught the Korpor by surprise and drove it to the ground. It heaved up against the weight of the writhing mass that savagely clawed into its sides, then pain erupted from its shoulder as teeth sank into it. The Korpor roared savagely and reached back, grabbed the head of the creature and twisted to the right, snapping its neck with a loud crack. The Korpor let the creature drop to the ground with a thud and was surprised to see it was an Omthagrod, the huge body covered in red and brown fur, its head turned at a negative angle, showing a long wolf-like snout and a slack mouth filled with sharp yellow teeth.

The Korpor slowly turned, snarling deeply as it glared at a second Omthagrod that crouched a few paces away, saliva hanging from its mouth as it prepared to leap. The animal looked into the Korpor's eyes and instantly fell forward, howling in pain as it flopped around on the ground. The Korpor stepped forward and plunged its claws into the side of the creature's head, puncturing the bone as if it were made of parchment. It turned to stare at the remaining four Omthagrod while squeezing its fist, crushing the skull of the one it held. The Korper pulled its claws from the Omthagrod's head, brains leaking out as it did so, and the creature twitched even in death.

The remaining Omthagrod bellowed in pain from the Korpor's glare and stumbled back into the darkness of the trees before turning and loping away. The Korpor listened until it was sure they were not coming back, debating whether or not to chase them. Its heart beat quickly and it smiled as it retracted its claws. This little battle was just what it had needed to bring itself out of its dark thoughts.

The Korper licked its wounds and they healed almost immediately, but it could not reach the entire gash on his shoulder so it opened its mouth, filled its palm with saliva, then carefully reached back and rubbed the viscous liquid into the ugly wound. The flesh fused together and the pain disappeared almost immediately.

The Korpor stretched the mighty muscles in its back, its joints cracking loudly, then looked down at the dead Omthagrod at its feet. The Korper realized it was very hungry, so it reached down and lifted the arm of the dead Omthagrod with one paw, swiped quickly with the claws of its other paw and severed the arm with a spray of blood. It held the furry limb up to its mouth but closed its nose slits at the terrible stench and dropped the arm in distaste.

Casting out its senses for other animals, the Korpor heard the distant footfalls of a deer and saliva dripped from its mouth in anticipation of the sweet flesh. It took off at a fast run, cutting between trees without slowing down, yet moving almost silently. It inhaled the sweet air and an ugly smile grew on its face as it spotted the small mule deer eating leaves from a bush. The Korpor collided with the animal, rammed its claws into the deer's side and pulled out its still beating heart. The Korpor studied the organ briefly before raising its arm and slowly crushing it, letting the warm blood trickle into its mouth. Energy flowed into is body, but the joy of the kill quickly faded away as it thought of the dead Aleph Null.

The Korpor threw the crushed heart to the ground and raised its head to the sky and howled, the sound lonely and filled with anguish.

Chapter 1

Sid looked up at the side of the cliff where the trail led from the Miq forest floor of the Srithian Wood up to the tunnel opening from which they had originally emerged after passing through the mountain only the previous day. His eyes watered as he thought of all that had happened in just one short day, of how much had been lost – his mother, his good friend Richard, thirteen of the mysterious Haissen, and his power of Numbers.

It was late morning and they had all just made the decision to travel to the Trith Nation after Sid had found the secret message in the Black Manuscript: *Trith, Circle, Zranh, Raith,* and *Death*. He didn't yet know what the words meant, but if he were going to defeat Tris, he had to find a way to get his power of Numbers back.

They had made their way through the Miq forest from the obelisk clearing, everyone happy to leave the site of the epic battles they had just endured. Sid glanced at Crowdal, Agnes, Writhgarth, Tulman, and Nik, surprised and thankful to have such loyal friends. He then turned in a small circle to look at the thirteen remaining Haissen, a full murder who surrounded the group protectively. They had fully dedicated themselves to Sid's safety after he had cured them of their disease and in doing so, fulfilled a millennia-old prophecy.

Sid subconsciously reached for his Numbers only to be reminded they were no longer inside of him. Their absence felt like a gaping hole in his mind. The Unnamed One had ripped Sid's power of Numbers from him just as he had used the awesome power of Black Numbers to cast it into the obelisk, imprisoning it for eternity. Sid looked over his shoulder and saw the thin thread of power reaching from him back to the obelisk, so he still had hope he could get his power of Numbers back. He owed it to his mother, who had sacrificed her life to give him the chance to defeat those who tried to do him and his friends harm.

Sid's throat constricted and he blinked back more tears as he thought of his mother, who he believed had died when he was six years old, but had actually been kidnapped by the Oblate and held prisoner for the past ten years. They had been reunited only briefly before being torn apart again, this time forever.

Writhgarth coughed and spit to his side as he glared at the trail leading up the rock wall of the cliff. "I don't look forward to passing through the tunnels inside that mountain again. More importantly, I don't want to climb down that cursed chimney shaft in the cliff on the other side."

Sid came out of his thoughts and realized Writhgarth was right. He had forgotten about the chimney shaft and didn't see any way they could all make it down alive. They had barely survived climbing the shaft, and going down would be twice as dangerous because they could easily slip as they put their weight onto any of the hundreds of shallow grooves carved into the rock.

Sid ran a hand through his hair and nodded to Writhgarth, "I agree, I think we need to find another way."

Crowdal sighed and took off his pack, sat down gingerly and put a hand to his left side where the Masteen Vorn Maghuur had broken his ribs. Crowdal's face was bruised and purple from the powerful punches he had taken from the Masteen, but Sid knew he would heal quickly. It was one of the many things that truly amazed him about the Trith.

Crowdal leaned back against his pack and stretched his legs out with another sigh. "The Trith Nation is to our southwest, so the only other route I can think of is to follow this valley north until we reach the sea, then follow the shoreline west until the mountains no longer impede us. We should then be able to angle south and west. I've never gone this way, but I once saw a map that showed a rough outline of this area and it seems like our only other choice."

Sid looked up at the cliff face on this side of the mountain then turned in a circle, taking in the cliffs that surrounded them to create the small valley in which they now stood. "Sounds good, Crowdal. Anything is better than going down that cliff on the other side. Come on, let's get going, then." He turned and immediately began retracing the route back to the obelisk clearing.

Crowdal slowly got to his feet and gingerly put his pack back on and brought up the rear as the group followed Sid.

After a short distance, Sid stopped and tilted his head back to look up at the sky. He was again amazed that the Miq trees completely blocked out the sun. The immense trees surrounded them, their trunks so large at least eight houses could fit inside just one. The forest floor was covered in giant brown Miq needles, each as long as a person's arm. All sound was dampened in the forest, creating a hush all around them.

As he walked, Sid thought of Tris and wondered if he had survived the brutal wounds he had suffered during the battle. While Sid didn't see it happen, Crowdal had told him how his mother had stabbed Tris in the shoulder with the Rissen blade and Writhgarth had impaled him through the back with his sword. But before Crowdal could finish him off, Tris had somehow disappeared into thin air. Sid worried about the possibility of facing Tris again, especially when his own Numbers were no longer with him.

Tris had been his best friend all through childhood, which made it hurt even worse when Sid had found out that Tris had been an agent of the Oblate the entire time and was now the Black Robe.

Sid came out of his thoughts as he entered the clearing with the obelisk. The dead bodies of the Masteen and his death squad were piled like so much garbage near the far side, which was more than they deserved. The blackened area where his mother, Richard, and the thirteen Haissen who had perished in the battle had been cremated beckoned him forward. Sid came to a stop and stared down at the ashes, feeling ill that so much death had occurred. His mother had saved his life by giving him the power of her blood and Numbers, providing him the strength to overcome the entities inside the obelisk as well as the Unnamed One, the giant creature created millennia ago by an unknown master of Black Numbers. The selfless act had cost his mother her life but she had done it without hesitating. Tears fell from Sid's eyes and coursed down his cheeks and this time he didn't feel embarrassed. He let the tears flow until there were none left. Sid felt Agnes leaning against him, her head on his shoulder. He noticed that his friends were also standing next to him with their heads bowed, the silence a true tribute to their loss.

Crowdal tilted his head, his face wet with tears and a silent moment passed between them. They had been through so much together and he was truly the best friend Sid had ever had, and Sid suspected that Crowdal felt the same way.

Sid started to speak but had to cough several times to get his voice to work. "Let's get going; I don't want to spend another night in this clearing."

Writhgarth nodded, "Me neither; if I never see this place again it will be too soon." He spat onto the ground as if to emphasize his distaste.

The group broke apart, preparing to leave. Sid looked into Agnes's eyes and managed a small smile. She leaned forward and kissed him lightly on the mouth then stepped away to leave him alone for a few moments. He glanced back down at the charred spot on the ground and silently said goodbye one last time then turned to see that his friends were ready, so he started toward the other side of the clearing. He heard Nik start to say something and then a smack and yelp. Sid smiled, knowing that Tulman had slapped Nik on the head to shut him up.

Sid reached the massive Miq tree line on the north side of the circular clearing and entered the deep forest without pausing. He wondered where this new path would take them.

Chapter 2

Tris nudged the variable into place and the equation faded slightly, wavering as if between darkness and light until it finally winked out of existence. He sat back with a curse and kicked at his desk, sending a ceramic cup of dark red wine crashing to the floor.

No matter what he did, he could not get the Black Numbers to work; they remained elusive, just out of his reach. He had been trying to solve for the Black Numbers ever since he had returned to his Oblate chamber a few days ago following the disastrous failure in the obelisk clearing. He had not only been stabbed in the shoulder by Lorielle with the Rissen blade, he had been skewered through his back with a sword by the witless Vringe. He had barely managed to form his portal equation to escape in time to avoid being decapitated by the Trith, returning to his Oblate chamber in defeat.

But at his lowest point he had found a surprise: he had somehow succeeded in grabbing a portion of Sid's Black Numbers before he had escaped. They bubbled inside of his mind, deliciously full of a power he had dreamed his whole life of obtaining. As a boy he had felt, deep down, that he was going to be the Aleph Null. When he had failed his Proofing, he had been so angry he had killed his family servant, stabbing the woman until she had no longer been recognizable as human. His mother had quietly cleaned up the mess, never looking him directly in the eyes. The Black Numbers had not been his destiny that day, but he vowed back then to harness their power by any and all means necessary.

Now he finally had the Black Numbers inside of him and he could not manipulate them. They remained as rooted inside him as gems buried in bedrock. The Numbers were visible, beautiful and touchable, but he couldn't hold them or move them at will.

Tris felt a twinge in his shoulder as he reached down to pick up his quill. He rotated his shoulder in a slow circle and winced at the pain. When he had returned from the Srithian Wood he had used multiple equations to mend his broken body; and with the help of a traditional healer, he was now almost as healthy as he had always been. But he still felt this persistent pain in his shoulder. The Rissen blade had been plunged so deeply into his shoulder, that no matter how intensely he probed the area with his mind, he could not find the final bit of damage that was causing the pain.

A soft knock sounded at his door.

Tris put the quill back down on the beautiful Miq desk and sat back in his chair. "Enter."

The door immediately opened and an armed human guard blocked a man in a blue robe from coming through the open door. Tris was briefly startled that the guard was not a Haissan, before he remembered that the

inhuman sword masters were no longer here in the Oblate. He missed
having them as his servants and still wondered what had happened to
them after he left the obelisk clearing in the Srithian Wood.

He had used the portal equation to return to the clearing this
morning but it had been deserted except for the dead men piled
haphazardly on the edge of the clearing, covered with thousands of flies.
Upon closer inspection, he was not surprised to see they were the
Masteen and his death squad. In the center of the clearing he had seen a
large pile of cold ash and reached down to pull out a charred brass
buckle. These must have been the dead members of the Aleph Null's
party. Tris searched the area but didn't find any more evidence as to what
had happened to Sid. He had repeatedly reached out to the Korpor, but
had made no connection and had to assume the Korpor was also dead. It
was a pity; he could still have used the powerful creature. After realizing
he couldn't get any new information from the battle site, Tris had
returned to his chamber to figure out what he wanted to do about Sid.

Since Tris had the power of Black Numbers inside him, he
technically no longer needed Sid. But he suspected he would still need
access to Sid's mind in case it contained a key to unlocking the Black
Numbers. As much as he would like to just forget about Sid, to wash his
hands of the stench of his mediocre mind, he couldn't take the chance.
He had to complete the scouring of Sid's mind to ensure he had every
variable of the Black Numbers. Then he would end Sid's miserable life
once and for all.

The man remained standing silently in the hall and Tris waved him
in, forgetting he had been still standing there. The Blue Robes - what was
he going to do with them? They were worthless mathematically, each
possessing a power of Numbers equivalent to that of a dog. But he
supposed that even dogs could be useful.

"Yes, Black Robe?"

"I told you, no more covering your face with a hood."

The man reached up and hesitantly pushed back his blue hood to
reveal the completely ordinary face of a middle-aged man.

Tris couldn't believe pathetic people like this were the best the
Oblate had. He was still frustrated that the beautiful and semi-talented
Red Robe, Agnes, had turned against him, choosing the weak embrace of
Sid over him. He looked back down at the document on his desk and
said, "Gather the Blue Robes for a meeting."

The man bowed slightly, "Yes, Black Robe."

He remained standing until Tris waved him away. The man backed
up until he was through the door, then turned and almost ran down the
hall.

Tris sighed, then stood up and rotated his shoulder again to try and
alleviate the pain, but as usual, it didn't help. He changed into richly-
tailored black trousers and a tight-fitting white shirt. He quickly combed

his thick blond hair and looked at himself in the mirror. He knew he was handsome - beautiful even. He thought about how plain and boring Sid was and it still annoyed him that he had had to pretend to be his friend for so many years. It had been difficult knowing he was so much better than Sid in every way.

Tris slipped a thick gold ring onto his right index finger and turned reluctantly away from his image in the mirror. He strode to the back of his chamber and pressed a stone in the wall. It clicked and a door opened almost silently. He made his way through a damp, narrow hallway, passed through another door, climbed twenty-four stone steps and stepped out onto the Black Robe platform high above the thirteen Blue Robes gathered below. Except for the middle-aged man he had just sent to gather them, they all covered their faces with thick hoods. Old habits were difficult to change.

Tris didn't even bother telling them to remove their hoods. They weren't worth his effort. He spoke loudly and clearly. "This will likely be our last gathering like this, for changes are in the works and the Oblate will soon be remade in my image, stronger and better than it ever was. But before I can do this, the Aleph Null must be found. He is a danger to our world and must be captured and rendered powerless."

Most of the Blue Robes nodded their hood-covered heads in excitement.

"For now, each of you will return to your post within the kingdom you represent and use your influence within the court to put together an army to aid in the capture of the Aleph Null. He is likely somewhere to the north and travels with the traitorous Red Robe and a ragtag group, including a Trith. You will command your armies to move in that direction. But if you find the Aleph Null, do not engage with him. Contact me immediately with his location instead. We must close this trap carefully and effectively to ensure the Aleph Null does not slip through our fingers again."

One of the Blue Robes raised a hand, looking fat inside of his robe.
Tris sighed. "What?"
The Blue Robe's voice cracked as he asked, "Why do we need armies to capture the Aleph Null? It seems like overkill, doesn't it?"
"I don't care what you think, I am the one making the decisions. Do not presume to question me about things you cannot understand."
The Blue Robe immediately bowed his head. "Of course, Black Robe. I apologize."
Another Blue robe hesitantly raised a hand.
Tris sighed again, raising his voice as he asked, "What?"
In a timid voice, the Blue Robe asked, "How do we contact you?"
"*This way.*"
Every Blue Robe jolted as one and looked around to see if anyone else had heard his voice.

Tris raised his hand and snapped his fingers loudly, "Up here."
They all looked up at him.

"There you go, welcome back. I have imprinted an equation into
your minds that will allow you to communicate directly with me no
matter where you are."

The Blue Robes began whispering in alarm so Tris sent an equation
that gently excited the pain sensors in the nerves of their arms and legs.
They all cried out in pain.

Tris deactivated the equation. "I swear; you are worse than children.
Now be quiet or I will kill you all just to get some silence."

The room instantly became so quiet that Tris could hear water
dripping from the ceiling and hitting the floor somewhere in the shadowy
parts of the large chamber. He growled deeply, "That's better."

He projected a simple equation into the air in front of each Blue
Robe. "As I was saying, if you want to contact me, create this equation
and speak to me inside your head. When finished, add this Alpha symbol
at the front of the equation to close it. Now memorize it and try
communicating with me."

After a few moments he heard four of them tentatively speak within
his mind. He pointed tiredly to the four and had them stand to the side of
the room. "So only four of you could muster the miniscule mathematical
ability to activate the equation?" Tris felt one more faint nudge against his
mind but it was too weak to make it all the way through. He waited a little
bit longer and when he didn't get any more activations he slapped his
hands against his legs in frustration. "Well I was hoping for at least half
of you to succeed. That was too ambitious it seems." He felt fear emanate
from the remaining nine Blue Robes as he said, "I have no further use for
the nine who failed. And as you know, there is no leaving the Oblate
once you are in."

He sent a single Number into each of the brains of the nine Blue
Robes who had failed him and felt himself grow harder than he had been
in ages as he listened to their screams of pain. Tris let the screams
continue, relishing the sounds until one of the Blue Robes suddenly
collapsed to the floor, interrupting Tris' enjoyment of the process. He
sighed and expanded the numbers inside their brains and sliced viciously
down. The remaining eight Blue Robes collapsed simultaneously to the
floor, dead.

Tris motioned to the remaining four, "Remove your hoods."
They all quickly slid them back.

Tris studied them, not surprised they were all young. Two men and
two women looked anxiously up at him.

"You all did well. Where are you posted?"
The man on the left calmly said, "Tauben."

The man standing next to him couldn't have been more than a few
years older than Tris, but where Tris was handsome, this man was

overweight and pallid of skin. He looked around the room to avoid making eye contact with Tris as he answered, "Uragon, Black Robe."

The woman next to him was attractive in a plain sense, neither beautiful nor ugly, but possessing a sexuality that Tris could sense from where he stood. She looked fearlessly at him and with an obvious sexual invitation in her voice to match her smile, she said, "I am from Paigon, Black Robe."

Tris vowed to have his way with her before he sent her away.

The last Blue Robe was as ugly a woman as he had ever seen, and she glanced to the floor as she mumbled, "Yathen, Black Robe."

Tris nodded to all four. "You will leave today, but you will not travel by horseback. Time is short and I can't wait the weeks it would take for you to get back to your posts, so I will transport you there. Gather your things and meet me in my chamber before the sun sets."

They all left the room and he sat in silence for a few moments. He didn't expect much from them, but if they could each raise even a small force, it would be helpful to him in trapping Sid. He was irritated he hadn't implanted a tracking equation inside Sid when he had a chance. But if he were honest with himself, he'd never expected to fail in the first place.

He slapped his hand against the Miq desk and stood up quickly. The chair tipped backward and tumbled from the platform, bursting to pieces on the stone floor below him. He looked over the edge and grinned. That had been fun. He slid the Miq desk to the edge and shoved it over. He leaned out quickly to watch it crash loudly to the floor. Feeling better, he left the platform and returned to his chambers.

While he had never been to the capital cities of the kingdoms, he had gotten the coordinates from the Korpor before he had lost contact with the creature. Within a short period of time a knock sounded on the door and he said, "Enter."

The door opened and all four Blue Robes filed silently into the chamber and stood expectantly in front of him.

Tris created the portal equation, adding in the coordinates for the capital city of Urgaer in Uragon. Although the portal equation came easily to him now that he had created it so many times, it still required a lot of energy. The air pressure changed, causing his ears to pop, and a swirling darkness filled the space in the middle of the room. Three of the four Blue Robes gasped and stepped back from it. The fat young man from Uragon was the only one who stayed silent and firm. There might be more to him than Tris initially thought. He came around his desk and sat casually on the corner and pointed at the man, "You first, fatty. Step through and don't fail me. I can twist that communication equation and kill you at any time if you choose any other course of action once you leave here."

The young Blue Robe swallowed heavily and nodded once. He

hesitantly stepped forward but stopped at the edge of the portal and looked fearfully into it.

"I am closing that equation at the count of two. One…"

The man quickly stepped through and disappeared with a slight thump of air.

Tris shook his head in disgust. "Why I keep any of you, I don't know." He changed the equation for the coordinates of Tauben and motioned to the next man. "Your turn."

The Blue Robe stepped forward immediately and entered the dark space without pausing.

Tris repeated the process for the ugly woman and she walked slowly through the portal to her home.

Finally, he turned to the last woman. She was prettier up close and radiated her sexuality even stronger in the small chamber. He looked her up and down, letting his eyes rest on her large breasts. She flushed slightly and her nipples grew hard under his stare, pushing against the robe.

He patted the edge of the desk, "Come here."

She immediately stepped to his side and said in a husky voice, "What does my Black Robe desire?"

Tris ran his hand up her stomach and cupped one of her heavy breasts, pinching the nipple hard.

She gasped in pleasure and leaned into his hand.

Tris flipped her around and shoved her violently forward so she was bent over the desk, holding herself up with her arms. He yanked her robe up and saw she was naked underneath. Her body was full and soft as he ran his hands down her backside and between her legs.

She breathed heavily, her long hair hanging over her face as she looked back at him.

Tris dropped his trousers and thrust violently into her, relishing her breathy gasp. He grabbed her hair and pulled it hard, eliciting a sharp cry of pain as he repeatedly plunged into her until sweat ran down his face, savoring her cries until he erupted inside of her with a roar. He leaned briefly on her back to get his breathing under control, then let go of her hair and pushed himself brusquely off her and pulled up his trousers. He changed the equation of the portal to the countryside outside of Serenpaigg, the port city of Paigon, and returned to his chair behind his desk, waving dismissively. "Get out of here."

The woman straightened out her robe, her face red with anger at being dismissed so callously after sex. She opened her mouth to say something, but seeing his dark look she changed her mind and walked stiffly into the darkness without a word.

Already forgetting her, Tris changed the equation and stood up and strode into the portal. The air crackled and he found himself standing in the killing field outside of Reilen castle, its walls towering far above him. Since this had been as close as the Korpor had ever come to the castle of

Reilen, it was as close as Tris could arrive.

He approached the huge double gate and when he was challenged by two guards, he swept them aside with a simple air equation, without breaking his stride. Shouts arose and armed men quickly surrounded him, holding wickedly sharp spear points against his body. One of the soldiers misjudged the pressure he exerted and punctured the skin of Tris' arm, causing blood to trickle down and drip to the ground. Tris slowly turned to glare at the young man and the soldier's head blew out backwards, showering the ground with blood and brain matter.

The soldiers, all battle-hardened men, quickly jumped back from Tris and warily held their spears toward him.

Tris spoke calmly, "Gentlemen, if you would kindly point the way to King Ottoe's chambers, I would be most appreciative."

One of the soldiers hesitantly pointed a shaking finger to the main doors of the castle across the courtyard.

"I know that's the entrance to the castle, you stupid, pathetic dullard. Where is he inside?"

The soldier spoke haltingly, "Second floor, through the hall to the right."

"Thank you. You may return to your posts now." Tris turned and they quickly separated to let him through. A soldier started to protest but was quickly silenced by another.

Tris approached the castle and created the same simple air equation that had gained him entrance to the castle walls and sent it at the doors, causing them to blow open. The guards inside jumped back but quickly rushed him with swords drawn. Tris casually waved his hand to send the same equation and the men were blown off their feet, sliding across the polished white and black speckled floor until they hit the far walls. They remained still, whether they'd been knocked unconscious or were dead, Tris didn't care and walked past them without a second thought.

He climbed the wide marble stairs, curving upward as he took each step until he arrived on the next floor. Two more guards awaited him here and attacked without warning. Tris created a wall of Numbers, one of the first things he had ever learned to do with his Numbers, as it was simple and done without real math. The swords bounced away from him as they impacted the Numbers shield.

The guards were unprepared to hit something hard, as Tris carried no shield, so as their swords flew from their hands, they stared in confusion at Tris, who waved his hand for them to get out of his way. The older of the two, with tinges of grey in his hair, stepped back, but the younger guard attacked Tris with a yell.

Tris drew a small dagger and stepped forward, jabbing quickly into the young man's stomach, his hand a blur as he repeatedly stabbed him with short, quick motions. Blood spurted out, splashing the numbered array he surrounded himself with as he put one hand to the guard's

shoulder and stepped calmly back. The young man looked down at the
blood running freely from his shredded stomach, then crumpled to the
floor, his eyes already glazing over.

The older guard raised his hands in surrender and stepped back as
Tris released his protective array, causing the blood on the array to drop
to the floor with a splat. Tris bent down and cleaned his knife on the
trousers of the dead guard before standing and returning it to a hidden
sheath in his sleeve. He nodded once to the older man and made his way
down the hallway.

There was only one set of doors at the end, which were guarded by
two very large men who eyed him impassively, secure in their strength
and abilities. Tris stopped a few paces from them and motioned at the
door. "Kindly open these. I have business with the king."

The men didn't even acknowledge him.

Tris shrugged. "So be it." He created two simple mathematical
arrays and activated them around each guard. The air hummed with
power. Tris then moved the arrays, with the men inside, out of his way.
When the guards felt themselves sliding across the floor, they tried to
draw their swords, but their elbows immediately hit the walls of the arrays
and for the first time, their eyes showed confusion. One reached out and
touched the invisible walls surrounding him, while the other punched at
the array and grimaced in pain.

Tris walked past them without a glance and opened the double
doors with a flourish.

King Ottoe looked up from a parchment he was reading on his
ornate glass-topped table. He wore glasses, which he lowered so he could
look over them. "Who are you?"

Tris casually walked to the table and sat down in one of the chairs,
propping his feet up on the edge of the beautiful glass top as he studied
the man. The king was middle-aged, slightly overweight and dressed
richly in dark burgundy trousers and a white shirt that flared out at the
cuffs. His shiny black boots clicked on the marble floor as he tapped his
foot angrily under the glass table.

King Ottoe yelled out, "Guards, remove this man!" When no guards
came into the room he stood and marched to the door. His back
straightened when he saw his elite guards standing to the side. "Why are
you just standing there?"

They tapped against the array, the sound thick and hushed in the
corridor.

Tris watched the king from his sitting position and called out in a
bored tone, "If you are finished over there, we have business to discuss."

The king yelled for more guards but no one came into view.
Confused, he turned and headed for the wall to his left where two swords
hung, one crossing the other. He lifted the top sword from its mount and
held it in a two-handed grip as he slowly approached Tris. "I don't know

what you did to my men, but I will kill you unless you tell me what is going on here? Who are you?"

Tris picked at the fingernail of his index finger. "I am the Black Robe of the Oblate and now the ruler of Reilen."

The king laughed harshly. He was obviously a man who had battled many foes to keep his throne and would not be intimidated. "Is that right?"

Tris needed to control the king so he could get what he really came for: the legendary Hunters of Reilen, who were feared across all of the lands, and in service to only the King of Reilen. Tris sent his thoughts into Ottoe's frontal lobe and wrapped an equation around the area of the personality and submission center of his brain. The equation was complex and would affect his thoughts with pulses of mathematically induced control. He activated the equation and Ottoe jerked once, his eyes briefly losing focus before clearing again. Tris glared at the king, "You now want to serve me and only me."

King Ottoe hesitated, his face twisting with a mighty internal struggle. His body tensed and shuddered until his shoulders finally collapsed and he weakly said, "Yes, I do."

"Good. Now, sit."

King Ottoe walked stiffly to the chair behind his desk and sat down.

"Good king." Tris eyed a decanter of Reilenea on the desk, the most exclusive liquor in all of the lands and made only in this castle. He motioned toward the Reilenea with his index finger, "Pour me a glass."

The King of Reilen did as he was told, lifting the decanter and pouring a small amount of the golden liquor into a fine crystal glass.

"More!"

Ottoe tilted the decanter again and filled the glass, his hands shaking slightly as he put the decanter down and slid the glass across the desk.

Tris lifted the glass and sniffed, smiling as the peaty scent filled his nose. He took a sip and immediately felt the warmth of the liquid move down his throat and settle in his stomach. He motioned to Ottoe. "This is truly remarkable. Remind me to get a few cases of this the next time I'm here."

Ottoe nodded, although his eyes briefly narrowed. Tris knew that since Reilenea was aged for more than 50 years, there were only a few cases available each year, with each bottle worth more than even the richest noblemen could afford. It was truly a drink for kings.

Tris held the glass between his hands to warm the liquid as he studied the king. "Now to the business at hand: I need the services of all your Hunters of Reilen. Since they serve only you, I need you to officially order them to serve me."

Ottoe's mouth twitched a few times, then he mumbled, "The Hunters do not really exist."

Tris leaned forward, surprised the king could still lie. He adjusted the equations in the king's mind, causing the man to spasm a few times. "Do not lie to me, Ottoe."

The king's face tensed as if he didn't want to speak, but he was not strong enough to resist and finally said, "Yes, Black Robe."

"Well, go and fetch them."

Ottoe stood and walked stiffly from the room.

Tris released the two elite guards from the array outside of the room. "Guards, come here."

The two huge men stepped into the room and bowed slightly, having overheard much of what had transpired.

"You two have been promoted to my personal guards. What are your names?"

The tallest one had brown hair hanging to his shoulders and was quite young. "I am Paul. At your service, lord."

The other was slightly shorter but more muscular and quite a bit older. "I am Ben. At your service, lord."

"Good. From now on you will protect and serve only me."

Both men bowed, this time much deeper, their facial expressions no longer impassive.

"Gather some pack men and enough supplies for at least two fortnights in the wilderness. Include warm clothing and extra boots and gloves. Even though it is almost summer here, I don't think spring has even arrived yet where we're going."

Ben asked, "Do you want horses, too, lord?"

"No, if I wanted horses, I would have asked for them."

The two guards saluted and left the room. He could hear them barking orders down the hall and the sounds of many running feet fading away. He not only didn't think horses would be useful if they had to cross the difficult terrain he suspected they would encounter, he didn't want to expend the extra energy needed to transport them to the Srithian Wood.

Tris finished the rest of the Reilenea. He really wanted another glass, but restricted himself. He had much to do and didn't want to be impaired in any way. He thought of the Hunters of Reilen and admitted that he knew very little about them. They were mysterious and many people did not believe they truly existed. But he had access to some rare texts that mentioned them.

They were supposedly chosen for service at birth and their training had already begun by the time they could walk. They were said to be able to move silently and almost invisibly through any terrain, even in populous cities, and they killed by any means necessary, true masters of dealing death. Now that Tris no longer had the Haissen, he needed the next best thing; although not even he was certain who would win in a fight between the Haissen and the Hunters of Reilen. It would be interesting to find out.

Hearing a single set of footsteps approaching down the hall, Tris turned to see Ottoe enter the room, followed by thirteen women wearing grey, tight-fitting clothing that did little to hide the curves of their bodies. They halted in the center of the room and Ottoe bowed. "Lord, may I present to you the Hunters of Reilen."

Tris was angrier than he had been in a long time. All of this effort for just thirteen women? All his plans for recapturing Sid depended on his controlling a large force of the Hunters of Reilen. He leaned forward and glared at the king. "I said I wanted the Hunters of Reilen, not thirteen *women*," he said snidely.

A woman with grey, close-cropped hair and a weathered face with eyes that glinted dangerously stepped forward with her arms crossed. "We are the Hunters of Reilen, *sir*." She matched his snide tone as she said 'sir'.

Tris briefly considered reaching for his Numbers to kill this woman, but he forced the anger back and gritted his teeth, hissing, "Step forward, old woman."

She moved in a blur and was by his side before he could even take a breath, holding a short knife to his neck. She whispered in his ear, "I do not know what you did to our king to make him order us to serve you. I should kill you now."

Tris formed a thin barrier of numbers around himself and shrugged nonchalantly, saying, "Go ahead."

She instantly sliced at his neck and stabbed at his side with another knife he hadn't seen, her hands moving so quickly he could barely register their movements. She stepped back when her blades hit against his barrier of Numbers and he didn't appear harmed in the least. She looked at him with her head cocked slightly, "Why aren't you dead?"

He sat back and crossed his legs, smiling. "I am not dead because I choose not to be. I am your master from this day forward."

The woman glanced at his unmarked neck and side, then down at the blades in her hands. She turned to King Ottoe, who nodded for her to do as told, so she turned back to Tris and stiffly bowed, "We are yours to command."

He raised an eyebrow.

Her face remained expressionless as she breathed out, "Master."

Tris smiled and clapped once. "Good girl. From this day forward you will be known as simply the *Hunters*. You will travel with me and help me hunt the Aleph Null pretender. We leave as soon as you are packed and ready."

The woman stood straight. "We are always ready."

Tris turned to Ottoe, who stood uneasily to the side. "You will run everything while I am away just as you've always done. No one will know what has happened here, but you will never forget that I am the true ruler of Reilen now." He narrowed his eyes. "Do not disappoint me, Ottoe."

The former king nodded rigidly, "I will not, my lord."

Ben and Paul returned with five large men who each carried massive packs on their backs, each almost as large as the men themselves. The men stood strong, trained for just this purpose when horses or mules were not available or practical.

Tris stood up and walked around the table as he concentrated on creating the equation for his portal. It appeared with a pop of air pressure, twisting and turning along the edges of the hole in space. The Hunters of Reilen didn't react in any way, their faces expressionless. He motioned them forward, "Off we go."

The Hunters leapt through the portal so quickly that he had to blink a few times to verify they were gone. He turned to the king. "Well, they certainly are quick, aren't they?"

Ottoe nodded but didn't reply.

Tris motioned for Paul and Ben and the five pack men to follow him as he stepped through his portal equation and into the obelisk clearing in the Srithian Wood.

The Hunters were fanned out and waiting for him.

Paul and Ben stepped through the portal followed by the pack men, and Tris dismantled the equation, causing it to wink out of existence. He felt his energy levels drop considerably after creating the portal equation so many times today; first for each of the Blue Robes and now for this last one.

Tris waved his arm tiredly to the Hunters. "Tell me what happened here and, if you can, find out where the Aleph Null pretender and his group went."

The older woman pointed toward the north. "We already did. There was a battle here. The victors initially made their way to the mountains to the south but returned and went north."

Impressed by them even more, Tris motioned them to move.

"Then let's go."

Chapter 3

Sid heard Crowdal call for a halt and stopped walking. He immediately put his hands to the small of his back and stretched, grateful for the break.

Crowdal pulled off his pack, speaking at the same time, "Why don't we make camp for the evening? I think we could all use the rest."

No one complained as they dropped their packs to the sandy ground. The thirteen Haissen split up, six of them facing back the way they had come while the remaining seven went up the beach a few hundred paces to guard it from that direction.

They had come upon the ocean around midday. It had been a surprisingly short walk from the obelisk clearing and everyone had cheered as they had stepped from the tree line onto the sandy beach. The Srithian Wood was basically a long canyon with a narrow exit at the ocean. They had turned west and followed the beach for the remainder of the afternoon.

Sid looked up at the Kulkraken mountains rising almost straight up from the beach – a wall of impenetrable stone making a climb impossible. The mountains stretched out in the distance along the beach for as far as Sid could see and he had the feeling he and his friends would be following the mountains for a long time before they would be able to turn south into the Kuldragg forest.

Having never seen the ocean before, Sid really wanted to explore the water's edge so he made his way toward a rocky outcropping that jutted out into the ocean. As he climbed up onto it, he heard a yell and turned.

Cupping his hands to his mouth, Writhgarth shouted, "Be careful on those rocks! The ocean can be a mighty bitch."

Sid signaled that he understood and turned back, not really paying attention to the warning. He looked out at the calm ocean, amazed he couldn't see any shoreline across it. He had never imagined in his life that there could be a body of water this large. The salty tang in the air smelled wonderful and he felt calm and as close to relaxed as he had felt in ages.

The deep water along the point was relatively calm as he made his way further out onto the rocks, looking at all the fascinating sea creatures living in the many shallow pools in the pockmarked stone. He saw small, multi-colored fish darting quickly around the pools; strange, red, hard-shelled creatures with bony legs and two scary-looking pinchers that snapped out at him while backing away as he swirled his hand by them; and strangest of all, blue and red flowers with thick, prickly spikes growing out of them.

He continued on, kneeling to gaze in wonder at a new type of sea creature in every pool of water he saw until he suddenly realized he was almost near the end of the rocky point. He stepped to the edge of the rocks and watched the deep foamy water swirl around just below his feet, rising and falling like a living, breathing entity.

He saw the largest pool of water yet at the very end of the rocks, so he took the final few steps and knelt down. It was about as deep as he was tall and was completely filled with hundreds of the prickly flowers growing along the sides and covering the whole bottom. He reached into the cold water to lightly touch one of them and as soon as he grazed the flower it quickly closed upon itself. As he swirled his hand in the water, a snake-like creature with a huge mouth full of sharp teeth lunged at him from nowhere. Sid jerked his hand out of the water before it could bite him and the creature retreated back out of view. Sid leaned over the edge of the water to get a closer look and saw the creature's head peeking out of a hole in the side of the rocky pool, its mouth opening and closing constantly. It was an eel! He had seen one in the Orm-Mina summer market that a band of traveling folk had put on display. That one had been thin and short while the one in this pool was at least three times as long and as thick as his leg. It was beautiful in its ugliness and radiated a deadly intent as it stared up at him. He realized he had been lucky to pull his hand out of the water in time.

A distant shout reached him from shore and Sid quickly looked back the way he had come. His friends were yelling and pointing past him. He was too far away to hear what they were saying but he knew something was very wrong. The hairs stood up on his neck as he jerked his head back toward the open ocean. Where previously it had been relatively calm, now a wall of water raced toward him, already at least six times his own height and growing taller as it approached.

Sid jumped to his feet and sprinted toward shore, leaping over rocks and pools of water without slowing down, hoping he wouldn't twist an ankle and fall. He heard his friends urging him to run faster and he pushed his legs to move even quicker as he heard the water crash onto the rocks behind him with a roar. He saw his friends climbing the rocky cliff face to get as high as they could above the beach, which made his fear more real. The six Haissen who were closest split up again. Three stayed back and three sprinted toward him.

He was in trouble.

The three Haissen reached him before he was halfway to the shore and turned to fall in step with him as they raced the wave, the crashing of the water behind him terrifying. Sid and the three Haissen reached the shore and leapt from the rocks to the beach just as the water hit their backs. They were swept up in the foamy water, tumbling end-over-end, arms and legs hitting the sandy ground over and over. Sid hadn't had a chance to take a big breath of air before the water caught him and he didn't know for how much longer he could hold his breath. Just as he was about to give up, he hit the ground hard but instead of tumbling, he found himself being dragged along the sand until he was lying flat on his stomach as the water retreated back down the beach.

The Haissen were already on their feet and pulled him to a sitting position. He gulped in sweet air, amazed he was alive. He looked into the strange white faces of the Haissen and nodded his thanks, but they didn't respond in any way.

Crowdal ran up and knelt down next to him, concern showing on his face. "Sid, are you alright?"

Sid looked up and smiled weakly, then spit out some salty water. "Yuck, that tastes bad." He flexed his arms and legs and aside from a rash on his arms from being dragged up the sandy beach, he didn't think he was injured. "Yeah, I got lucky, I guess."

Writhgarth soon arrived to stand by Crowdal, and Agnes knelt to Sid's right. The little man turned his face and spat, wiping the corner of his lips with a finger. "You were lucky, indeed. If you hadn't been warned, that monster wave would have tumbled you across those rocks and you would have been broken open like a melon thrown against a brick wall. Next time, respect the bitch."

Sid nodded as he pulled off his boots and tipped them to let the water run out. "I've never seen the ocean before. It never crossed my mind there could be waves like that." He looked up at his friends. "Thank you. You saved my life and I'll never forget it."

Crowdal pointed toward Tulman. "Don't thank us, it was Tulman who saw the wave and first yelled to you."

The tall mercenary glanced down at Sid and nodded slightly before turning away to look out over the ocean. His eyes were hooded and he seemed lost in his own thoughts.

Sid struggled to pull his wet boots back on and finally stood up with his hand outstretched. He still didn't feel like he knew Tulman, even after all they had been through together. The bald man was an enigma. On the surface he looked like any other mercenary – tough and scarred from many battles, dressed in simple, well-worn leathers, with the countenance of someone who had often faced death and wasn't afraid of it. But Tulman also had very intelligent eyes that could stare down the toughest of men and make them back down, yet showed the depth of character of someone who had felt both love and loss.

Tulman turned his gaze from the ocean to look down at Sid's outstretched hand. His eyes softened and he shook it briefly before letting it go and walking away.

Sid watched the large mercenary sit down on the sand against the cliff wall and pull a stone from a leather pouch. He began running one of his many knives along the surface, the repetitive rasp of steel on stone a comforting sound.

Sid looked up at Crowdal who shrugged and said, "He is an interesting man. I think there is more to him than anyone knows."

Sid had to agree with Crowdal. He glanced back at Tulman and was glad the Captain was on their side. He was not a man Sid would like to have as an enemy.

Nik had pulled a small box from his pack and Sid realized it was a fishing kit. Excited, he forgot about his close call with the wave as well as his wet clothes. He stepped over to Nik and knelt down. "How's your arm feeling?"

Nik moved it in a slow circle and only winced a little as he completed the turn. "It's sore and I won't be using my bow for another few days, but overall I am feeling pretty good, especially compared to yesterday."

"That's excellent. You got lucky that the guy who did that only bruised you."

"You have that right. At least I killed the bastard."

Sid pointed at the fishing kit. "Hey, you wouldn't by chance have two sets of hook and line, would you?"

Nik smiled. "You have to ask? I take my fishing gear almost as seriously as I do my bow set." He opened the kit and pulled out a square piece of wood with a long, thick line wound around it many times and secured with a roughly-shaped hook. He tossed it to Sid, flashing a wide smile as he took out a second one for himself. "Let's go find some long sticks and catch us some fish for supper."

Excitement raced through Sid. He loved fishing and was anxious to see what types of fish they would catch in the ocean. He was used to fishing in the small river by his house in Orm-Mina where he caught the occasional catfish if he fished the deeper parts of the river. He followed Nik up the beach, his eyes cast down to the sand looking for anything that could be used as a fishing pole. They were lucky and quickly found a few tree branches that had fallen from somewhere up the steep rocky mountain that bordered the sea. They each picked one and used their knives to carve off the small branches and irregularities until they had serviceable poles. They raced back to the rocky outcropping, laughing as each tried to beat the other there.

Nik won by a few steps and he clapped Sid's shoulder. "Good race. Now let's get these lines in the water. Biggest fish wins a day of no camp chores."

Sid grinned. "Deal."

Nik climbed up onto the rocks and walked out to one of the shallow pools of water.

Sid eyed the rocks warily, then looked out to the ocean to search for incoming waves, but the water was calm again. He saw that Nik had only gone out fifty paces or so which didn't seem too dangerous if another wave came in, so he climbed up and made his way to Nik who was perched over one of the shallow pools of water in the rock. Nik suddenly jabbed his hand into the water and pulled out a small red fish about the size of his palm. It squirmed in his clenched fist until he set it on the rock and quickly cut it in half. He grinned up at Sid as he handed him the head portion. "Here, this ought to catch you a big one."

Sid took the fish head and ran his hook through the mouth as it dripped blood. He quickly tied the line to the end of his stick, using a special triple knot that his father had taught him when fishing in the river. He estimated he had at least thirty feet of line.

Nik walked further out onto the rocky point until he found a spot where the rock jutted out a few paces into the water. He carefully climbed onto the outcropping and with practiced ease gathered his line in one hand and flicked the stick with his other, sending the bloody fish tail at least ten feet out into the deep water with a splash.

Sid stayed where he was and threw his line out, watching the fish head sink. He prepared himself for the long wait he'd often had back home, but before his bait was even half-way to the bottom, he saw a huge shape dart out of the depths and grab his fish head. The line played out until it was at the end and his stick was pulled hard down into the water.

Sid gripped the wood and stumbled forward at the unexpected strength and weight of the fish pulling him. He teetered on the edge of the rock but regained his balance enough to step back a bit from the rocky edge. The fish pulled left, then turned back to the right, constantly drawing the stick down to the water. Sid heard the wood crack slightly and he lowered the rod until it was pointing to the water to reduce the stress on the wood. He knew he had to get the fish to shore quickly or risk losing it, as there was no way he would be able to pull something so heavy from the water to the rocks without it breaking the line. Sid edged his way toward the beach one step at a time until he was only a few paces from the shore. The fish fought even harder as it sensed the water getting shallower, then Tulman was wading into the ocean, waving to Sid with a hand. "Angle it over toward me and I'll try and grab it."

Sid nodded, sweat dripping down his face as he fought to pull the huge fish toward Tulman. After three tries, he was able to get it close enough for the tall mercenary to lunge into the water and wrap his arms around it. Sid got his first glimpse of his catch as Tulman backed up the beach while struggling to hold the squirming fish. It was huge, its tail dragging the sand as Tulman came to a stop quite a way from the water's edge and dropped the thing. It flopped around until Writhgarth stepped forward and efficiently stabbed its head with his knife, instantly killing the fish.

Sid jumped down to the sand and ran over to stare in amazement. The fish had brown spots and was as long as Sid was tall with a mouth large enough to engulf a person's head.

Tulman eyed Sid appreciatively. "That is a fine catch. I've caught many of these fish before, though rarely one this big. It will make a fine feast for us. You can cut steaks as thick as this from its side," he said, holding his hands widely apart.

Sid was amazed by the joy in Tulman's voice as he spoke. Then, as if Tulman suddenly realized how he was talking, he quickly shrugged, mumbling, "Let me know if you need help cleaning it," as he trudged away to sit against the cliff again.

Nik yelled out in excitement as he pulled a yellow fish about the length of his arm from the water. He turned toward shore and held it up with a huge smile on his face, which quickly faded away when he saw them all standing on the beach next to Sid's huge catch. He muttered something unintelligible, removed the hook from the fish's mouth and angrily tossed it back into the water before marching back to shore. Sid started to apologize, but Nik put up his hand to stop him as he stared at the fish for a few moments. Then he walked away, still muttering under his breath.

Writhgarth laughed deeply and slapped Sid on his lower back. "That look on Nik's face was worth a copper piece if it was worth ten!" He motioned Sid away. "Go on and change into dry clothes, I'll get this fish cleaned and on a fire."

Sid said thanks and made his way over to his pack where he had dropped it earlier by the cliff face. Thankfully, the wave hadn't reached this high up the beach and it was dry. He dug around and pulled out a fresh shirt and trousers.

Agnes walked up as he was pulling on his dry shirt. "Need any help with your trousers?" She glanced down and winked when she saw him blush.

Sid felt himself stir in his pants and wished they were alone. They had not really had any time to talk privately or be together since this morning when they had left the clearing with the obelisk. But even so, they had touched hands once while walking today and intertwined their index fingers briefly before letting each other go. It had made his heart pound quickly and he found himself unable to think of anything but her for most of the day.

He started to smile at her when thoughts of his horrible rape by Rugger in the hut, as well as his violent sexual encounters with the Korpor suddenly intruded into his thoughts, causing a blackness to come over him.

Agnes noticed the change on his face because her suggestive smile immediately fell away, replaced with concern. She reached out to him, but the conflicting emotions he felt made him pull slightly away from her. She started to say something but turned away instead and walked up the beach with her head down.

Sid didn't know what to say so he didn't say anything and mentally kicked himself for being a fool as he watched her walk away. But he still couldn't make his legs move to go after her. He angrily dropped his wet trousers to the ground and pulled his right foot free. He kicked them violently away but the trouser leg stuck around his left ankle and whipped back up to slap him in the face. He hopped on one leg trying to free the wet trousers from his foot and fell backward to the sand. The familiar anger that always simmered just beneath the surface of his mind flashed out. He viciously pulled his foot free and flung the trousers behind him causing sand to cascade down onto his head. The anger faded away just as quickly as it had come. He shook his hair back and forth in embarrassment and looked quickly around, but thankfully no one had noticed what had happened. He took a deep breath and slowly pulled on his dry trousers.

He was such an idiot.

Chapter 4

The rocks were slick with green algae from the constant mist that rose from the waterfall as it crashed into the small pool of water. Drax removed his trousers and carefully stepped down to the water's edge and dove in without pausing. He swam underwater for a few strokes before coming up in the center, kicking his legs to tread water while he wiped his eyes. He craned his head back to look at the water rushing over the small cliff, sad that this would likely be the last time he swam here.

The sun was close to the horizon and would be setting soon, so with practiced ease, he swam into the waterfall itself, the harsh beating his body took from the falling water invigorating him. He was quickly through the waterfall and inside a small cave lit from the fading sunlight that filtered through the waterfall itself, causing the stone walls to flicker with deep red and orange colors.

"Took you long enough to get here," a deep male voice echoed off the ceiling, difficult to hear over the falling water.

Drax looked up and saw Walter sitting on a rock ledge against the side wall, dangling his feet into the water. Drax smiled apologetically and rolled his eyes as he swam over to sit on a rock shelf just under the water below where Walter sat. "I was delayed by Jormi. He kept asking me questions about the final exam and no matter how much I helped him, he wouldn't leave the room."

Walter shook his head. "That guy is never going to be a Fahrin Druin. He doesn't know Faltic from Lartic acid; much less that one will kill, while the other is used to make a cough medicine. You waste your time helping him."

Cupping his palms together half under water, Drax squeezed them together to spurt water up into the air. "I know, but I can't just tell him to bugger off. He is a good guy."

Walter snorted. "Well, good guy or not, he's an idiot and will never make it through the final exam tonight." He lifted a leg and hung it over Drax's shoulder.

Drax caressed his foot absently. "Where do you think we will be assigned after we graduate tomorrow?"

"I don't care, as long as it is in one of the major cities. I guess if I got to choose though, I would love to be stationed down south in Serenpaigg or Osengraeth. The warm weather and sun would be a nice change from Bildenhall."

Drax looked up at Walter. "Do you think we will get stationed in the same city?"

Walter reached down and ran his fingers through Drax's curly black hair.

Drax reached up and took Walter's hand in his. Walter's white skin contrasted with his own dark brown skin and a lump formed in his throat at the thought of being separated from him.

Walter leaned down and kissed his head. "Whatever happens, we have had an amazing five years together here in Bildenhall. Even if we are sent to different places, we won't be apart forever."

"I know, but that doesn't make it any easier."

They settled into an uneasy silence until the sun set and filled the cave with darkness.

Walter kissed Drax's head again and stood up. "It's time." He dove into the water and swam under the waterfall leaving Drax alone in the dark.

Drax sighed and pushed himself into the cold water and swam through the waterfall and headed for shore. The air was getting cool and mosquitoes whined around him as he climbed out of the pool and toweled off.

Walter was already dressed and pulling on his boots while slapping at mosquitoes. "We need to hurry; the final exam will be starting soon."

Drax nodded and quickly pulled on his clothing, then slipped into his sandals as he shook water droplets from his hair.

Walter grinned as he motioned up the trail. "Come on, I'll race you." He slapped Drax on the shoulder and took off up the narrow trail.

Drax sprinted after him as best as he could in his sandals, cursing himself for not wearing boots. But he did his best and followed his best friend and lover through the forest, leaping over large tree roots and dodging low-hanging branches. They soon broke out of the trees and onto the manicured lawns of the manor house that was the secret Fahrin Druin training facility and ran to the main door. It was locked, as usual, and they knocked quietly, trying to get their breathing under control.

The door soon opened and a stern woman in a brown robe hissed for them to hurry to their exam room down the hall.

They came to a tall, wooden door and opened it as quietly as they could, just enough to slip through the opening. Fourteen young men and women glanced at them, some rolling their eyes, and the Faouthger at the front of the room pointed angrily to two empty desks upon which sat a single sheet of costly parchment.

Drax slid into his desk and put his head down so the Faouthger wouldn't have any more reason to be angry at them besides being late to his final exam.

The Faouthger cleared his throat and spoke in a quiet voice. "Now that Mr. Drax and Mr. Walter have seen fit to arrive, we will begin." He pointed to a small window in the ceiling. "You will have until the moon is fully visible in that window to complete your exam." He then turned to the wall behind him where a large cloth hung and pulled it down to reveal a wall of slate filled with two hundred chemistry questions written in chalk - everything they had been taught over the past five years. "You have one piece of parchment and a small bottle of ink for your quill so there is literally no room for errors." He nodded quickly, "Begin."

Drax had not needed to study for the exam because he not only innately understood everything that was taught to him, he never forgot anything. In fact, he remembered every single moment he had ever lived and could recall any instant with total clarity. So he glanced once at the chalk board, then put his head down and quickly wrote the answers to every question without pausing or looking up again. He wrote down the last answer and placed the quill in its holder as he lightly blew on the parchment to dry the ink.

The Faouthger looked up from his desk with an irritated expression on his face. "What is wrong, Mr. Drax?"

Drax felt his face turn red. "Nothing, Faouthger. I am finished."

The Faouthger stood up and leaned forward on his desk. "You are close to expulsion for being late to my exam, do not push me further. Now, get back to work."

Drax squared his shoulders, then stood up, carried the piece of parchment to the Faouthger's desk and set it carefully down.

The Faouthger's face turned red and he raised his hand to strike Drax when his eyes were drawn down to the parchment. It was so full of writing that no space was left unused and there was not a single scratched out or re-written word. Everything was perfectly written the first time. The Faouthger leaned forward and motioned him out of the room with a quick jerk of his hand, not looking up from the parchment.

Drax saw Walter staring at him in awe, and quite a few others openly glaring at him, so he shrugged his shoulders, quietly left the exam hall and made his way to his small room. Maybe he shouldn't have shown his true intelligence like that. He had done that on the first test he had ever taken here and had hated the jealous glares from the other students when he had scored 100%. So for the past five years he had always made sure he worked slowly and never got more than 90% on an exam. He was not sure why he didn't do this now – maybe it was because it was the last exam he would ever take and he no longer cared what his fellow students thought of him. He had Walter and that was all that mattered.

He must have fallen asleep, for the next thing he heard was Walter letting himself into the room and bright sunlight was streaming through the window. Drax sat up and wiped sleep out of his eyes. "Hey, how did it go for you?"

Walter plopped down in a chair and pushed his blond hair away from his face. "I stopped by last night, but you were sound asleep."

Drax sat up straight. "What time is it?"

"Close to mid morning."

Drax shook his head. "Really? I can't believe I slept through the night."

Walter put his feet up on a stool and leaned back with his arms resting across his stomach. "Well, the results were just posted. The highest score was an 88% by yours truly." He smiled and tapped his stomach with his hands.

Drax looked at him in confusion. He knew he had not gotten even one question wrong.

Walter grinned at the look on Drax's face. "Aside from you, that is, who scored a perfect 100%."

Drax relaxed and Walter looked at him shrewdly for a few moments. "How did you do it?"

"Do what?"

"Don't play stupid. You know what I'm talking about. You wrote non-stop and so quickly that I thought you were just goofing around. But then you handed in your exam before I had even completed ten of the questions."

Drax started to shrug but Walter cut him off. "I said don't play stupid with me. I always thought you were smarter than you tested, but thought maybe it was just because I liked you. Tell me, what is going on."

Sighing, Drax stood up and looked out the window. Before he could answer, someone pounded on the door. He stepped over and opened it, surprised to see the Faouthger himself standing there.

The old man pulled his hand back from the door and gruffly said, "Follow me, Mr. Drax," then turned and started down the hallway.

Drax looked back at Walter, who nodded his head toward the open hall and whispered, "Hurry up, idiot. The Faouthger never comes down here, so it must be really important."

Drax started to reach for his sandals when Walter hissed at him, "Forget your shoes, hurry after him."

"Right, right." Drax sprinted out the door and saw the Faouthger turn the corner of the hallway. He pumped his legs faster, slid around the corner and ran out the door of the building at full speed, letting the door bang open and then closed again. He quickly caught up with the Faouthger on the lawn and fell into step behind him.

They walked in silence across the lawn and entered the tree line. Drax didn't dare ask any questions as he followed the old man deep into the dark forest. The sunlight filtered only occasionally through the trees and they followed no trail. Getting worried he was really in trouble, Drax was about to ask where they were going when he spotted an ancient stone building through the brush. There was no door, nor any indication it was even a usable building; it looked like a small mausoleum. They stopped when they had reached it.

The Faouthger turned to Drax. "This is the Frahnndem of the Fahrin Druin."

Drax stopped breathing. He had read of the Frahnndem in an ancient scroll he had found hidden deep within the lowest level of the unused section of the library four years earlier. He had easily understood and memorized everything that was taught to him, so he often secretly searched the off-limits areas of the library for any kind of additional knowledge. The cracked and brittle scroll from this memory had briefly mentioned the Frahnndem, describing it simply as the 'House of the Master'. He hadn't understood the reference then but hearing the name now made the short hair on his neck stand up.

The Faouthger stepped back with a hiss. "Your face shows that you've heard of this place. How can that be?"

Drax put up his hands. "I merely ran across a reference to it in an old scroll."

"That is impossible; there are no written references to this place." The old man's voice rose in volume and he pulled a long and wicked-looking blade from his sleeve. "Now tell me the truth or I will kill you here."

A deep and commanding voice filled the area. Drax turned his head and behind him he saw an opening in the stone wall and a huge figure filled the space. "Put down your little knife, Xandis, and leave us."

The Faouthger's face instantly filled with terror and he turned and fled into the forest.

A deep sigh emanated from the figure as he watched the old man disappear into the brush, then he turned to Drax and said, "Come with me. We have much to discuss."

Drax watched the figure turn and disappear into the darkness inside the doorway. He was more scared than he had ever been in his life but he forced himself to take a step forward, then another until he was able to peer into the darkness. He did not want to enter, but he did not want to run away like the Faouthger had, so he squared his shoulders and stepped through the dark opening, hearing the door close behind him with an ominous thud.

Chapter 5

Melinda felt a hand touch her forehead. It was soft and warm as it moved down to caress her cheek. She tried to open her eyes, but they remained closed no matter how hard she tried.

The soft voice of a woman spoke into her left ear, her warm breath a physical sensation Melinda had not felt in a long time. "It's alright, Melinda." A warm, wet cloth was placed across her eyes and moved gently around before it was removed. "Now, try and open your eyes."

Melinda did as she was told and the soft, yellow light of a candle came into view, the flame flickering gently, casting shadows against the wall. It was a sight so beautiful that she sobbed, relieved to be out of the nightmare world she had been stuck in for so long.

A hand touched her cheek again. "Welcome back, Melinda."

She tilted her head slightly toward the voice and saw her grandmother, Prennia, sitting close by her, smiling gently as she removed her hand from Melinda's cheek.

"Why are you here?" It wasn't the first thing Melinda had wanted to say and it came out in a harsh rasp.

Prennia's smile faded briefly but returned as quickly. "It is good to see you awake." At the confused expression on Melinda's face, she continued. "You have been unconscious for seven days. We did not know if you would ever awaken again."

Melinda closed her eyes. The last thing she remembered was walking through the tall, grassy prairie with Crowdal, Writhgarth, and the mercenaries Nik, Richard and the huge Captain Tulman. They were supposed to meet up with Sid and Agnes and her Haissan, who were leading their horses away from the main trail to try and throw the Masteen and his men off their route. She had been so tired that she had fallen quietly behind until she suddenly found the world spinning. She had experienced nothing more until just now, except for constant nightmares, in which she didn't know what was real and what wasn't.

"Here, drink some water."

She opened her eyes and struggled to sit up, succeeding with Prennia's help. She took the wooden mug and started gulping down the water, but Prennia quickly took it away.

"Slowly, dear. Too much, too soon is not good."

As a healer, Melinda understood, so she nodded. "Sorry, you are right." Prennia gave her the cup again and she drank more, but only in small sips until she finally felt a little more clear-headed.

Prennia patted her thigh. "You look much better. Do you think you could handle some quail broth?"

Her stomach growled loudly at the thought of the broth, which Prennia must have heard, because she smiled and motioned with her hand to someone behind her. Melinda turned her head but didn't see anyone. She then looked around her, surprised that she was in a small cave, one that was warm and comfortable. A smokeless fire burned in the center, thick animal pelts covered the floor, and candles provided a warm light throughout the space. But there was not even a hint of natural sunlight so they must be pretty deep underground. She turned back to her grandmother. "Where am I?"

"You are back in the Branstall Wood where we first met, though underground in our summer home."

"The Zranh live underground?"

"Yes, dear. While we spend most of our time in the wooded areas of this land, we live underground for safety. That is why no one in the outside world knows of our existence, other than as rumor and stories told around campfires."

Melinda had not known this about her people. Her mother had never fully discussed her heritage, wanting Melinda to live as normal a life as possible.

"What happened to my friends?"

"They were fine the last time the Quadrant saw them."

Melinda looked at her, confused, so Prennia explained. "I sent a group of four Zranh trackers, which we call a Quadrant, to follow you in case you fell to the Raith world. They caught up with you in the prairie and had to bargain with the Trith to take you back here. He was quite protective of you and only let the Quadrant take you back here because he knew you would die if you weren't returned."

Melinda smiled at the thought of Crowdal and how imposing he must have seemed to the Zranh. While he could be terrifying to anyone who didn't know him, Melinda knew just how gentle he could be. "So they were all fine, then?"

"Yes. They were heading toward the Kulkraken mountains when the Quadrant left them. I'm sorry, I do not have any further information."

Melinda sighed deeply, wishing she were back with her friends, hoping they were all still safe.

A young man entered the cave and set a steaming bowl of broth by Prennia, leaving silently and quickly. The smell made Melinda's mouth water. She couldn't remember the last time she had eaten. Prennia handed her the small bowl and Melinda spooned some broth into her mouth, slurping the hot liquid to avoid burning her tongue. In that moment, it was the most wonderful food she had ever tasted. She finished the broth and then laid back down, feeling full and sleepy.

Prennia pulled a soft deer hide up to her chin and patted her hand. "Get some real sleep, now. We will talk more when you next wake up."

Melinda nodded, her eyes already closing. She didn't dream and when she heard the soft rustle of the deer hide being pulled further up her body she opened her eyes. A young girl no more than twelve or thirteen years old jumped back when she saw Melinda staring at her.

"I am sorry for waking you, Leillireph."

Melinda sat up, finding she now had the strength to do this herself. She looked curiously at the young girl. "Why do you call me 'Leillireph'? My name is Melinda."

The girl hesitantly stepped back to Melinda's side. She was nervous, her eyes constantly looking away from Melinda. "You are Leillireph."

"Eithes, you may leave us now" Prennia's voice was kind but the girl jumped up like she had been slapped and she hurried away with her head down. Prennia sat down in her spot. "Please do not be angry with Eithes. She only knows you by your title."

"Title? What are you talking about?"

"We can talk about that later. How are you feeling?"

Melinda sighed in exasperation. "Tell me what you meant by 'title'."

Her grandmother studied her for a few moments before nodding assent. "The title of 'Leillireph' is old, dating back to the beginnings of our race many thousands of years ago." She closed her eyes as she continued, "It means Mother of the Blood – She Who was First."

"What does that even mean?"

"It means that you carry the power of the Ancients within you, the blood of the First, she who can enter the third frequency of the Raith world. You are Leillireph, Melinda."

Out of reflex, Melinda pushed hair from her eyes and barked, "No, I do not accept that. I am a healer and only a healer." But even as she said this, she knew she was lying to herself. The things she had done – entering the Raith world at will and with ease, killing her father and all the mercenaries who had shot arrows at her and her friends in the woods; she could no longer deny who she was. She was Zranh.

It was as if Prennia saw the acceptance written on her face, for the old woman nodded slightly and whispered, "You know this to be true, don't you?"

Melinda felt a warm energy fill her, the familiar heat of the Raith shift, but she pushed it back. It was still there, burning inside of her as hotly as ever, a part of her as much as her mind and body. She felt calm for the first time in her entire life, a sense of peace washing over her. She was Zranh; she accepted it fully and completely. She turned away from Prennia for a moment and when she faced her grandmother again she smiled slightly. "So, what happens now, grandmother?" It was the first time she had used that word and it brought tears to Prennia's eyes.

"Now, you get some more rest, and when you next awaken, we will go for a walk and discuss all that has happened to you, as well as what we will do next."

"But, I'm not tired anymore."

Prennia eyed her skeptically. "You should be after what you've been through."

Melinda threw off the deer hide and swung her legs over what she now saw was a stone ledge not far above the floor of the cave. She felt almost normal, not weak like she thought she would. In fact, she felt strong. Melinda pushed herself up to a standing position and Prennia reached out to steady her but Melinda brushed her grandmother's hand away. "I don't need your help." She took a few steps, quickly gaining her full balance and spun around, raising her hands. "See?"

Prennia studied her carefully, disbelief clearly showing on her face. "You were unconscious for more than seven days; the Quadrant carried you, day and night, to get you back here, moving into and out of the Raith world at regular intervals to speed up the trip as you faded away. You had been in the Raith world for much too long before the Quadrant caught up with you, longer than anyone has ever tried. You are lucky to even be alive."

"Well I am alive, and I want to get some fresh air and see the outside again." She turned left and started walking when she heard Prennia cough behind her. Melinda turned her head and saw Prennia pointing the other way. She felt herself blush but lifted her chin high and turned around, walking quickly past her grandmother who fell into step behind her.

It turned out they were far underground. As she walked, she saw four side tunnels, but Prennia kept her moving forward. After a few hundred paces she came to a wall with a ladder leading both up and down into dark openings. She turned her head and her grandmother tilted her chin upward so Melinda climbed the old wooden ladder. Some of the rungs were missing, so she had to pull herself up with her arms. She was soon inside another tunnel, much narrower than the previous one. The air was slightly warmer up here, and to her right she saw stone pots glowing with a soft light leading far into the distance. It was dark to her left so she followed the lights, eventually coming to a dead end.

Melinda turned to Prennia, who motioned to her left. "You should know how to exit and enter our secret home. Press the indent above you while twisting it at the same time."

She eyed the wall and immediately saw what her grandmother was referencing. Reaching up she felt a tingling sensation in her palm the closer she got to the spot. Melinda hesitated briefly, then pressed down hard with her hand and twisted at the same time. A small piece of the ceiling pivoted open, the grating of stone against stone loud in the small passage.

"There are small stones embedded in the wall where you can put your hands and feet. If you are too tired to climb, we can go back to your room."

Melinda rolled her eyes and leapt up to the third stone and grabbed it with her left hand while reaching for the fourth stone with her right. She put her feet against a lower stone and climbed quickly through the hole in the ceiling. She had to climb two more body lengths before she poked her head above the floor opening in the next tunnel. It was semi-dark in this tunnel although she could see a hint of daylight far away, so she carefully climbed out of the hole and hunched down on her feet to wait for Prennia.

Her grandmother slowly pulled herself out of the hole, a little out of breath.

"The older I get, the more difficult this becomes. I used to be able to climb this just like you did." She pressed and twisted a spot next to the hole and the stone pivoted shut until the floor was smooth again with no indication that there was an opening. "Follow me and don't exit the tunnel until I say it is safe. We don't light any torches or candles on this level so we don't draw attention to our home."

Melinda nodded and followed her grandmother until they were at the opening to the outside world. Prennia stayed completely still as she listened. After several moments she motioned Melinda forward into a gully at least forty paces wide with a shallow, gurgling stream running through it. Turning around, Melinda saw they had exited from a narrow opening in a small, rocky cliff.

Melinda stepped forward and sat down on a rock by the edge of the stream. The area was beautiful, almost surreal in its magnificence. She closed her eyes and tilted her face to the sun, basking in the warmth. The bubbling of the water was like music and the birds twittering in the branches above brought a smile to her face. She tilted her head back down and opened her eyes when she heard a strange sound.

Prennia gave a cry and disappeared.

Melinda jumped to her feet and spun around, anxiously searching the area when she felt her skin prickle. She immediately let the heat of the Raith world fill her. The sounds of nature in the gully disappeared and everything around her slowed down as she completed the time shift. She heard soft footsteps behind her and spun around and gasped when she saw three Zranh approaching her, crouched low and holding black-bladed knives.

When they saw her spin toward them they halted.

Melinda heard two people struggling in the water and turned to see Prennia and a young man locked in combat, Prennia holding the arm of the man trying to jam his blade into her face.

Melinda felt an icy anger fill her. She growled deeply in her throat and the three Zranh stepped hesitantly back. Then one of them strode forward and spoke angrily, "You are an abomination. You must die."

"Who are you?"

The leader stood up tall. "I am Quin, Gorepeth of the south Quadrant."

Melinda smiled coldly and whispered, "Good, because I wanted to know who I was going to kill." Then she let the heat of the Raith world utterly fill her body.

The eyes of all three men widened in fear before they stopped moving as the world around Melinda came to a complete stop. She basked in the sensation of the full Raith world for a few moments, then quickly ran over to Prennia who was frozen in her struggle with the Zranh. The knife was almost touching her face and the mouth of the Zranh holding the knife was split in a grimace as he pushed the knife lower. Melinda carefully pulled Prennia's fingers open and slid her free of her attacker. She slowly backed up with her grandmother until she was able to gently set the old woman onto the ground, folding her legs so she was in a comfortable position.

Melinda stood up, ran back to the man in the stream and pulled his fingers viciously back from the knife handle, the bones of his fingers snapping loudly in the silent landscape. Melinda took the Zranh's blade and slashed upward and across his neck, slicing it deeply.

Melinda walked calmly to the other three Zranh who seemed like living statues. She gripped the heavy knife and was about to ram it into each man's mouth like she had done to her father when he had tried to kill her, but she held back when she noticed that one of the Zranh was no more than thirteen or fourteen years old, his face more a child's than a man's. The anger left her as quickly as it had come and she stepped back and screamed in frustration.

She could feel the exhaustion of being in the Raith world setting in and realized she hadn't recovered from her previous injuries as much as she'd thought, so she quickly pulled a coil of rope from the belt of one of the Zranh and cut it into sections, then roughly tied their hands behind their backs. She tied their feet together for good measure, and then hit each one in the back of the head with the handle of the knife. In the time shift of the Raith world, they didn't react or fall down.

Melinda walked over to her grandmother, sat down in front of her, then let the heat flow from her body as she let the Raith world go. The loud sounds of the forest assaulted her after the complete silence of the Raith world. Her grandmother disappeared briefly because she was still in the partial Raith world, but she quickly reappeared, her face showing shock, eyes wide and face red from her recent exertion.

Melinda knew her grandmother had just experienced something entirely different than she had. The four Zranh who had attacked them were in a partial Raith shift, the common method they used to attack and kill others. Prennia had shifted into the partial Raith world to fight the Zranh, but since Melinda could stop time completely, Prennia had been fighting for her life one moment, and the next she was sitting on the ground with Melinda next to her. Prennia looked toward the stream in time to see the Zranh whom she had been fighting spurt blood from his neck and fall forward into the water. Her eyes widened as she turned back to Melinda. "You made the full shift into the Raith world, didn't you?

You entered the third frequency."

This was the second time Prennia had mentioned the third frequency. She would have to ask her grandmother what it was but right now she was too tired to do more than motion to their left.

Prennia followed her motion and at the sight of the three unconscious Zranh, she let her shoulders relax. "Are they dead, too?"

"No, just unconscious with their hands and feet bound."

Prennia took Melinda by both hands and leaned forward. "Thank you, dear. You saved our lives and held back from killing them all. That shall help us put an end to the small but vocal portion of Zranh who do not trust you."

Melinda chuckled without humor. "Vocal? I would say they are a little beyond just being vocal."

A group of at least twenty Zranh quickly filed out of the tunnel opening and surrounded them. Melinda jumped up and was about to make the full shift again when she felt Prennia grab her wrist. "No, Melinda. These are friends."

Melinda eyed the Zranh as she sat back down.

Prennia motioned toward the three bound Zranh. "Take them to the Woydthan chamber and guard them."

One of the larger Zranh motioned toward the body in the creek. "What about him?"

"Bury him with full ceremony and tell Sarih he died nobly."

At a raised eyebrow from the man, Prennia sighed. "She doesn't need to know about his betrayal."

The Zranh nodded, respect showing in his eyes, and turned away to do as she had ordered.

Melinda was amazed by the way Prennia ruled with such strength and compassion.

Prennia stood, her back straight although her exhaustion was evident by the slow speed at which she moved. "Come, Melinda. Let's get back to your room. I don't know about you, but I could use some rest."

Standing up with a creak of her own knee joints, Melinda took the old woman's hand and helped her back into the tunnels, wondering just what her future would hold with the Zranh.

Chapter 6

Crowdal leaned forward, stretching his hands toward the small fire to warm them. It was the third day they had been on the beach, and they were taking a short break after walking for most of the morning.

Each night they had camped as close to the cliff face as they could to stay above the tidal line. The big fish Sid had caught two days earlier provided an enormous amount of extra meat so Writhgarth had soaked the remaining fillets in ocean water over the first night, and then last night he had covered red-hot coals with some wet driftwood and seaweed to smoke and dry the fish.

Crowdal's mouth had watered at the smell of the smoking fish, wishing at that moment he still ate meat. To take his mind off the fish, he had walked down to the water's edge and found a large clump of seaweed that had just washed ashore, succulent pods hanging thickly from it. He rinsed it in the ocean to get the sand off, then dried it over the coals along with the fish. The little grape-sized nodules had shriveled enough for it to be folded into thick packets. As he worked, Writhgarth had wrinkled his nose and commented he would rather eat sand than the strange-looking plant. But Crowdal had merely smiled, knowing that seaweed was not only filling and good for him, it actually tasted pretty good, too.

Crowdal removed a packet of the dried seaweed from his pocket now and took a bite, chewing it slowly as he glanced up at the ever-present mountains, then back down at the beach, which stretched endlessly ahead of them. He sighed, already tired of the sand. The air was cold and the sky was grey and filled with heavy, low-hanging clouds that completely blocked out the sun, just as they had the previous day. A cold rain had fallen most of the morning and even though it had stopped, the air still hung heavy with moisture. He held the packet of seaweed in his mouth as he dug in his pack with a shiver and pulled out a thick wool shirt. He slipped off his rain-proof coat and pulled the wool shirt over his existing shirt to protect him from the chill that seemed to reach deep into his body no matter how many layers of clothing he wore.

He wasn't sure exactly how far they would have to go before the mountain range ended and they could turn inland toward the Kuldragg forest, but he suspected it could take another half a fortnight. He had never been this way but based on the crude map of this area he had once seen, it was his best guess.

Sid glanced at Crowdal, then motioned his head. "We should probably get moving again. If I sit here much longer, I'm going to fall asleep."

Crowdal nodded and stood up, kicking sand over the small fire they had built to warm themselves while they rested and ate.

Nik stood also and looked up at Crowdal, his head barely rising above Crowdal's waist. "Hey, big guy. How much longer do you think we will have to walk along this cursed beach?"

Crowdal looked ahead of them again then shrugged his shoulders. "My best guess would be six or seven days; maybe more, maybe less."

Nik rolled his eyes. "Thanks for being so exact."

Crowdal shrugged; he had no answers.

Nik pulled the collar tighter around his neck. "Great, six more days of wind and rain. I'm so tired of this."

Tulman walked past and growled, "Well if you stop talking and start walking, we may actually get off this beach in my lifetime."

Nik quickly picked up his pack and started after Tulman, awkwardly trying to get his left arm through the straps.

Crowdal and Writhgarth grinned at each other before falling into step behind Sid and Agnes, who were keeping distance between each other. Something had happened between them; they hadn't said a word to each other in days. Crowdal suspected it had something to do with young love. They had only known each other a fortnight or so, yet they had experienced some pretty intimate moments in that short amount of time. They hadn't had time to really get to know each other, so even a single comment could be easily misinterpreted. Crowdal thought of Melinda and some of the arguments they had had, some based on something as minor as a word said at the wrong time.

At the thought of Melinda, Crowdal gritted his teeth and fought down the rising anxiety he constantly felt for her. He had no idea if she was alive, or whether he would see her again. The Zranh had told him they were taking her back to the Branstall Wood so they could heal her. But they would only be staying there until autumn and Crowdal didn't know if he would be able to get back there in time. It was already approaching early summer and the days were passing by too quickly. He pushed hair away from his eyes and tucked it behind his left ear so he could see better, remembering Melinda doing the exact same thing. Gods, he missed that woman.

So lost in his thoughts was Crowdal, that he almost didn't notice they were nearing a change in the beach. He called a stop and studied the area ahead. The smooth, sandy beach ended abruptly at a line of boulders that rose from the ocean all the way to the mountain face. Some were huge, while others were small and jagged.

Crowdal climbed up onto one of the larger boulders and looked ahead. The rocky beach narrowed considerably and extended as far as he could see, though far ahead it looked like it curved sharply out to a point in the ocean.

He jumped back to the sandy beach. "Looks like we are done with this sand for a while."

Nik cheered, but Crowdal shushed him. "There are a number of dangers to watch for as we move forward. Watch each step so you don't twist an ankle. One wrong placement of a foot and you could be laid up for a few days; time we do not have. Secondly, the seashore narrows so we need to be aware of the tide changes so we don't get trapped or swept away." He motioned forward. "Let's travel single-file from now on and be ready to help someone if they start to fall. I'll take point," he looked at Tulman, "and you take the rear, Tulman. From your eyes I can see you are familiar with the ocean and know what to watch for with the tide."

Tulman nodded once, his eyes flicking toward the water. Crowdal suspected the mercenary Captain had a story worth hearing someday.

"Everyone ready?" At nods from all around, Crowdal tightened his pack so it would not throw him off balance and started forward, climbing rock after rock and sliding down or jumping carefully from each. They would have to slow down considerably from this point forward.

By the time the sun was approaching the horizon in front of them, they had made their way to the sharp turn in the beach. The tide was creeping closer to them as they walked, but fortunately the beach expanded inland at the sharp turn, giving them a place to camp where the rising water would not reach them. Crowdal stopped and pointed at the area higher up. "Let's make camp up there. We should be safe from the tides." He immediately turned and climbed up where the boulders were large and provided enough space for them all to lay down and rest.

Sid sat down with a sigh. "Gods, it feels good to rest. Those rocks are brutal to climb over all day."

Writhgarth chuckled. "You should try doing it being as short as me."

Nik laughed outright. "There's a reason that Vringe usually never leave the comforts of the city."

Writhgarth nodded seriously. "Aye, that is true. But I was never comfortable sitting on my arse. Give me a sword and a purpose and I am a happy man."

Nik pointed to his left where dried wood lay piled on a ledge a few dozen feet away, evidence that others had used this spot to camp, and winked at Writhgarth. "I have a purpose for you: how about helping me gather some of that wood for a fire?"

Writhgarth grinned, then shrugged. "Wish I could help you, Nik, but these hands are made for wielding a sword, not collecting firewood. Plus, I have supper to prepare."

Rolling his eyes, Nik turned to gather the wood alone when Sid stood up and said, "I'll help you, Nik."

The mercenary clapped him on the shoulder. "Good man."

Crowdal slid his pack to the rocky boulder he was standing on. He had an uneasy feeling and didn't know why. He made his way to where Tulman sat and knelt on one knee next to him and quietly asked, "Want to take a little exploratory hike with me out to that point?"

Tulman nodded slowly. "You feel it, too? That something is not right?"

Crowdal nodded. "Definitely."

The big mercenary stood up. "Let's go have ourselves a look, then."

Crowdal stepped over to Writhgarth and leaned down so he could speak quietly. "Tulman and I are going to go out to the end of the point to see what we can see."

Writhgarth looked in that direction. "I'll keep an eye on everyone here. Be careful."

Crowdal stood and joined Tulman, who was facing the ocean. "Let's get moving before it gets too dark." He slid down the large boulders and worked his way to the main beach area, Tulman by his side. They set off, moving as quickly as they could and by the time the sun was completely down they'd reached the end of the point. The cliffs were only a dozen feet from the open ocean and the waves crashed close to them, spraying them with freezing water and making the rocks slippery. The tide swirled up and down just below their feet as they crawled forward until they could see around the corner, shielding their eyes from the ocean spray.

Tulman swore loud enough for Crowdal to hear over the roar of the crashing waves, and he had good reason, for in the distance they could see a large bonfire blazing on the shore. He counted at least four dozen men eating, drinking and laughing as they passed around huge jugs. They wore thick pelts of some kind of smooth-skinned animal and all had long bushy beards. They were hard-looking men and not anyone he wanted to meet.

He glanced over at Tulman and saw him glaring at the men with a blaze in his eyes, one Crowdal had seen many times in men who faced an adversary they badly wanted to kill. He tapped Tulman on the arm and motioned back the way they had come. Tulman hesitated briefly before nodding assent.

They edged back until they could stand without being seen, then carefully made their way back to camp through the darkness lit only by the light of the moon reflected low off the ocean. As they entered the makeshift camp, they stomped the burning wood of the fire until it was out.

Nik yelled out, "Hey, why'd you do that?"

Tulman clamped a huge hand over his mouth and glared at him. "Be quiet."

Nik nodded, his eyes bulging as Tulman slowly removed his hand.

Crowdal knelt down and spoke quietly. "We made it to the point and on the other side there is a large group of very unpleasant-looking men camped on the beach. They don't seem the type to welcome visitors, so we must decide what to do."

Sid glanced up at the mountain and then back the way they had come. "What can we do? We can't climb this mountain and we can't go back. Maybe we can try and wait them out and see if they leave."

Agnes raised her hand. "I don't think waiting is a good idea. What if they are coming this way? We would have nowhere to go."

Sid nodded agreement. "You are right, Agnes, I wasn't thinking."

Her eyes softened as she looked at him and something seemed to pass between them, for Sid slid his hand along the rock to touch her hand and she closed it in hers.

No one seemed to notice, but Crowdal did and couldn't help himself from smiling slightly. "Agnes is right, we can't just hope they go away; it's too risky."

Writhgarth motioned to the Haissen who stood a dozen paces away, just barely visible in the faint moonlight as they faced the beach in a semi-circle around their camp. "We have them; can't we just fight our way through? I have seen them bastards fight and don't think a few men would present much trouble for them."

Crowdal considered that Writhgarth might be right. But in his experience, anytime you put yourself into a situation where you had to fight there was substantial risk for things to go wrong and for people to die, even if you had Haissen on your side. A stray arrow could kill as easily as a direct sword strike. And with Sid being without his power of Numbers, the risk was just too high. He said as much and Writhgarth nodded in agreement.

Sid looked at the moon, which was already approaching the sea. "Crowdal, what if we snuck by them?" He pointed at the moon. "This far north, the moon doesn't seem to fully rise into the sky like it does back home in Orm-Mina. I think it will be setting soon, and like last night, it should get pretty dark then."

Crowdal didn't really like the idea, but there were really no other options. He clapped Sid on the shoulder, almost knocking him sideways into the rock. "Sorry, I didn't mean to clap you so hard."

Sid chuckled, rubbing his shoulder. "No problem. I take it you like my idea?"

Crowdal looked at the moon, then back to the group. "It will be dangerous, but I think it is our best option. The moon will be down shortly, so if we do this, we need to do it soon."

Agnes was the first to say she was in, quickly followed by Writhgarth and Nik. Tulman remained silent, but he nodded his agreement.

Crowdal gave a low whistle and one of the Haissen turned its head. Crowdal motioned it over and said, "Gather your Haissen."

It didn't move until Sid repeated the request.

The Haissan turned and leapt lightly across the rocks, and within moments all thirteen Haissen stood around them, their white faces hidden in their hoods.

Crowdal spoke to the whole group so the Haissen knew what was going to happen. "We are going to try and sneak past the large group of men on the other side of that point. Now, as we near the point, the beach almost disappears and the waves will be crashing very close to us, so be careful of the rocks, they will be very slippery." He looked at Sid and Agnes. "Crawl on your hands and knees if you have to, but most importantly, be as quiet as you can. Sound can carry very easily."

He motioned at the Haissen. "I would like at least half of your murder to go ahead of us while the other half remains with the group. That way, if we are discovered, we can better fight them. Agreed?"

The Haissen nodded as one.

"Good. Gather your packs."

They were ready to go in moments. Seven Haissen led off, moving so quickly and lightly on their feet that they seemed to glide across the rocks. Crowdal led the group, followed by Sid and Agnes, Writhgarth, Nik, Tulman and the remaining six Haissen.

They worked their way up the coast, carefully climbing the rocks as they went. The closer they got to the point, the narrower the area got until the cliff wall was very close to the water's edge. The waves were larger than earlier, completely drenching them with spray as they crashed against the rocks only paces from them.

Crowdal heard a yell and quickly looked behind him. Nik had lost his balance and was teetering on a rock, the water from a wave knee-deep and swirling around him. He began tilting backward, flailing his arms wildly. Then a Haissan was next to him, pulling him forward to safety while clamping a white hand over his mouth to silence him. Nik hugged the Haissan but the creature dropped its arms and slipped from his grip. Nik looked at his bare arms, shook his head and lowered himself so he could crawl across the rocks instead of walking. Crowdal caught Nik's attention and put a finger to his lips for him to be quiet, then turned back.

He reached the apex of the point and inched his way forward until he could see around the edge. The fires had burned down and the men were settling in for the night. Some were already sleeping and the few remaining awake were quietly talking by the fires. Crowdal squinted and gasped when he saw two men raping a young woman. She was completely nude and on her hands and knees as they violated her. It was a sight that sickened Crowdal and he wanted nothing more than to run over and cut the men to pieces, but he crawled backward instead, feeling shame and anger, until he could talk to the group as quietly as possible over the constant roar of the ocean.

"We need to wait for a while, they are… still active."

Sid spoke, frustration in his voice. "If I still had my Numbers I could imprison them all in a simple array so we could just walk past them."

Agnes lifted her hand. "I can do it."

Sid looked at her and asked, "You can?"

"Yes, although I've never made an array that big, so it will take some time for me to figure out the mathematical equation necessary to stabilize the binding structure to keep such a large array from stretching too thin and snapping from the stress."

Sid got excited. "I can still help with the math part, even if I'm powerless." He leaned in and put his mouth close to her ear and spoke for some time until she nodded.

Agnes put her mouth to his ear and said something that Crowdal couldn't hear. The crash of the waves made it necessary for them to huddle close so they didn't have to raise their voices so much. As they did this, Crowdal saw them holding hands.

Finally, Agnes pulled away and said, "I think I understand it. What about the modifier?"

Sid leaned back to her ear and she nodded as he spoke.

"That will be easy." She let go of his hand and crawled forward until she had a clear view of the barbarian men. Her face darkened when she noticed the men raping the woman.

Crowdal could not tell if she was doing anything until he heard a cry of alarm reach them from the men's camp. Crowdal crawled forward and saw the men running around in a small circle in a frenzy, some pounding at an invisible wall. To the back he saw that the men who had been raping the woman were lying unmoving on the ground while the woman crawled hastily away, covered in blood. What Agnes did to them, Crowdal didn't know, but he turned and caught her eye.

Agnes shrugged. "They didn't deserve to live." She slumped in exhaustion. "The array should hold them but I'm afraid I won't have the strength to do anything like that again for a while. Sid used to make it look so easy, but I'm not quite at his level."

Crowdal touched her shoulder. "You did great. Can you walk?"

She nodded and Crowdal helped her back to the group, no longer bothering to hide himself from the men on the beach.

"Agnes did it. They are all imprisoned. But we should hurry in any case."

Sid put his arm out for Agnes to hold, concern for her showing clearly on his face.

Crowdal turned to the Haissan standing closest to him. "Go secure the camp to ensure there are no lookouts that were missed."

The Haissan turned to Sid, who nodded for it to go, and with a slight motion of its head to the other Haissen, seven of them sprinted across the rocks.

Crowdal looked at Sid, again amazed that he commanded such loyalty from the Haissen. They would die for him without question or concern. He turned back to the camp and saw the Haissen fanning out to explore the entire area. Two Haissen ran up the beach, disappearing into the darkness before quickly melting back into the light of the fire in the middle of the camp. The leader of the Haissen turned and motioned that it was all clear.

Crowdal quickly stood up. "Alright, it's clear. Let's go."

They walked into the camp and the men imprisoned in the array glared and shouted at them with murder in their eyes. They were large and filthy men, most with thick beards and rings in their noses, cheeks and eyebrows. They pounded against the invisible array, spittle flying from their mouths as they bellowed.

Nik stopped at a pile of items by the fire, varying from crude cups to animal pelts and clothing. He nudged them with the toe of his boot and glanced at Sid. "It looks like they are marauders." When Sid looked questioningly at him, Nik pointed at the men. "I've run across men like these. You may think mercenaries are bad, but we usually live by rule and law, working for employers who pay us to do specific jobs. These scum just rove around and steal and pillage from anyone they run across. They often hit small villages and destroy them completely, raping their women and children." He turned and spat at the nearest marauder, but it hit the array and ran slowly down. The man smiled cruelly at him, his teeth blackened and broken.

Nik spotted something and ran around the array to peer more closely into its center. He cursed loudly and motioned the group over.

Crowdal joined him and looked where he pointed and gasped. Lying amidst the men were five filthy women wearing no clothes and cowering on the ground. The men saw them looking at the women and laughed as they pulled them by the hair to a standing position. They pulled out long knives and slowly slit the women's throats. Blood flowed freely and the men pulled the gurgling women forward and shoved them against the array, the blood running thickly down the invisible wall.

Sid cried out as he pounded his fists against the array, his eyes wild.

The men laughed as they threw the dead women to the ground. One of the men held up the blade he had used and licked the blood from it.

Sid turned to Crowdal, his eyes tearing up. "We can't let these men live."

Crowdal felt his stomach knot up at the thought of more killing, but then he looked at the dead women – who were actually just girls no more than twelve or thirteen years old, and anger welled up from the pit of his stomach. He turned to face the rest of the group and saw the same looks on their faces.

Crowdal pulled Sid and Agnes back until they were a hundred paces from the camp. "You two stay here. At my signal, you cancel the array, Agnes." She nodded, her eyes hard and her back straight with no sign of exhaustion showing anymore.

Crowdal turned and drew his sword as he walked back to the camp where Writhgarth, Tulman, Nik and the thirteen Haissen all stood with swords out. Without a word they spread out in a line until they each had room to fight, then Crowdal raised and lowered his arm. He felt the air pressure change slightly, the only indication the array was gone.

The marauders, all holding pitted and warped swords, stayed still for a few moments, the only sound the waves crashing on the shore. Crowdal counted more than fifty of them, the odds not in his small group's favor. He glanced at the thirteen Haissen and quickly changed his mind, knowing what they were capable of.

Then, as one, the men screamed and charged with their swords held high, sand flying up from their boots as they ran, splitting up in groups of four or five to attack each of them.

Crowdal waited, still and calm until five men were just a pace away, then he kicked savagely at the nearest one, sending him flying back at least five paces where he landed in an unnatural position and didn't move again. Crowdal quickly skewered another, pulling his sword free from the man's stomach in time to block two enemy swords with quick flicks of his wrist, then spun and swept his blade in a deadly arch. Two marauders immediately stumbled backward, their intestines spilling to the ground as they collapsed. The remaining man looked at his four comrades, killed before he had even come to a stop. He looked up at Crowdal with fear in his eyes, eyes that opened briefly in surprise as his head fell to the ground. Crowdal kicked the decapitated body back and ran over to Nik, who was struggling to hold back three of the marauders.

Crowdal kicked one in the back so hard the man's spine snapped. One of the remaining two spun toward the new threat and died as Crowdal rammed his sword so hard into the man's gut his blade sunk to the hilt. Crowdal pushed the man back and pulled his sword free as Nik cut the sword arm from his foe. The man's scream was cut short as Nik stepped forward with a two handed downward strike, the blade crunching entirely through the man's skull and coming to rest in his upper torso. Nik yanked his sword free with difficulty and turned to look for another adversary, his sword dripping brain matter and blood.

Crowdal raised an eyebrow at Nik's violent strike, gaining new respect for the man who always seemed more ready to laugh than to fight.

The area was suddenly quiet except for the distant crashing of waves. Crowdal looked around and saw Writhgarth and Tulman standing by eight dead men. Tulman was bleeding from a wound in his thigh and Writhgarth held his hand over a bloody shoulder. The Haissen had killed the rest of the men, at least thirty bodies lying at their feet. The strange creatures stood quietly as if they didn't even see the death strewn around them.

The stench of blood and filth made Crowdal nauseous as he walked over to Writhgarth and Tulman. "You are hurt, let me see."

Tulman shook his head. "I can dress my own wound. Take care of Captain Writhgarth."

Crowdal turned to his friend. "Come on, let's get near the fire so I can get a better look at that."

Writhgarth followed him, muttering about the filthy man who struck him from behind.

Motioning to a piece of driftwood, Crowdal asked Writhgarth to sit while he retrieved his pack, but as he turned, he saw Sid and Agnes dragging it over. He couldn't help smiling at their awkward struggle to drag a pack that was as large and heavy as them. He stepped forward and picked it up. "Thanks, guys. I've got it." They were breathing hard and didn't protest.

Sid sat by Writhgarth. "Is there anything I can do to help?"

Crowdal motioned at the shoulder. "Cut the cloth away from the wound." He rummaged through his pack until he found his medical kit, a dark wooden box with a beautifully worked brass hinge and hook that kept the lid closed. His mother had made it and given it to him when he had left. He rarely had use for it, as he healed so quickly, but it was nice to have for situations like this. He wished for the thousandth time that Melinda was with them. Her healing skills were unmatched. But she wasn't here, so he turned to Writhgarth as he set the box on the ground and opened it. "I need to rinse and sterilize the wound. This will not be pleasant."

Writhgarth grunted. "Get on with it."

He pulled out a thick glass bottle and pulled the cork free with his teeth. A sharp alcohol smell burned his nose. It was pure and strong, too strong to even drink. He carefully poured a few drops at a time into the wound. While it wasn't very deep and shouldn't affect Writhgarth very much, he needed to make sure it didn't get infected.

Writhgarth hissed but didn't move, a testament to his strength.

Putting the cork back into the bottle, Crowdal set it down and removed a needle and coarse black thread. "Do you want a piece of leather to bite on while I close it up?"

Writhgarth glared at him and Crowdal grinned despite the situation.

"I'm glad you find this so amusing, Trith. Now if you've had enough fun, can you finish up so I can get on with my life?"

Crowdal sewed the wound shut as quickly as he could. The stitches were jagged and would leave an ugly scar, but looking at the scars on the Vringe's face, he didn't think Writhgarth was a man who cared. He placed a clean cloth against the wound and tied it on with strips of leather. "Try not to use your left shoulder for a few days or those stitches could tear out; it's not a serious wound though, so you will be fine."

Writhgarth nodded his thanks, pulled a flask from his belt and took a long swallow of water. He motioned with his good arm at the dead men all around. "What do we do with them?"

Tulman walked up, not even limping, and spat on one of the bodies. "We leave 'em here to rot as a warning to any others."

Sid motioned at the five dead girls. "We need to bury them, though. They deserve it."

Crowdal felt tears in the corners of his eyes. "That they do."

By the time the sun rose, they had buried the five girls in graves as high up the beach as they could, covering them with rocks to keep any scavengers from getting to them. They stood in silence for a few moments then Crowdal motioned with his head at the bloody mess behind them where the marauders lay in their own blood. "Come on, let's get out of here."

Nik motioned at the camp. "Should we take their food?"

Writhgarth spat to his side. "I will not touch anything those foul men had."

For once, Nik didn't have a sarcastic reply.

No one spoke as they started walking up the beach. The smell of death quickly faded and Crowdal looked back to see black vultures already circling above the bodies.

The ugly birds would feast this morning.

Chapter 7

Waves crashed relentlessly onto the sandy beach with a repetitiveness that irritated Tris. He and his party had been following Sid's trail along the beach for days, always coming upon their old campsites but never catching up with them.

Not for the first time, he wished he could use his portal equation to jump ahead. But since he had never been to this area, he could not attach the equation to anything. In anger, he had forced his group to continue walking through the first three nights to try and catch Sid, and even though the Hunters, body guards and pack men didn't show much fatigue, he had tired himself by creating so many portal equations, especially the final one to get them all to the obelisk clearing in the Srithian Wood, which had required a tremendous amount of energy.

He felt his eyes closing as he walked, sleep pulling at him. He stumbled and caught himself from falling onto the rocks. It was almost sundown, so he called a stop for the night.

Paul and Ben set up his sleeping roll and the pack men made a fire and began preparing food. The Hunters never stayed in camp during the night. He had no idea where they went, but they always reappeared in the morning.

Tris laid down and closed his eyes, asleep in moments.

The light from the sun on his closed eyelids woke him. He opened his eyes and sat up, his shoulder aching and his neck popping as he turned his head in a circle.

Paul handed him a mug of steaming tea and he took it without a word, warming his cold fingers on the sides of the mug. The sun was just rising above the cliffs along the beach. The rays didn't warm him in the least but the sight of the sun was welcome after so many cloudy and cold days. But just as quickly as the sun had appeared, a fog rolled in and blocked it, bringing with it a cold mist that made him shiver. He could create an equation to protect him from the weather, but it would just be a waste of energy.

He motioned Ben over. "Get me a thicker coat."

The huge man dug into one of the packs and produced a thick long-coat that protected the wearer's legs from wind and cold and handed it to Tris.

Tris put it on over his existing coat and within moments he felt warm for the first time in days.

One of the pack men handed him a charred piece of meat stuck on a stick. It steamed as he bit into it, juices running down his chin. The meat filled him with energy and he quickly finished it, tossing the stick into the fire. He stood and stretched, feeling almost normal for the first time in days. He walked a few paces away and dropped his trousers, speaking over his shoulder as he did his business, "You'd better be ready to move out by the time I finish."

The pack men burst into a flurry of activity and the camp was packed up by the time Tris stood up and buckled his trousers.

They started up the beach again and it soon became so rocky that they had to slow down even more to make their way over the rough terrain. The sun hung low in the sky by the time they came to a point where the beach narrowed and arched out into the ocean. They carefully made their way around it and immediately came upon the scene of a mighty battle. The massive fire pit was cold, and scattered about the beach were bodies that were cut to pieces. Tris stopped by the closest one and saw that birds had eaten the eyes and much of the face. Flies crawled inside the sockets and mouth, buzzing angrily when he kicked sand at them.

The Hunters quickly moved about the area and the older woman, who he had found out was named Gee, glided up to him. "Looks like a band of marauders were massacred. She pointed farther up by the cliffs. "There are five graves up there."

Tris started forward, speaking curtly, "Show me."

He was led to a group of graves covered carefully with rocks. "Dig them out. I want to see who they are."

Gee whistled the pack men over and told them to dig. The big men quickly did as they were told, throwing rocks over their shoulders until they reached the sand, and then digging furiously with their hands until they reached the bodies.

Tris leaned forward expectantly as the pack men brushed wet sand from the faces to reveal young women, their throats cut. Relief washed through him that Sid wasn't one of them and he turned and walked away. He heard the pack men begin to refill the graves and he bellowed out, "Leave them for the birds."

Tris led the way up the beach, knowing he was catching up with his old friend.

Chapter 8

Drax stepped through the dark doorway and into a narrow hallway that led to his right. Faint light reached him, revealing a rough-hewn stone floor damp with water. He slowly made his way down the short hallway until he came to a stairwell that curved down into darkness. The huge man was nowhere in sight and he hesitated, wondering why he was following a man he had never met into a dark stairwell. If he was as smart as he thought, he would turn around and get as far away from here as he could.

The deep voice of the man echoed up the stairs, "Do not hesitate, young Drax. Follow me now or run away and live a mediocre life. I will close the door I'm holding at the count of five. One, two, three…"

Drax ran down the dark stairs and came around the final turn just as the man reached five and was pulling the door closed. Drax reach out and stopped it with his foot.

"You cut it pretty close." The man pushed the door open and motioned Drax through. "Welcome to the Frahnndem."

Drax pushed aside his fear and stepped through the doorway and into a chamber lit by flameless braziers that gave off a dull, yellow light. The chamber was circular and maybe thirty paces across. Four closed doors lined the walls at even intervals. Shelving and cubby holes filled every bit of wall space and were filled with books and scrolls. In the center of the chamber was a long, rectangular table with two backless stools on which to sit. A ladder with wheels on each end that sat in tracks leaned against the wall, and Drax saw right away it could be pushed around the room even while someone was standing on it. There was more wealth of knowledge in this room than he had ever seen before. The library in the Fahrin Druin training facility had only a fraction of the books and scrolls held in this room.

He turned to the man in awe. "I've never seen a room with this many books in my life."

The man chuckled. "Actually, this is the smallest one of five within my home."

Drax widened his eyes, unable to comprehend what the man had just said. He saw a massive book on a shelf across the room and found himself almost running over to it. The spine was at least a hand-span thick. He ran a finger lightly across the ancient leather, the dry and cracked material making his heart race. How much knowledge was in this one volume alone? He turned his head to the man. "May I?"

The man hesitated, then nodded yes, although he looked a little irritated.

Drax carefully slid the book from the shelf, his eyes widening even further at the immense weight as he pulled it free and carefully walked to the table to set it down. The book was at least four hand-spans in length by three in width, and he had to use both hands to open the cover.

Before he could bend down to read, though, the man placed a hand on the cover and pulled it closed again. "You will have time enough later to examine this, for now I need you to follow me." He turned and walked to the middle door across the room and opened it. He turned to Drax and motioned with his head for him to follow.

Drax glanced back down at the book with longing, then sighed quietly and walked over to the man whose name he had yet to hear.

He was led down a series of hallways to a smaller room containing only a fireplace and two soft chairs facing each other, angled toward the fire, each with a narrow table next to it. But the floor was covered with books and scrolls, some of the books stacked as high as Drax was tall, precariously balanced so it seemed only a small nudge would send them collapsing to the floor. The man motioned him to take a seat as he closed the door.

"It is always cold this far underground, so I spend most of my time here in this room."

Drax chose the chair to the right of the fireplace, but before he could sit, the man said, "No, that one is mine." Drax quickly sat in the other chair as the man turned and removed his heavy cloak and hung it on a hook on the door. Drax was shocked to see that the man was standing on stilts. Using the wall for support he stepped off of them with practiced ease and set them against the wall before turning to face him.

Drax didn't know what he was expecting the man to look like, but nothing prepared him for what he saw.

The man was short, no more than Drax's height and had used the stilts to make him look like a giant. He had a sunken-in upper body with a narrow waist, and his legs looked as thin as young willow saplings. Drax couldn't help staring in wonder as the strange man limped over and stopped by his chair, holding out his bony hand.

When he spoke, his voice was as deep and powerful as earlier. "It is time we were formally introduced. My name is Baldrick, and as you may have guessed, I am the Frahnndem."

Drax took the man's hand and shook it lightly, worried about harming him. But the man squeezed his hand with some strength before releasing it so Drax could sit down in his chair.

"I imagine you find my appearance strange." When Drax started to shake his head no, the man held up a hand to stop him. "No need to say anything. I wear those stilts only when I open the main door for one of the Fahrin Druin to offer me a promising candidate. They have degenerated into a pathetically simple group who only respect strength and power, which I am irritated by more than you can know. Unfortunately, as I've not yet allowed one of their offerings through my door, I've worn the stilts too often for naught. Tell me, are you worth the effort of being brought down here, Mr. Drax?"

Drax felt his mouth hanging open so he closed it and wiped a bit of drool from his mouth. This was all so very strange that he honestly didn't know how to respond.

Baldrick noticed his confusion and sighed loudly. "Come now, Mr. Drax, use that big brain of yours or I will be forced to rid myself of you."

It was like a physical slap and Drax sat up straight. He was in the strangest situation in his life but one that intrigued him. Plus, the threat was real. He knew there was likely only one way out of here and that was to do what this man wanted. He swallowed twice to try to get enough moisture back into his dry mouth to speak and finally managed to say, "Yes, sir. I am at your service."

Baldrick roared, "I don't need a servant. I need someone who can think and act, who can use their brain to the limits of possibility and then go even further." He lowered the volume of his voice to conversation level and continued, "I have watched you for a while now and I have seen you actively trying to be mediocre when I know you are far from it. I should flay your skin from your body for that."

Drax felt his cheeks flush. Aside from Walter, he had never had anyone see him for who he really was. A weight lifted from him, a heaviness he had forgotten was even there.

Baldrick must have seen the change in him for he nodded with a gruff exhalation of breath. "Welcome to the Frahnndem, Mr. Drax. Unfortunately, we are short on time so I will review my history briefly and then explain what I need from you."

Drax felt like he was in the right place for the first time in his life and shifted forward in his chair, anxious to hear what Baldrick had to say.

The man tilted his head and looked up to the ceiling as he spoke. "To begin at the beginning is no easy task, for I do not even know where that point in time is anymore. I do know I was born in the age of Ulon, the name really more of a concept than a memory for me now. I mostly remember it as a time of war and death, of bloody battles and ravaged lands with no kingdoms or borders. Armies of black-armored men from the north clashed with giants from the west and humans from the south in endless cycles of struggle." As he spoke, he reached to the table next to his elbow, picked up a short ivory pipe and tapped it onto a marble plate to empty old tobacco from it. He reached into his shirt, pulled out a small cloth sack with a drawstring and opened it.

"An evil man controlled the army of humans; more than 20,000 of the hardest men the world had ever seen, then or now." He packed the pipe with a pinch of sweet-smelling tobacco. "His army was losing to the black-armored hordes from the north so he did the unthinkable." Baldrick stuck a thin taper into the fire and when it was lit, he put it to the pipe and sucked in, the small flame pulling down into the pipe until he removed it and shook out the flame with an exhalation of thick blue smoke. "Where was I?"

Drax immediately said, "The evil man did the unthinkable."

"Yes, that's right." His eyes got a faraway look as he smoked in silence for a few more moments, then continued, "He created a creature that was not of this world, a creature made from the power of Black Numbers that was so massive and violent, it would crush his enemies to the north and the giants to the west."

Drax broke in. "But how could he create a creature from Black Numbers? Only the mythical Aleph Null could possibly do something like that. And how do you know all of this?"

Baldrick narrowed his eyes. "I know this because that evil man was me."

Chapter 9

T he forest floor turned from flat and clear of brush, to hilly and damp with thick, stout trees that grew so closely together it was impossible for the Korpor to see far in any direction. Birds of all sorts chirped and twittered in the tree branches above, and like the numerous robins running across the ground, stopping and listening before plunging their beaks into the dirt and pulling out a worm or grub, the Korpor had not had a problem hunting for food. Just that morning it had caught a deer hiding in a thick copse of trees, the meat tender and rich, filling the Korpor's stomach for the first time in days.

The Korpor had made its way slowly through the forest, having no real place to be. It had spent the entire previous day sleeping against a large tree. At one point, a small bird had landed on its head, hopping around while chirping softly, waking the Korpor from a deep sleep. But it had ignored the bird and closed its eyes again, drifting back into a dream it couldn't remember after awakening. More than ten uneventful days had passed as it rested and ate and rested some more.

A roar echoed down the long ravine where the Korpor was drinking from a shallow stream, yanking its thoughts back to the present. It lifted its head and cocked it sideways, listening intently. In the distance it heard multiple, heavy footsteps approaching. The Korpor quickly climbed up the side of the ravine to see what was making such noise. Thick trees blocked it from seeing any distance, so the Korpor leaned against a tree and waited for whatever approached to come into view. The sounds grew louder and closer until the Korpor finally saw a group of humanoids marching toward it. They passed by just a few dozen paces away and the Korpor studied them, intrigued.

The humanoids walked on two legs and wore no clothing, despite being hairless. Their skin was a mottled orange and brown, their faces similar to a human's, yet different enough that the Korpor couldn't recognize them as any race it had ever encountered. Their foreheads were non-existent, so their eyes rested where a human's cheeks would have been, and their heads sloped back in a wedge shape. The Korpor raked its claws against the tree without thinking and even though the sound was minimal, the creatures stopped as one and turned to look at it.

The beings stared at the Korpor in curiosity. They showed no fear, nor did they fall to the ground in pain from the Korpor's gaze.

One of the individuals turned and approached the Korpor, coming to a stop within reach of it, sniffing with a nose that jutted out at a sharp angle. The strange being curled up a thick lip in what might have been a snarl or smile and reached out to touch the Korpor's cheek with a large muscular hand. The creature then screeched in short bursts and the Korpor flinched slightly at the harsh sounds. Soon, it was surrounded by the rest of the creatures, eight in total, all touching it in different places. This was the strangest encounter it had ever had in its thousands of years of existence. It had always struck terror and pain upon any living thing it saw.

One creature slipped a hand between the Korper's legs and held its flaccid penis, then slid a finger into its vagina before quickly removing it and sniffing it. Under any other circumstances, the Korper would have rammed its claws into the creature, but it was curious what might happen next.

The creatures screeched softly to each other until they finally stopped touching the Korper and stood back in a semi-circle, facing it. One stepped forward and a male-sounding voice whispered in the Korpor's mind, *"Can you understand me?"*

The Korpor cocked its head and replied, *"Yes I can. What are you?"*

"We are the Myrss. My name is Cryff. What are you?"

"I am the Korpor."

Cryff tilted his head. *"And what is your name?"*

The Korpor scowled. *"I am the Korpor."*

Cryff narrowed his eyes. *"The Korpor. How strange. The Korpor, why do you enter our territory?"*

"I go where I please."

The Myrss screeched angrily to each other until Cryff raised his hand for silence. *"The Korpor, you are not welcome here. You will leave here."*

Looking at each of the Myrss, the Korpor wondered if it should kill them all and be done with this situation. But instead, it decided to see what they would do if it stayed. So it bared its teeth and snarled, *"I will stay here for as long as I please."*

The one called Cryff struck the Korpor across the face with a blow so strong that the Korpor's head struck the tree trunk next to it. The weight behind the blow was incongruent to the fist itself, as if the Korpor had been struck by a much larger creature. The Korpor touched its face and the sight of the thick blood on its paw caused an instant bloodlust to flow through it. With a deep growl, the Korper struck out at Cryff, raking its claws in a blow that should have taken his face off in a bloody clump. But Cryff put up an arm to block the strike and it felt like the Korpor had struck a thick tree. Pain radiated through its paw and up its arm.

The Korpor stared in confusion at Cryff.

"You will leave now, the Korpor."

Vibrating with rage, the Korpor struck at Cryff with its other paw and connected against his head, but Cryff didn't even flinch from the blow. The Korpor lunged forward, wrapped its arms around the Myrss and attempted to throw him against the tree, but it couldn't budge the creature. It might as well have tried to pull a large oak tree from the ground.

The Korpor stepped back and felt its rage quickly dissipate as Cryff simply waited for the Korpor to either strike again or leave the area.

For only the second time in its long life, the Korpor backed down from a confrontation. The Unnamed One had been the first to prove unbeatable, now these strange beings. Flexing its claws, the Korpor nodded once and stepped through the ring of Myrss, who parted to let it through. It glided through the forest and didn't look back as it quickly made its way west, shaking the pain from its arm and wondering just what kind of beings it had just encountered.

The Kuldragg forest was not proving to be the quiet place it needed to rest and figure out its future.

Chapter 10

Sid crouched down to stretch his knees, the popping of his joints loud as he bounced up and down to loosen the stiffness. He hurried to catch up with the group, which was going around a sharp turn to the left where the mountain rose straight up into the clouds, forming an imposing stone wall.

He craned his neck back to stare in wonder at the thousands of white seabirds nesting far up the cliff, wheeling about and calling to each other as they flew. After a few thousand steps, Sid made it around the bend and heard a cheer from Nik.

He stopped in his tracks at the sight ahead of him. The mountains that had risen from the sea for so long fell sharply away to the flat expanse of a grass and boulder plain that led inland. He squinted his eyes and in the distance he could make out the line of a dark forest stretching as far as he could see to the west.

Nik fell to his knees and kissed the beach a few times, then raised his head and sputtered sand from his lips. "Yuck. I probably shouldn't have done that." At seeing everyone staring at him, he shrugged. "What? Can't a guy show happiness at finally getting off this cursed beach?"

Sid agreed with him, though he didn't go so far as to kiss the sand. He looked ahead and saw there was a small fishing village not too much farther up the beach. Crowdal and Writhgarth spoke softly together, gesturing toward the village as they spoke.

Sid stepped over to them. "Should we approach the village? I wouldn't mind a warm bed and bath for a night."

Crowdal looked at Writhgarth once more and said, "I agree with you, Sid. But Writhgarth doesn't think it would be a good idea."

Writhgarth spat to his side. "Aye, we do not know anything about these people. We are as far north as we can get and I've never heard of any people living out here. I say we just cut inland now and head for the Kuldragg forest."

Crowdal nodded. "I understand your reasoning, but we really could use some supplies."

"Then we'd better be careful. Don't tell anyone where we are from or who we are."

Crowdal pointed to the small stone pier that the people of the village had built. "Let's enter the village from the pier..., what is Tulman doing?"

Sid looked and saw Tulman hurrying toward the pier.

Crowdal motioned them forward. "Come on, let's see what's going on."

The Haissen split up, with six of them leading the way, five staying to the rear, and two staying close to Sid. Even knowing they now served him, it still made him feel uncomfortable knowing just how deadly they were. But he was also very thankful to have them with the group. It definitely made him feel safer, especially since he no longer had access to his Numbers.

It took much longer to reach the pier than he anticipated; distances were difficult to judge along the beach. As they approached, Sid curiously studied the stone-built structure that stretched about thirty paces out into the rough, gray waters. It was built in a backward "L" shape which Sid instinctively realized was to protect boats from the never-ending wind and waves that battered the shore, although there were no boats tied up now. He had never seen a pier before and started toward it, but Crowdal pulled him back. "Stay off of it; it might not be safe."

Sid nodded reluctantly and turned to see a muddy trail led from the pier up a small hill, hiding the village from view. Tulman's tracks were visible in the mud, disappearing over the top of the hill. The area was quiet except for the slap of waves hitting the pier and shore.

Sid got a feeling something was very wrong.

Six of the Haissen sprinted up the hill and were soon back. One of them hissed, "The village appears to be empty. Tulman is searching every building."

Crowdal started up the trail with Writgarth, and Sid followed with Agnes, Nik and the remaining Haissen. Sid crested the top of the hill and stopped to take in the village. It was smaller than he had expected. The trail he was standing on led right through the middle of the village and exited into a vast expanse of barren scrub brush and boulders, out toward the forbidding darkness of the Kuldragg forest. The village consisted of a couple dozen worn, stone structures that clustered around a small village square.

The Haissen were right, the village was deserted. The doors of many of the buildings had been chopped up and scattered on the ground; some were blackened and charred, and most of the thatched roofs had been burned or torn away. Some of the buildings themselves had fallen to the ground in a pile of rubble. A banging sound reached them, and in the distance Sid could see a worn shutter striking the wall of a home as the wind hit it, the sound eerie and lonely. He saw Tulman step from a building and turn to walk to the next.

Crowdal turned to Nik. "Do you know why Tulman is doing that?"

Nik shook his head. "I have no idea."

Crowdal looked torn, then said, "Let's give him his space. He is obviously searching for something."

Sid walked over to the closest building and peered through the doorway. The room was small with a dirt floor and a broken wooden table lying against the wall. In the corner he spotted a bit of red sticking up from the ground. He took three steps and pulled it from the wet dirt. To his surprise it was a crude doll, barely recognizable as a doll, but probably some child's dearest possession. He brushed as much dirt from it as he could and carried it outside, coming to a stop by Crowdal and Writhgarth.

Sid heard Writhgarth say, "I would bet it was those marauders we dealt with who did this. Bastards."

Crowdal shook his head. "No, this village was destroyed years ago, there is too much overgrowth for this to have just happened."

Writhgarth glanced around and nodded, "You are right, I didn't notice that."

Sid felt Agnes step up close to him and he could feel her shivering, whether from the cold wind or the evil that had occurred here, he wasn't sure. He put an arm around her and showed her the worn doll, feeling tears run down his cheeks. These poor people had worked hard to survive in this barren terrain, using the bounty of the ocean to feed them and the animals of the land to cloth them. Yet it had probably only taken a day for them to be wiped out by whomever had done this.

Agnes turned the doll in her hand and looked at Sid, tears in her eyes, too. Her voice was soft as she said, "It breaks my heart to know some child held this very doll. Why is there so much evil in this world?"

Sid had no answer so he just held her tighter.

Tulman exited a broken building on the other side of the village and turned to stare back inside.

Sid looked up at Crowdal. "I think we should go talk to Tulman and find out what he knows."

Crowdal nodded and they all started making their way over to Tulman. The mercenary Captain didn't move or acknowledge their arrival. He just stared into the darkness of the building he was standing in front of.

Clearing his throat, Sid touched Tulman's shoulder.

Tulman reacted as if Sid had punched him, spinning around and drawing his sword in a single move, the action so quick that Sid didn't even have time to react. But two Haissen had stepped forward and knocked Tulman's sword to the ground with a clatter, holding both of their blades to his neck.

Sid watched Tulman's eyes change from blazing fury to shock in a moment. Sid motioned to the Haissen, "Remove your swords."

The swords disappeared with a swish of air and Tulman slumped his shoulders, the first time Sid had ever seen anything remotely like weakness from the man. "Tulman, what's going on?"

Tulman's hands shook as he bent down and picked up his sword, placing it slowly in its scabbard. He looked at everyone, his eyes haunted and empty. The silence stretched out until he let out a breath and motioned at the building over his shoulder. "This was my family home. I grew up in this village. My father and mother, and my brother and his family all lived in this house. I knew we would come here as soon as we started traveling along the coast, but I didn't expect to be so affected by the emptiness after all this time."

Crowdal stepped forward and put his hand on Tulman's shoulder. "I am sorry. When was the last time you were here?"

Tulman looked at the sky, his face twisting in fury and sorrow. When he spoke, his voice was raw and deep. "I was last here eighteen summers ago. I saw the birth of my nephew, Wult, but my brother's wife died soon after the birth." He pointed to a hill in the distance outside of the village. "I helped dig her grave over there. I stayed the summer to help my family, but when autumn came I had to go look for work. When I returned the following year, the village was destroyed and everyone was dead." He closed his eyes and when he reopened them, they were glassy from barely controlled tears. "I buried the remains, most of them nothing but scattered bones after a year of scavengers having free reign. I have not returned since."

Sid felt himself on the edge of tears again. He never thought of Tulman as a man who had family. He was such a tough and solitary man that it was hard to imagine him having a history.

Tulman glanced down at Sid. "I apologize for drawing my sword on you." They were simple words but carried a heavy burden in their tone. "I will take my leave and you will not hear from me again."

Sid looked up at Tulman, "I would prefer to have you by my side."

He stared at Sid for a long moment before nodding his head once in agreement and walking up the path toward the end of town.

Sid watched him angle up the barren hill and kneel by a stone marker.

Crowdal sat on a relatively dry section of the ground and motioned them all to join him. "Let's give the poor man some time. We might as well eat something while we wait."

Writhgarth grunted. "Like you ever need a reason to eat. I swear, you would stop to make a grass and dirt salad in the middle of a battle if your stomach had any say."

Crowdal bit into a piece of cheese while Writhgarth pulled out a packet of dried fish and passed it around, taking a large fillet for himself.

Sid ate his fish and noticed an old well in the center of the village. He gathered up everyone's water skins and walked over to see if it still had water in it. He set the containers on the ground and peered over the side. It was dark inside the well and many of the stones at the top were missing. There was still a bucket and wheel intact, although the rope was frayed and partially rotted. Sid picked up the bucket and dumped out some dirt and pebbles, then gently lifted it over the edge of the well. He grabbed the wooden handle and slowly cranked it backward, the wheel squeaking as the bucket lowered to the water far below. He let it fill with water and hoping the rope held, slowly cranked it back up and pulled the full bucket to the stone edge. The water looked clear, so he took a small sip, prepared to spit it out if necessary, but to his surprise it tasted more pure than any water he had ever had, so cold that it made his mouth numb. He drank until he couldn't drink anymore, then lowered the bucket three more times to fill all the water skins.

He turned and called for his friends to join him. Soon everyone had drunk as much water as they could, even the Haissen. It had been a long time since they had been able to completely slake their thirst.

Tulman wandered back to join them and smiled for the first time when he saw the well. He ran his hand along the stone, "Ah, I remember you." He lifted the bucket and drank deeply, his entire front soon wet from the sloshing liquid. He splashed his face, grinning with delight. "Have you ever had water this cold and good?"

Crowdal laughed and said he hadn't.

Tulman gestured to the well. "This water will purify your spirit and make you as healthy as a mule – at least that was what my ma used to say. It was my job as a kid to be lowered into the well every spring to fix any of the crumbling rocks after the long cold winter. I remember once I leaned too far out and the bucket flipped, dumping me into the water at the bottom." His eyes had a faraway look as he continued, "I treaded water and yelled for my pa to lower the bucket. It only took a few moments, but in that short time my whole body became numb from the icy water and I barely had the strength to hold onto the bucket as I was lifted up. I was given a blanket and as soon as I was warm again, I climbed back into the bucket and was lowered back down." His eyes cleared and he shrugged, "That was a long time ago." He gazed around the village one last time and then motioned with his head, "Come on, let's get out of here."

Crowdal studied Tulman for a few moments, then headed back to where he left his pack and swung it onto his back, looking up as the sun peeked through a break in the clouds. "We should make it to the edge of the forest by dark."

The rest of them gathered their own packs and followed Tulman up the little hill leading out of the village.

Sid glanced at the worn headstones clustered on the top of the barren hill, many of them leaning, some broken and laying on the ground, all that remained of the people of this lost village. They continued out into the vast expanse of rough terrain filled with boulders, rocks, and stubby grass that crunched loudly as they stepped on it. Not far from the village, Sid stumbled on a small rock and fell to his hands and knees, and as he pushed himself back to his feet he saw a piece of metal sticking up from the ground. He bent back down and pushed the scrub grass away from the metal and saw it was the edge of a sword. He followed it back until he saw the edge of a haft, most of it buried.

Crowdal looked back at Sid and stopped. "What is it, Sid?"

Looking up briefly, Sid said, "I think it's an old sword." He looked back down and dug around the haft, the dirt crumbling away until he was able to wiggle it free and wrap his hands around it. He pulled up, straining to get the rest of the sword from the ground until it came free with a shower of dirt. Sid stood up and held the sword out to look at it.

Everyone crowded around him, including Tulman, who had a dark look in his eyes as he said, "Give me that."

Sid handed him the sword and Tulman twisted it in the light as he brushed more of the dirt away. The blade was rusted and pitted and the haft had tatters of leather hanging from it. Tulman threw it into the grass in disgust and turned to Sid. "That was a fucking raider sword. I was not more than fifteen years old when a small raiding party attacked us in the night. We drove them out here and finished them off, but not before they'd murdered my uncle and four others." He wiped his hands on his trousers as if they were unclean, then turned and made his way forward, cursing as he went.

Sid exchanged a glance with Crowdal, then started following Tulman and the Haissen. Sid thought of the long history of this forsaken area so far north of any existing civilization, of the generations of people who had lived and died out here, including all of Tulman's family. A sadness filled him and stayed with him until they drew near the forest. Sid turned his head to the right for what seemed like the hundredth time to look at the tree line stretching as far west as he could see, like a colossal castle wall. They stopped a few hundred paces from the forest edge just as the sun set. He tried to peer into the trees, but the forest was impenetrable and dark, making him shiver with fear.

Sid wondered if any man had ever set foot in it and if so, if they had ever made it back out.

Chapter 11

Melinda held the small wooden cup of hot tea out to Prennia, who took it with trembling hands and leaned over to inhale the bitter Hartroot steam, a root that Melinda knew helped increase blood flow.

Prennia's mouth drooped on one side and as she took a small sip, the tea dribbled out. She struggled to speak, but when the words didn't come out, she concentrated hard and slowly said, "Thank you, Melinda."

Melinda knew her grandmother's failing health was her fault. Prennia had been training her for the past few days in the proper ways to enter the Raith world, working with her night and day with barely a stop for food or rest, as if she knew her time was short.

Melinda had learned more than she thought possible, but she had not been able to dissuade her grandmother from continuing with the training, even when she looked like she would collapse at any moment. Although she was exhausted, Prennia had told Melinda that the Raith world existed on different frequencies. Most Zranh only had the ability to enter the first frequency, a level where time cycled at a slightly slower rate. Some, like Prennia had mastered the second frequency, which allowed her to slow time even more. But most children born in the last twenty years or so could just touch the first frequency, creating more of a wobble in time that allowed them to move as a blur while still remaining visible to others.

Melinda was different. She could enter the third frequency, where the base level of time existed, allowing her to completely move about a plane of existence that no others could touch. She had asked Prennia if there were more than three frequencies and the old woman had paused, looking lost in thought, then she hesitantly nodded, saying there was an ancient Zranh song that mentioned something called 'negative frequency,' but it was only referenced once in the long song and no one knew what it meant.

Melinda had been intrigued, but Prennia had moved on to discussing how Melinda could conserve her energy by cycling between the first two frequencies of the Raith plane, and when she must fully enter the third frequency, she should only stay for an extremely limited amount of time.

As they had talked, Melinda had asked about the Zranh being assassins, and her grandmother had chuckled.

"Melinda, we are not assassins. That is just an old tale told by humans to explain what they don't understand. We never kill unless we must, and that is very rare. And how would we remain hidden if we killed for profit? That would mean working for others which is something we would never do."

Melinda nodded, knowing just how easily people accepted rumor over fact, and she felt ashamed for even asking the question of her grandmother. But Prennia had patted her knee with a smile and they had moved on to practicing how to phase quickly between the first two frequencies. Melinda had quickly understood the nuances of the shifting pattern and had found she wasn't even tired at the end of the practice session. But Prennia had grown pale and had collapsed to the floor, as if something inside of her had suddenly snapped. Melinda had helped her to the bed and had immediately rushed out into the surrounding woods, where she had thankfully been able to find Hartroot growing on the shady side of a ravine. She had returned and made the medicinal tea, but she feared it was too late to do lasting good.

Prennia took the last sip of tea and set the cup on the stone floor.

Melinda leaned forward and felt the pulse in her grandmother's neck. It was quick and uneven. "Lie back, grandmother."

Prennia nodded and let Melinda help her lie down, holding Melinda's hand, smiling as best as she could. She spoke slowly, concentrating on each word before saying it, "I am so glad you are here, Melinda. It warms my heart to know our people will be in such good hands."

Melinda squeezed her hand slightly. "You will be fine once you sleep for a while."

Prennia patted her hand. "You are a healer; you know the truth. My time in this world has come to an end."

Melinda felt a tear fall down her cheek, knowing Prennia was right. She pulled a soft deer-hide blanket up to her neck. "Sleep now. I will be here when you wake up."

Prennia shook her head. "Not yet, little one." It was a term of endearment her grandmother had begun calling Melinda the previous day and to her surprise, Melinda found that she didn't mind it. "You have learned everything I can teach you about the Raith world, but I have said very little so far about your people and what you must do next." She spent the remainder of the day speaking quietly with Melinda, telling her everything she could about the Zranh. "And finally, you must find the Aleph Null again. He and the Trith are linked with the Zranh." She fell quiet and Melinda leaned closer to her.

"How so, grandmother?"

Prennia refocused her eyes. "When you were all here before, during the time you were fighting your father, I entered the second frequency and studied your friends, for I was drawn to them. The Trith vibrated on a strange frequency that was similar to the Aleph Null and the Zranh, yet different in some way I couldn't understand. The Aleph Null had a frequency that existed on a level I've never seen, yet is complimentary to the Trith and the Zranh. If they survived the Srithian Wood, then they will be compelled to travel to the Trith Nation. You must find out what this means; you must travel to the Trith Nation, but you must also lead our people to our ancestral home in the Muldragg forest. They are both to the northwest."

So much speaking had taken the last of her energy reserves. Her eyes lost focus and she breathed out, faintly saying, "Remember, you are Leillireph." Prennia looked up at the ceiling of the cave as if she saw something and didn't look back down again.

Melinda leaned forward to check her pulse but knew she would not find one. She caressed her grandmother's cheek for a few moments and let the tears fall. She had only known her for a short time, yet had grown very close to her. She felt a presence and looked up into the tearful face of the young Zranh girl named Eithes, accompanied by an even younger girl named Goris, whom she remembered from her first time meeting the Zranh.

Eithes asked in a timid voice, "Is she gone?"

Melinda nodded and closed her grandmother's eyes. "Gather our people."

The girls stood straight and answered as one, "Yes, Leillireph." They turned and quickly disappeared out of the chamber.

Melinda took a deep breath, knowing everything had just changed. She was now the leader of the Zranh and she was surprised the idea didn't frighten her.

The next day was a blur to Melinda. They buried Prennia with the highest honors in a ceremony that lasted into the night. Just before sunrise, every Zranh had knelt before Melinda, touched their lips to the ground and said 'Leillireph'. After the last one had done this, Melinda spread her arms. "The final thing Prennia said to me was that we must leave this place and travel to our ancestral home in the Muldragg forest." They all nodded in agreement, but Melinda held her hand up. "She also told me I must travel to the Trith Nation. So I will lead us that far, then I must leave you."

One of the older Zranh stepped forward. "We will accompany you wherever you go."

Melinda shook her head. "No, you must all continue to our home for the winter. If we show up in the Trith Nation, there will be violence, and that is something I cannot have."

"We are not afraid of the Trith."

"I know, and that is not my issue. Prennia told me I must meet up with the Aleph Null at the Trith Nation, that it was important to our future. Just me."

The same Zranh started to speak but Melinda held up her hand to stop him. "It is decided."

When none of the Zranh argued, she waved them away. "Prepare for our departure. We leave by mid-day." She watched the Zranh fade into the trees until she was alone. She couldn't wait to find her friends again but a part of her was frightened of what lay ahead.

Chapter 12

Drax sat back, stunned. "What do you mean you were the evil man? I thought only the Aleph Null could wield the Black Numbers?"

Baldrick raised his right eyebrow.

"You mean you were the Aleph Null?" Drax asked, incredulous.

"No, I am *the* Aleph Null and have been for many millennia."

"But how can that be? I heard the Aleph Null was found just this spring by a Fahrin Druin in Yisk who lost her arm to his power."

"Yes, I heard that too. It is something I have been fearing for thousands of years." He cocked his head. "Tell me, what is the mission of the Fahrin Druin?"

Drax responded without hesitation, "To search for the Aleph Null and kill him or her immediately." It was something that had been drilled into him over and over for the past five years. He continued, "It is why the Fahrin Druin are trained in combat, in chemistry, and in every method there is to kill. The Fahrin Druin are to rid the world of anyone with exceptional mathematical abilities to ensure none become the Aleph Null."

Baldrick puffed on his pipe, eyeing him through the blue smoke. "And have you ever thought about why the Fahrin Druin do this?"

"To rid the world of the Aleph Null."

"No, I mean, *why* do they hunt the Aleph Null?"

Drax shrugged. "Because the Aleph Null is evil and will destroy everyone in the land."

Baldrick shook his head. "No, that is what you were taught. Come on, think. Why were you trained to do this?"

Drax had secretly questioned this simple tenet of the Fahrin Druin. It had always seemed strange that a whole organization would exist for millennia to search for someone who had possibly never existed. He had never vocalized this doubt though, fearing he would be cast out.

Baldrick tapped his foot impatiently. "Well?"

Taking a deep breath, Drax said, "I think you started the order of the Fahrin Druin to search the land for the Aleph Null because you do not want another person to have the power of Black Numbers like you do."

"And why is that, do you think?"

Drax leaned forward and whispered, "Because you know first-hand the destruction that the Aleph Null could unleash upon the world."

Baldrick grunted in irritation. "It took you long enough to finally come to that conclusion." He tapped the ashes from his pipe and set it down. "Yes, I know just how seductive the Black Numbers are. I almost destroyed everything that existed in this land."

"What stopped you from doing so?"

Baldrick sat quietly, his eyes growing distant for a few moments until he pointed to a small ceramic container on the fireplace mantle. "That contains the ashes of my wife, who was taken from me many millennia ago. I had stood on a field slick with black mud, soaked with even blacker blood, surrounded by the mutilated bodies of more than a thousand of my own men. Most had been torn apart to the point where I did not know which pieces went with which body. The stench was," he paused, his face drawn and his voice a whisper, "indescribable in its putridity. The creature I had created to destroy my enemies had gained a sense of its own self and returned to kill its maker. It had torn through my army as if they were stalks of wheat until it got to me. With a scream of rage, it had charged me, casting aside my private guard in a bloody massacre, their swords having no effect on its other-worldly skin – skin made from the essence of my Black Numbers."

He paused again, this time for much longer. His face contorted in anguish and when he looked at Drax, his eyes were red and swollen. "My wife had fled our tent with our infant son in her arms just as the beast rose above her. She threw our son as far from her as she could just as the creature smashed her to the ground. I had known then that I was to blame. As the beast attacked me, I cast it into a mathematical prison from which it could never escape, filling it with a constant pain to remind it of the misguided love I once felt for it; a love based on depravity and control. I had allowed the power of Black Numbers to supersede my sense of right and wrong, and worst of all, I never should have been so over-confident as to bring my wife and son to that battlefield. I created an equation that burned to ash what was left of my wife and scooped up what I could. I then walked away from that place of destruction with my son in my arms and disappeared into the Kuldragg forest, one of the deepest forests in the land. After a few centuries, my son left to live his own life and I came here to build this underground prison, a place from which I have never left. I created what has since become the Order of the Fahrin Druin to be my insurance that no person ever attained the power of Black Numbers again."

"What happened to your son? Did you ever see him again?"

Baldrick didn't reply at first, his eyes glazed again as if lost in a deep memory. Finally, he nodded. "Oh, yes, he returned often for the first few thousand years, and we frequently lived together here, sometimes for fifty to a hundred years at a time. He helped me build the Order of the Fahrin Druin, and he scoured the land for every book, manuscript and scroll you saw in the other room. But a few hundred years ago he grew bored and went off again. Last I heard, he was living in Uragon."

Drax sat up at this. "He's still alive?"

"Yes."

"Then that means he has the power of Black Numbers, too?"

"Yes." Baldrick slumped in his chair. "Which brings me to you."

Drax was still trying to digest the incredible story when Baldrick's last words registered with him. "Me?"

"Yes, Mr. Drax. You. Within you is a brain more developed than any I have ever seen. You are the only one I hope will be able to withstand what I need to do."

Drax felt an icy coldness fill his mind and he shook his head. "Look, I would like to help you, but I don't think I am the man you are looking for. I'm just a student of the Fahrin Druin."

"No, that is the one thing you are not." Baldrick leaned forward and whispered, "Time is almost up for me. I feel my body giving out, decaying from a disease that not even my power of Numbers can halt. Unfortunately, the two new Aleph Null have come into being just when I am at my weakest. Chance, I suppose. I do not have the strength to hunt them down but you can, with my help."

"Wait, two Aleph Null? What do you mean?"

Baldrick sat back in his chair and picked up his pipe again, toying with it. "There is one who was recently born who is a true Aleph Null, and another who has…acquired the Black Numbers. Both are traveling toward the Trith Nation as we speak and must be destroyed. I have created a map and infused it with the power of Black Numbers. After I am finished with you, it will bind with you and show you where the true Aleph Null is at all times. Unfortunately, it will not show you where the second Aleph Null is, as he hasn't activated his Black Numbers yet."

Drax didn't like the 'after I'm finished with you' part of what Baldrick had just said. Not really wanting to know the answer, he asked, "Is your son the true Aleph Null I must destroy?"

Baldrick shook his head. "No, my son is of no concern to you. He has never used his power of Black Numbers for ill."

Looking into the ancient man's eyes, Drax saw madness and pain, a combination that scared him beyond measure. He feared this man and suspected he would be killed if he didn't agree to help. But more importantly, Drax believed Baldrick, so he placed his hand over his heart and bowed slightly. "I am yours to command."

"Good, then let's begin. Come and kneel at my feet."

Drax did as he was told and only flinched a little when Baldrick placed cold hands on his head. Baldrick's voice became even deeper, more of a rumble than actual words, "This will hurt, but do not move."

Closing his eyes, Drax took deep breaths and thought of Walter, his lover's image calming his racing heart. He felt nothing from Baldrick and relaxed even more, pretending it was Walter touching his head instead. But instead of a caress, pain worse than he had ever known shot into his mind. Colors flashed in bursts behind his closed eyes, each one causing him to scream until he thought he could no longer scream. He saw negative images of numbers race through his mind, moving so fast that he couldn't see them as anything more than a blur after a while. The numbers moved from his brain and he cried in relief, but then pain flared in different parts of his body, lingering in each place for a long time before moving on to another. The agony felt like it would never end. And it didn't end, it just kept moving to different parts of his body, lingering in one place until he couldn't take it anymore, lingering even longer, then moving on again.

Drax screamed and cried as the agony moved to yet another area of his body. He began to shake uncontrollably, his body going into shock, and yet the torture continued, now encompassing his entire body at once. It continued to grow until he wished he would die.

And then the pain ended.

He waited, expecting the agony to start again, the moments passing slowly. Eventually, he sighed in relief as it seemed his ordeal was finally over.

Then the pain shot through him yet again, this time even worse than before. It moved through his brain, remaining longer this time. Then it moved on to every part of his body just as before, only this time the agony extended past his level of endurance, pushing him beyond what any human could take. He felt his heart beating erratically, and he no longer convulsed as the pain moved through his body; it was as if his body and pain were one. How much time passed, Drax could not tell, but it no longer mattered. He relived moments of his life, saw images that brought a smile to his face and smelled each memory as if he were actually there. And the pain continued, moving through his brain and body a third time, only now he no longer cared.

The pain ended and Drax waited for it to begin again, but when it didn't, the lack of pain felt wrong and he found himself almost wishing it would start again, missing it.

He opened his eyes and found he was lying on the floor, his clothing wet with sweat. He let out a breath, unaware he had been holding it in the first place, and pushed himself shakily to a sitting position. The room spun around him and he took deep breaths to get the nausea under control.

Drax heard the thump of a body hitting the floor and turned to see Baldrick lying on his side, blood pooling around his head. He scrambled over and rolled Baldrick to his back, relieved when the man opened his eyes.

Baldrick lifted his hand. "Help me up, if you please."

Drax carefully pulled him to his feet and settled him back into the chair.

Baldrick raised a finger to touch the wound on his head and looking at the blood, he said, "Now that was much worse than I had expected." He looked Drax up and down. "You appear to be alright. Better than me, it would seem."

Drax gave a small smile. "Well, I am a bit younger than you."

Baldrick snorted and motioned Drax closer. "Don't get smart with me, boy. Now, let's see if this worked." He reached out and smacked Drax across the face with an open hand.

Drax's head flew sideways from the blow and he raised a fist to strike the little man, but stopped short and opened his eyes wide at the realization that he hadn't felt any pain from the blow. He put a hand to his cheek and when he felt that light touch, he looked at Baldrick in confusion.

Baldrick smiled. "You didn't feel any pain from the slap but you do feel the light touch of your fingers, don't you?"

When Drax nodded, Baldrick said, "Good. The deepest of pain sensors within you are dead, so be careful you don't cut your finger off or otherwise injure yourself without knowing it. Now for the next test." He stared at Drax for a long time and finally slapped the arm of his chair in triumph, and exclaimed, "Excellent, you didn't explode!"

Drax leaned back in alarm. "What?"

Baldrick filled his pipe as he spoke. "I just sent a number of destructive equations at you, any of which would have burned out or blown your brain out the back of your head and you didn't even feel a thing, did you?"

Drax put a hand reflexively to the back of his head and Baldrick laughed outright at him. He pulled his hand away, expecting to see blood, but his fingers were clean. He had felt a soft tickle in his brain but had attributed it to the nausea. He looked at Baldrick. "What did you do to me?"

"I did something wonderful to you. Because your brain is so amazing, so much better developed than anyone I've ever seen, I was able to rearrange it and infuse it with the essence of Black Numbers, something no ordinary brain would have been able to withstand. You are no longer fully human, Mr. Drax."

Stunned to his core, Drax felt like he was going to throw up. He swallowed, climbed into his chair and looked at Baldrick like he was the monster he said he had been long ago. "So what am I, then?"

"You are now what I call a meta-human. That means that you are on almost even footing with the Aleph Null you will hunt down. I have used up most of the power of Black Numbers that remained in me after so many millennia to do what I just did for you. It is a pity I could not do more."

Drax leaned forward when he saw the skin of Baldrick's face start to turn brown.

Baldrick arched his back and cried out, his eyes wide and filled with pain. The pipe fumbled from his grasp and fell to the table with a hollow clink as he reached for the arms of the chair and gripped them hard. After a few moments, the pain seemed to fade a little and Baldrick coughed, his lungs sounding hollow. He wiped at his mouth with his sleeve and looked at the thick blood on it. "Hmm, that is new." He dabbed at his mouth once more before continuing weakly, "It seems I have even less time than I had anticipated. Now, where was I? Yes, your changes. The main thing I did was change the molecular structure of your body, infusing you with the essence of Black Numbers, similar to what I did when I created that creature so long ago. But where that creature had a brain the size of a walnut and felt nothing but rage, you have the unprecedented ability to use almost all of your brain where most people are lucky to use only a small percentage. So I utilized your brain to make you impervious to the power of Black Numbers. The Aleph Null cannot harm you with their power, now."

He stopped to get his breathing under control but failed. His body convulsed for long moments and Drax had to rush to hold him down to keep him from falling to the floor.

Baldrick opened his eyes after his body quieted down and whispered, "I must finish."

Drax shook his head. "No, you must rest."

Baldrick sighed softly. "I will rest for eternity very soon. It seems I made a calculation error in how much energy I used up and went past the point of no return. My body is collapsing upon itself and there is nothing I can do to reverse the process."

He reached up a hand, touched Drax on the ear and whispered, "You also have more abilities. I enhanced your hearing and eyesight by lengthening and restructuring the molecular makeup of each. I also sped up your metabolism so you will heal quicker, even faster than the mighty Trith. You are also stronger and faster than you were by a factor of ten. These were all easy attributes to add and had nothing to do with what was most important: your immunity to the power of Numbers. In the next room you will find everything you will need for your journey, including the map that is now bound to you and will show you where the true Aleph Null is."

Baldrick began to cough and this time didn't stop until the sound was nothing more than a raspy exhalation. Drax held his hand but could feel his skin rapidly drying up and the muscles dwindling away. The old man sank upon himself and breathed out, "Do not fail me," before closing his eyes.

Drax leaned forward but he could actually hear the man's heart stop beating and the blood stop flowing through his veins. He looked down at Baldrick with sadness and quickly jumped back when his feet burst into flame. The fire rapidly moved upward until nothing but the black outline of Baldrick's body was burned into the chair.

Drax stood in the center of the small room, his hands shaking, then sat down heavily in the other chair and stared at the outline of the man incinerated into the chair opposite him, all that remained of the original Aleph Null. It seemed impossible that Baldrick had been talking with him just moments before, a man who had lived for thousands of years, and he was now nothing but carbon molecules adhering to the chair.

Drax felt a sense of purpose fill him, warming his mind with a soft reassurance of fate. He felt truly alive for the first time in his life. He had always felt different from everyone around him, that he was meant for something great. But the world around him had constantly beaten him down with its mediocrity, making him think life was nothing more than one tedious event after another. But now he knew there was a reason for him to exist and he embraced his metamorphosis. From this moment forward, he was on a path that had been laid out for him by intention – a path he would follow no matter where it led.

He stood and bowed low to the outline of Baldrick, then left the room and quickly found the chamber filled with food, weapons, clothing, and chemistry supplies. On a table was the map, more detailed than any map he had ever seen. He reached out a finger, and when he touched it he felt a flash within his mind. When it cleared, a red mark pulsed slowly on the map up on the far northern coast, just on the northern edge of the Kuldragg forest: the indicator for the Aleph Null's location. Just outside of Bildenhall he saw a black mark pulsing in time with his heartbeat, obviously his own location. He stared at the map and quickly memorized it, then rolled it carefully up and put it into his inside coat pocket.

He took his time packing what he needed and stared longingly at all of the books and manuscripts, wishing he could stay for a millennia and read them all. But he had to do what Baldrick had given his life for. He fingered the small bottles of chemistry supplies and packed them in his travel kit out of habit. No Fahrin Druin would be caught without a full chemistry kit.

Drax then retraced his route out of the underground complex and stepped outside, closing the door tightly behind him. He was surprised to find it was early morning. He had been inside for almost a full day.

The birds twittered loudly around him as he turned north and left at a quick jog.

A thrill coursed through him as he began the hunt for the Aleph Null.

Chapter 13

Glaub gathered the last of his clothing and placed it into his small personal pack. Just a few days earlier he had been in the Black Robe's chamber and had approached the strange portal that the Black Robe had created, pausing to study the mathematical structure. The Black Robe had thought he had been scared and called him 'fatty'. But Glaub had ignored the insult, like he had done his whole life, and stepped through the portal, in the process memorizing its exact mathematical structure.

As the counselor to King Jass of Uragon, he had used his position to convince the King to give him twenty of his best men, making up a story about a minor nobleman who had stolen money and gone on the run. The king had balked at first, saying it was something his soldiers could do, but Glaub had said only he knew the man's face. The king had relented, quickly losing interest in such mundane matters. Glaub had requested Captain Shaw and ordered a full supplement of horses and pack animals to be ready for departure this morning.

He had spent the time before bed last night studying and modifying the portal equation, making it more stable and less uncomfortable to step through. It had been a simple adjustment and had required only a small amount of concentration. He had made the portal appear and stepped from one part of his chamber to the other; a small test, but enough for him to know he could do it again without much effort. He had never seen this type of equation in his long years of life and had been surprised to run across something new. It would definitely come in handy.

He had hidden his true mathematical skills from everyone in the Oblate, especially the new Black Robe. When the young Black Robe had asked them all to recreate the communication equation, he had forced himself to act the fool, showing just enough skill to be accepted but ignored.

The truth was he didn't want any position of true power; he much preferred to stay in the background, living the simple life of a farmer or fisherman. But over the past year, strange events had occurred that had forced him to infiltrate the Oblate as a Blue Robe so he could keep an eye on things. When the Oblate had sent the simple creature called the Korpor to Proof him, he had pretended to feel pain during the Proofing, while also using an equation to dull the Korpor's sexual receptors to hide his true identity as an Aleph Null.

Glaub sat back in the plush chair in his chamber now and grimaced at the thought of the journey he would soon have to endure at the Black Robe's whim. He despised the Black Robe and his disgustingly dark mind that reveled in the pain and submission of others. He had known so many people like this through his long life, people who thought, because they were powerful, they could do anything they wanted to those who didn't possess those shallow traits. But at the same time it was so easy for him to manipulate people like Tris. Glaub was overweight and physically ordinary in most ways, so he blended easily into the background of life, which allowed him to gather information of every kind.

His servant, Charly, poked his head into the room. "They are ready to leave, Glaub," using his first name with the comfort of a true friend.

On the outside, Glaub looked no more than twenty-five years old. When the Oblate had sent him to this court to be the new counselor to King Jass, Charly had become his new servant. Glaub had quickly realized Charly was a good man and they had become instant friends despite the disparity in their stations within the court.

Glaub grimaced as he pushed himself up from the chair. "So be it. Tell me again, why am I doing this?"

Charly grinned. "Because maybe you will lose some weight, fatty."

He grinned at the reference. He had told Charly of the Black Robe's idiocy as well as his childish efforts to demean him, although he didn't call him the Black Robe, he had just said it was some senior official. They often shared their grievances, as Charly was made fun of because of his arm, which was really more of a club since it ended at his wrist. It had been cut off after a horse had stepped on his hand, crushing it beyond repair. "Maybe I will, though I hate traveling and do not think it is worth the effort."

"You took the counselor position knowing full well what it entailed." Charly often poked fun at him, though without rancor or maliciousness.

Glaub grimaced again as he pulled on the long travel boots. "The price of power, blah…blah…blah." He pointed at the long cloak hanging from a hook on the wall and Charly grabbed it without a word and walked over to hand it to him. "Thanks, Charly." He cinched his boot laces tightly and tied them, standing up when he finished, looking down at his feet and the shiny black boots. "I look stupid in these."

Charly whistled softly and grinned again, something he did so often. "I think you are a sexy bastard."

Rolling his eyes, Glaub took the offered coat and small pack, motioning his head. "Come on, let's get this over with."

Charly instantly became serious and followed him through the door, closing it behind them with a thud.

He followed the beautiful halls of Uragon castle, the green and white marble so exquisitely crafted, that he often found himself just standing for a few moments in the middle of the hall, taking in the beauty. He had spent the previous two decades as a fisherman in Ulkengor, a mid-sized city far to the north of Urgaer, where he was now. It had been a rough but fulfilling period of his life. But over the past year he had enjoyed all that court life had to offer, especially the rich food. He looked down at his substantial belly and tried to suck it in with no effect. Maybe this journey would be good for him.

Glaub came out of his thoughts as he stepped through the door to the stables, already breathing hard. He had traveled to Undaluag twice over the past year for the secret bi-annual Oblate meeting, traveling under the guise of a counselor on business, but he had always made the trip in the comfort of a horse-drawn carriage.

He eyed the horses lined up in the courtyard and gritted his teeth at the thought of sitting on one of the creatures for the next few fortnights.

Captain Shaw saluted as he approached. "We are ready at your order, sir."

Glaub nodded. He had traveled with Captain Shaw to Undaluag over the past two trips and he liked the man. "Which of these beasts is mine?"

Shaw motioned to a huge brown stallion that stood proudly to his right. Glaub looked up at the gigantic creature, knowing he would never be able to climb into the saddle. The stirrup was as high as his chest, but the Captain saved him from embarrassment by placing a short step by the side of the horse. He nodded his thanks to Shaw and used the step to reach his foot up to the stirrup. He rocked back twice to get the momentum to step up and swing his leg over the horse, gripping the saddle hard to keep from going over the other side. He saw a few of the soldiers roll their eyes but he ignored them.

Shaw motioned a soldier to stow the step onto one of the pack mules as he slid smoothly into the saddle of his own stallion, a horse even taller than Glaub's own.

Glaub motioned for the Captain to go, and Shaw yelled, "Move out!"

The horse immediately started forward and Glaub gripped the leather reins as he leaned back, off-balance. He used the reins to pull himself back to an upright position, something that normally signaled a horse to stop, but his horse ignored his clumsy use of the reins and followed Shaw's horse without any guidance from him, which relieved Glaub. He had ridden horses many times in his long life but had never gotten the hang of the process; he far preferred using his own legs to travel.

They exited the stable yard and trotted around the eastern edges of the castle courtyard, the ground muddy and churned from the constant horse traffic of a busy castle. Soon they turned the corner and entered the main courtyard, a vast expanse of open space where villagers and traveling folk set up stalls to sell everything from food to clothing to trinkets. They made their way through the throngs of people to the double gates, and as they exited the castle grounds, Glaub looked back, already wishing he was sitting in his comfortable chambers eating a thick steak. Not paying attention, he suddenly slid forward and his testicles slammed into the pommel as the horse stepped down from the level area of the gate onto the wide road that led east. The pain made him nauseated and he had to swallow twice before he was sure he wouldn't throw up. It was not an auspicious start to the journey.

He had studied the maps and had planned their journey carefully. While he could have used the portal equation he had just learned to travel anywhere in the land, he had to keep up the outward appearance of a counselor to King Jass, as well as the secret appearance of a lowly Blue Robe so he could let things between the Black Robe and the new Aleph Null play out. He was curious about the new Aleph Null and wondered if his father was also tracking the situation. He supposed he could have just killed the Black Robe and gone off on his own in search of the Aleph Null, but he had never killed anyone with his power of Numbers and didn't want to start now. Plus, he had been quite bored over the past few centuries and had to admit he relished this new turn of events.

They would travel the main road east for a day and then cut northeast through the great Uragon farmlands until they came to the Gon river, which they would follow to the Paigonian Sea. It seemed a likely area where the Aleph Null could be found. He couldn't imagine the Aleph Null would travel north or west any further than the Paigonian Sea, as there was nothing but the Muldragg forest to the north and desolate, rocky plains to the west all the way to Ulkengor. And north of Ulkengor was the Grimstone desert, a place that supported no life other than the occasional traveling band of the violent Ortenn folk.

They would make their way around the north side of the Paigonian Sea and if they didn't find the Aleph Null there, they would follow the western shores of the Bertol Sea northward. That was as far as he would most likely have to go, unless the Trith that traveled with the Aleph Null was leading him to the Trith Nation that was in the southern portion of the vast Muldragg forest. But that scenario was unlikely, as the Trith were not known for their hospitality. Glaub had spent some time with them long ago and although he had been treated well, they didn't accept strangers into their midst often.

The jingle of a bridle made him look out over the fields of wheat that stretched out for as far as he could see. Further up the coast from Urgaer were the fields of Uragon Leaf, the most prized tobacco leaf in all of the lands.

The previous summer he had the good fortune to be able to purchase a small Uragon Leaf farm on the coast midway between Urgaer and Ulkengor. He had been in court when the neighbor to a farm that had mysteriously been left without owners was requesting permission to take the land as his own. The court had immediately assumed the neighbor had killed the owners of this farm and initiated an investigation. In the meantime, Glaub had requested a favor from King Jass to allow him to purchase the land for a small sum. This was granted without trouble and Glaub had hired a poor local family he knew to move there and farm it for him, splitting the profits 50-50. Maybe when all this current excitement started to become dull to him, he would travel to the farm and live a simple life again. Last autumn he had taken delivery of the first bushel of his prized Uragon Leaf and a good portion of it was in his private pack now.

Up ahead, the main road curved southeast toward the border of Paigon, and a smaller track led on to the northeast, cutting between the borders of two different farm fields – one corn, the other wheat. A steady wind blew from the coast, warm and damp as it ruffled his coat.

He was getting warm so he pulled his coat off as he rode, struggling to keep his balance as he did so. He finally pulled it free and felt the breeze immediately start to cool him. He handed his coat to Charly, who rode next to him. "Could you store this away for a while?"

Charly nodded and turned his horse to ride to the rear of the column where the pack mules were.

Glaub tilted his head to the sun, enjoying the warm rays on his skin. Riding in a carriage was more comfortable, but he had to admit there was something enjoyable about riding a horse, a closeness to the nature around him. Then he felt a sharp jab of pain in his posterior where the saddle dug into him, reminding him why he didn't ride horses. He sent a mathematical query into his body and was aghast at how unhealthy he had let himself become.

Glaub created a series of complex equations and sent them into his body to restructure the tissue and muscle that was damaged and weak in his buttocks and thighs, and then added an equation to build extra muscle in the spots where the saddle dug into him. He stopped short of removing the fat in other areas of his body, deciding he would do only a bit of body sculpting each day so as to not arouse suspicion, but enough to speed up his weight loss and rebuild his muscles. At least the pain in his buttocks was now gone and he sighed with appreciation.

Charly rejoined him and motioned to the trail ahead of them where the corn grew. "It would have been nice if it were later in the season. Fresh corn on the cob would sure have tasted good tonight."

Glaub felt his mouth salivate at the thought and he agreed. "Maybe on the way back through here it will be ripe."

"You don't think this little trip will take all summer, do you?"

"It very well might, although maybe with some luck we'll find the rogue nobleman sooner rather than later."

Charly shrugged. "Whatever, it is just nice to be away from court for a while."

"That it is, Charly."

They traveled for the rest of the day, talking quietly on occasion, but mostly just enjoying the ride. As the sun fell from view, they camped along one of the corn fields, enjoying the roasted partridge the soldiers had quickly shot down with expertly-aimed arrows throughout the day.

The weather held over the next three days, staying mostly cloudy but with no rain to make it uncomfortable. Glaub had used equations to continue rebuilding the muscles of his body while ridding himself of fat. By the fourth day, Charly had stopped to stare at him.

"You are looking remarkably fit already. This little adventure is really doing wonders for you."

Glaub accepted the compliment. "It helps that I'm not eating all that rich food at court."

His friend nodded seriously. "You look good. Keep it up."

He had never told Charly who he really was or what he could do with mathematics. In all the millennia he had been alive, he had only confided in one person: his wife Natalie, and that had been five centuries ago. She had loved him for who he was and they had lived together as husband and wife for three decades. They hadn't had any children and she had died relatively young from a blood vessel that had burst in her head. They had been sitting in the grass together, enjoying a beautiful autumn day, his arms around her as she laid back against his chest and they talked about little things. When she hadn't replied to him at one point, he had leaned forward to kiss her head and when she hadn't responded to that, either, he had turned her face toward him and had seen a smile on her face, her eyes open, but no life in her. He had tried to use his Black Numbers to bring her back, but not even he could reverse death. He had lived a solitary life ever since, keeping his friendships and love affairs short. He would never love another again.

He came out of his thoughts as they reached the top of a large hill and he saw a wide river in the valley below.

Captain Shaw called a halt and approached Glaub and Charly. "We've reached the Gon river. We have some sunlight left. Do you want to continue on up the river for a while yet or make camp?"

Glaub gazed across the river, its water calm and reflecting the soft light of the low-hanging sun in beautiful shades of gold. He shifted his gaze to the northwest. From the vantage point on this hill he could see the river snaking to the east, then back again to the west. From the map, he knew the river did not travel in a straight line, and if they followed it, they would add days onto their journey. But if the Aleph Null was coming this way, he would probably be following the river. "Let's camp down by the river tonight and get a fresh start tomorrow morning."

Shaw saluted and called out orders. They began the slow descent to the river basin, letting the horses pick their way carefully to avoid any slips on the steep grassy hill. It didn't take them long to reach the bottom and make their way to the water's edge. The men quickly set up a simple camp. Three men threw out fishing lines and within a short time had pulled in three massive fish. It was enough to feed all twenty-two of them.

Glaub crawled into his small tent, a simple water-proof blanket hung over poles, and was asleep in moments. The mosquitoes grew thick in the evening so he pulled his blanket over his head to keep the whining insects from biting him.

The next morning dawned with a cloudless sky. Dew covered everything as Glaub climbed out of his blankets and stretched his arms over his head, the bones in his back cracking loudly but his muscles no longer hurting. The soldiers were quietly sitting by two fires eating fish and talking softly.

Charly glanced at him from where he was sitting by a fire and laughed once in reply to something a young soldier said, then stood up and carried a steaming mug over. "Morning. Here's some hot tea. It's pretty cool out still, so why don't you go on over and sit by the fire while I get you some fish for breakfast?" He turned and went across the camp to where an older soldier was cooking a freshly caught fish over the flames of a large fire.

Glaub ambled over to the spot Charly had recently vacated and sat down. The young soldier who had been talking with Charly glanced at him out of the corner of his eye but didn't acknowledge him. He knew that soldiers rarely interacted with members of the court and he wished, not for the first time, that he was just an ordinary civilian again and not a counselor to a king. He sipped from the simple wooden travel mug and relished the hot tea, feeling it warm him from the inside.

Charly arrived with a steaming plate of fish. "They ran out of leftover fish, so this is a fresh one caught this morning."

He took the plate and broke off a piece of fish, blowing on it briefly before taking a bite, then breathing out and moving it quickly around his mouth to cool it more. It was a little oily but the rich flesh was tender and delicious. He quickly finished off the two large fillets and handed the plate back to Charly, who took it to the river to clean.

Glaub heard the young soldier mutter softly to himself and caught the words, "rich asshole". He felt himself flush in embarrassment and anger but didn't say anything. He had to keep up his role as counselor to the king no matter how unpopular it made him with the soldiers.

Suddenly a soldier ran into camp, yelling, "Attack!"

The soldiers dropped their cups and food, springing to their feet with swords drawn.

Glaub heard the thud of many horses approaching at a run. He ran back to his tent with Charly by his side and grabbed his own sword. It was a blade he had owned for more than two thousand years, made as a gift for him by the mysterious Haissen when he had visited their home island of Haisissei.

Charly's eyes widened when he saw the beautiful blade but he didn't ask any questions, instead pulling a short sword from his own tent.

They both faced the approaching thunder of horses that came around the bend, at least fifty riders dressed in furs and wielding wickedly thick swords.

Glaub's own soldiers formed a line and eight archers stepped forward. At a signal from Shaw, they let loose two quick volleys, released so quickly that the first arrows struck after the next arrows were loosed. Ten of the attacking men fell to the ground with arrows in their throats. Six of the attackers took arrows to their chests but kept on riding, screaming in anger as they raised their swords.

Why they were attacking, Glaub didn't know. He had heard occasional reports of attacks around the farms of this area but they were rare this close to Urgaer. He felt the strange calmness before battle that he had always felt, and, glancing at his friend, he saw Charly was composed, as well. How a man reacted before a battle said a lot about his character.

The attacking men were quickly upon them and Glaub's men sprang into action, ducking under sword strikes while stabbing upward. In the first pass, fifteen more attacking men fell dead or wounded from their horses, while four of the king's soldiers who had not been fast enough to avoid the attackers, dropped to the ground in sprays of thick blood.

The horsemen turned their horses for a second run, trampling tents and supplies as they did. Two of them spotted Glaub and Charly and kept riding forward instead of turning, their horses kicking up dirt as they charged.

Glaub and Charly stepped a few paces away from each other and faced the two riders. The men grinned grotesquely as they leaned forward and swept down with their swords.

Charly dropped to the ground and rolled away from the horse's hooves, and that was all Glaub saw as he swung his sword hard against the downward strike, shattering the man's sword with a crash of steel on steel. The Haissan blade, made by folding the steel more than two hundred times, continued through the broken sword and sliced the man's arm cleanly off, blood showering down on Glaub as the horse and rider continued past.

Glaub turned to find Charly facing the huge man, who was still on his horse, and swinging hard strikes down at his friend. Charly rolled under the man's horse and came up on the other side already spinning to stab upward. Even though he only had one good arm, he thrust with incredible power and his sword pierced the man's thigh and continued through to enter his stomach. Charly twisted the sword viciously and pulled it free with a yell. The rider dropped his sword, then toppled from the horse with a thud.

Hearing a horse behind him, Glaub spun around and stepped to the side as it went past, the armless attacker slumped in his saddle, unconscious or dead.

Charly grinned at Glaub and motioned toward the rest of the fight going on in the center of camp. "Come on, let's help out."

They both ran toward the chaotic battle. Glaub only counted twelve of his soldiers left, each fighting one or more men on horseback and struggling to get an advantage against the extra height of their adversaries. The young soldier who had called him a rich asshole blocked the constant strikes from two huge men, retreating as he did so. Glaub knew his soldier would not last much longer, so he quickly made his way over to him and ran his sword into the side of one attacker, pulling his sword quickly out and leaping up at the second, stabbing him in the throat. It had happened so quickly and both men slid from their saddles and hit the ground in a heap of bloody furs. The young soldier stared at Glaub in awe, and Glaub saluted him with his sword before turning to take in the rest of the battle.

They were still outnumbered by at least fifteen, so with hardly a thought, Glaub sent simple equations into the remaining attacking men, wrapping the equations around their ear canals to make them feel dizzy and clumsy. It was enough for his remaining soldiers to quickly finish off their attackers without anyone suspecting anything out of the ordinary.

The ground was slick with turned up dirt mixed with blood. Moans filled the area from the injured and dying. The soldiers walked through the area stabbing any remaining injured attackers while stopping to attend to their own injured men.

Captain Shaw saw him and Charly and walked wearily over to them, holding a hand to his bloody left shoulder. "You two are not injured?"

Glaub shook his head.

"Good." He gazed around the camp, his eyes hooded with anger. "Unfortunately, eight of my men weren't so lucky."

"Who were these men who attacked us?"

Shaw shrugged. "I think they were Ortenn folk from the north. They have been moving further and further south over the past decade, but I didn't know they'd made it this far down."

Glaub had known who they were but had to pretend otherwise. He had come into contact with the wild Ortenn folk of the northern Grimstone Desert over the centuries but had managed to avoid them for a long time, until now.

Shaw motioned at the remaining men. "With only twelve of our contingent left, you must make a decision. Do we continue with the mission or return to Urgaer for reinforcements?"

Glaub had no wish to backtrack and lose a fortnight. He squared his shoulders and looked Captain Shaw in the eyes. "We need to continue on."

The Captain nodded immediately, respect showing on his face for the difficult decision Glaub had just made. "We will spend the day here tending to the wounded. We will then send any who are too injured to continue with us back to Urgaer and we will carry on." He turned and barked orders, his men responding without question.

Charly turned in a circle, taking in the destroyed camp. "Well, I suppose I should start gathering our things. Looks like much has been destroyed."

Glaub nodded and turned his head to assess the bloodshed with sadness. Just when he'd thought the lands were getting more civilized, he'd been reminded just how brutal people could be.

Nothing ever seemed to change.

As he was turning to go back to his sleeping area to help Charly, sudden pain lanced into his mind, pain worse than any he had ever felt. His vision wavered briefly and the pain lessened to a dull throb at the back of his head before winking out of existence. In confusion and disbelief, he reached out to Baldrick and found only emptiness.

He fell to his knees and cried out, his voice nothing but raw pain, then lowered his forehead to the dirt and sobbed.

His father was dead.

Chapter 14

Dark. That was the only word Sid could think of as he gazed at the wall of thick, black trees that stood before the group. He could see nothing beyond the initial trees, as if the world would cease to exist once they stepped into the forest.

He turned and looked back toward the thin, grey line of the ocean far in the distance and wished they could turn around, even if it meant following the beach again. But Crowdal said that cutting through this forest would save at least a fortnight of travel, so they had to do it.

As if reading his thoughts, Crowdal placed a hand on Sid's shoulder. "This really is the quickest way to the Trith Nation."

Sid nodded. "I know, but it looks so…forbidding."

Crowdal gazed into the forest and squeezed Sid's shoulder. "That it does. But we should be able to cut southwest and avoid having to go too deeply into it."

"Is there such a thing as not going too deep into it?"

"I am not sure, but let's hope there is." He glanced at the sky and said, "We are wasting daylight. I am going to kick out the fire."

Sid shivered and pulled his coat tighter around himself. The temperature had gone up slightly after they'd left the coast, but the ever-present wind chilled him to the bone.

Agnes stepped beside him and pulled her own coat tight, her brown hair blowing around her face in the wind. She reached up and tucked it behind her ears but it didn't help so she pulled her hood up and tied it tightly. She spoke without looking at him. "We shouldn't feel much of this wind once we get into the forest. That's something at least."

A strong gust of wind hit them as if to emphasize her words. The trees swayed back and forth, creaking loudly, and a large branch snapped from high up and fell right toward them. Before Sid could move, one of the Haissen who never left his side yanked he and Agnes violently back by the collars of their coats. The branch landed with a thud right where Sid had been standing, its broken end sticking straight into the ground. He gasped, knowing it would have impaled him if it hadn't been for the amazing reflexes of the Haissan. He turned to thank the Haissan but it was scanning the area and ignoring him.

Crowdal ran up. "Are you two alright?"

"Yes, though it was a close call. I think we should get out of this wind soon. It isn't safe to stay here much longer."

Crowdal agreed and whistled. "Time to go."

Writhgarth, Tulman and Nik swung their packs over their shoulders and with the remaining Haissen, they walked single file into the Kuldragg forest in what had become their standard formation: six Haissen leading, followed by Crowdal, Sid and Agnes with two Haissen next to them, then

Writhgarth, Nik, Tulman and the remaining five Haissen to the rear.

Sid glanced up as he entered the forest, worried another branch might crash down on them, but the wind was no longer noticeable as soon as they entered the trees, as if its job were done and it had chased them away. He rolled his eyes, feeling stupid for even thinking it.

After only a few dozen steps, Sid looked back and was shocked he couldn't see the place where the forest opened out onto the field of scrub brush from where they had just come. The trees not only grew thickly together, they varied by species, some gnarled and twisted, others growing straight up, tall and thick. But one thing was similar among all the trees: they all were very old. He did not see any new growth. The forest floor was covered with a thick layer of brown leaves and that was all. Sid looked up again and noticed there were no trees with needles. He missed his Miq tree back home.

Sid was jolted back to the present when he stepped in a rut and stumbled forward into Crowdal. He looked up at his tall friend, who turned around in alarm. "Sorry, I wasn't watching my step and tripped." Crowdal just nodded and turned forward again. Sid noticed his eyes never stopped scanning the forest, heavy with worry. Sid found himself looking around more carefully; if Crowdal was worried, then he had better be, too.

The air was still and damp, filled with the smell of rotting vegetation and something else he couldn't quite place. He sniffed and it hit him: it smelled like the dead mice he would find in the corners of the kitchen where his father had put poison down. It was a sickly sweet smell that nauseated him. But where it had been a localized smell of death back then, here it seemed to permeate the entire forest.

Agnes nodded slightly when he glanced over to her. "I smell it, too. Death."

Sid felt goosebumps rise along his arms as he walked; he was sure they were being watched. He didn't hear or see anything, though, as they stepped over dead and rotten trees that had probably fallen hundreds of years before. They trudged along for what felt like half a day, although it was difficult to see the sun through the thick canopy of branches overhead. He followed Crowdal around a massive tree that was short in height but so wide it looked like a building, staring in wonder as he passed it, wondering just how long it had stood in that spot. As he turned forward again, he saw what looked like a small opening through the trees to their left. He tapped Crowdal's arm. "Look over there, it seems to be a clearing."

Crowdal peered in that direction and whistled softly. The Haissen in front of him quickly returned. He pointed to his left. "Check that out. It might be a nice spot to rest for a bit."

The Haissen quickly sprinted away, following Crowdal's order. Sid had felt uncomfortable having the Haissen look to him for orders. So a few days earlier he had spoken to a Haissan and told it that he wanted them to do what Crowdal asked without verifying with him every time. It had given the faintest of nods and turned away without a word. Since then, the Haissen had carried out Crowdal's commands without looking first to Sid.

The Haissen quickly returned and one hissed, "It is safe."

They turned left and moved quickly toward the clearing hoping they would get to rest.

Sid stepped around a tree and gasped when he saw what was in front of him. A small ring of stones, no more than three paces in diameter sat in the exact center of a perfectly square clearing surrounded by tall, straight trees. The ground was covered with black stones, each fit so tightly together that it looked like a floor inside of the House of Healing instead of a clearing in the middle of a forest. Sid hesitantly stepped onto the outer-most stone, expecting something bad to happen, but it was solid. He felt Agnes take his hand as she looked around in wonder.

She looked back at Sid with a smile on her face. "Look: it is a perfect square." She pointed at the stones. "Each stone is a perfect square, and each side of the clearing has the exact same number of stones."

Sid quickly did the math and saw she was correct. He looked back at her. "What do you think it means?"

Agnes shrugged. "I have no idea. Something religious, maybe?" She let go of his hand and went to her knees so she could run a finger along the stone closest to her. She looked up excitedly. "These cuts are not done by hand. They are too perfect and there are no tool marks. I think someone powerful created this, maybe with the power of Numbers." She looked around the square. "But I've never heard of anyone having power like this." Glancing up at him, she said, "Except for you, that is."

Sid looked for the faint line of light that always flowed out of him back toward the obelisk in the Srithian Wood, and immediately saw it was outside of the square, leading back the way they had come. But to his surprise, it did not enter the square where he now stood. He walked sideways a few paces and saw the line move with him, but staying outside the square. It seemed to corroborate Agnes' hypothesis that this square clearing was created by someone who had the power of Numbers.

Writhgarth dropped his pack and lay his head down on it, crossing his arms on his stomach. "Ah, this feels good." He looked at Nik. "Hey Nik, why don't you make us some of those bready meat things you are so anxious to start selling in the city."

Nik dropped his own pack and nodded. "I think they would taste good right about now. I'm so hungry I could even eat your smoked fish, and I swore yesterday that I would never eat fish again for as long as I lived."

Writhgarth rolled his eyes. "Blah, blah, blah, that's all I hear when you speak."

Nik laughed as he pulled out some meat, cheese, and bread from his pack.

Tulman was fast asleep already, snoring loudly as he lay by the ring in the center of the square.

Sid made his way over to the ring of stones and leaned over the edge but pulled back immediately. Using more caution than he had before, he leaned over again and whistled softly. It was a smooth hole that fell away to darkness.

Crowdal walked up next to him. "What is it?"

Sid motioned for him to look.

Crowdal leaned forward and his eyes widened. He picked up a small rock and dropped it in, listening for a long time, but never heard it hit bottom. He turned and called everyone's attention. "Be careful around this ring of stone. It is a hole that doesn't appear to have a bottom."

Nik ran over to look, as did Writhgarth. Both backed away when they saw the ominous depth of the hole.

Sid could not think of any reason why it would be there. This was a strange place in every way.

Nik soon called them over for food and Sid's mouth watered. They had not eaten all day and the bready meals looked delicious. He took one from the small pile Nik had made up and bit into it with relish. Around a mouthful of food, he asked, "What do you call these, again?"

Nik shrugged. "I haven't settled on a name yet."

Writhgarth tore a hunk of bread from the loaf and bit into it. "They do taste good, especially when traveling, but I've said it before and I'll say it again – this is how bread should be properly eaten."

Nik lifted his hand with the food in it. "You are the one who asked me to make them, but suit yourself, old man. New ideas and new ways, that is what I say."

Grunting in mock-disgust, Writhgarth covertly picked up one of the bread concoctions and turned away so Nik couldn't see him eating it.

They all soon finished eating and repacked the remaining food, preparing to leave soon. Tulman opened his eyes and sat up, looking refreshed as he picked up a hunk of bread and took a bite while putting on his pack.

Sid marveled at how Tulman could fall so quickly asleep, stay asleep for just a short period of time and awaken instantly refreshed. As he pulled the straps tight on his own pack, Sid felt a strange tug against his mind. He spun around, looking into the trees all around him and saw movement to the southwest. He gasped and the Haissen immediately fanned out in a circle around them, facing the same direction.

Nik started to say something but Tulman clamped his hand over the young mercenary's mouth.

Heavy footsteps approached, crushing leaves and branches in a manner showing whomever was approaching didn't care about stealth.

Images of the Unnamed One flashed through Sid's mind, memories of the giant creature smashing trees as it had drawn near the obelisk clearing. Sweat ran down his face and he trembled until he realized that it was a group coming toward them, not the nightmare of the Unnamed One.

Crowdal drew his sword and pushed Sid and Agnes back from him so he could fight if needed. The Haissen also had their swords out, casually held in front of them, waiting without fear for whatever approached.

Nik grumbled about there always having to be something that disturbed them, and Writhgarth spat to his side, agreeing with him for the first time in a long time.

Sid looked all around as a strange group of creatures came to a stop outside of the square. They had orange and brown skin that seemed to move with the diffused light of the forest. Their faces were unlike any Sid had ever seen, with mouths, noses and eyes that were compressed at the bottom, and no forehead to speak of as their heads sloped back sharply where a forehead should have been. They didn't make a sound as they stood on the outside of the square clearing.

Crowdal looked at Sid. "I am not sure, but I think these are the Myrss."

Writhgarth spoke from behind Sid. "My father once read to me from an ancient book about these people. If I remember, they went extinct long ago."

Nik waved his bow at their guests. "I am pretty sure they aren't extinct."

Sid noticed the Myrss staring at him, some of them glancing behind him then back at his face. He wondered if they could see his thread of Numbers reaching away from the clearing so he turned to Crowdal, "I want to check something."

Crowdal spoke, barely moving his mouth. "Move slowly if you do move."

Sid took a step to the side, then another. The creatures followed him with their eyes, some glancing outside of the clearing as he moved, and Sid turned to see they were staring at the thread of power as it moved parallel to him. He glanced back to Agnes. "They can see the thread of Numbers that connects me to the obelisk."

Agnes turned to follow their gazes and saw he was right. "That is strange."

Sid didn't feel any sense of danger from them, so he stepped forward until he was at the edge of the square, only a few hand spans from the nearest creature. He sensed the two Haissen just behind him, his ever-present guard, making him feel relatively safe.

The strangely colorful being closest to him cocked its head, its eyes filled with emotion. He heard Agnes take in a breath of air.

"I can hear them speaking in my head, but they are speaking directly to you, Sid. Can you hear them?"

Sid felt the barest touch against his mind but then it disappeared. He turned to Agnes. "No, I thought I felt something for a brief moment, but then it was gone. You can hear them actually speaking?"

"I can. They say you are connected to the (E)." She listened for some time. "They are called the Myrss. They ask you to step forward out of the square."

Crowdal whispered, "Sid, don't do it."

But Sid felt himself stepping out of the square without a thought. They knew about the (E) of the obelisk. They might have information about how he could get his Numbers back.

Chapter 15

Tris stopped on the hill outside of the abandoned village and looked across the expanse to the distant outline of the Kuldragg forest. He was amazed Sid would willingly enter that place. The Kuldragg forest was mentioned a few times in the books he had read in the Oblate library, although only in general terms. No one had ever really explored the dark forest, so almost nothing was known about it.

Not for the first time, he wondered where his old friend was going and why he seemed to be in such a hurry. There was nothing this far north as far as he knew, just rugged coastline, the forest, and after that, unpopulated hill country. If Sid had wanted to go south, he could just have retraced his route from the Srithian Wood, so there was obviously something out here he was intent on finding.

He turned to his Hunters. "Is he heading directly for the forest?"

Gee nodded immediately. "Yes, we tracked him for a distance and his trail doesn't deviate."

"Good, let's move out."

The ground was strewn with rocks and boulders with a course, straw-like scrub growing between them. It would have been very slow-going if they didn't have the narrow track to follow. They reached the forest by mid-morning and saw the old campsite just on the edge of it. The ashes of the fire were cold, but the tracks were still fresh, no more than a day or two old.

They immediately entered the forest, Tris walking quickly and without worry, for nothing scared him.

Sid's trail through the forest was easy to follow, especially with the Hunters tracking him, and Tris pushed them to move as quickly as possible. As he walked, he continued working on solving for the Black Numbers, using every mathematical technique he had ever learned, but no matter what he did, the structure of the Black Numbers remained elusive and unsolvable. He had once found a small book in the Oblate library where the author discussed something called nonfigurative chaos theory, but the mathematics she'd conjectured were needed to implement her theory didn't exist yet. Tris wondered if the Black Numbers he took from Sid were a similar set of theoretical mathematics.

He came to a fallen tree trunk that was slick with a strange red moss. The Hunters had leapt lightly over it, but as Tris put weight on his hands to climb over it, they slipped out from under him and he fell to his stomach against the slimy wood. One of his bodyguards put out a hand but Tris slapped it away angrily and pushed himself up, and as he did, he saw a shadow move between trees in the distance.

Tris instantly created a thin mathematical array around himself and slid to the other side of the tree trunk. Before he could say anything, three of the Hunters sprinted away, disappearing into the trees in the blink of an eye. The leader, Gee, stared after them, so he stopped by her side and waited without speaking. He didn't have long to wait before the three Hunters returned and stopped in front of Gee, totally ignoring Tris. He seethed but held his tongue when one of the Hunters said, "We found the tracks of a single Omthagrod but it seems to be gone now."

Gee nodded once and turned to Tris. "It appears we are being followed by a single Omthagrod. I will send out two scouts to try and locate its pack before they can attack us."

Tris shook his head. "No, don't waste any effort on them. They obviously aren't a threat if they stay hidden, and we can't waste the time. We will keep moving."

Gee stared hard at him, obviously not agreeing with his order, but she was a professional, so she turned and motioned once with her hand and the Hunters started off again.

Tris followed Gee, already turning his mind inward to the continued problem of solving for the Black Numbers. The afternoon passed quickly, yet he was still no closer to a solution, making the ever-present anger inside of him bubble close to a release. He held it back with effort as the pack men set up the camp for the night. The forest grew unnaturally quiet as darkness settled in. The Hunters faded away into the dark outside of the fire-lit camp, leaving him and his bodyguards and pack men for the night. He had asked Gee where they went during the nights but all she would say was they didn't leave the camp unprotected.

A plate of cold meat and bread was handed to him and he settled next to the fire to eat. The pack men finished setting up the sleeping shelters and settled down to eat, sitting on the edge of the camp as was their place, quietly talking to each other. Tris' two bodyguards stood behind him, never relaxing.

Tris placed the final piece of meat into his mouth and tossed the plate across the campsite toward the pack men. One of them leapt to his feet to retrieve the plate, but froze when a piercing howl rose in volume from somewhere in the dark forest.

Tris activated his mathematical array but didn't bother standing up, confident in his Hunters' ability to handle anything out there.

In the distance he heard a series of roars that were quickly cut off, then silence filled the camp. The pack man slowly picked up the plate and returned to his mates to clean it, his eyes wide from fear.

Tris waited for some time but heard nothing more, so he ambled over to his sleeping spot, crawled under his blanket and fell asleep almost instantly.

He awoke to the diffused light of dawn filtering through the tree branches above him. Stretching his arms out, Tris threw back his blanket and stood up, arching his back to get the knots out, hating having to sleep on the ground. He could have created a portal equation and returned to his Oblate sleeping chamber each night but he didn't want to expend so much energy twice a day.

The pack men were already awake, as usual, quietly preparing breakfast, and Tris' bodyguards stood at attention not far from him.

Stepping to the edge of the campsite, Tris urinated against a tree and when he turned, the Hunters were back in the camp. He hadn't heard them, but then again, he never heard them moving. Pushing his member inside of his trousers, Tris casually asked, "So, what was that ruckus last night?"

Gee shrugged, "Just the pack of Omthagrod circling to attack the campsite."

Tris waited for more information and when none came, he turned away and pulled on a thick wool shirt. Even he was impressed by their casual reference to the Omthagrod. He assumed they had killed every one of the beasts, yet they didn't feel the need to tell this to him, as if it was not even worth mentioning. Tris had never seen an Omthagrod but had heard many stories about them, specifically about their often fearsome attacks on small settlements that left only a handful of survivors, the rest massacred and eaten. They were among the most feared creatures in the land.

The pack men quickly prepared for departure, handing Tris a plate of hot meat that he ate quickly before tossing the plate back to them. When they were ready, Tris motioned the Hunters to lead the way.

Chapter 16

Melinda accepted the mug of grass tea from Eithes and when the young girl started to back away, Melinda motioned for her to sit next to her.

Eithes stepped forward and folded her legs smoothly under her as she sat next to Melinda on the ground.

"You do not need to serve me tea or food all the time, Eithes; I am quite capable of doing these things myself."

The young Zranh picked up a small pebble and turned it in her fingers, not looking Melinda in the eyes. "I am yours to command, Leillireph."

Melinda started to object but stopped, knowing there was no use arguing with the young girl. She patted the ground next to her. "Sit by me."

Eithes hesitated but finally slid over next to Melinda.

"How old are you, Eithes?"

"I am thirteen, Leillireph."

"Thirteen? That is impressive!"

Eithes looked up at Melinda through the dark brown hair that always hung over her face. "You don't need to say that. I know it is."

Melinda laughed outright. "You are a smart young woman."

Eithes smiled for the first time.

She had been watching the young Zranh over the past two days and had seen her usually sitting by herself when she wasn't serving Melinda. Sometimes she spent time with Goris, who was a little younger, but not often enough for them to be considered good friends. "Eithes, do you have any family?"

Eithes put her head down and didn't reply, so Melinda cupped her chin and raised her head. "Answer me, please."

Tears fell from the young girl's eyes and she shook her head. "No, Leillireph."

Fearing she already knew the answer, she whispered softly, "Where are they?"

Eithes wiped the tears away, her face hardening. "They are dead."

Melinda felt her heart break. There was so much pain and sorrow in the world, but it wasn't right for such a young child to be alone. "Do you have anyone else?"

She motioned to where Goris was sewing a rip in her sleeve. "Goris and her parents let me sleep in their space if I want, but I usually sleep alone."

Melinda knew the girl was cared for by the Zranh as a whole, but she needed something more. She needed a purpose to her life, so Melinda stood up and motioned Eithes to her feet. "Eithes, I would like you to help me with something."

Standing, Eithes said, "Anything, Leillireph."

"I require the services of someone who can be available to help me day or night. Do you know of anyone who might be able to take on this important responsibility?"

Eithes looked around the camp and finally pointed to a young boy about her age. "Jaith would be a good choice. He is strong and works hard."

"No, he is not my first choice."

Eithes looked around some more and started to point at Goris when she suddenly turned, her eyes widening. She straightened and proudly said, "I would be honored if you would choose me, Leillireph."

Melinda studied her carefully, as if she were debating the offer in her mind. Then, in a harsh and commanding voice, she asked, "Do you, Eithes, choose to serve me as my personal attendant?"

Eithes stood even straighter and tilted her head up. "I do, Leillireph."

"Good. Gather your things and keep them with mine. You will sleep in my space so you will always be available to me."

The young girl nodded and said, "Yes, Leillireph." She walked away, pride in her step and her back straight.

Melinda smiled as she watched her for a few moments, then she sat back down and gazed through the trees without really looking at anything. They had been traveling northwest through the Branstall Wood for the past three days, following the normal route that kept them from encountering any population centers. They would continue to the southern-most edge of the Kuldragg forest and then travel west inside the edges of the forest until they reached the Wilder Hills. They would then travel northwest to the northern tip of the Bertol Sea. It was here they would split up; the rest of the Zranh would travel northwest to the deepest parts of the Muldragg forest, while Melinda and Eithes would go southwest to find the Trith Nation. It was a long journey that would take at least a fortnight.

Eithes returned with her small travel pack and stood hesitantly a pace away.

Melinda motioned her forward. "From now on you will treat my space as your own."

Eithes stepped forward and set her pack down. "May I make you some food, Leillireph?"

"No, thank you. We will be leaving very soon." Melinda stood up. "In fact, I am ready to leave now."

Eithes immediately picked up Melinda's tea cup and used a leaf to wipe it out before placing it into her pack. The rest of the Zranh had stood up when Melinda had and were ready to depart.

Melinda saw some of the older Zranh smile when they watched

Eithes roll up Melinda's blanket, and they nodded slightly to her, respect showing in their eyes. But six of the younger men eyed her coldly as they sat against a large tree. She had been keeping an eye on them since Prennia's funeral and knew she had to take care of this situation now or they would foment discord within the Zranh. They obviously did not accept her as their new leader.

She casually made her way over to them and a hush fell over the area as all of the Zranh stopped what they were doing to watch the scene unfolding before them. Melinda stopped a few paces away from the six men, who openly sneered at her. "You six, on your feet now."

The men looked at each other and ignored her request. One of them took a huge bite of a plum, the juice running down his chin. He wiped at it with a hand and flicked it at Melinda. An angry murmur came from the Zranh behind her but she put her hand up to quiet them.

"I issue a formal challenge of Raithegren."

A few of the Zranh hissed in astonishment. An older man named Rollew, who was the second-highest ranking Zranh and now Melinda's second in command after her grandmother's passing, stepped forward. "Leillireph, no. None of these six are worthy of the challenge."

Melinda nodded in respect to him but motioned him away. She knew she was risking everything, but she had to do it. The Raithegren challenge was only issued when leadership of the entire clan was at stake. The winner would have undisputed leadership.

The six men stood up and grinned. The largest one motioned to himself and his comrades, "Which of us do you issue the Raithegren to?"

Melinda raised an eyebrow. "One? No. I issue it to all six of you at once."

The Zranh all around them shouted in alarm. Rollew stepped close to her, his eyes showing fear. "That is a suicidal challenge, Leillireph. No one can defeat six Zranh at once."

Melinda touched his arm. "It has been decided."

The six young Zranh openly laughed at her as they each pulled their Kryppen blades from their sheaths and spread out in a half-circle. The rest of the clan formed a large circle around her and the six men.

Rollew spread his arms, his eyes showing sad acceptance. "The Raithegren is official. Per the law, this challenge is to the death."

Melinda whipped her head around to the man. "What? No." She hadn't wanted to kill these men, she had just wanted to defeat them and earn their respect.

The six Zranh laughed at her fear and the tallest one mocked her. "Are you afraid to die?"

Rollew glared at the Zranh who had just spoken, then turned to Melinda. "I am sorry, Leillireph, the rules are absolute. Death is the only way to leave the circle."

Melinda closed her eyes, feeling sick to her stomach. Prennia had briefly mentioned the Raithegren but hadn't gone into any detail. She wished now that she had asked her grandmother for more information, but at the time she had been too overwhelmed to do so.

The tallest stepped forward. "Without your grandmother here to protect you, you are no better than an Ousler."

The clan muttered angrily at the insult; Ousler was the term they used for anyone not of the Zranh.

Melinda felt the familiar anger that had been a part of her life for so long spring to life again. These six Zranh would never accept her, much like her father had not accepted her and had, in fact, tried to kill her. She turned to Rollew. "Please take your place in the outer circle." He did as he was told and Melinda faced the six Zranh and spoke in a clear voice. "The Raithegren begins...now."

The six men shifted into the first frequency of the Raith world, disappearing from view. Melinda felt heat instantly fill her as she followed them. The world around her slowed down and everything became quiet. The clan in the outer circle also shifted so they could witness the challenge, although some of the younger members only blurred into and out of the first frequency, unable to fully shift.

The six men grinned at her as she completed the shift. The biggest one pointed at her with his Kryppen blade. "You do know that death in the Raith world is incredibly painful and slow, don't you?"

Melinda ignored him and felt the heat reserves inside her burning as hotly as they ever had, but she didn't shift to the second frequency yet. The biggest man charged her, staying in a crouch and moving fast. She waited, standing perfectly still until the last moment. As he sliced at her neck, she stepped slightly to the side and slid her Kryppen blade into his abdomen, pulling the blade out so quickly that he didn't even know he had been stabbed.

He turned to face her and stumbled as he did. Looking down, he saw the thick blood discoloring his tunic and put his hand over the wound. He shouted in rage and motioned to his five friends. "Don't just stand there!" He stumbled toward her as his friends charged.

Melinda heard Eithes scream and start running to her aid. She couldn't let Eithes get involved, so she let the heat fill her and she shifted to the second frequency. Everything slowed down again. Although everyone around her still moved, it was as if they were trying to move while under water.

Melinda was surprised when two of her opponents shifted to the second frequency, their eyes hooded in anger. But she was shocked when Eithes did, as well. The young girl stumbled forward as she shifted, looking around in wonder.

Five of the Zranh in the outer circle, including Rollew, also shifted as they were the only remaining members who had the ability to enter the second frequency. They narrowed their eyes at Eithes, unaware she had the power to do such a thing.

Eithes started to run to Melinda's side, but one of the two men in the circle stepped forward and grabbed her, holding his Kryppen blade against her neck. He grimaced as he held her. "Eithes, you are breaking the rules by entering the Raithegren. For that, you will also die."

The other challenger who had shifted started forward, a confident grin on his face as he held his Kryppen blade pointed at Melinda.

One of the witnesses in the circle yelled out. "Let Eithes go, Sulden."

Sulden turned and shouted, "She entered the Raithegren, therefore she now must kill or die to leave it. It is the law." He tilted Eithes' neck back as he prepared to slit her throat.

Eithes looked at Melinda with a serenity that rocked Melinda to her core, accepting her death with calm dignity.

The other man lunged at Melinda and she let the heat within her explode outward. Time completely stopped around her. The Zranh who was lunging at her was suspended above the ground in mid-jump, his Kryppen blade almost touching her side. She stepped the other way and plunged her own Kryppen blade into the back of his neck in the traditional killing method of the Zranh. She removed it as quickly and ran over to where Eithes was being held.

Melinda stopped and carefully pulled the blade away from Eithes' neck. It had already broken her skin but the cut was shallow. She pulled Eithes from the man's grip and carried her to the edge of the circle where Rollew was standing, his face frozen in anguish. Melinda lifted his arms and wrapped them around the young woman, then returned to Sulden. She had no sympathy for a man who would so casually slit an innocent girl's throat, so she stepped behind him and tilted his neck back, just as he had done to Eithes, and pulled her blade across his throat, cutting so deeply she almost severed his spinal cord.

Looking at her remaining opponents, she hesitated briefly, weighing her options before finally making a decision. She removed their knives and tied their hands behind their backs. As for the biggest one she had already wounded, she walked over to him and stabbed him in the back of the neck without emotion.

Melinda walked to the center of the circle, sat down cross-legged and put her knife away. She took deep breaths to calm herself, then let the heat dissipate, fully leaving the Raith world.

The world around her burst into motion and noise. The Zranh of the circle, including Rollew, who now held Eithes, appeared one by one as they left the Raith world, followed by the three men she had tied up. The three Zranh she had killed fell to the ground in a spray of blood, their deaths complete after their shift.

The Zranh stood silently and stared at her with open wonder on their faces and then, as one, every member of the clan fell to their knees and put their heads to the ground, including the three Zranh she had tied up. They stayed like this, unmoving, until Melinda uncrossed her legs and stood up.

Melinda spoke clearly and loudly, "The Raithegren is complete. Rise to your feet."

Rollew approached her, holding Eithes' hand. He bowed to her when he came to a stop. "You are truly Leillireph."

Eithes hesitated, staring at Melinda with a mixture of awe and fear until Melinda held her arms out and Eithes almost leapt into her embrace, tears streaming down her face. Melinda stroked her hair then pushed her back so she could look at her neck. "You will be fine. Go and gather some Pectun moss for the cut and come back to me so I can bandage it."

Eithes nodded and ran away into the woods.

Melinda walked over to the three Zranh who still knelt with their heads bowed to the ground, hands tied behind their backs.

Rollew glanced at them and asked, "Why did you not kill them?"

At his words, the three Zranh stiffened visibly but did not look up.

Melinda stared at them for a long moment without speaking. The silence had a power to it, as if even the slightest sound would signal the men's death. Melinda motioned to the Zranh named Pronni, the woman who had led the Quadrant to rescue her. It had been only a few days earlier she had found out Pronni was her cousin.

The young woman proudly stepped forward and stood at attention in front of her. "Yes, Leillireph?"

"Untie these men."

She did as she was told without question, cutting the men's bonds. But she stayed close behind them and didn't put her Kryppen blade away.

Melinda motioned the three men to stand and step forward. They did as they were instructed, their faces drawn and filled with guilt and shame.

One of them fell to one knee. "My name is Gareth. Forgive me, Leillireph. I accept death as punishment."

The other two joined him and repeated what he said, giving their names as Rutho and Kireth.

Melinda spoke clearly for all to hear, "You will not die this day."

All three looked up with puzzled expressions.

"Do you want to re-enter the Raithegren with me?"

They paled and quickly said no.

Melinda gave them her harshest glare. "Then your acts from this day will be erased from memory and you are full Zranh with full rights as part of the clan. But, there is one thing you will have to do."

All three said, "Anything, Leillireph."

She pointed at the three dead Zranh. "Bury them without honors and destroy their Kryppen blades. All memory of them will be erased from our histories."

The three men nodded. "At once, Leillireph."

Melinda turned to face the others. "Prepare for departure as soon as they are finished."

Eithes returned with the moss and Melinda quickly bandaged the small cut on the girl's neck, then said, "You will be fine. Pack up our space. I will be back shortly."

Eithes nodded and quickly began packing up their things.

Melinda walked deep into the woods and in an isolated spot, bent over and vomited until she had nothing left in her stomach. She sat down on a rock and closed her eyes as a violent sob wracked her body.

Chapter 17

Drax had been following the Brass river northwest all morning and had enjoyed a relatively easy journey so far. As he had traveled, he had explored his new abilities. The first part of the morning had almost been unbearable, his enhanced hearing making every sound of the land almost too loud for him. A single bird twittering on a branch had felt like the Faouthger blowing his whistle directly into his ear. A frog croaking along the shoreline had sounded like the roar of a bear. He had put his hands to his ears as he ran, which only helped a little. In desperation, he had tried to ignore the background sounds and had eventually been able to reduce the volume enough to keep himself from screaming.

As he had run, he had found he never got tired. After a number of leagues, he still hadn't even been winded, so he had settled into a casual jog that was quick enough that he would make good time, but slow enough for him to still be able to stay aware of his surroundings and any dangers that might be present. Criminals and bands of outlaws could be found anywhere, so Drax never stopped listening and looking as he ran. The constant tinkling of the chemistry vials he had taken from Baldrick's supply room had begun to irritate him almost immediately. After a few leagues he had dropped the specially made belt of glass vials to the ground without breaking his stride.

He had also checked the map frequently, amazed to see his location marker moving along his route. He was already halfway to Death Falls, which bisected the Paigonian and Bertol Seas, a journey that should have taken at least seven days on foot. He felt strong and almost god-like as he ran, reveling in his new abilities.

Drax bounded over a large boulder along the river and leapt to the next one, landing softly. The river began to narrow up ahead and as he ran around a sharp corner, he saw tall cliffs rising on both sides, creating a gorge where the water ran fast, shooting high into the air as it hit the sides of boulders. He came to a stop, unsure of where to go. He studied the cliff sides and decided the best course of action would be to climb them and follow the river from the top.

The rocks were slippery from the spray of the water as he carefully reached up to a handhold in the rock. He pulled himself up easily, surprised by his own strength. He dangled by one hand, then swung over and pulled up at the same time so he could grab a higher ledge. He repeated the process and was soon pulling himself over the top of the cliff. Pine trees grew right up to the edge, the scent of the needles bringing a smile to his face. It reminded him of walking with Walter through the woods behind the Fahrin Druin complex.

He stood up and turned around to look back down the way he had come. He pulled back a little, surprised at just how high he had climbed.

The river looked narrow from up here, the sound of the rapids a hushed roar.

The crack of a twig sounded in the distance, which Drax's superior hearing told him had come from about thirty paces upstream. He crouched and peered through the woods, the pine trees making it difficult to see any true distance.

A hushed, fearful whisper reached his ears. There were at least two people coming toward him, so Drax leapt up, caught a branch from one of the trees and silently pulled himself up to a crouch. He saw movement about twenty paces away and tightened the muscles in his eyes to make his vision zoom closer to them. He had found this new skill the previous day when he had heard a bird singing but couldn't see it. He had zeroed in on the location and spotted a flash of red in a tree at least fifty paces away. Out of habit, he had narrowed his eyes to try and better see it. Suddenly, he could see the bird as if he were only a dozen feet away. He had practiced the skill since then, so it now came naturally to him.

The two people, a young man and woman, both in their late teens, glided forward and stopped right below his tree.

"Liella, I don't want to go any closer to the edge." The young man was trembling from fear.

The young woman rolled her eyes. "Oh come on, how are you ever going to get over your fear of heights?" She was plain-looking, but her eyes flashed a wicked gleam as she challenged him.

He backed up a step. "Maybe I don't need to get over it. I am quite happy with how I am."

"I'll let you touch my breasts if you look over the edge, Tumm."

He glanced at her breasts pushing against her dress and gulped, then looked back to the cliff edge.

Drax thought about making his presence known but something stopped him. Maybe it was the voyeur in him, he didn't know. But he kept silent.

Tumm took a step toward the cliff's edge, his hands shaking as he rubbed his palms together nervously.

"That's it. Just a few more steps." She walked with him, and for each step he took, she unbuttoned her dress from the top down.

He kept glancing at her and then back to the ledge. By the time he reached the edge, he was sweating profusely.

Liella smiled at him and pulled her dress to the side, revealing a breast to him.

Tumm couldn't take his eyes from the breast and licked his upper lip nervously as he reached out a hand, but she stepped back just out of his reach.

"Not until you look over the edge, Tumm." She giggled when he gulped air, his chest heaving.

He leaned forward until he was able to look straight down and it was as if he suddenly became drunk. His body started to sway and instead of leaning back, he kept going forward, his eyes rolling back in their sockets.

Drax leapt to the ground in an attempt to grab him, but was too late. Tumm fell forward, his arms moving in circles, and was gone.

Liella screamed out and lunged forward, but Drax pulled her back as he heard a thud and splat, as if a melon had been thrown to the ground. He leaned over the edge of the cliff and felt sick to his stomach at what he saw.

The young woman leaned over the ledge with him and screamed again when she saw her companion's body cracked open on a large boulder, blood spattered everywhere.

She looked at Drax in confusion, then collapsed to her knees, hands over her eyes, sobbing.

Drax knelt down beside her. "Where is your home, Liella?"

She looked up at him, her eyes wet from tears. "I only wanted him to get over his fear of heights."

Nodding, he caressed her shoulder. "It was an accident, that's all." He noticed her breast was still hanging out of her dress, so he carefully pulled the cloth over it and buttoned it up. She didn't even notice him doing it. "Liella, let's get you back home." He stood up and she didn't protest when he pulled her gently to her feet.

Drax led her a dozen steps away from the cliff, then let her arm go and pointed the way he had seen them approach from. "Do you live that way?"

When he turned back, she was running toward the edge of the cliff, which she leapt from, her dress fluttering in the breeze for a moment before she was gone. He ran to the edge, his heart pounding, knowing what he would see. But when he looked down, there were no bodies and the boulders were clean of any blood.

He stood up, not believing his eyes. Where were the bodies? Looking over the edge again, he rubbed his eyes and just stared at the river.

Shaking his head in wonder, he stepped away from the edge and heard a twig snap in the distance. He furrowed his brow when he heard scared voices whispering to one another. He hid behind a tree and within a few moments, Liella and Tumm approached the same spot.

"Liella, I don't want to go any closer to the edge."

"Oh come on, how are you ever going to get over your fear of heights?"

Drax watched them repeat the exact same actions, this time without his interference, and she immediately jumped off the cliff after Tumm. He walked to the edge and sure enough, there were no bodies.

He heard the twig snap again and heard the voices approaching. Not wishing to relive their deaths yet again, he silently entered the woods and then he ran, always keeping the river to his right until the sun dropped

low into the sky, the cliffs gave way to a gentle hill, and the river became
flat and slow-moving again. He stopped when he found a grassy area that
led down to the river's edge, and sat down, breathing only a little harder
than normal.

It had been one of the strangest experiences he had ever had. He
had physically touched Liella. His fingers had lightly brushed her nipple
as he had pulled her dress up to cover it. He had spoken with her. He had
seen Tumm's dead body and then they both had reappeared at the top of
the cliff, only to repeat the same actions. Maybe it was his new abilities
that let him see the spirit world?

He pulled a hunk of dried deer meat and some bread from his pack
and ate it slowly, staring out across the river as he thought about what
had happened. He closed his eyes and mentally reviewed every text he
had read about the spirit world, and while most of the theory was based
on fear of death, there was one section of an ancient scroll that
postulated that the spirit world was tied in with Black Numbers and the
Aleph Null. But other than that single reference, there was nothing more
said in the scroll. Drax took another bite of meat and concluded it might
very well be true. He had been remade by Baldrick - the original Aleph
Null, and now he had witnessed this extraordinary event.

The sun set and the light faded slowly away until it was dark. He
wasn't tired; in fact, he had not slept in more than two days, yet he felt as
fresh as he normally did after eight hours of sleep. But he knew that
traveling in the dark could be dangerous, so he just sat where he was.
Then he noticed the darkness fading away to be replaced with a greenish
light. His enhanced vision let him see in the darkness almost as clearly as
if it had been daylight. He listened to the sounds of the insects and small
animals that moved about as he looked around in wonder.

A skunk waddled up to him and sniffed his trousers. He reached out
and petted its head and the skunk leaned into his hand for a few
moments, making small happy sounds. Drax pulled a piece of dried deer
meat from his pack and fed it to the animal in small portions. The skunk
gently took each piece of meat with its paws and ate with gusto. When
the meat was gone, Drax smiled and stroked the narrow white stripe
between the skunk's eyes. "Sorry, buddy. That's all I can spare. You go
on now."

The skunk twitched its nose as if it didn't believe him, then put its
paws on Drax's chest and sniffed his mouth.

Drax laughed as he gently pushed it away. "I said I don't have any
more food for you."

The skunk twitched its nose, then finally lowered itself to the ground
and shuffled away, its snout low as it sniffed for more food.

Drax pulled out another piece of meat and nibbled on it, feeling
guilty for withholding it from the skunk. As he looked around, he decided
he might as well continue his journey, so he popped the last bite into his

mouth and brushing his hands on his trousers, he started jogging along the river. As the moon reached its zenith he reached a long, wide bend in the river and stopped to consult his map.

It was a good spot to leave the river and head straight north toward the Kuldragg forest, so he refilled his canteen and waded across the river, then turned north and started running again. As he ran, he kept increasing his speed until he almost felt like his feet weren't even touching the ground. It was invigorating and he grinned, then tripped on a small rock and tumbled end over end, the contents of his pack scattering across the ground all around him as he slid to a stop.

He shook his head and as he wiped dirt from his cheek, Drax felt blood drip onto his face. He held his arm out and saw a jagged gash all the way from this elbow to his wrist, blood pulsing thickly out of it. He dug through his pack for his health kit but couldn't find it, then looked anxiously around the ground and saw it a few paces away. By the time he got it opened and pulled out a clean cloth, he was surprised to see that the bleeding had stopped and the gash had begun to fuse together. Within a few more moments, the gash closed completely. He wiped the blood away and saw a nice new scar. Flexing his arm back and forth, he could barely tell he had injured it, and a smile of wonder spread across his face.

Drax washed the rest of the blood away, then gathered up his supplies and refilled his pack, noticing that the buckle on the flap had broken. He cut a strip of leather from one of the inside pockets and used it to tie the flap tightly closed, tugging on it a few times to make sure it held. He then started off at a fast run, but not the full out sprint he had done before. He would not run that fast again unless he had to.

Before sunrise, he saw the southern edge of the Kuldragg forest loom in front of him. He continued on until the sun rose over the horizon and he came to a stop at the boundary between the grassy fields and the tall wall of trees of the forest.

Taking a sip of water, he pulled his map out and saw that the Aleph Null was in the western interior of the forest. He figured he could reach him by the end of the day.

Still not tired, he ate a chunk of cheese as he entered the forest.

Chapter 18

Sid stepped from the square and the Myrss placed a heavy hand on his head, the skin rough and warm but hard as stone. He felt a pressure in his mind but nothing more, and from behind him, he heard Agnes speak.

"His name is Cryff and he says you are tethered to the (E)."

Sid nodded, feeling a slight chill at the mention of the entities that existed inside of the obelisk in the Srithian Wood. He looked pleadingly at Cryff, "That's right, I am still connected with them. Can you help me regain my Numbers?"

Cryff just stared at him.

Agnes spoke in a hushed voice, "He says you have the Numbers inside of you and asks why you cannot see them?"

Sid looked back at Agnes in confusion. "What does he mean? I felt the Unnamed One take my Numbers."

Cryff never moved, but his body began to vibrate, causing Sid's head to vibrate as well in his grasp. Then the vibration stopped and the strange creature removed his hand from Sid's head.

"He says you have your Numbers."

Sid felt for his Numbers, but like usual, he could find no indication of them and he screamed out, "No, I don't! They are no longer in my head!"

Cryff didn't react in any way to his anger.

Agnes said, "He says you have your Numbers, but they are in the space within space. They cannot help you yet."

Cryff turned then and marched heavily away, followed by his party until they disappeared from view.

Sid wanted to run after them, but Agnes touched his shoulder. "Don't, they will not respond anymore. I tried until they were out of sight."

"I don't understand. I can't feel my Numbers; how can they still be in my head?"

Agnes lightly touched his cheek. "We will figure it out."

Nik stepped forward, still looking into the woods. "Now those were some ugly people." He uncharacteristically squeezed Sid's shoulder. "Like she said, we'll get you your Numbers back."

Sid nodded and thanked them both, then turned away, feeling defeated. "We should get moving before it gets dark."

Crowdal put his sword away, still staring in the direction in which the Myrss had gone. "It seems strange they couldn't seem to enter this square. I wonder if they know something we don't about it."

Pulling the pack straps tight against his shoulders, Sid responded without looking up from what he was doing. "I think this place has a mathematical base, maybe similar to the obelisk clearing in the Srithian Wood. Whatever it is, it affects the stream of Numbers connecting me with the obelisk." He looked up. "And they knew about the (E), the Essence of Black Numbers. I have to believe them when they say my Numbers are still inside of me."

Crowdal glanced down at him, his eyes looking troubled. "So why do you think the Trith can help?"

Sid shrugged. "That's what the Black Numbers manuscript said, although I am not certain of anything, anymore."

"I know my people, and mathematics is as foreign a concept to them as eating with a fork and knife."

Writhgarth was passing by and quipped, "Ain't that the truth."

Crowdal grinned and spoke to Writhgarth's back as the little man walked away, "Well if you would prepare a proper meal sometime, maybe we could actually use utensils." He looked back at Sid and continued, "I hope the manuscript is right, then. The Trith are not easy to be around."

Sid shrugged. "We'll find out one way or another, I guess. How long do you think it will take to get to your home?"

"I am not sure, maybe 20 days."

"That long?"

"Maybe even longer."

Sid grunted as he shifted the pack to a more comfortable position and retightened the straps. "We might as well get moving, then."

Crowdal spoke louder. "Are you all ready to go?" When everyone nodded, he motioned the Haissen forward and six of them immediately glided out of the small square, followed by the rest of the group in their standard order.

Sid felt a small warmth in his mind as he stepped off of the paving stones of the square and into the forest proper. It wasn't unpleasant and he wondered if he really did have his Numbers still inside him. It was enough to give him strength and hope.

They marched single-file for the rest of the day, no one speaking in the semi-darkness of the forest, not even Nik. The deeper they moved into the forest, the deeper the gloom seemed to settle on everyone. It was as if the forest was an entity that didn't like their presence, although Sid knew it was silly to think so. He felt his feet sink into a particularly thick area of leaves on the forest floor and as he pulled his foot free, he caught a strange scent, almost like urine and sweat. He turned his head in different directions trying to pinpoint where it was coming from.

Agnes, who was walking just behind him spoke quietly, "Do you smell that too, Sid?"

He turned to her and nodded. "I can't figure out where it is coming from, though." He stumbled on a dead branch that was partially buried in the leaves and fell face-down to the ground. He lifted his head and the smell was much stronger, giving him a bad feeling.

Agnes helped him to his feet and saw the look on his face. "What is it?"

He looked carefully all around them. "I don't think we are alone."

The Haissen all pulled out their swords, facing outward, eyes scanning the area. The area became silent as everyone stood still.

Sid felt a chill run down his back as he slowly turned in a circle, scanning the forest carefully. He was sure they were being watched.

After a few more moments, the Haissen all flicked their swords into their scabbards, the motion fluid and beautiful, and returned to their usual positions.

Nik put his bow away. "This forest is really giving me the creeps. I almost wish there had been something out there; at least we could fight it."

Tulman casually slid his own sword into this scabbard and spoke calmly. "Stop whining and start acting like the soldier you are."

Nik saluted but as Tulman walked away he made a face at his back.

Tulman spoke as he walked, not turning around. "I saw that."

Nik paled and quickly slid the arrow back into his quiver. He caught Sid looking at him and whispered quietly, "That man sees everything."

Tulman spoke loudly from where he stood near the rear of the group, "And hears everything. Now stop messing around and get into position."

Nik quickly closed his mouth and went back to stand by Tulman.

Grinning despite the oppressive presence of the forest, Sid faced forward and nodded to Crowdal. His friend motioned to the Haissen up front and they immediately started forward.

Sid still couldn't shake the feeling they were being watched and followed, but if the Haissen were not worried, he would trust their instincts and abilities.

They walked in silence for the remainder of the day until Sid noticed the light starting to fade and assumed the sun was close to setting, even though he couldn't see it through the thick canopy of trees. He was about to suggest they stop for the night when Crowdal raised his hand, signaling the Haissen to stop.

Crowdal motioned around the area. "This looks as good a place as any to make camp."

Sid quickly unloosened the straps on his pack and let it drop to the ground. He stretched his back muscles, happy to be free of the extra weight. "I'll gather some wood for a fire."

Crowdal nodded his thanks as he cleared the ground for a smooth campsite.

Sid walked through the damp woods, a Haissan shadowing him, and didn't have to go far before he had collected an armload of wet sticks. He saw a large branch that had fallen long ago, its leaves gone, the wood slick with moss. He grabbed a part of the branch where another smaller branch stuck out and gripped it like a handle and dragged it back to camp while balancing the sticks in his other arm. He caught movement in the distance, but when he turned to get a better look, he couldn't see anything. The forest was playing tricks on his eyes.

He soon entered the camp and Nik quickly took the large branch from his grip, pulling a small axe from his belt. "I'll chop this up."

Sid nodded his thanks and dropped the bundle of sticks to the ground with a clatter. He knelt and arranged the sticks in a pile, putting the smallest twigs at the bottom and stacking progressively larger sticks on top until he had a rough triangular shape. He hadn't found any kindling; neither birch trees with their highly flammable bark, nor pine-needle branches, which were also excellent for starting a fire. The wet wood he had found would not be easy to get burning.

Agnes sat down next to him. He motioned to the wood. "You wouldn't be able to get that burning with your Numbers, would you?"

She quickly nodded and closed her eyes. The wood suddenly burst into flame but the fire immediately started to sputter. A few moments passed, then the flames flared up and burned so hotly they turned almost blue.

Agnes opened her eyes and smiled. "Is that good enough?"

Sid grinned and quickly added some of the larger pieces of wood Nik had chopped up until the fire was large enough to be self-sustaining despite the wet wood.

Writhgarth placed his metal spit over the fire and hung a small cast iron pot filled with water from it. He carried the pot with him everywhere, despite the added weight, because he liked making stew so much.

By the time it was fully dark, they had all eaten and were sitting around a fire that had turned to coals, shifting color constantly.

Exhausted, Sid stood up. "I'm heading to bed. 'Night everyone."

Agnes stood up, as well as Nik, Tulman, and Writhgarth, all echoing his announcement. Crowdal pushed a stick around the coals then dropped it into them and stood up, too. They didn't have to take turns standing guard, as the Haissen never slept.

Sid pulled his blanket up to his chest and put his head on his bundled up coat as a pillow, something he had done since he had been a kid.

Agnes lay down on her own blanket close by him.

They had not talked much over the past few days but they seemed to be getting along better again. He thought of her smile and soft touch when she had taken his hand earlier in the day. He had gently squeezed her hand and gotten a return squeeze, no words needed as they walked.

He closed his eyes and listened to the soft swaying of the trees around them. Then he felt Agnes slip her hand under his blanket and briefly rest it on his stomach. Before he could cover it with his own hand, she slowly slid it downward until she touched the waist of his trousers. He stopped breathing, wondering what she would do next. Before he had time to ponder this, she slipped her fingers inside his trousers and gently wrapped her fingers around him.

He instantly swelled and was soon rock hard in her hand. He looked over at her and as she stared into his eyes, she started sliding her hand up and down, slowly at first but speeding up as he gasped softly. The pleasure built within him and he closed his eyes, his mouth open so he could breathe without making noise.

He felt movement and opened his eyes to see Agnes' head disappear under his blanket, her warm, wet mouth enclosing him. He suppressed a moan, trying to stay silent as she slid her mouth to his base and flicked her tongue in a circular motion. When she began moving in a regular up and down motion, it became too much for him and he went over the edge. She soon slid back up from under the blanket and rested her head on his chest, a wicked grin on her face.

Sid had never even known something like this could be done and he found himself amazed by her in a whole new way. Thoughts briefly flitted through his mind of the Korpor doing something similar when it had Ringed him, but at that time his consciousness had been floating above the moment and he had felt nothing but horror at the bloody image.

Sid caressed Agnes' soft hair and leaned down to kiss her, tasting himself on her mouth. She closed her eyes and returned his kiss with passion. He found himself getting hard again and looked around the camp, thankful to see that everyone was asleep. He slowly rolled on top of her, pulling the blanket over them. She giggled quietly and he put a finger to her lips. She reached down and he lifted himself so she could unbutton her trousers and slide them down. She then grasped him and guided him into her.

This was his first time with a woman, but he instinctively knew what to do as he began moving into and out of her. The warmth of her enveloped him, a feeling beyond anything he had ever experienced before. The orgasms they had each experienced back when they had first touched each other, combining their mathematical equations to hide them from the Masteen and Black Robe, had been beyond powerful, but it had not been personal and physical like what was happening now.

She closed her eyes and her breathing quickened until she quietly whimpered and arched her back. He slowed down, letting her enjoy the moment. She finally opened her eyes, and a feeling of love washed over him as he gazed at her. He had stopped moving, forgetting he was still inside of her when she softly whispered, "Please, don't stop."

He immediately started moving again and soon erupted inside of her. She felt it happening and wrapped her legs tighter around his waist. When the orgasm subsided, he leaned his face down to hers and simply whispered, "Wow."

Agnes caressed his face and kissed him. They stared into each other's eyes for a long time. Eventually, his hands began to ache from holding himself above her for so long, so he rolled to his back and she put her head on his chest. They fell asleep like this and he couldn't have been happier.

The morning light filtered through Sid's closed eyelids, bringing him out of the dream he had been in, a dream that faded as soon as he opened his eyes. Memories of what had happened washed over him and he looked down with a smile. But it disappeared when he didn't see Agnes next to him. He looked over to her empty bedroll and then quickly scanned the camp, not seeing her anywhere. Panic filled him and he jumped to his feet, ready to yell out, when Agnes pushed a bush aside and walked into camp.

She saw him and smiled. "Good morning."

Relieved, he grinned back and kissed her quickly.

The rest of the camp soon came to life as Writhgarth pushed his blanket aside and stood up, arching his back to crack it. He nodded to Sid and Agnes and began stirring the coals and blowing on them to try and get a flame going before adding some more sticks. Crowdal and Tulman disappeared into the brush, going in different directions, and eventually returning after relieving themselves.

The group sat around the fire drinking hot tea and eating bread and cheese for breakfast. Sid and Agnes didn't feel comfortable displaying any affection around the others, but they sat close together.

Nik snored under his blanket the whole time until Tulman got up and kicked him lightly. "Get up, you worthless excuse for a soldier."

Nik mumbled from under the blanket, "Alright, alright." He pulled the blanket from his head and sat up, grumbling. His hair stood out at every angle from his head as he rubbed his eyes and yawned. He finally made it to his feet and stumbled behind a bush, dropping his trousers before he was even out of view.

Crowdal grinned. "I've never seen anyone who hates mornings more than him. Why did you hire him? He doesn't seem the mercenary type."

Tulman grunted through a mouthful of bread, took a swig of water and swallowed. He wiped his mouth and replied, "I almost didn't, but he was friends with Richard, whom I trusted completely. Plus, he's the best bowman I've ever seen in my life. I swear he could shoot a mosquito out of the air."

Sid shrugged. "I like Nik. I don't think he has a bad bone in his body."

Tulman stared at him, his eyes hooded. "You are wrong. Don't get that man angry." He glanced behind him to make sure Nik was still gone. "He hides a darkness behind that likeable façade I hope you never see."

Sid exchanged a glance with Crowdal. "What do you mean?"

But Tulman would say no more and Nik soon entered the camp,

buckling his trousers. He slapped at a mosquito on his neck and flicked away the crushed insect as he sat down by the fire and grabbed a hunk of bread and cheese, biting into each without worrying about making one of the hand-held concoctions he bragged would make him rich.

Tulman stood and started rolling up his blankets, so Crowdal and Agnes did the same.

Sid studied Nik, unable to see any traces of the darkness Tulman had cautioned them about. Nik noticed Sid looking at him and asked, "What?" through a mouthful of bread.

Sid quickly looked down at his hands. "Nothing. I should get my stuff packed up."

Nik went back to his meal as Sid stood up and stepped to his blankets.

Agnes was rolling her blanket tightly and tying it with a thin piece of string. She motioned at his blanket. "I poured some water on the, ah, spills on your blanket. They should be dry by tonight."

Sid blushed, knowing exactly what she was referring to as he rolled up his blanket. "Thanks. I…well thanks for…everything."

She laughed softly as she stood up. "You don't need to thank me. Believe me, it was my pleasure."

He grinned and finished tying his blanket roll, shoving it into his pack along with the coat he used as a pillow.

Nik had quickly finished his bread and held the remaining cheese between his teeth as he packed his stuff.

Crowdal kicked some dirt over the fire and tamped it down with his feet until only a thin line of blue smoke curled up.

As they moved out, Sid looked back at the small area, thinking how quickly a little one-night camping spot could feel like home.

The forest soon enveloped them as they left their little safe haven. As Sid turned to face forward, he thought he saw motion in the distance, but, again, when he looked, there was nothing there.

Chapter 19

Staying low to the ground, the Korpor moved slowly and carefully as it stared through the forest toward the group of people trudging single file. It ignored the Haissen, the Trith and the humans. It ignored the Vringe and the Numbers woman. It ignored everyone except the Aleph Null. Or what had been the Aleph Null.

It had followed the strange Myrss for a while after its encounter with them, curious about creatures that were immune to its stare. They had known it was following them, but they didn't seem to care in the least. The Korpor had only run across one other creature that hadn't feared it, and that had been the giant, monstrous being that had hunted the Aleph Null all the way to the Srithian Wood. The Korpor had not waited around to see what would happen back then, knowing nothing could defeat the creature. When the bond between it and the Aleph Null had snapped, the Korper had assumed the creature had indeed killed the Aleph Null.

But then last night it had seen the Aleph Null in the flesh as he encountered the same wedge people the Korper had been following. It had sent out its thoughts to the Aleph Null, but had not sensed him or his Numbers. He was technically no longer the Aleph Null, yet he was alive. Confused, the Korpor had followed the boy, never letting him out of its sight. A few times it had gotten too close and had almost given itself away. The mighty Haissen had drawn their swords at one point and it had stayed perfectly still, emptying its mind of all thought. They had stared in its direction for a long time and it was sure they would come investigate its location, but then they had put their swords away and continued on.

The Korpor had kept its distance ever since, except for one time when the Aleph Null had left the group to collect sticks. It had crept close to him, sniffing constantly and sending out its thoughts, but still had encountered nothing of their previous bond. Sid had looked right at the Korper at one point, but it had stayed still and he had returned to his camp.

It had watched Sid copulate with the Numbers woman that night, the scent of his seed reaching the Korpor even from the distance between them, and it had shivered, remembering the scent very well. It had sniffed the spot after the group had left, the scent of his seed very strong. It felt an intense anger fill it at the thought of the Aleph Null copulating with the human woman. The boy was its property and always would be.

That had been two days earlier. Now, it laid down on the forest floor to look under a low-hanging branch at the group camped by a stream in the distance. Then the Aleph Null had told the Trith that he was going upstream a distance to bathe.

The boy had left the camp with a single Haissan by his side.

The Korpor crept wide of the camp and approached the boy and Haissan from the north, moving silently and slowly until it was only a few paces from them. The Aleph Null was scrubbing his armpits with some kind of simple soap, the water of the stream running white with the foul-smelling stuff, while the Haissan stood silently on the side of the stream.

As the boy dunked himself under the water, the Korpor leapt at the Haissan. The Haissan was incredibly quick and spun around, its sword hissing in a deadly arc, but the Korpor had caught it by enough surprise to get close enough to swipe its long claws viciously out; it tore the Haissan's head from its neck in a spray of blood and the Haissan crumpled to the ground as the Aleph Null popped up from under the water.

The Korpor turned in a feral crouch, then leapt into the stream.

Chapter 20

As Tris had suspected, Sid and his group had kept moving southwest through the Kuldragg forest. The tracks were getting fresher and fresher; they were now no more than a day old.

He was thinking about getting his hands on Sid again, this time for the last time, and just long enough to tear through his mind and verify whether or not Sid had any special key to unlocking the power of the Black Numbers. He was so lost in his thoughts that he bumped into the back of Ben, who had stopped suddenly.

He shoved the large guard in anger. "What are you doing, stopping like that?"

Ben turned and apologized, pointing ahead of them.

Tris stomped forward and stopped next to Gee, who was facing forward, her eyes narrowed. "What is it, woman?"

She ignored him and motioned to the woman on her right, whispering, "Go, tell me what is out there."

The young woman sprinted forward and quickly disappeared into the forest.

Gee turned to him and nodded her head in the direction of the forest. "We feel a presence out there. We will find out what it is and deal with it."

Irritated by her demeanor he stared ahead, impatiently waiting for the Hunter to return.

Suddenly a scream rose ahead of them, turning to a blood-curdling screech that went on for many moments before being cut off.

Tris saw Gee's eyes narrow as she clenched her teeth. She turned and motioned three more Hunters forward. "Find out what happened."

The three Hunters glided forward, long knives held in each hand. Within just a couple of moments they disappeared from view, so adept were they at blending into the forest.

Silence filled the area around them and stretched for so long that Tris found himself leaning forward in anticipation. Then screams erupted, filling the place where they stood, pure terror and pain in them until they faded away and silence descended again.

Tris rolled his eyes when Gee motioned all of the remaining Hunters forward. "Why? You apparently have no clue as to what's out there, why keep sending more Hunters to die?"

Gee glared at him, her fingers flexing on her two knife handles.

He put up a hand. "Stay here. I'll take care of this."

Her face turned red from anger and she was barely able to nod assent, her eyes flashing with rage.

Tris would have to decide soon what to do with her. But for now he put her out of his mind and created a simple mathematical array around himself, invisible but so strong that nothing would be able to harm him. He walked confidently forward, pushing branches out of his way and not bothering to be quiet.

Within a hundred paces he came upon the first dead Hunter, her body torn to shreds and her entrails scattered about the ground. Her face was frozen in a scream.

He looked about and saw another Hunter in a tree, her legs dangling by mere strips of flesh, so deeply cut and gouged were they. Her head had been ripped off and lay at the base of the tree.

Curious, Tris stepped over the head and on the other side of the tree he came upon a third Hunter, this one not even recognizable as a woman, her face and brain gone, leaving an empty skull red with blood and tissue.

In the distance he saw the final Hunter's body in a similar state of ruin.

Despite the dead bodies, he could find no evidence of what had killed them. He turned in a slow circle, taking in the area, when he saw it.

A creature shimmered in front of him and then materialized into a solid form. It stood about his height, its skin pure black and shiny smooth. He raised his eyes and was startled to see it was a female, her face amazingly beautiful, yet not entirely human in nature, and her mouth red with blood. Her arms and legs were thin but muscular, and as she stood in front of him, she clicked what looked like sharp talons together, each pure red and like a scythe, still dripping thick gore from her recent kills.

Tris let his eyes trail down her body to see she was not wearing clothing. He focused on two perfect breasts, each full and heavy, with stiff nipples. He felt himself growing hard in his trousers and let his gaze drop lower to the spot between her legs and his erection throbbed even harder at what he saw.

With difficulty, Tris trailed his eyes back up to her face and she hissed confusedly at him, turning her head to the side as she glared at him.

He moved forward until he was just a step from her and leaned forward until his face was almost touching hers.

She pulled back slightly as he looked into her eyes, not blinking.

Without thinking, Tris dropped his shield of Numbers and reached up to touch her face, causing her to pull back even more. He touched her again and she let him this time, so he leaned forward until he touched her lips with his, the blood on them making him want her even more. He had no idea why he was doing this and briefly thought he should stop, but the thought was fleeting; he could think of nothing but her.

The kiss went unreturned, her lips unmoving. But then she responded, moving her lips slightly, and then with increasing urgency. He slipped his tongue between her lips and felt hers touch his. Sharp teeth pricked his tongue but didn't puncture it.

When he finally broke the kiss, she looked at him for a long moment, then took his hand.

He let himself be led away and didn't notice the air shimmer around them or the Hunters behind him calling his name and moving about the area in confusion, not seeing their trail.

A veil of darkness descended upon him, then was gone as he found himself in a cave that had thick animal rugs on the floor and in the corner, a soft bed made from piled animal skins.

She turned to him and removed his clothing so quickly that he was naked before he knew what was happening. She led him to the bed and pushed him down, straddling his hardness and settling onto it in one fluid motion.

He bucked against her and grabbed her breasts with both hands as he stared into her eyes.

She put her bloody hands to his thighs as she leaned back and rode him, her talons scoring his flesh.

Tris clenched his teeth and time seemed to fade away as he fucked her in every way possible, over and over, never tiring and never stopping. Just as he was about to reach orgasm, it would fade slightly, leaving him trying harder to attain it once again. He didn't notice this as he explored every part of her, never getting enough of her scent, her body and her sounds of bliss that filled the cave as she went over her peak untold times.

Chapter 21

Refreshing, ice-cold water ran down his face as Sid sat up in the stream. But as he rubbed his eyes and opened them, he saw a blur of movement and was slammed to the bottom of the shallow stream by an immensely heavy creature. He hadn't even been able to take a breath as he felt the back of his head strike the pebbly bottom. He looked up but couldn't make out what was holding him under, its blurry visage wavering through the water as he kicked and twisted. He felt thick fur as he grasped at the arms and tried to pull them away, but it was like trying to move a rooted tree.

He was going to die.

Sid began to convulse as his lungs tried to get more air. His vision began to fade, whatever strength he had left now gone. He lay under the water, unmoving, and as the stream calmed down, he could have sworn he was looking at the hideous face of the Korpor.

With a heave of strength, he was pulled from the water and hung limply above the stream. He slowly lifted his head to stare into enormous blue eyes that glared at him with barely controlled rage.

The Korpor opened its mouth and snarled at him, its teeth sharp and yellow. It sniffed his face, its gill-like nasal openings flaring wide. Sid struggled weakly and opened his mouth to scream, but the Korpor threw him over its white-furred shoulder and sprinted up stream. He bounced against the creature's back, the wind knocked out of him, the ground a blur beneath him.

How had the Korpor found him again? It didn't matter, he realized with a sickening certainty, for he could no longer use his Numbers to fight the creature.

Sid thought he heard yelling in the distance, but it was too faint for him to be sure. He soon lost track of time, eventually closing his eyes, feeling too tired to care what happened to him.

He awoke to the familiar smell of the musty forest floor. Turning his head, Sid opened his eyes to see he was lying on his side against a rotten tree branch that was half buried by brown leaves and moss. He sat up and looked around in a haze, realizing he was alone in the forest but had no idea where he was. The trees swayed slightly from a constant breeze, the creaking and moaning of the wood an eerie sound.

Then he remembered the Korpor and scrambled to his feet, detritus flying everywhere as he spun in a circle, wildly looking for the creature, hoping it had left him alone long enough for him to escape. The forest around him was thick with trees and brush so he couldn't see very far in any direction. He didn't even know which way to run. Pushing long hair from his eyes, he realized it didn't matter which way he went as long as he went somewhere else, so he crept forward, trying to be as quiet as he could. He heard no sign of the Korpor and pushed away the fear that threatened to overtake him. There wasn't time for that if he wanted to live.

After a few hundred steps he came upon a large tree surrounded by smaller trees and brush. He worked his way forward until he could slip through the bushes and lean against the rough bark of the tree and was mostly hidden from view. His breathing came in ragged gasps, so he closed his eyes and concentrated on slowing it down until it was almost back to normal.

Sid whimpered softly when he heard a soft step not far away. He slowly slid his back down the tree until he was sitting on the ground, trying to be as small as possible. He heard another step, this time much closer. He held his breath, trying to be as quiet as possible.

Then a soft voice said, "Come out of there, Aleph Null."

Sid jerked his head up at the voice, not expecting it. He had thought it had been the Korpor hunting him. He didn't recognize the voice, but the fact it had called him Aleph Null frightened him almost as much as if it had been the Korpor.

He stood up and with shaking hands pushed the brush aside and stepped out of his hiding spot.

A young, dark-skinned man stood only a pace away, holding a knife at his side. He bowed slightly. "Well met, Aleph Null. I have traveled a long way to kill you."

Sid stepped back, his eyes widening. "Kill me? Why?"

"Because, you are the Aleph Null. It is nothing personal."

Sid breathed out, "Fahrin Druin."

The man raised his eyebrows. "No, I am not technically Fahrin Druin. I am…something more." He raised his knife and stepped forward but whipped his head around and quickly sliced to his left just as the Korpor slammed into him, throwing the man to the ground.

The Korpor straddled him while pinning his arms with its huge paws, then opened its mouth with a low growl, its long teeth dripping saliva as it lowered its face to the man's.

Sid wanted to turn away and run, but he couldn't stop looking.

Then, to Sid's astonishment, the man pushed his arms up against the Korpor's paws and started lifting them away from the ground. The Korpor's muscles bulged beneath its fur as it pushed down, but no matter how hard it strained, incredibly, the man kept forcing his arms up until he gave a violent heave and threw the Korpor from his body.

The Korpor fell to its back and slid a few paces across the leaf-covered ground, its face showing shock. It flipped itself to its feet with another growl, it's eyes wide open to inflict as much pain as it could on the man.

The man climbed slowly to his feet and faced the Korpor without fear, holding his knife casually at his side again. He spoke calmly, "I don't know what you are, but if you leave now I won't kill you."

Sid was startled to realize the man was staring at the Korpor and not showing any pain from its gaze.

The Korpor bared its teeth and clicked its long claws together, its face contorted in rage as it moved to its left. Without warning, the Korpor leapt at the man and lashed out with a blow that would have torn him in half, had the man not moved from his spot in the blink of an eye. The Korpor landed awkwardly and took two steps forward before regaining its balance. It spun around just in time to raise an arm to block a knife strike and roared in pain as the knife sliced into its arm, blood spurting from the gaping wound.

The man struck repeatedly at the Korpor, his arm moving so quickly that Sid grew dizzy trying to follow the strikes.

The Korpor backed up, swiping at the man but not hitting him as he ducked and swerved, relentlessly slicing and stabbing at the Korpor. Bleeding from a dozen places, the Korpor bellowed in frustration, then turned and sprinted away through the brush.

The man watched it go, then calmly turned to face Sid, not even breathing hard.

Sid stepped back, his arms up in front of him. "Who are you?"

The man bowed slightly. "My apologies. My name is Drax. I couldn't let that creature kill you."

Sid's eyes bulged. "You don't know what that creature is, do you?"

"No, should I?"

Sid shook his head in amazement, forgetting to fear the man. "That was the Korpor."

"Ah, the Korpor. I've heard about it." He glanced in the direction where the Korpor had run and said, "Interesting creature."

Sid gawked at him and in a trembling whisper, said, "The Korpor has lived for thousands of years and as far as I know, it has never run from anything. You should be dead right now."

Drax smiled and shrugged. "Well I am not. Unfortunately, I have to kill you now. And don't even try and use your power of Black Numbers on me. They won't work against me."

Black Numbers? He wanted to kill him because of his Black Numbers? Suddenly tired of everything, Sid slumped his shoulders. "Don't worry, I lost my power of Numbers. I am just a normal man now."

Looking at him with his head cocked, Drax stopped moving forward. "You mean you are not the Aleph Null?"

"Not anymore. And even if I was, I believe you when you say there is nothing I could do to you. To be honest, I would rather die by your blade then be in the control of the Korpor again." He sat down, wrapping his arms around his knees.

Drax looked at him quizzically. "Why do you say such a thing?"

Sid felt a tear fall down his cheek and angrily wiped it away. "It's not your concern."

Drax put his knife away, doing it so quickly that one moment he was holding it and the next it was gone. He sat down across from Sid. "I have to say, I was expecting to find a monster, not someone like you."

"Why do you want to kill me?"

"I don't want to. I was tasked to do it by someone who knows what the power of Black Numbers in the wrong hands would do to our world. Again, it is not personal."

Sid felt confused and angry, so tired of everyone wanting to kill him. "You are just one of many who want me dead, all because I once had some abilities that I never wanted in the first place."

Drax studied him carefully for long moments, his face tilted slightly to the side as if listening for something. Finally, he sat back with his arms on the ground behind him. "I can hear your heart beating and it tells me that you are telling the truth." He looked troubled for the first time.

Sid felt his anger sliding away as he studied Drax, noting he was not much older than Sid was. He had an honest and kind face, making him someone Sid found comforting despite his threats. Remembering the Korpor, Sid looked quickly around, scanning the forest for any sign of the white creature he hated and feared above all others. Turning back to Drax, he was surprised to find that he felt safe in the man's presence. "So, what happens now?"

Drax picked up a dead leaf and started picking it apart. He threw the empty stem away and picked up another, repeating the action as he asked, "What's your name?"

"It's Sidoro. But my friends call me Sid."

Drax hesitated. "May I call you Sid?"

Sid nodded, thinking how strange this situation was. Here was a young man who had been sent to kill him, had fought the Korpor and won, yet sat across from him asking if he could use his shortened name.

Drax continued, "I am not sure what I need to do, Sid. I don't sense that you are a bad person, and if you truly no longer have your power of Numbers, then there really is no reason to kill you. May I ask you a question?"

"Yes."

"Is there any chance you will regain your power of Numbers?"

Sid didn't see any reason to lie to him, so he said, "I don't know for sure, but yes there is a possibility I can."

"If you do get them back, what then?"

"I will track down and kill an old friend who has killed scores of people in his quest to obtain my power of Black Numbers."

Drax nodded. "Did this person, by chance, recently acquire your power of Black Numbers?"

Sid straightened up at this. Could Tris have actually succeeded in stealing some of his power of Black Numbers when he had so viciously entered his mind back in the Srithian Wood? "Why do you ask?"

"Because there is a second person I am to hunt and kill, a person who has acquired the power of Black Numbers instead of being born with them, like I assume you were."

Sid felt fear fill him at the idea that Tris had access to his Black Numbers. There would be no stopping him if that were the case.

"By the look on your face, I see I am correct in my assumption."

Sid nodded slightly.

Drax pinched his nose and closed his eyes as if he had a headache, then opened them to look at Sid again. "So if you get your power of Numbers back and kill this 'friend', then what?"

"I don't want anything else other than to return to my simple life with the woman I love and not be bothered by anyone."

Drax stared at him for a long time, never blinking. Finally, he said, "I believe you are telling me the truth. It appears we have a similar path to travel, as I too must hunt down this friend of yours."

"He is no friend. While we've known each other our entire lives, our friendship was all a lie. He is now the Black Robe of the Oblate."

"The Black Robe of the Oblate? I know much about the Oblate, and if this person is the Black Robe, then it makes it that much tougher for us to succeed because no one knows who is in the Oblate or even where it is located."

"Maybe I can be of help there. I not only know what he looks like, I wouldn't doubt if Tris is hunting me even after his defeat a fortnight or so ago. Knowing him as I do, I suspect he does not want anyone but himself to have the power of Black Numbers."

Drax sat still as he considered everything, then he seemed to make a decision and stood, holding his hand down to Sid. "I will not kill you, Sid."

Looking up at Drax, Sid breathed out in relief and reached up to grasp his hand. He was pulled to his feet and they stood facing each other.

Sid found that he liked Drax, despite the feeling that he was somehow not entirely human. His movements were too quick, his breathing almost unnoticeable, his strength unnatural. But he liked him and that was good enough for Sid. He let go of Drax's hand and asked, "If you help me find my friends, you may travel with us. We must first go to the Trith Nation, then find a friend who was taken from us. If I get my Numbers back, I will gladly travel with you to hunt Tris. But like I said earlier, I suspect he is trying to find me right now to finish what he started, which would make things easier for both of us."

"I accept your offer, Sid. While I would like to keep an eye on you to make a final conclusion on your character, I believe my initial analysis of you is correct. It seems our paths must run parallel for now." For the first time, he looked like a normal young man.

Sid slowly turned in a circle, trying to find any reference point that he recognized, but all he saw was uninterrupted forest in every direction. "Unfortunately, I have no idea where I am in relation to my friends. The Korpor took me and I passed out as it ran."

Drax pointed to his left. "I passed close by a small group as I tracked you here. They are about a half-morning's walk in that direction."

Feeling hopeful for the first time, Sid couldn't help himself from grinning. "Then lead the way."

Drax nodded. "Stay close to me in case the Korpor doubles back."

Sid looked around as he fell into step behind Drax. "Don't worry, I will."

***

In the distance, the Korpor leaned around a large tree and stared after the Aleph Null and the non-human as they made their way through the forest. It slowly blinked its left eye, followed by its right eye, then it started following them, moving almost silently from tree to tree. Blood dripped into its eye so it formed a globule of spit, let it drip onto its paw and rubbed the wound with it, causing the bloody cut to knit together until there was just a thin scar.

It had never hated anyone as much as it hated the dark-skinned non-human that had taken the Aleph Null from it.

But it also felt something strange.

It felt fear.

Chapter 22

Crowdal yelled Sid's name for what seemed like the hundredth time as he pushed his way through the brush. He heard similar shouts from the group all around him.

Earlier that morning, Agnes had stood up in camp and expressed worry that Sid hadn't returned from his bath, so they had made their way upstream and found the Haissan that had been guarding Sid crumpled in a heap, its head torn viciously from its body, with Sid nowhere to be seen. There was no evidence that Sid had been killed so they assumed he had been taken, and whoever had taken him must have been incredibly deadly to kill a Haissan like that.

They had to assume that whoever had abducted Sid had carried him upstream to the north, as they had not seen any tracks going east or west from the spot where the Haissan had been killed, and their camp was to the south of the stream. So they had spread out in a wide line on each side of the stream, everyone accompanied by at least two Haissen, as they searched for any signs of their friend.

Crowdal yelled Sid's name again, feeling a deep sense of hopelessness descend upon him, and then, to his shock, he heard Sid yell back from a distance. He whipped his head in the direction from which Sid's voice had come, and yelled his name again, this time getting a quick reply. Crowdal turned and called out to the group, "Sid's over here!" He ran forward, covering ground quickly with his long strides until he saw Sid up ahead pushing his way through the brush, accompanied by a young, dark-skinned man.

Sid grinned when he saw Crowdal and ran forward, laughing and crying at the same time.

Crowdal bent down low so he could embrace him. "Sid! Thank the gods you are alright."

"I'm fine, Crowdal." He pushed back from Crowdal as the rest of his friends arrived, the Haissen quickly surrounding them and facing outward, scanning the area for threats.

Agnes pushed forward and hugged Sid, kissing him quickly before checking him over. "Are you injured?"

"No, I'm fine."

Crowdal looked at the stranger and tilted his head toward the man. "Sid, who is this?"

Sid looked behind him and motioned the man forward. "Everyone, this is Drax. He saved my life."

The man stepped hesitantly forward, looking uncomfortable.

Crowdal reached out his hand and the man looked up at him with a strange look before taking it. "Thank you, Drax. We are in your debt."

Drax shrugged. "It was no big deal."

Sid chuckled without humor. "No big deal? Wait until you guys hear what Drax did."

Crowdal touched Sid's arm. "Come on. Let's get back to camp and you can tell us what happened."

Sid nodded and they backtracked until they re-entered the small camp. He sat down with a sigh and said, "It feels good to sit on my own blanket again."

Agnes sat down next to him, relief showing on her face.

Crowdal noticed Drax standing just outside of the camp, so he extended his arm. "You are welcome in our camp."

Drax stepped forward, then stood perfectly still.

Crowdal studied him briefly. Drax was of ordinary height, his dark skin very smooth, and if Crowdal had to guess, he would say he was no more than twenty years old. But there was something strange about the way he moved, going from complete stillness to motion in quick bird-like movements.

Crowdal turned from him and sat down across from Sid, with Writhgarth standing close-by with a grin on his face. Nik stood a short distance away, staring at Drax.

"Do you need some water or food?"

"No, I'm fine."

"Tell us what happened."

Sid looked around at everyone like he was hesitant to start speaking. Finally, he took a deep breath and softly said, "The Korpor took me from the stream."

Agnes gasped loudly, looking wildly around. Sid touched her knee. "It's alright. I don't think it will come back anytime soon."

She looked at him, her face pale. "How can you be so sure?"

Sid pointed toward Drax. "Because of him."

Everyone turned to stare at Drax, who looked down, avoiding their eyes.

Crowdal asked what they were all wondering. "He saved you from the Korpor? How?"

So Sid recounted his story, and by the end, everyone was staring at Drax in open wonder.

Crowdal couldn't believe what he had heard. But he believed Sid, so he stood up and stepped over to Drax, towering over him as he extended his hand. "Thank you, Drax. We are all in your debt. Our camp is yours and you are welcome here without reservation."

Drax took his hand, squeezing it firmly. Crowdal usually kept his handshake limp so he wouldn't harm anyone, but with this man he felt incredible strength and got the feeling he was holding back so as to not harm Crowdal.

Drax released his hand and his eyes softened. He smiled for the first time and seemed to relax. "Thank you. I heard Sid call your name out in the forest. May I have the honor of calling you Crowdal?"

Laughing, Crowdal slapped him on the shoulder. "You may call me anything you want, but yes, Crowdal would be wonderful." He motioned him forward. "Come, sit and break bread with us."

Drax stepped forward and sat down by Sid and Agnes. She smiled. "My name is Agnes." Drax nodded as she pointed and introduced him to everyone, each stepping forward to shake his hand. When she introduced Nik, the mercenary seemed to glare at Drax for the briefest of moments before he turned away, ignoring his outstretched hand.

Crowdal wondered at Nik's reaction, but then food was passed around and he could think of nothing but taking a bite of the crusty bread, even though it was stale and slightly moldy in places. It was still bread, which he loved more than any other food.

Drax tilted his head toward the Haissen standing around the perimeter of the camp and softly asked, "Who are they?"

Sid turned his head where he was looking. "They are the Haissen."

Drax's eyes grew wide and he drew in a quick breath. "That is amazing. I read about them but never knew they actually existed. Is it true what is written about them, that they are unbeatable with a sword?"

Sid remained quiet for a moment as he glanced at Crowdal. "They are unmatched with any sword but Crowdal's. He has defeated three of them."

Drax looked at Crowdal, astonishment showing on his face, then he lowered his head in true respect.

Crowdal nodded, feeling uncomfortable. He got the feeling he wouldn't last even a few moments against this man if that time ever came.

The light began to fade as the day ended, and everyone soon laid down on their blankets for the night. Crowdal motioned to an empty area. "You can sleep there, Drax. Do you need a blanket?"

Drax shook his head. "I don't sleep. I'll stand guard with the Haissen tonight." He walked away without another word, blending into the darkness.

Crowdal wondered just what kind of man Drax was.

If he was even a man.

Chapter 23

From her vantage point atop the last of the Wilden Hills, Melinda looked down upon the gray waves of the Bertol Sea as they rolled and crashed against the shore with relentless fury, fueled by the high winds from the west. Her hair blew all around as she stood atop a large boulder, her cloak whipping about her with a constant flapping sound.

She tilted her head to see the Zranh camp below her, close to the sea shore. Melinda knew the moment had come when she must split from the Zranh and go her own way to the Trith Nation. But now that the time had come, a part of her didn't want to leave her people, a people she had grown to love in the short time she had been with them. She had climbed this small hill hoping she would get some clarity in her decision.

They had traveled along the edges of the Kuldragg forest and through the southern edge of the Wilden Hills without incident. It had been an easy journey, giving her time to really get to know the Zranh; especially Eithes and Rollew. She thought of the older man like an uncle, knowledgeable and always willing to share everything with her, never treating her with anything but respect and kindness. But she would miss Eithes the most. The young girl had become like her shadow, always close by but not intrusive in any way, like the little sister she had never had. As much as she would like Eithes to accompany her to the Trith Nation, it would be much too dangerous and she would not risk the girl's life. Maybe, after all this business with Sid and Crowdal was finished, she would return to the Zranh and ask Eithes to live with her permanently.

Melinda shaded her eyes as she looked to the west where the lower Muldragg forest touched the western edge of the sea. She could see the trees growing tall and thick in the distance, but from her discussions with Rollew, she now knew that this was like a small, wooded area compared to the deeper parts of the vast Muldragg forest, where there were places not even the Zranh dared go. He had told her the approximate location of the Trith Nation in the lower Muldragg forest. The rest of the Zranh would go to the ancestral home of the Zranh in the far northern reaches of the forest where no humans or Trith ventured.

She caught movement in the distance out of the corner of her eye. She quickly turned, narrowing her eyes against the wind, and inhaled sharply when she saw a group of people heading straight toward their camp. She couldn't tell for sure, but from this distance it looked like dozens of people. She caught the flashing of steel in the light and knew they were not peaceful in nature, probably raiders.

She took off at a run down the hill, leaping small rocks without slowing down. Without thinking, she shifted through the Raith frequencies like her grandmother had taught her, slowing down time in intervals so as to not fatigue herself, yet arriving back at the camp much quicker than if she had just run in normal time.

She released the frequencies and stepped to the middle of the camp, calling out for everyone to pack up immediately. The Zranh responded without question, packing so quickly that Melinda had barely gotten her breathing under control before they finished.

Rollew stepped next to her. "What is it, Leillireph?"

Pointing to the south she said, "There is a large group of armed people approaching. They will arrive shortly."

He nodded and turned away, motioning to the others without speaking. They immediately started northwest at an easy run, following the shore. Eithes fell into step beside Melinda, holding out her pack. Melinda took it with a nod and put it onto her back as she ran. They continued like this until they reached the far northern tip of the sea. The edges of the Muldragg forest started here, with the Bertol Sea now at their backs. Rollew motioned for a stop, and Melinda drew them into a circle around her.

"I have to leave you here. You will follow Rollew to our home in the northern Muldragg forest. I must now go to the Trith Nation. As she spoke, Rollew stepped into the circle.

"We will wait for you in the Zranh homelands for as long as it takes for you to return. But you will not travel alone."

Melinda started to object but he cut her off. "You are Leillireph – by Zranh law, you cannot travel a long journey alone." He turned back to the circle. "I need a Quadrant to volunteer."

Pronni immediately stepped forward, along with Saulian, Nren, and Oeth, the members of the Quadrant who had rescued Melinda on the great, grassy plains.

Rollew bowed to them. "Pronni, you are the Gorepeth. Keep Leillireph safe from all threats."

Pronni bowed even lower, her hand over her chest.

Melinda was going to protest but knew it would not only be useless, it would also deeply offend the Zranh. She was now Leillireph, so she stood straight and nodded briefly to Pronni and the rest of the Quadrant, then turned her gaze to the rest of the Zranh in the circle. In a firm voice she said, "May the Raith world keep you safe. Until we meet again."

The Zranh dispersed with no further ceremony and Melinda felt a sadness fill her, but she hardened herself and turned to pick up her small pack. Eithes was already holding it out to her, her young face resolute and radiating strength. Melinda took the pack and motioned her to join the Zranh. "Thank you, Eithes. Now go with the rest."

Eithes just stared at Melinda, her lips pressed firmly together as she shook her head. "I am going with you, Leillireph."

"No, Eithes. It is a journey filled with danger. You must go with the Zranh."

The girl didn't respond, her face like stone.

Melinda saw the Zranh disappearing into the wooded area that bordered this side of the sea. Rollew was last to leave and his eyes said all she needed to know, so she nodded to him and he disappeared into the woods. Turning to Eithes, she said, "It is good to have you with me. I can use a strong warrior such as you."

The young girl's eyes shined with pride as she stood tall and straight.

Pronni stepped forward. "We must leave now, Leillireph."

Melinda slipped her pack over her back and tightened the straps. "The Trith will not be expecting our arrival, especially if the Aleph Null is not yet there. You will not kill any Trith, do you understand?"

Pronni nodded quickly, "Yes, Leillireph."

Melinda motioned her hand. "Then let's go." She started running toward the tree line, going at an easy pace they could keep up all day. Adrenaline flowed through her at the thought of seeing Crowdal, Sid and Writhgarth again. She just hoped they were all still alive and well.

Chapter 24

Glaub sat up and glanced around the quiet camp. It was well past midnight and everyone slept except for two guards. He slipped from his blanket and as he stood, Charly opened his eyes and sat up.

"Is everything alright?"

Glaub nodded. "Just need to relieve myself. Be back in a bit."

Charly smiled. "The fish didn't agree with you, hey?"

"No, now go back to sleep." He walked to the guard on the edge of the camp. "I will be back in a while."

The guard nodded but didn't reply, as it wasn't his place.

Glaub walked up-river until he was far enough away, then created the simple portal equation he had learned from the Black Robe and stepped through it into a small study. It was dark, so he created an equation for light and the room lit up as brightly as if it were day.

His father's chair was in front of him, a blackened silhouette burned into it. He stepped forward and touched it with his finger, bringing it to his nose and sniffing it. He sent out his Black Numbers and immediately sensed the residual power of his father's Numbers in the ash.

This was all that remained of his father, Baldrick – The first master of Black Numbers.

He sat heavily in the other chair and stared at the incinerated form of his father opposite him. He had not seen his father in at least a century. They had not been on bad terms; they had just known each other for so many thousands of years that they hadn't found it necessary to see each other very often anymore.

Glaub had always thought of his father as the one certainty in his life, that he would be there forever. Glaub had never even considered the idea that he would ever be without his father. Now here he was, in his father's empty chambers and alone in this world for the first time in his very long life.

Leaning forward, he picked up his father's pipe from the small table next to his chair and turned it to look at the bottom of the bowl. He smiled at the simple three-word inscription, 'For you, Papa." Glaub remembered making the pipe when he had been only eleven years old, carving it from an ancient piece of ivory he had unearthed while digging an irrigation trench to bring water to their garden from a nearby stream. His father had smiled when he had accepted the pipe from Glaub's outstretched hand, something his father rarely did. He had examined it carefully and a tear had fallen down his cheek when he had read the inscription that Glaub had so carefully carved.

Glaub touched the pipe stem and it felt cold, devoid of life now that his father was dead. He took out a handkerchief, carefully wrapped the pipe in it and placed it in his pocket. Then he stood and left the room and made his way to the library. His mathematical light followed just above him as he walked directly to the back part of the room where the oldest manuscripts, books and scrolls were kept, and reached high up on one of the shelves to removed one of the scrolls. He carefully set it on the table then returned to the shelf and reached to the back of the empty cubby, moving his hand around until he felt an object with his fingers and carefully pulled it out. He looked down at a locket and chain, tarnished so badly he could barely tell it was made from pure silver.

With shaking hands, he managed to unclasp the small latch and open the locket's tiny door. He leaned forward to look at the faded drawing of his mother, so faint he could barely make out the outline of her face. He created a Black Numbers equation that would replicate the chemical makeup of ink and let it flow around the outline, darkening the lines until his mother's image looked back at him for the first time in more than seven centuries. She was beautiful and happy in the drawing, her eyes looking almost alive as they stared back at him. He had hidden the locket in the back of the cubby so long ago that he had nearly forgotten it was there. He curled up the chain and grabbed a small wooden box from the table, emptying out the Uragon tobacco his father had kept in it. He then he placed the locket inside and put the box into his pocket.

He concentrated and sensed that the Black Numbers equation his Father had created to protect the rooms from entry by anyone else was still active even after his death. With a last look around, he spoke out loud for the first time since he had arrived, "Until we meet again, Papa."

He created the portal equation and stepped through it, arriving back to the edge of the stream he had left only a short time earlier. He closed the equation, still chastising himself for never thinking of using his power of Numbers to transport himself like this in all his long life. The fact that he had learned the equation from a kid not even in his twenties made it even more embarrassing. He never was too old to learn new things, he guessed.

Turning to walk back downstream, he saw a shape rise up from the darkness. He stepped back in alarm when Charly stepped into view.

"Sorry, Glaub. I didn't mean to startle you."

Chuckling in relief, he put a hand over his heart. "You gave me quite the start. Don't do that."

Charly cocked his head slightly and motioned behind Glaub. "So, do you want to tell me how you appeared out of thin air?"

Glancing behind him, Glaub cursed himself for being so careless.

But Charly put up his hands. "Don't be angry. I just came out here to see if you were alright when you didn't return after so long."

Glaub thought of creating a lie to explain what he did but suddenly felt tired of being alone, especially now that his father was gone. He stepped forward and put a hand on Charly's shoulder. "I won't lie to you anymore."

His friend looked at him calmly. "Good, I was getting pretty tired of pretending I haven't seen the things I've seen over the past year."

"What things?"

"Oh, you know, things like you never having an injury, even after I see you get hurt; or how you recently lost so much weight and gained so much muscle so quickly." He pointed behind Glaub, "And, just now, you appearing out of thin air."

Glaub squeezed his friend's shoulder. "I am sorry for keeping secrets from you. But you must promise me you will tell no one a word of what I will tell you."

Charly nodded quickly.

"I mean it, Charly. No one can know about me."

This time, Charly stood straighter and said, "I promise on my life."

"My name isn't really Glaub. It is Baldrick the Second. But I have not gone by that name in more than three thousand years."

Charly's eyes widened. "You are serious, aren't you?"

He nodded.

"So, how old are you?"

"I honestly don't know anymore. Many ages of man. How many, I don't fully remember."

Charly stepped back, looking at him like he was crazy. Finally, he shrugged and grinned. "Alright, old man, so how did you appear out of thin air?"

Glaub created the portal and Charly stepped back, his mouth agape. "Take my hand and see for yourself."

Charly tentatively grasped his hand. "Now what?"

"Now we walk through it."

Charly's eyes grew wide as he stared at the swirling darkness in front of them, then he nodded.

Glaub led him through the opening and they stepped into his chambers back in the Castle.

Stumbling forward, Charly looked at Glaub. "Are we really back home?"

Glaub nodded.

Charly sat down heavily on the chair where Glaub normally sat. All that came out of his mouth was, "How?"

"I am a master of Mathematics, specifically of Black Numbers. I can do pretty much anything I want. Traveling here like we just did is just a simple mathematical equation that bends the molecular structure of space together, like you would fold a piece of parchment, so we could step between great distances as if they were next to each other."

Charly nodded his head in understanding and said, "I have no idea what you just said."

"Then why did you nod like you did?"

His friend grinned. "I don't know; maybe because I am just a servant with no education, but I understood that you understood what you were talking about, which was enough for me."

Glaub chuckled. "You are a strange man, Charly." He instantly became serious. "There are some people who would do very bad things if they knew about me and what I can do. I need to stay Glaub – the simple counselor to King Jass – until I get to the bottom of all that is happening." He pointed at Charly. "That means no talking about this again, even if we are alone. Do you understand?"

Charly stood up from the chair and stepped forward with the most serious expression he had ever used. "I promise, on my life."

"Alright, let's get back to camp before everyone goes out looking for us."

Charly grinned. "We don't want them thinking we are…you know, a couple of…"

Glaub rolled his eyes. "Only you would say something like that, Charly."

He created the portal again and this time Charly walked through it no differently than if he were going through a real door.

They arrived in the darkness and made their way back down stream, chatting as if nothing had happened as they passed the guard and entered the camp.

***

Only a few paces from where they had rematerialized, Captain Shaw stepped into view and watched them fade into the darkness downstream. He thought of his father, the greatest man he had ever known. His father, who was once a Numbers man and Blue Robe in the Oblate long ago.

Chapter 25

The forest was beginning to thin out as Drax stopped and looked back at the group in which he now found himself. They had called another stop, the second one today, and it wasn't even close to sunset yet. It was very difficult to move at their slow pace but he was working hard to get his new abilities under control, to accept that he was different now. He had noticed the strange looks he had gotten from the different members of the group over the past two days since he had joined with them, looks of wonder, fear, and distrust. He had been confused by their reaction, not thinking he was any different from them. He was just Drax, the one who had studied for five years to be a Fahrin Druin, who had loved another man, and who had wanted nothing more than to sit and read everything he could get his hands on.

But that was before; a time when he hadn't really known about the real world, a world that included Aleph Null, monsters, giants, and most amazing of all, Haissen.

He walked up to one of the enigmatic beings at the head of the column and stood by its side. The Haissan wore a brown cloak with a hood that hid most of its features. Drax casually leaned forward to look at it more closely and was amazed again by its pure white skin, green eyes that were close to being true squares, and round, toothless mouth. They were truly one of the strangest beings he had ever seen. He had not yet dared to speak with one and they had not engaged him in conversation either.

They both stared into the forest in front of them until Drax asked, "Why do they all look at me so strangely?"

The Haissan turned its head slightly, the white skin of its face barely showing behind its hood. It was silent for some time, then it hissed, "They fear you."

"Why?"

"Because you are like us, but not us."

Drax thought about the statement, at first thinking it meant everyone in the group. But then he realized it was referring only to the Haissen. "You mean I'm like you Haissen?"

"Yes and no."

He realized that speaking with a Haissan was difficult. They didn't seem to consider saying anything more than they had to, as if they didn't think making themselves understood was important. But he thought he knew what it meant. His body was now different from humans. Baldrick had called him a meta-human but that didn't fully describe what he had become. Everything around him seemed to move so slowly that he could anticipate movement in others and react before they even made the decision to act. Drax listened to the incredibly slow beat of the Haissan's heart, of the blood flowing smoothly through its veins similar to his own body. He could imagine how he seemed like a Haissan to the others.

He turned and left the Haissan, knowing it didn't care if he were there or not. As he stepped into the camp, Nik looked up and then quickly away again, his face showing anger and distrust. He found Nik attractive in a rough-around-the-edges sort of way, but that wasn't what seemed to cause the discomfort between them. What it was, though, he had no idea.

Sid blushed when Agnes cupped his ear and whispered that she wanted to share his bed that night. Drax turned away, sometimes hating his enhanced hearing. He didn't like being party to other's intimate moments.

Crowdal stepped next to him, towering above him like a tree. He had never met a Trith before and was a little in awe of him. He had read much about the Trith and none of it matched up with what he saw in Crowdal. He was kind, gentle and smart, whereas the Trith were supposed to be rough, violent, and not known for their academic prowess. Crowdal motioned toward a large clearing with only a few trees in it. "It's been a while since I've practiced throwing a knife. Feel like joining me?"

Drax could hear the Trith's heartbeat quicken. He was interested in seeing what Drax was made of but also a little scared, so Drax smiled and motioned toward the area ahead, saying, "Sure, I could use a little practice."

Crowdal raised an eyebrow. "Somehow, I don't think you do." He then laughed and motioned to Writhgarth, Tulman and Nik. "You want to join us for some knife throwing?"

Writhgarth quickly got to his feet, as did Tulman and Nik, joining them in the clearing. Sid and Agnes followed, too.

Crowdal pointed to a tree about fifteen paces away. "That looks like a good one; it's a Wilden tree, so the wood is soft."

Drax nodded, pulling out a couple of the smaller knives he had taken from Baldrick's supplies. They were sharp and weighted nicely for throwing.

Crowdal pulled two knives from a boot sheath, both at least twice as long as Drax's own. But in the Trith's huge hands, they looked small. Crowdal motioned with the knife at the tree, "Let's aim for that knot about halfway up."

Drax nodded. "You first."

Crowdal lifted his arm over his head and threw the knife in a single motion. It flew end-over-end and hit just outside the knot. He swore under his breath and quickly flung the second one, this time hitting the knot dead center. "That's better. Guess I was a little rusty." He motioned to Drax.

Wanting to see just what the others could do, Drax nodded toward the Vringe. "I defer to you all."

Writhgarth threw two knives, one hitting close to Crowdal's in the center, the other a hand-span to the upper left. He shrugged. "Whoever I would have thrown at would be dead enough for me."

Tulman grouped his throws within a hand-span of the knot, and Nik landed both of his knives so closely together in the knot that the handles were touching.

Crowdal whistled in appreciation and clapped Nik on the back.

They all turned to Drax.

The changes Baldrick had made to him were incredible and he knew he would never miss the knot in the tree. In fact, he could hit any spot as easily as if he walked up to the tree and pushed the knives into it. But he knew from being a student with the Fahrin Druin that no one liked him when he excelled because it made them all realize just how mediocre they were. So he threw the blades clumsily on purpose. One knife bounced off the tree, hitting it handle-first. The other stuck a couple hand-spans from the knot at an angle, then tilted down and fell from the tree. Drax shrugged and turned away when Sid stepped forward, shaking his head.

"You don't need to pretend you are terrible, Drax. Try for real this time."

"I don't know what you mean."

Sid motioned toward the tree. "I saw you fight the Korpor. The way you used your knife, I know there is no way you could miss that tree."

Crowdal raised his arms. "I'm with Sid. And I do not like a person who doesn't try his best; we have no use for someone like that."

Drax looked at them with interest, having never been asked to excel. Of course, they may ask it of him now, but he knew they would turn on him as soon as he showed them up. So be it. He might as well make it spectacular and get it over with. He retrieved his knives, along with everyone else's blades from the tree and walked back. He held them up, "Do you mind if I throw yours, too?

Writhgarth shrugged. "Be my guest."

The others agreed, too.

Drax walked past them another forty paces, then turned.

Everyone quickly joined him, not wanting to be in the direct flight of the knives. Crowdal shook his head. "You don't need to try this far out. You'll be lucky to even hit the tree from here."

Drax shrugged. "Worth a try." He lined up facing the tree and as he looked at it, the tree seemed to zoom up to him and he felt connected to it. He calculated the trajectories needed, and holding five knives in each hand, he threw them in rapid progression with both arms, the first knife arcing high, and each of the remaining knives moving in a slightly lower arc. All ten knives hit the tree at the same time in a tight grouping dead center of the knot, yet none touched.

No one spoke or made a sound, they all just stared at the tree. They all turned to look Drax as one, their eyes wide.

He waited for their faces to turn angry from fear and humiliation, but to his surprise, Crowdal laughed with genuine humor and clapped him on the back. "That was the most amazing thing I've ever seen."

Everyone else honestly congratulated him, shaking his hand, except for Nik, who turned away with a scowl to retrieve his two knives.

Drax was overwhelmed, having only felt this accepted by Walter. He tentatively smiled as he shook hands and thought he just might become part of the group. Then he glanced across the clearing at Nik as he pulled his knives free from the tree.

Crowdal saw him looking. "I wonder what is up with Nik. I've never seen him act like this. He is usually a happy guy."

Tulman nodded and quietly said, "I think I know. Before he worked for me, he had a Captain who had gathered a team of mercenaries to help a rich nobleman in Paigon. After the job was completed and they were paid, the Captain hired another team of mercenaries to murder everyone in their sleep and take the money. Nik and Richard were on watch and were the only two who escaped, but not before the Captain went to the City Patrol and accused him and Richard of killing the other team members. Nik has not been able to enter the cities of Serenpaigg or Osengraeth since then, upon penalty of death."

Writhgarth looked confused. "What does this have to do with Drax?"

Tulman motioned at his skin. "I believe the murderous Captain was dark of skin like you, Drax. So Nik hates all dark-skinned people because of it."

Nik walked past, not looking at anyone, and went to sit by the fire.

Tulman looked at Drax. "I'll have a word with him." He turned, but Drax grabbed his arm.

"No, I think it should be me."

Tulman nodded, respect showing in his eyes.

Drax walked into the camp and knelt on one knee by Nik. When the mercenary didn't look at him, Drax cleared his throat. "Nik, may I have a word with you?"

He glanced sideways. "No."

"I just want you to know that..."

Nik whirled on him, his knife out. "One more word and I'll cut out your tongue."

Stunned, Drax put up his hands and stood, then backed away. There was no talking through hate like that. He would just keep his distance.

The rest of the group had given them privacy and soon entered the camp. They saw the look on Nik's face and Tulman began to walk over to Nik, his face set in stone, but Drax motioned him to stop. The Captain hesitated, then nodded and turned away.

Crowdal called for them all to prepare to head out again. The temporary camp was soon packed and as soon as the fire was put out, Crowdal motioned the Haissen and they began marching through the forest.

By the time the sun hung low in the sky, they came out of the Kuldragg forest, stepping through the last of the straggling trees and stopping at the edge of a steep hill that led down to a beautiful, brown, grassy valley below with a small river winding through it. As far as Drax looked in the distance he saw nothing but rolling hills and valleys, some of the hills so tall they could almost be classified as low mountains if it weren't for their rounded grassy tops.

He pulled out his map and saw they had reached the eastern edge of the Wilder Hills. The Bertol Sea was to the southwest.

Crowdal came up behind him, and looking over his shoulder at the map he whistled in appreciation. "That is the most detailed map I've ever seen. May I look at it?"

He handed it up at Crowdal, "Sure, just be careful with it."

Gently taking the map in his huge hands, Crowdal studied it closely. He lowered the map and pointed at the marker indicating Sid's location, which was their location. "What's this strange mark?"

"That marks the spot where Sid is at any given time."

Crowdal's eyes widened. "Really? How does it work?"

"I'm not sure. This map was made by someone who was very powerful."

The Trith studied him, looking like he was going to ask more questions, but he turned his eyes back to the map instead. "According to this, we are about fifteen days from my home." He pointed at a spot on the map west of the Bertol Sea, in the southern portion of the Muldragg Forest. He handed the map back. "I would be careful who sees that thing. I would bet there is not another map that is its equal in the land and some might kill to get it."

Drax nodded his understanding and put it safely away in his coat pocket.

Crowdal made his way back to the group and said, "We need to cross these hills and then head southwest into the Muldragg Forest. We should reach the Trith Nation in a fortnight or so."

Writhgarth eyed the hills and spit to his side. "Great, hills. I hate climbing up and down hills."

Crowdal motioned to his back. "Would you like me to carry you?"

Writhgarth growled at him and turned away.

Crowdal caught Drax watching the exchange and winked good-naturedly at him before motioning them to start descending the steep hill.

The grass was coarse and fairly tall, but it made for relatively easy-walking. They took their time and when they reached the bottom, they walked over and stopped by the small river. It was shallow and clear, its bottom made of pebbles. Shiny fish swam lazily against the current in such numbers that they couldn't see the bottom of the river in some areas.

Sid looked up at the sky and saw that the sun would set soon behind the hills to the west and said, "We might as well make camp here. Hey Nik, feel like joining me in catching some of those fish?"

Nik nodded, a grin on his face as he dropped his pack and quickly pulled out two fishing kits. He tossed one to Sid. "I don't think we will even need to fashion rods here. Just toss out the lines with worms and pull them in." He found a large flat rock and tipped it over, revealing two fat night crawlers, tossing one to Sid.

Sid caught it and anxiously jogged upstream to an area where the small river turned sharply, creating a wider and deeper area in which to drop his line.

Nik walked into the shallow water downstream. "You aren't going to get anything over there, it's too deep."

Sid waved him away. "Smallest fish does chores tonight?"

Nik yelled back, "You are on."

Drax watched them both, envying their easy relationship, something he had had with Walter and he missed every day. He often wondered where Walter had ended up being posted. He thought of trying to find him after all of this was over, but a part of him worried it would not be the same ever again between them.

Nik whooped as he splashed through the river, vigorously pulling in his line until he reached into the water and pulled out a large fish and carried it quickly to shore. "Hey Sid, you are not going to beat me this time!"

Sid waved at him, quietly sitting on the embankment, his line sitting in the deep water.

Nik unhooked the fish and tossed it toward the fire where Writhgarth was cutting some semi-rotten potatoes. "Hey, would you mind filleting this for me?"

Writhgarth sarcastically replied, "Sure, I'll get right to it after I prepare everything else for our meal."

Tulman stepped over and picked up the fish. "I'll do it."

Writhgarth nodded his thanks.

Nik found another worm and splashed back out into the river. He caught five more fish and Sid had yet to get a bite. He grinned as he dropped the last one on the ground. "Boy, I sure am tired from catching all of these fish."

Sid waved his hand. "Yeah, yeah, yeah."

Drax quietly walked over to where Sid sat on the ground. "Do you mind if I join you?"

Sid motioned him to sit.

"What are you trying to catch?"

"I don't know really. I just know that the largest fish usually like the deeper water. But to be honest, I don't think I'm going to have any luck."

Drax looked up and noticed that the sun had completely set behind the tall hills to the west, making the hilltops glow against the sky. "It's going to be dark soon, maybe we should head back."

Sid glanced at him, then nodded. "I suppose."

He began to pull the line in when there was a mighty splash just below them under the steep bank. Sid yelped as the line started to pull quickly through his fingers.

Drax quickly reached out and grabbed it, stopping the line instantly.

Sid let go and looked at his palm where it was bleeding. "Ouch, that stings. Thank you. Can you pull it in?"

Drax felt the constant pulling against the line, but it was nothing more than a light tug for him. He began pulling it in when a huge splash of water erupted below them and the line broke. Without hesitating, Drax leapt into the water, disappearing under it. He saw a huge shape and wrapped his arms around it, feeling thick, armor-like skin. Even under the water, he could see it was not a fish. Instinctively, he closed arms around its jaws to keep it from biting him as he walked along the bottom of the river. Feeling the ground rising up, he finally broke the surface and saw he was almost completely around the corner, the camp ahead of him. He heard Sid shouting, then running feet as everyone in the camp arrived, holding torches.

Drax stepped out of the water and walked a few paces inland before dropping the creature to the ground and heard gasps from everyone as they jumped back.

He looked down to see a reptile with short legs and a long mouth filled with teeth. It was as long as Drax was tall and darted at him, snapping its huge jaws at his legs. Drax jumped forward onto its back and wrapped his arms around the jaws again. He looked calmly up at Sid, who stood wide-eyed staring at him.

"This is technically your catch, Sid. What do you want done with it?"

Sid gulped. "I ah, I don't even know what it is."

Tulman stepped forward, holding a torch closer. "That is a Cilman; they are good eating."

Looking at Tulman to see if he was joking and seeing that he wasn't, Sid eyed the dangerous creature. "I'm not eating that. Can you just kill it?"

Crowdal stepped forward. "You are not going to kill it if you aren't going to eat it." He grabbed its tail and then pinched the jaws shut with his other hand. "I've got it Drax. Will you grab a torch and give me some light?"

Drax let go of the Cilman and stood up, watching Crowdal easily pick it up and carry it back toward the deeper water. He grabbed a torch and followed him, holding it high to provide as much light as possible.

Crowdal leaned down and gently set the head in the water, letting go of the tail last. There was a soft splash as the Cilman dove deep.

Crowdal stood and nodded his thanks for the light as they returned to the camp.

Agnes motioned her head toward the river. "Are we safe this close to the water?"

Crowdal moved his eyes to the Haissen who ringed the camp. "There's nothing to worry about with the Haissen keeping watch."

She looked at the Haissen and then relaxed.

Nik walked up and slapped Sid on the back. "Looks like I won. You get to wash the dishes."

"No way, that Cilman was way bigger than your fish."

"Maybe, but it wasn't a fish, and you didn't technically catch it." He motioned at Drax, "He did."

Sid was about to argue when the Haissen leapt into motion, cutting at the air.

Drax quickly looked into the darkness and saw the Haissen cutting arrows out of the air as they arced from across the river.

One of the arrows made it through the Haissen perimeter, heading straight for Nik, who didn't see it coming. Drax leapt at him, moving faster than the arrow and caught it just as it hit Nik's neck, the tip barely penetrating his flesh.

Nik yelled in surprise and pain, looking quickly down at the arrow, expecting it to be buried in his neck. When he saw Drax holding the arrow's shaft, his eyes grew wide.

Drax pulled the tip out and dropped the arrow while scanning the area. He counted at least ten people in the darkness of the opposite shore. They all held bows, which they were constantly shooting. The Haissen cut all of the arrows down until the people stopped shooting and faded away into the deeper darkness.

The Haissen held their ground, anticipating the retreat was a ruse to get them away from the camp.

Crowdal was standing in front of Sid and Agnes, his sword out, with Writhgarth and Tulman facing the backside of the camp.

Fearing there might be poison on the arrow tips, Drax stepped over to Nik. "Are you feeling alright?"

Nik put his hand to his neck and felt the wound, then pulled his hand back and looked at the small amount of blood on his fingers. He looked up at Drax and nodded, his face showing myriad emotions until he finally held out his hand, "I feel fine. Thank you for saving my life."

Drax shook his hand. "It was my honor."

Nik flushed, looking embarrassed.

Drax asked, "What?"

"It's just, I am ashamed for treating you as I did. My hatred for another caused me to assume you were the same. I am sorry."

Knowing it had taken a lot for Nik to say this, Drax nodded then turned away, saving him from further discomfort.

Drax left the fire-lit camp and walked out into the darkness so he could see better. Scanning the hills around them, he saw movement to the north as four figures descended the hills without using torches. He looked across the river and saw at least ten of the attackers hunkered down in the grass. It was clear in the other directions, which meant they might be able take this opportunity to escape. But something about this whole attack bothered him. Why would such a small group attack them now instead of waiting for their reinforcements to arrive? Unless the attackers weren't related to the people approaching from the north.

He returned to the camp and stopped by Crowdal, who was talking with Writhgarth, Tulman and Nik. "Excuse me."

The four turned to him and Crowdal asked, "Yes, Drax?"

He pointed to the west and said, "The ten attackers are hunkered down in the grass across the river and there is another small group of people approaching from the north."

"Did you see how many?"

"I estimate about four. They move without using torches, which indicates they don't want us to know they are coming."

Crowdal swore under his breath. "It seems we have camped on someone's land and they don't like it." He turned to Writhgarth and Tulman. "Should we make a run for it or stay and face them if they attack again?"

Tulman looked around the camp. "This place is not easily defended. We would do better to try staying ahead of whoever is after us."

Writhgarth shook his head. "We have no idea of the lands around us. We could walk right into a trap. I say we stay and see if we can reason with them or fight if need be."

Crowdal turned to Sid and Agnes, who had stepped into their meeting. "What do you think?"

Sid ran a hand through his bangs, pushing them back and sighed. "I don't know. They already attacked once and the Haissen kept them at bay. I think it might be best to stay put and see if we can wait it out till morning."

Crowdal nodded. "I think that is the best plan, although a part of me agrees with Tulman. Ok, let's put out the fires so we aren't such easy targets." He motioned at Drax. "I saw you catch that arrow meant for Nik. Can you repeat that if needed?"

Drax nodded immediately. "Of course."

"Good, I want you to watch over Sid and Agnes. The rest of us will join the Haissen at the perimeter. Nik, don't shoot anyone unless we are attacked again; we don't know yet if the ones approaching us have bad intentions."

Nik checked his quiver. "I have ten arrows left. Let's hope they are peaceful."

The four of them went to the northern perimeter and Drax stepped closer to Sid and Agnes. "Agnes, you are a Numbers woman, right?"

She nodded. "Yes, why?"

"Is there any way you can use your abilities to protect us?"

She slapped her leg in embarrassment. "Yes, of course, I should have thought of it; I can create an array around us like I did to the marauders on the beach. Nothing should get through it."

"Can you do it for our whole camp?"

She was quiet as she closed her eyes. They moved rapidly behind her lids for some time, then she opened them. "Yes, I think I can do it for the whole camp. It will be difficult, as the greater the area, the more energy is needed to create it. But I've done the calculations and believe I can do it, although I am not sure how long I can maintain such a large array."

Drax put up a finger. "Hold one moment."

He sprinted over to Crowdal. "I have an idea."

Crowdal looked down at him. "Anything would be welcome right now."

"Agnes can build a mathematical array around us all that will protect us from any weapons, but we need to return to the center of camp so Agnes doesn't need to build a large array. We can safely see what happens, and if both groups are here to kill us, we can fight back then. But they may not be on the same side. By not engaging with both at the same time we can gain some perspective and maybe not have to kill anyone."

Crowdal's eyes widened as he nodded quickly. "That's a great plan, Drax." He turned away and spoke to the closest Haissan. "Get everyone back to the center of camp."

The Haissan disappeared into the darkness without a sound.

Crowdal motioned toward Writhgarth, Tulman, and Nik. "Come on, let's get back to Sid and Agnes."

When they approached Sid and Agnes, Crowdal stopped next to her. "Are you sure you have the energy to do this?"

Agnes tilted her chin up and spoke with conviction. "Yes, I've done the calculations five times. I may not be of much use for a while afterwards, though."

"Alright, be ready to activate it at my word."

Agnes nodded and Sid leaned close and whispered to her, "I wish I could help."

She smiled softly. "I know you do. But I will be fine."

Drax turned away and in the distance he saw the Haissen moving quickly toward the camp. "The Haissen approach."

Crowdal raised his arm and called out, "Come as close as you can."

The Haissen backed up, their swords out, until they formed a tight circle around the group, leaving a space for Crowdal and Sid near the edge in case they needed to speak to the approaching groups.

No one made a sound as they waited. A slight breeze moved the grass, making a soft swishing sound.

Drax stared north and saw that the four people were getting close. He tilted his head to look across the river and saw the ten in that group creeping forward. He whispered, "They are almost here."

Agnes closed her eyes and stood still as she concentrated.

Drax sensed the array come into existence, the Numbers vibrating at a frequency he could feel, and without having to test his hypothesis, he knew he could walk through the array as if it wasn't there. Baldrick had, indeed, made him invulnerable to Numbers. He heard the soft padding of footsteps approaching, and then the four people entered the campsite.

They brandished swords, their faces covered with the skulls of some massive wolf species that must have been at least twice the size of any wolves Drax had ever seen in the south.

He heard splashing water and knew the ten in the other group were running toward the camp. He turned his head in time to see them slide to a stop opposite the wolf people. They were dressed similar to the four across from them, although they wore the skulls of eagles on chains around their necks. In their hands, they also held swords now.

The two groups faced each other, barely noticing Drax and his party.

One of the wolf people stepped forward and calmly said, "You were warned about entering our lands and killing our people."

With a scream of rage, the eagle people charged.

Chapter 26

He lay in the arms of his beautiful lover. She stared at him, never blinking or smiling, but her touch said all he needed to hear. Her scythe-like talons lightly stroked his arm, so sharp that with even the slightest pressure she could have sliced him to the bone.

He tilted his face to look at her, marveling at the obsidian hardness of her skin, shiny and inflexible, as if she were a statue instead a living thing. Yet she moved fluidly and had a softness to her touch that excited him beyond measure. He felt himself stiffen as she caressed his member with her sharp red talons and without pausing, she mounted him, put her hands to his chest and slowly rode him.

He closed his eyes, not caring if he ever left this bed.

Or did he?

Who was he?

He felt a faint memory try to push through the intense pleasure he was feeling, an image of…what? It faded away as she pinched one of his nipples hard, twisting it. He looked up at her and saw barely controlled rage in her eyes. Any trace of the memory faded completely, even the knowledge that it had been there at all.

She released his nipple and reached behind her to touch him in the place he loved and he couldn't stop from moaning. Closing his eyes, he let the pleasure grow and grow. He began to shake, unable to handle the intense ecstasy. He felt his heart beating wildly and his breathing came in ragged gasps, sweat pouring down his face. He didn't want this to stop.

Then his heart gave out. He felt it beating irregularly before it completely stopped. His pending orgasm peaked at the same time and he died as he went over the edge.

His vision faded.

In the barest corner of his waning consciousness he felt his chest being struck over and over.

He sucked in a ragged breath and opened his eyes, his chest throbbing from the beating.

She looked down at him, still straddling his body, with her fist raised to strike him again. She leaned forward, stroking his arm with her talons.

He felt like they could slice him to the bone if she added just the slightest bit more pressure.

She slid her nails down and began to lightly stroke him to full hardness, then she began to ride him slowly.

The pleasure built within him and he never wanted this to end.

Then the barest hint of a memory surfaced in his mind. This time it flared briefly, showing him an image of equations and Numbers that twisted and turned in his mind.

Pain erupted and he opened his eyes to see her glaring at him as she twisted one of his nipples.

The memory of his Numbers faded and she stopped the pain, quickening her rocking back and forth on his member.

This time, though, he felt the memory still peeking out from the recesses of his consciousness, even as his orgasm built and built and they bucked against each other harder and harder.

Then his heart stopped beating and he died.

He felt his chest being repeatedly struck and consciousness slowly returned.

She pulled him into her arms and lightly stroked his arm with her talons.

This time, though, the memory was still there and he grasped at it, holding on with everything he had as she stroked him to hardness and began to ride him.

Chapter 27

The two groups collided with a clash of swords in front of Sid and his friends. It was dark, but Sid could see well enough by the light of the moon.

The eagle warriors struck at the wolf warriors with nothing but pure hatred, hacking instead of fighting, taking hits instead of blocking if it meant they could strike their enemies at the same time.

The wolf men stayed calm, relying on their advanced sword techniques. The battle moved toward the array as the wolf people calmly and precisely cut down their enemies. Suddenly, blood sprayed against the array as a man wearing an eagle chain struck down at a wolf man who had bumped against the array without seeing it, throwing him off balance. The eagle warrior pounced, striking down at his enemy again, splitting both the wolf and human skulls right in front of Sid.

The victor looked directly at Sid and screamed as he pulled his sword free from the dead man's skull, hacking at Sid in a berserker-like fury but striking the array over and over instead. His sword snapped so he pulled a knife and stabbed at Sid repeatedly to no effect. Finally, exhausted, the man slumped against the array, still weakly stabbing at it.

The battle was suddenly over and the camp was silent. The remaining three wolf-skull warriors, now covered with blood and gore, saw their last remaining adversary slumped against the array and calmly walked over and stabbed him slowly through the heart, the act almost gentle.

They looked up at Sid and his friends and put away their swords. They removed torches from their packs and lit them, bringing a warm light to the camp.

The tallest of them reached up and removed his wolf skull, revealing the handsome face of an older man, hair streaked with grey and ending in a ponytail. Some blood had sprayed against his face through the mouth and eye holes of the wolf skull, leaving his face red in those places. His companions removed their wolf skulls also, showing they were all older men, one of them with hair so white, and a face so wrinkled, that Sid wondered how he could still wield a sword.

The tallest stepped forward and held his hand palm up in the universal sign of peace. "We will not harm you."

Crowdal, who stood next to Sid, towered over the man. "Who are you?"

The man looked up at Crowdal, his face not registering surprise at seeing a Trith. He bowed slightly. "I am Fultun."

Sid turned to look up at Crowdal. "What do you think? Should we have Agnes cancel the array?"

Crowdal nodded, so Sid turned to Agnes. "You can cancel it now."

Agnes closed her eyes briefly, then opened them again. "It is done."

Crowdal stepped forward and stopped in front of the three men. "My name is Crowdal. We do not mean to be on your land and are only passing through."

Fultun appraised him and then the rest of Sid's group. "You are free to travel through our land." He motioned to the two men standing next to him. "These are my brothers, Fondan, and Rilston." He looked down at his fallen brethren with sadness. "And this was my other brother, Jol. We are of the Jaess people and welcome you to the Jaesswithrien, our ancestral valley."

Crowdal bowed, "I am sorry for your loss."

Fultun leaned down and closed his brother's eyes, then stood. "He died a warrior's death and will be honored. It is better than dying of old age in bed."

Crowdal nodded. "That is a very Trith sentiment." He introduced everyone, ending with Sid, then motioned at the ten dead men around them. "These men attacked us earlier this evening. Who are they?"

Looking down at the man at his feet, Fultun used his toe to turn the dead body over to reveal a barbaric-looking man, his entire face covered with hair except for his eyes. "These unfortunate souls are the Gults, a primitive race who do not understand anything but violence. We have tried to reason with them over the centuries, but they do not understand communication. We leave them alone when we can, but sometimes they grow bold and attack our people and destroy our homes in a berserker fury that is impossible to deal with except through death. We have been tracking this group for most of the day." He looked up at Crowdal. "Unfortunately, you and your friends got caught in the middle."

Sid stepped forward. "Would you like to join us for a meal?"

Fultun nodded. "We would, but first we must bury my brother, and then these poor ten souls."

Sid nodded. "We will help you." At the man's acceptance, Sid turned and got a small shovel from his pack. Nik and Crowdal also carried small shovels and retrieved theirs. Within a short time, they had helped the men dig a pit large enough to hold the ten dead Gults, covering them with the freshly dug dirt.

Fultun returned and easily picked up his dead brother. He carried him a short distance away from the river, where a large boulder rose out of the ground, and set him gently down.

Sid started forward, but Rilston stopped him with a hand to his chest. "It is Fultun's responsibility to bury our brother."

Sid nodded in understanding and left the man to dig his brother's grave in peace.

They reentered the camp, dirty and hungry. Writhgarth was busy cooking up the fish, and had already arranged some old bread and cheese to make a meal enough for all.

Fultun eventually entered the camp, his face streaked with dirt and sweat and sat down cross-legged.

Writhgarth pulled all of the cooked fish from the fire and placed them onto a board in the middle of the bread and cheese.

Fultun looked at the fish, eying it carefully. "You got lucky that all you caught were these fish. That river holds a danger."

Sid grunted as he picked up a fish and cut into it with his knife. He pulled out some of the flesh and popped it into his mouth. "We know. I caught one of the things."

The old white-haired man named Rilston glared at him. "We do not like liars."

Shocked by the accusation, Sid forgot to chew the food.

Fulton put up his hand. "My apologies. Rilston is a bit old and doesn't understand humor very well anymore."

Sid chewed and swallowed. "We really did catch one of the Cilman. Well, actually Drax caught it by diving into the river and wrestling it to shore."

Fulton looked at him sharply. "I see from your expression that you tell the truth. Tell me, did you kill it then?"

Crowdal spoke up. "No, I released it back into the river."

Rilston cackled. "No foreigner would do that. Especially a Trith. You kill everything you see without reason."

Crowdal stared at the old man. "While that may be true of most foreigners, it is not true of us."

A tense silence filled the camp as the two groups stared at each other. Then Fultun laughed, the sound easy and contagious. "Well met, Crowdal. We are in debt to you then, for we revere the Cilman and they have protected our lands in return since the dawn of history." He removed a large flask from his pocket and took a small sip, then poured a small amount of the liquid to the ground. "For the Cilman; may they continue to protect us."

He handed it to Crowdal, who took a small sip and coughed. Wiping his eyes, Crowdal croaked out, holding the flask as if it were on fire, "What is this?"

Fulton laughed. "That is Jaess Dram. It'll put hair on your chest."

Crowdal passed it to Sid, who raised it to his mouth and took a tentative sip. It burned going down but was smooth and tasted like peaty moss and wood smoke. He licked his lips. "That is really good." He handed it out to Fultun who indicated it was to be shared with everyone so Sid passed it to Agnes.

They spoke until the moon was straight above them. Sid was fascinated by the ancient culture these Jaess people maintained so far to the north and would have enjoyed spending more time with them. They were friendly and honest, with even Rilston eventually warming up to the group. It was a relaxing time of laughter and many tales, something they had rarely experienced on this journey. But he was getting light-headed from the Dram and finally had to excuse himself and go to sleep.

As the sun started to rise, he opened his eyes to see the Jaess had left sometime in the night. Everyone was still sleeping, except the Haissen who stood still and silent around the perimeter. He sat up with a groan and put his hand to his forehead as pain lanced through it.

"Had a bit too much to drink, hey?"

Sid turned his head slowly and saw Drax sitting by the fire, poking a stick into the embers. "It seemed like a good idea at the time."

Drax nodded, grinning. "I've been there, believe me."

It was one of the few times he had seen what seemed to be the real Drax. Sid liked this side to him. He got to his feet and swayed, still feeling off balance, and licked his lips. His mouth was dry and tasted like he had been eating dirt.

Drax handed him a water skin. "Here, drink as much as you can. You are very dehydrated."

Sid tilted the skin back and the cool water tasted better than he could have imagined. "Where did the Jaess go?"

Drax pulled the stick from the fire and looked at the red tip, then pushed it back into the coals. "They left just a bit ago, before dawn."

It was too bad; he would have liked to have said goodbye. Looking around, Sid stumbled over to a small bush and relieved himself, then walked over to the river to sit for a while along the peaceful shore. By the time he returned to camp, the others were getting up.

Writhgarth got some water boiling for tea, then pulled out some of the leftover fish and held it out to Sid.

Just the sight and smell of the fish made Sid's stomach turn, so he crawled back under his blanket and ignored Writhgarth's chuckle.

"I thought he would like some fish. I know I do after a night of drinking."

Crowdal said something, but Sid felt sleep overtaking him.

He awakened much later, the sun already high in the sky. His mouth was dry again, so he pushed himself to a sitting position and drank all the water from his water skin, the cool liquid making him feel a little better.

Nik grinned at him as he worked on restringing his bow. "Welcome back, Sid. How's your head?"

Sid realized, thankfully, that his headache was mostly gone. "Much better, thanks. I've never felt like this before. What happened?"

"Hangover, that's what happened. You drank enough Dram to drop a horse."

"Ugh, I'm never doing that again."

Nik laughed outright. "Spoken like everyone who's woken with a hangover. It's a promise that we all tell ourselves but break without a second thought the next time we find ourselves in the same situation."

"Well not me. I'm never drinking again."

"Sure thing, mate." He turned his attention back to stringing the bow.

Sid looked around the camp. Writhgarth and Crowdal were gone, and Tulman was sleeping. He heard footsteps and Agnes touched his back. "How's the mighty drinker?"

Sid grimaced. "Terrible. Why didn't anyone warn me to stop. I have never had liquor before."

She looked at him incredulously. "Seriously?"

He nodded. "Beer a few times, but just with food."

She grinned. "Well now you know. I don't expect you'll drink that much again any time soon."

"Gods, no." He looked around. "Is there any bread left?"

"I'll check. We were pretty low last I looked. I swear Crowdal could eat a loaf a day." She went through the main food pack and pulled out a chunk of black bread. "This is all that's left. I hope we come across a village soon so we can get more."

Sid took the bread and nibbled at it. Just as he finished, Crowdal and Writhgarth returned carrying a large sack each. "Where were you guys?"

Writhgarth dropped the sack, sweating from the exertion. "We went to see if that group that attacked us had left anything worth taking after they were killed."

Crowdal set his sack down and started pulling out loaves of ugly brown bread, much of it moldy in parts. He removed some chunks of cheese in the same condition, as well as what looked like some kind of dried meat Sid could not identify.

Writhgarth motioned at his sack. "Same stuff in here, too. We should be able to cut off the moldy parts. If we get really low on our own food, which we are getting to that point soon, we will have to rely on this stuff and whatever we can catch or kill ourselves."

Agnes looked through the bread. "It seems to be made from some type of grain but I have no idea what kind." She nibbled at a corner of a bread loaf and looked thoughtful as she chewed. "It is actually quite good in a primitive kind of way." She looked at Writhgarth and Crowdal. "I just gave Sid the last chunk of our bread and was telling him that I hoped we'd reach some kind of village soon to buy some more."

Crowdal stared at Sid in horror. "You ate the last piece of bread? How dare you?"

Sid shrugged. "It's not my fault you didn't eat it all."

Drax entered the camp holding three dead rabbits by their back legs, already skinned and gutted. He thought Crowdal was really angry and leapt in front of him, protecting Sid. "There's no need for violence now."

Crowdal looked down at him and laughed. "We were only joking, Drax. You never have to fear any harm will come to Sid when I'm around."

Drax nodded and turned away without a word. He dropped the

rabbits by the fire and pushed sticks through them and hung them high over the flames so they would slowly cook.

Sid whispered to Crowdal, "How did he kill them? He doesn't have a bow, nor do I see any knives on him."

Crowdal bent down. "I would guess he caught them with his bare hands."

Sid started to grin but saw that Crowdal wasn't joking.

Crowdal walked over to Drax. "When you finish cooking those, we should at least try and get a half day of travel in."

Drax nodded and lowered the rabbits closer to the fire. They started to sizzle, juice dripping into the fire causing it to constantly flame up.

Crowdal eyed the dead rabbits, a sad look flashing briefly across his face and Sid remembered his friend telling him the story of why he stopped eating meat; of how he had snared a rabbit and held it up, and how it didn't struggle as it twisted in his grip, just staring at him without fear. It was still strange for him to think of Crowdal not eating meat, but he had come to accept this quirky part of his friend.

After a short while, Crowdal called out, "Get packed up. We will head out as soon as those rabbits are cooked."

Sid didn't really feel like traveling today, but it was his own fault he felt so poorly. He picked up his blanket and shook it out, snapping it to get the dirt and grass off, which blew back onto Agnes in the breeze.

She hollered out, putting her hands over her head. "Hey, watch what you're doing."

"Sorry, I didn't realize the wind was blowing that way."

She picked up her blanket and walked a pace in front of Sid and shook it out, covering him with grass and dust, then placed her hand over her mouth in mock despair. "Oh, sorry, I didn't even think of the wind." She smiled sweetly at him and walked back over to her area.

Nik chuckled but didn't say anything.

Sid brushed his hair roughly to get all the grass out and shrugged at Nik, a grin on his face.

Drax pulled the rabbits from the fire and wrapped them in a small blanket and stuffed them in his pack.

Crowdal looked around the camp. "Everyone ready? Alright, let's go."

Sid looked up as thunder rumbled in the distance. He saw dark clouds rolling over the huge hill to the south and could see rain falling even from this distance, darkening the air all the way to the ground. Lightening crackled over the hill and thunder sounded at the count of eight. The storm was still a good distance away, but it was moving their way. He stopped and pulled his rain coat from his pack. Everyone followed his lead, except for Drax and the Haissen.

It looked like their journey was going to get uncomfortable.

Chapter 28

Melinda felt at home now in the forest, at the feeling of soft ground underneath her feet thick with the dead remnants of the trees and life about her. She glanced up to see the sun shining down on her through the branches of the pine trees. The forest wasn't dense here just west of the Bertol Sea, so she could see some distance around her, the trees growing tall and straight.

From what her grandmother had said, the deeper one traveled into the Muldragg forest, the more densely together the trees grew. The forest itself stretched from the Bertol Sea north all the way to the Olduur Mountains, then west to the ocean.

She thought back to her days of talking with Prennia back in the Branstall Wood, listening to her grandmother tell of the Muldragg Forest and how far away and mysterious it had all sounded to her at the time. To her, the Branstall Wood was deep and dark, and she had said that she couldn't imagine the Muldragg Forest could be much larger. Her grandmother had laughed and patted her hand, her voice light as she said, "Dear, these woods around us are like a nobleman's country estate compared to the true forests of this land."

She had looked at her quizzically. "Forests? There is another besides the Muldragg?"

Her grandmother had rooted around her possessions then and had finally pulled out a yellow and worn piece of parchment and unfolded it next to Melinda. Leaning forward, she had seen it was a crudely drawn map.

Prennia had pointed to where they were and then moved her finger north, "This is the Kuldragg Forest. It is a forest we never venture too deeply into. When we travel from here to our home in the Muldragg Forest, we travel along just the southern edge of the Kuldragg Forest."

Melinda turned her head. "Why"

Prennia had stared at the map and said in a low voice, "Because there are strange and dangerous things deep in the heart of that forest that not even we Zranh are willing to face." She dragged her wrinkled finger to the other side of the map. "And here is the Muldragg Forest. See, it starts here by the Bertol Sea and stretches all the way up here. This is where our ancestral homeland is, next to the Olduur Mountains."

Melinda had stared in wonder, then pointed to a blank area above the forest. "What's up here north of the Olduur Mountains?"

"No one knows, really. The mountains are too large and harsh to cross." She leaned closer. "But there are tales of a lost land up there."

Melinda remembered staring at the blank area of the map, intrigued and amazed by the idea of a lost land that no one had ever seen. Then her grandmother had folded the map and handed it to her. "This is yours now. Keep it safe."

She smiled at the memory of her grandmother, wishing she had gotten more time to spend with her. The old woman was so different from her mother, who was just a shell of a person, never really living her own life, always in fear of the Zranh. Maybe someday she would see her mother again and show her the true Zranh and tell her she had nothing to fear.

Pronni held her hand up, her fingers all raised.

At seeing the signal, Melinda instantly shifted into the first frequency of the Raith world.

Eithes and the four members of the Quadrant quickly joined her.

Melinda stepped forward to Pronni's side. "What is it?"

The young woman stared straight ahead, her eyes narrowed. She pointed just to their left. "There, about fifty paces."

At first, Melinda didn't see what Pronni was pointing at. She let her eyes lose focus so she could see the whole area, knowing it was sometimes easier to see something out of the ordinary in the forest by not trying to focus on individual things; the thing that doesn't belong would often be easier to see then.

She saw it almost immediately; a tuft of brown cloth showing along the edge of a tree. She focused and realized it was the sleeve of someone's shirt.

Pronni glanced at her. "Should we engage or bypass?"

Melinda didn't turn away from where she was looking, speaking from the corner of her mouth, "Take the Quadrant and explore the entire area. I want to know if it is an accident we ran into whomever is out there, or if it is someone intending us harm. If so, I want to know why."

Pronni motioned quickly and the Quadrant spread out, fading into the forest without a sound.

Melinda heard Eithes step close to her and she put her hand on the girl's shoulder without thinking. Eithes didn't speak. Trained as a warrior from a young age, she knew the danger they faced. Even in the first frequency, they were not immune to harm.

The Quadrant quietly arrived back, one at a time. Pronni knelt down and cleared away a patch of dirt. She marked where they stood. "There are twelve of them." She marked the twelve spots in the dirt. "Nine carry short, fat swords and three carry primitive bows. They do not look like anything more than outlaws."

Melinda hated those who stole from others, usually killing innocent people in the process. She had healed her fair share of people who had come to the House of Healing after being attacked along the roadside. She had rarely heard of outlaws living so deeply in the forest though. There was simply no one to rob out here. No, these were not likely just outlaws, unless she and her Quadrant had stumbled upon their refuge. She kicked the dirt clear and pushed brown pine needles over it until the ground looked undisturbed. "Let's go around them. We will stay in the Raith world until we are sure there are no more of them."

Pronni nodded and led them to the right, picking their way carefully as to ensure they left no markings.

Melinda counted three men as they passed through the area but that was all. The rest were hidden well. When they were clear of the outlaws, she gave the motion to leave the Raith world. The sounds of the forest hit her immediately, a shock to her after the near silence she had been in for so long. She took a few dozen steps when she heard the swish of an arrow pass by, hitting the tree next to her head with a twang.

Four people stepped out in front of them, two holding bows with drawn arrows, all of them dressed in simple brown leathers. One called out clearly, although she couldn't tell which one it was. "Do not shift or we will be forced to do the same."

Melinda shook her head in response to Pronni's look, knowing she was about to shift to the Raith world again. She whispered, "Be ready to shift to the second frequency if anything happens."

Pronni gave the barest tilt of her head that she understood.

Melinda called out, "Who are you?"

A man stepped forward until he was a few paces from them. He was young, close to Pronni's age, and although he gave her a hard look, his eyes looked gentle. "We are Zranh."

Melinda narrowed her eyes and turned to Pronni. "Do you know these men?"

Pronni shook her head no.

Turning back to the man, Melinda studied him carefully, at his clothing, the way he and his people carried themselves with such confidence and ease, and she knew they were truly Zranh. She stepped forward until she was directly in front of him. "My Gorepeth does not recognize you, nor do I."

The man shrugged slightly. "I do not know you or your Gorepeth either, so we are at an impasse. I cannot let you enter into our lands until I can confirm your intent, even if you are Zranh."

Melinda motioned behind her. "We passed by a group of outlaws a short way back. Were you aware of them?"

He nodded. "Of course. We were just on our way to rid our home of their foul stench." He cocked his head. "We did not expect to run across you, though. Why do you travel through our lands without requesting permission first?"

Pronni stepped forward, her face showing just a hint of anger. "You know not who you speak with. The Leillireph goes where she wants."

The man's face blanched at the title, then every Zranh dropped to one knee and bowed their heads. He spoke without looking up, "Forgive me, Leillireph."

Melinda was shocked by their reverence. "Please, rise."

The man stood up fluidly, although he still looked shaken. "I did not know the Leillireph was reborn. Of course you are welcome to our lands. The elders will be most pleased to speak with you."

Melinda did not want to waste time by making a diversion, but she knew there was no way she could refuse the offer. To do so would be the ultimate insult. "My name is Melinda. This is my friend Eithes, and this is my Quadrant. What is your name?"

"I am Falweth. Gorepeth of the east quadrant at your service."

"Well met, Gorepeth. We would be honoured to meet with your elders."

He relaxed, then lunged forward and chopped an arrow out of the air next to Melinda. "It looks like we have attracted the vermin we were hunting. Excuse us." Disappearing from view, he shifted into the Raith world as did his Quadrant.

He reappeared in just a dozen heartbeats, his knife dripping thick, red blood. He smiled and casually said, "My apologies for the wait, we can leave now. Please join us."

Melinda glanced back and saw dead men lying behind her, each with a single puncture wound to the back of their necks. She turned and started following the Quadrant. By mid-afternoon they entered a clearing with a large pool of water. A small waterfall fell on the opposite side, the crashing of water creating a mist that had a rainbow inside of it.

Falweth led them along the stony shore and as he approached the waterfall, he held up his hand. "Our watch has already reported your arrival." He held his arm out. "You will enter first, as is the right of the highest rank, Leillireph."

Melinda stepped forward and was surprised that the entrance turned into the wall, protecting her from getting wet. Within a few steps, she entered a well-lit cavern that stretched far back, descending at a slight slope. Twenty Zranh knelt in front of her, heads bowed.

The Zranh in the front had white hair with skin as wrinkled as old parchment.

Melinda stopped in front of this old person and softly said, "Please, rise."

The head tilted up and an old woman gazed at her with milky white eyes. With effort, she pushed herself to a standing position, her back bent at a bad angle with her head pushed to the left. Her head barely reached Melinda's chest. A young child quickly handed her a cane which she accepted with a kind smile, lightly touching the child's head.

"Welcome, Leillireph. I am Eidle, Matriarch of the Border Zranh."

"Thank you, Eidle. May we please sit?"

The old woman shuffled to a simple wooden chair and sat down with some effort, motioning Melinda to sit in the chair next to her. The rest of the Zranh sat in a circle on the stone floor of the cavern covered with reed mats. As custom, Melinda's Quadrant stood behind her. Eithes sat at Melinda's feet, her back straight.

"Leillireph, we do not mean to be disrespectful, but we must have proof you are Mother of the Blood, the true Leillireph."

Pronni hissed, "You dishonor the Leillireph."

Melinda held up her hand. "No, Pronni. Eidle is correct in her request." She looked around the circle of Zranh. "How many of you can enter the first frequency?"

All except for the youngest raised their hands.

Melinda nodded. "Good. And how many can enter the second frequency?"

Of the twenty Zranh, only seven raised their hands, including Eidle.

"That is excellent. If you six will please stand." She turned back to Eidle, who was slowly pushing herself to her feet. "No, Eidle. You may remain seated."

Eidle sat back down. "Thank you, Leillireph."

Turning back to the six standing Zranh, she saw that of the six, most were older. Only two were her age or younger, including Falweth. Prennia had been correct when she had said the abilities were fading among the Zranh. She motioned them forward. "Please, stand over here."

The six Zranh did as she asked.

"I formally ask you to be witness for all Zranh, and upon your lives to be truthful of what you observe. Do you agree?"

They all nodded, the older ones trembling slightly.

"Shift to the second frequency now."

The seven disappeared from view.

Melinda felt the heat deep inside of her and tapped into it, shifting straight to the second frequency. The seven reappeared in front of her while the remaining Zranh were almost frozen in place. They bowed slightly to her, including Eidle, who looked a little pale from the effort.

"I won't keep you in this frequency for long, as I know it is difficult and exhausting. I will shift to the third frequency; while in it I will put you all back into your original sitting positions and I will stand right where I am now and return to the second frequency. Do you accept this as proof of my being Leillireph?"

They all agreed, although the youngest Zranh didn't look convinced, openly smirking.

Melinda let the heat loose and shifted to the third frequency. Every one of the seven Zranh became as still as stone. She reached from behind and dragged each of the six standing Zranh back to their places, carefully pushing them back to a sitting position. When she got to the youngest Zranh who had smirked at her, she decided he could use a lesson, so she dragged him out of the cave and pushed him under the waterfall for a few moments, then dragged him back soaking wet.

She returned to the original spot and let the heat dissipate, returning to the second frequency of the Raith world.

All six Zranh visibly flinched when they realized they were sitting down in their original places. In their second frequency, they had been nodding to Melinda's instructions one moment and then instantly found themselves sitting down in a different location. They looked at each other in wonder, and when they saw the youngest sitting there drenched and dripping water, they all laughed at him. To his credit, he didn't get mad, laughing with them instead. They all stood up and bowed low to Melinda. "We witnessed your ability; you are Leillireph."

Melinda turned to Eidle, who was looking pale but beaming at her. "Alright, lets return from the Raith world now."

They all shifted back, the room returning to full motion.

Eidle motioned at Melinda. "Let it be known that we seven bear full witness that Melinda is the true Leillireph."

Every Zranh bowed low, then stood up, cheering.

Melinda was shocked by the reaction, having expected them to be as quiet and reserved as her own clan. She hadn't even known there were other Zranh clans, so she guessed she shouldn't be surprised they might be different.

Eidle raised her hand for silence. "Go and prepare a feast for tonight. I will speak with Leillireph alone now."

Everyone filed out of the cave. When Melinda's Quadrant didn't move, she motioned them away, too.

Eithes was last to reluctantly leave.

Eidle watched the young woman exit the cave. "That one idolizes you."

Melinda smiled. "She is without family so I asked her to be my personal attendant, not because I wanted one, but because she needed someone who would love her."

The old woman smiled warmly. "You are truly the Mother of the Blood."

Uncomfortable with the deference of such a woman, Melinda looked away.

"Tell me, why are you traveling with just a Quadrant and an attendant?"

Melinda quietly told Eidle her story, ending with her plans to visit the Trith Nation to hopefully meet up with the Aleph Null.

"The Trith are a difficult people. You would do well to avoid them."

"I know, the one I mentioned has told me about his people's violent history. But it is something I must do."

"Then you should let me send a second Quadrant to escort you there."

"That will not be necessary, Eidle. My Quadrant is sufficient."

Eidle closed her eyes and leaned her head back. "Please accept my request. I am very old and will likely not see another winter. I must do what I can to ensure your safety. You are the future of the Zranh. Your children will strengthen the bloodlines of the Zranh for generations to come, breathing life back into our peoples."

Melinda snapped her eyes into focus. She had never really thought about having children, and Prennia had only mentioned it in passing. But listening to Eidle reference it right after talking about Crowdal made it hit home. She put her head in her hands, feeling a sob escape.

For the first time, she realized that she could not have a future with Crowdal.

Chapter 29

The Korpor sniffed in the darkness around the day-old camp by the river. The clouds were heavy and a cold rain fell, making the night pitch dark to any but itself. With its massive blue eyes, it could see everything around it in a low, blue light, the rain drops looking like fireflies as they streaked past.

It slowly blinked its left eye, followed by its right as it bent low in the mud and traced a water-filled boot print with a claw. It sniffed it and caught the faintest hint of the boy's scent.

The Korpor had followed the Aleph Null from a distance, keeping at least a day behind him. It didn't trust the hateful non-human who had appeared in the woods to drive it away from the Aleph Null. He had been too fast, too strong, and didn't react to its pain-inducing glare. Whatever the non-human was, the Korpor didn't want its next encounter to be a surprise.

It lifted its head and gazed at a hill in the distance, hearing the soft footfalls of four humans trying to stealthily descend it. The Korpor narrowed its pupils and made out their silhouettes, the swords glinting as they held them while walking, instead of keeping them sheathed, showing that these humans were hunting it.

The Korpor huffed in irritation, its breath showing in the cold rain. It didn't want to waste time killing the humans, but rage filled it at the idea they would dare to hunt it.

Baring its teeth, the Korpor growled, saliva dripping from its teeth and combining with the rain to run to the ground. It let its claws slide out of their fleshy sheathes, each as long as its paws and crouched low, moving into the tall grass outside of the camp, edging around and toward the four humans, who had reached the bottom of the hill and were moving through the grass toward the old camp.

The humans were only a hundred paces away when they stopped and turned their heads as if listening to something. The Korpor turned to look in the same direction and saw another, larger group of humans approaching from the other side of the river, at least forty of them. The four humans the Korper had been hunting turned and sprinted back the way they had come and the group from across the river let out yells and screams as they gave chase.

The Korpor watched, its anger fading away. Let them kill each other, it saved it the time of doing it itself. It returned to the old camp and searched the area, easily finding the direction the Aleph Null and his group had gone.

It stood up, staring in the distance, the rain sliding off of its fur. Behind it, the Korpor heard shrieks of pain and death. It glanced back but couldn't see the battle taking place. It retracted its claws and ran into the grassy fields toward a huge hill in the distance.

As it ran, thoughts filled its head of tearing the dark-skinned non-human to bloody shreds.

Chapter 30

He latched onto the memory, and even as the pain increased as she twisted his nipple harder, he wouldn't let it go. Images of Numbers trickled into his mind, then equations flowed in that were so long in their complexity that they felt warm to him, comforting. The pain moved from his nipples to his chest. He opened his eyes and saw the obsidian-colored female dragging a scythe-like talon in a trail down his stomach, blood welling up behind it.

He closed his eyes to block out the sight and pulled the Numbers closer to him, feeling them pulse with his pain. They entered him, filled him, seeped into his mind, pushing the fog of agony away.

And he remembered!

He was not He anymore.

He was Tris. He was the Black Robe. And he was the master of Numbers.

The pain moved lower and he opened his eyes to see the obsidian female holding his now soft penis with one hand, a sharp talon from her other hand touching the base of his testicles, her eyes no longer showing anger, as if she knew she had lost control of him. She started to pull the sharp talon across his testicles, and without thinking, he built a small array and wrapped it around them, snapping off the tip of her talon.

She screamed out and lashed at his face, her talons spread wide. He built a simple molecular field equation and used it to push her back until she struck the cave wall. As he raised his arm, she rose up the stone.

She struggled, her eyes glinting with anger and desire as he trapped her.

Tris remembered everything they had done together; the areas of each other's bodies they had violated, the pleasure and pain they had inflicted upon each other. He had no control before, but he did now.

He stepped off the bed and stood in front of the creature, fully studying her for the first time with a clear mind. She had the body of a woman, her breasts beautifully large, her sex soft and folded, inviting him to penetrate her. Her skin was obsidian black and shiny, any light that hit it completely absorbed. When Tris leaned close to her face and ran his finger around her lips, she opened her mouth to reveal rows of sharp teeth. He looked up into her eyes, eyes that were pure black with no pupils.

She was beautiful. Beautiful and deadly.

And he wanted her again. But this time on his terms. He moved the equation, using it to push her back down the wall and over to the bed while holding her immobile.

She looked up at him, challenging him. Inviting him.

He pushed her legs apart and she grinned, her sharp teeth glinting in the candle light. Using his Numbers, he added an array around his penis, including an equation that allowed him to feel sensations. Then he expanded it so the field was larger and longer and plunged into her. She hissed and gasped, trying to writhe on the bed but unable to. She screamed in pleasure and instantly went over the edge, her sex convulsing around his shaft.

Tris leaned down while still inside of her and kissed her mouth, running his tongue gently over her sharp teeth. Then he pulled away and whispered, "You are mine. I own you. I control you. I and only I will pleasure you." He expanded the array around his penis even more and she moaned. "Do you understand me?"

She blinked but couldn't move her head, so he released the equation that held her head immobile. She immediately nodded.

"Good. Can you speak?"

She hesitated, then nodded. She opened her mouth and her voice came out as a hoarse whisper, "Yes, I can."

Tris expanded the array around his penis a little more and she gasped. "You will call me 'Master'."

She nodded.

"Say it."

"Master."

"Good. What is your name?"

She looked at him questioningly. "Name? I have no name. I just AM."

Tris studied her carefully to see if she were lying, but could see she wasn't. "Are you alone?"

She stared at him, unblinking. "Yes. I am always alone."

Tris nodded and smiled. She was truly one of the most unique beings he had ever run across and she could be of incredible use to him. He leaned down and almost touched her lips with his. "Do you know what you are?"

She tilted her head slightly. "I am…Mithenzz."

He had never heard of this word and would have to do some research when he returned to the Oblate. He began moving inside of her and she sighed in pleasure, and as she did, he whispered, "I will name you. You are now, Obsidian."

She moaned as he thrust harder.

Tris expanded the array around his shaft a little more. "Tell me your name."

He quickened his pace and she breathed out low and raspy as she went over the edge again, whispering, "I am Obsidian."

Tris emptied himself into her with a roar, then laid on top of her, his body heaving as he got his breathing under control. He finally pulled himself free and stood up, looking down at her body and licked his lips, wanting her already again. But he turned away from her and looked around the cave. He found his clothing in a corner and got dressed.

Obsidian watched him from the bed, still trapped by his equation.

Tris walked about the cave and saw there was no exit. Solid stone covered every surface. "How do we get out of here?"

"I take us out."

He turned to look at her. "How?"

"I can move through air, through stone, unseen."

Running his hand along one of the walls, he was intrigued by the power she had. While he could have created a portal equation to get out of here, he wanted to experience what she could do. He turned his head and said, "Then you will do this for us now."

He released the equation that held her and she lithely got to her feet, stretching her body in ways that made him stare at her private areas with lust. He couldn't keep her around fully naked, it would be impossible for him to not think about her body.

"Put some clothes on."

She looked down at herself as if noticing her nakedness for the first time. "I do not like cloth against my skin."

"I don't care what you don't like. I said put some clothes on."

She immediately stepped to her right, opened a crude chest and pulled out a black cloak made from a thin material. She threw it around her shoulders, arching her breasts as she did, and cinched it around her waist with a belt. Her nipples showed as they poked against the cloth.

"Better. Now, you are my property. You go where I go. Understand?"

Obsidian nodded. "Yes, Master."

"Good. Take us out of here and back to the last place I was."

She stepped forward and opened her arms. "We must hold each other."

Tris stepped into her embrace, inhaling her musky scent and finding himself getting hard again. She felt his hardness and pressed herself against it, rotating her hips. He saw the air shimmer around them and then it grew dark, but only briefly. He sensed movement and then the air shimmered again and they were standing in the forest.

She held him still and ran a hand down to caress his hardness. She whispered in his ear, "I want you."

Tris forced himself to ignore his rising lust and he pushed himself from her. "Not yet, my pet. But soon." He turned to take in their surroundings and didn't see her eyes narrow briefly at being denied.

Chapter 31

Not for the first time, Sid gazed in wonder at the hills all around him that interconnected with grass-covered peaks and valleys, each seeming separate yet part of a whole system. Birch trees grew thickly in groves that often covered entire valleys, other times growing in certain areas only, leaving the valleys filled with nothing but tall grass. The sun hid behind heavy clouds that rolled across the sky like the tumbling surf of the sea. In the far distance, at the base of an angular hill, the sun's rays broke through the clouds in one spot, shining down upon the rocky river the weary group had been following for the past two days, causing the water to sparkle and shimmer.

It was the most beautiful realm Sid had ever seen. He breathed in the cool, damp air, so fresh and clean that he often found himself taking deep breaths without realizing he was doing it.

Over the past two days, the grass had started to turn from a pale brown to a green so deep and rich that he sometimes wondered if what he was seeing was real or a dream. The days remained cool but not cold, with rain almost a constant. One moment the clouds would look to be breaking up, like now, but the next moment they would close back in and belch out the rain they had come to dread again.

As if Sid had summoned the rain simply by thinking about it, he felt a raindrop hit his head, followed by another and another. Sighing, he pulled the hood back over his head as the rain fell harder. A wind kicked up, driving the rain at an angle, hitting him from behind. At least they were facing away from the rain this time. Earlier in the morning, the wind had come from the opposite direction, the rain lashing them in their faces so they had to put their heads down and hold their hoods tight to keep them from blowing back.

Writhgarth muttered behind him, "This rain will be the death of us."

Nik replied, though the rain drowned out his words.

Sid peered from under his hood and thought he saw something move up ahead. He reached out and pulled on Crowdal's coat.

Crowdal turned his head, squinting his eyes against the rain. "What is it, Sid?"

"I think I saw something move up ahead."

Crowdal raised his closed fist and everyone stopped. He made a quick motion and four Haissen sprinted forward, spreading out as they ran.

Sid put his hand over his eyes to keep the rain away as he looked around the valley, but now all he saw was the endless green grass and occasional copse of birch trees. "Sorry, I guess it was nothing."

But Crowdal didn't respond, his head turned to the left as he stared intently. Then he softly said, "Everyone, slowly kneel down." He lowered himself as he spoke, but even then his entire upper-torso stuck up above the grass line.

Sid peeked above the top of the blowing grass, still no longer seeing anything moving out there. Then, from out of the rain came the four Haissen. He crept forward so he could hear their report.

The lead Haissan hissed, "There is nothing out there."

Crowdal nodded. "Good. Let's resume then." He motioned everyone forward.

Sid thought he must be seeing things that weren't there in this never-ending rain.

They continued on, and as they trudged through the rain the hills grew larger and steeper. They reached the end of the valley by late afternoon and Sid tilted his neck back to take in the imposing hill in front of them, which was really more of a mountain that curved around the head of the valley, leaving nowhere to go but up a narrow gorge with a rocky center where water flowed fast and heavy from the rain. Rocks and boulders spread out at the base, likely brought down from eons of flash flooding.

The river they had been following for days curved to the left and exited into a small lake that butted up to the edge of the hill. He looked closer and wondered if his eyes were tricking him when he saw the water swirling wildly next to the hill. He pointed. "What's happening over there?"

Everyone turned to look where he was pointing and Drax said, "It is draining into the hill. I would suspect it enters into an underwater cave system that goes through the land mass, probably exiting out the other side of the hill. I've read about this phenomenon. Something similar exists in the Funglewood mountains in the south of Reilen." He turned to them. "I probably wouldn't swim in that lake, myself." His lips curved upward at his dry joke.

Crowdal smiled. "We will heed your warning, Drax."

Sid turned to gaze up the gorge, feeling uneasy as he remembered the flash flood that had almost killed him and Crowdal the day they had first met. And that had just been a small river, nothing like the grand scale of the defile in front of them.

As if reading his thoughts, Crowdal said, "Sid and I got caught in a flash flood outside of Oiro. I don't want us all to get caught in another, so let's make camp away from the gorge."

Writhgarth spit to his side, the black tobacco juice streaming out and hitting the ground with a splat. He wiped his mouth. "Aye, lets wait to see if the weather clears tomorrow before we try climbing that."

They all followed Crowdal a few hundred paces where they set up a simple camp in the rain, nothing more than water-proof tarps over sticks to keep them relatively dry. They ate cold bread and meat, unable to get a fire going, not even when Agnes tried to get the wood burning with her

Numbers, which were no match against the heavy rain.

The rest of the day passed slowly for Sid, even though he had Agnes to hold, each keeping the other warm. As night fell, he slept poorly, cold water dripping onto his shoulder. He didn't shift though, not wanting to awaken Agnes. The rain slowed to an occasional patter during the night, and by the time the sky lightened, the rain had stopped completely. The ever-present cloud-cover remained, and the temperature dropped so substantially that he could see his breath as he pulled his arm free from Agnes and crawled from under their tarp. He cupped his hands and blew into them to warm them as he stepped up to Drax, who was the only other one awake so early aside from the Haissen. Sid had never seen Drax actually sleep and wondered if he ever grew bored while everyone else slept.

"Morning, Drax."

Drax glanced sideways at him and nodded. "At least it is no longer raining."

Sid grimaced as he stomped his feet, feeling the cold all the way down to his toes. He noticed that Drax didn't seem to be affected by the low temperature, wearing only a light coat, neither shivering, nor showing any sign of discomfort. "True, but I'm not sure what I prefer – the rain or this cold."

Drax didn't respond as he gazed across the valley from where they had just come, his eyes narrow and piercing.

"What is it?"

Drax didn't respond, so Sid touched his arm. "Drax, what is it?"

He spoke out of the corner of his mouth, never looking away. "The Korpor follows us."

Sid whipped his head to where Drax was looking. He squinted when he thought he saw something moving but realized it was just a small deer feeding in the distance, its head bent down to the grass. He finally looked back at Drax. "I don't see anything but the deer. Are you sure?"

Drax nodded slowly. "Yes. It is six or seven leagues away, always keeping its distance, never getting too close."

Sid shuddered but wasn't surprised the Korpor was following him. Their connection from the Proofing and Ringing may be gone, but they were still connected by their history together. He blew into his hands again. "How long have you known it was following us?"

"For two days. I wasn't sure at first, but I backtracked last night for a number of leagues and caught just a glimpse of something white descending a hill far away." He glanced down at Sid. "It could only be the Korpor."

Sid shivered and his teeth chattered slightly, whether from the cold, or the name of the Korpor being spoken, he couldn't tell. Maybe it was from both. He heard movement and turned to see Writhgarth rubbing his hands together as he emerged from under his tarp and turned to walk a short distance to empty his bladder. Sid turned back to Drax. "We need to tell the group and figure out what to do." When Drax didn't respond, Sid turned away. Speaking with him was almost as difficult as talking with the Haissen.

He shivered again and figured he might as well see if he could have better luck in lighting a fire this morning, now that the rain had stopped.

As he got some dry sticks from Crowdal's pack, the giant opened his eyes and nodded at him. "I see the rain stopped. I'll help you make the fire." He crawled out from under the two tarps he had overlapped to provide enough coverage for him and stood up, his back popping as he did. "This damp cold is far worse than even the deep winters back home. It creeps into your bones."

"I know. Right now, I don't think I'll ever feel dry and warm again."

Crowdal grabbed a few larger pieces of wood he had kept under his tarp. "Come on, let's build that fire."

Sid grabbed his coat to stop him. When Crowdal looked down at him, he motioned him to bend down. "Drax just told me the Korpor is following us."

Crowdal cursed softly. "Is he sure?"

Sid nodded.

"Will we ever be rid of that thing?"

"It doesn't seem so. Let's hope we can stay ahead of it, at least."

Crowdal looked back down the valley. "Somehow I get the feeling the Korpor could catch us if it wanted to. I think it keeps its distance because it is afraid of Drax, but I will warn the Haissen to keep a closer watch to be doubly sure it doesn't sneak up on us."

Crowdal set the wood down and walked over to the closest Haissan.

Sid watched Crowdal speaking with the Haissan and hoped he would never see the Korpor again. Just the thought made him feel ill. He bent down and placed some dried moss on the ground. He used his flint to drop sparks, and on the fifth try, a spark caught. Sid bent low and blew lightly on it until it flared and a flame appeared. He added small sticks, slowly added larger ones until he knew the fire would be self-sustaining. He put his hands out and the heat felt wonderful.

Sid thought back to how easy it had been for him to start a fire using his Numbers, using just a thought to create a simple equation for fire that would start with even the wettest wood. He missed having his Numbers floating around his mind and the comfort they used to provide. Turning his head, he saw the ever-present thread of power stretching away from him to the northeast, back toward the obelisk in the Srithian Wood.

Agnes came out of the tarp and bent down next to him, kissing him on the cheek, then putting her hands out to the fire. "You started this with just flint and tinder? Sid, you could have woken me to start it with my Numbers."

"It's alright. I need to get used to doing things the old-fashioned way."

She leaned against him. "It won't be forever."

"We don't know that, do we? What if we get to the Trith Nation and nothing comes from it? I have no idea what I'm supposed to even do when we get there."

"What did the manuscript say again?"

"Just five words: *Trith*, *Circle*, *Zranh*, *Raith*, and *Death*. It isn't very helpful, is it?"

Agnes was quiet as she thought. After a few moments, she asked, "Trith and Circle definitely relate to the ancient ceremony where two young Trith become men through battle. Maybe it is a metaphor for what you must do, to battle for your Numbers?"

"But, who do I fight? A Trith?"

"Maybe. Or it may mean you must have an internal battle with yourself? Or it could mean something entirely different."

Sid moved his hands as he said, "That's the problem. It could be anything and all I have is that five-word clue."

Agnes was quiet again, lost in thought when Crowdal walked up to the fire. "The Haissen will stay extra vigilant, if that is even possible, to ensure it doesn't circle around us."

Agnes looked at him questioningly, then to Sid. "To ensure *what* doesn't circle around us?"

Sid whispered, "Drax said the Korpor is following us."

She visibly shuddered.

Crowdal glanced back down the valley. "I think we have enough resources to protect us from the Korpor. Drax defeated it once, and the Haissen are not afraid of it."

Sid motioned to him. "And you fought it before."

He grimaced. "I did, and I hope to never have to face it again."

Sid pointed at the mountain. "Then let's get up that gorge soon before it starts raining again. I'd like to get more distance between us and the Korpor."

Crowdal stood. "I agree. We can eat when we get over the mountain." He yelled out. "Everyone, get up and let's move."

Tulman quickly exited his tarp and nudged Nik's foot as it stuck out from his own tarp. "Up and at it, Nik." When there was no response, he kicked the foot harder and Nik mumbled that he was awake.

Sid hated to leave the warmth of the fire, but he was anxious to get going.

They rolled up their tarps and were soon trudging up the slope to the mouth of the gorge, making their way carefully over and around the rocks and boulders that spread out quite a way from the base of the chasm.

Sid stared up the steep gorge, the rushing of the water down to a trickle now that the rain had stopped.

He turned to his friends. "Well, this should be fun."

Writhgarth grunted. "I hate climbing, have I ever said that?"

Crowdal grinned. "Only a few dozen times a day." He became instantly serious. "Everyone, just climb slowly and watch every step."

The Haissen started up the gorge, followed by Crowdal, Sid, Agnes, two more Haissen next to them, and then Writhgarth, Nik and Tulman with the remaining Haissen.

Sid put his hands down to the rocks to steady himself as he climbed, his feet wanting to kick out behind him in the rubble. The grade increased as they climbed until they reached a point near the top where an almost vertical rock face blocked their ascent. It was about four times taller than Crowdal.

Crowdal asked a Haissan, "Can you climb that with a rope and tie it off from the top?"

The Haissan nodded and took the rope that Crowdal held out. Throwing it over a shoulder, it briefly studied the rock face, then leapt up and grabbed a small crack in the rock by its fingers. It swung lithely and pulled itself to another higher up, this one so small it could only grip it by the tips of its fingers. Sid watched in amazement as the Haissan quickly made it to the top, performing feats of strength and agility beyond the ability of humans.

Sid glanced at Drax, who had calmly watched the Haissan climb. He suspected Drax would have easily kept pace with the Haissan, although Sid wasn't sure he was entirely human either.

The Haissan disappeared from view for a few moments, then quickly reappeared and dropped the rope down.

Crowdal gave it a good tug, then motioned for Sid to step forward. "Drop your pack, then tie yourself at the waist. You want to pull yourself up, using your feet as leverage like you are walking up the rock."

Sid did as he was told and found it quite easy to climb that way. He quickly reached the top and pulled himself over with the Haissan's help.

He untied the rope from his waist and dropped it back down.

Agnes was next and quickly made her way up, barely breaking a sweat and grinning widely. "That was fun."

Nik came next but he couldn't get the hang of using his feet like they had, swinging off balance and hitting his shoulder hard.

Crowdal yelled up. "Lift your legs and put your feet flat against the rock, Nik. Yes, just like that. Now walk yourself up."

Nik swore as he awkwardly struggled, falling to his back when he reached the top, breathing hard. He untied the rope and tossed it over the edge without sitting up.

Everyone else made it up without a problem until it was just Crowdal down below. He tied the packs together and two Haissen pulled them up, untied them, then dropped the rope back to Crowdal.

He weighed at least three times what everyone else weighed, and the rope creaked loudly as he pulled himself up. Sid eyed the rope, hoping it wouldn't break and was relieved when Crowdal pulled himself over the top.

Before they continued on, Sid gazed out at the valley they had just climbed out of and from this great height it was even more beautiful. He turned and looked down the other side of the hill at a plain of grass. In the distance, to the south, he could just make out the sparkling water of a great sea. He turned to look west and saw another forest stretching for as far as he could see.

Somewhere out there was the Trith Nation and, perhaps, the answers to how he could get his Numbers back.

Chapter 32

Glaub raised his arm and called out to Captain Shaw, "Let's stop here for the night and climb Death Falls in the morning."

They had been following the shoreline of the Paigonian Sea for the past five days and were approaching the point where it met the Bertol Sea in a violent display of nature called Death Falls.

He could hear the roar from the water crashing down more than a thousand feet in a narrow defile that separated the two seas. The elevation changes between the two bodies of water occurred along a major fault line that divided the northern and southern parts of the continent. The tectonic changes were subtle and mostly unnoticeable everywhere, but here they were spectacular. While Glaub had studied many texts written about the phenomenon over the past millennia, and had visited the area countless times, he never grew tired of experiencing it again.

Captain Shaw motioned his men to make camp, then slid from his horse and walked over to help Glaub dismount.

"No, I am good, Captain." Glaub leaned forward, lifted his right leg smoothly over the saddle and dropped nimbly to the ground.

Shaw raised his eyebrows. "Impressive, sir. Just a few days ago you couldn't have done that."

Glaub patted his horse's side and said, "The exercise is doing me good. I even like this guy."

Shaw nodded with a smile, then grew serious, "Sir, we should ride inland to bypass the falls."

"No, that would waste time and energy. We will climb the falls tomorrow as planned."

Shaw looked like he was going to argue, but then nodded and turned away to tie up his horse.

Glaub watched him walk away and understood his reticence. The falls were dangerous, but this route would save them at least two days of traveling.

Handing the reins to Charly, he walked down the pebbly shore to the water's edge. The water was foamy and filled with branches and detritus churned up from the nearby falls. He gazed across the water and could see the other side of the sea for the first time in days, narrowing to a point here.

They had not come across the Aleph Null, nor had Glaub had any communication from the Black Robe in more than a fortnight.

He sighed, knowing he should make a report. He once again assumed the persona of someone who was insecure and weak, then activated the simple communication equation the Black Robe had given him. He made his thoughts quiver in fear as he said, "*Black Robe? Black*

Robe, are you there?"

The Black Robe's voice boomed in his head and he winced at the volume. *"Report, fatty!"*

"Black Robe, I'm sorry to...to bother you."

"Just give me an update, I don't have all day."

"Sir, I have secured a group of soldiers from King Jass and we have arrived at Death Falls between the Paigonian and Bertol Seas. We have encountered no sign of the Aleph Null."

"That's because he isn't down that far south. I swear, I am surrounded by morons."

"I am sorry, Black Robe. Please tell me how I can make it up to you?"

The Black Robe's voice seethed with barely-controlled contempt. *"Travel due north to the Muldragg Forest. The Aleph Null is moving in that direction. He travels with a Trith, so there is a good possibility he is going to the Trith Nation for protection."*

"Where are you, now?"

"That is not your concern."

The Black Robe abruptly cut off their communication. Instead of removing the alpha symbol like the Black Robe had instructed to close the equation on his side, Glaub scrambled the specific variables in the equation the Black Robe had snuck in to allow him to spy on Glaub. If the Black Robe found out he had done this, he could claim ignorance and say he had accidentally damaged the equation. It had taken all of his patience to play the part of a simpering fool to such a vile man, but while the Black Robe had been speaking, Glaub had mathematically followed the connection between them and knew exactly where the prick was. He removed his map and put his finger on the eastern portion of the Wilder Hills, midway between the Bertol Sea and the Sein Ocean.

He moved his finger across the map, trying to figure out where the Aleph Null could be traveling to other than the Trith Nation. There was not much to the west besides the Muldragg Forest. He went through his memory, trying to think of everything he had learned about the forest over the years. Ages ago, it had covered much of what is now Uragon. But over the past few millennia it had shrunken considerably as the people of Uragon had cut down trees along the edges of the forest and floated them down river to fuel the expansion of the cities. They had turned vast areas that were once rich forest into wastelands of rocky plains and desert. Only a small portion of the forest remained untouched, mostly the farthest reaches to the north along the Olduur Mountains.

Glaub knew the Zranh lived in different parts of the forest, but he didn't think the Aleph Null would be seeking them; he would likely not even know they existed. As much as he hated to agree with the Black Robe, if the Aleph Null was traveling with a Trith, he might just be making his way to the Trith Nation.

Glaub looked behind him and saw the soldiers sitting around a large fire, eating and talking softly. If only he wasn't saddled with these men; traveling with them made things more difficult and slowed him down greatly. He could just use the portal equation now to transport himself to the Trith Nation, but he needed to keep up with his affected role for a while yet. He had rarely interfered with human events throughout his long life, usually letting them do as they wanted as long as he wasn't impacted directly. But with a new Aleph Null coming into existence for the first time in thousands of years, he knew it was his duty to ensure that this person didn't use the power of Black Numbers to harm others, and the Black Robe was the only one who knew who this Aleph Null was.

As for the Black Robe, he would need to die after he had led Glaub to the Aleph Null. Glaub had encountered violent and evil people many times over the millennia, but none of them had the power to do lasting harm. Even the strongest warlord had quickly faded to obscurity, nothing more than a flash of violence in the long history of the land. But Glaub sensed the simmering power of Black Numbers inside the Black Robe, and although they were incomplete, in the control of one so malevolent, such power could be used to cause permanent destruction upon the land and all who lived in it. He wondered how the Black Robe had come by the Black Numbers, because he could sense they were not a true part of the man's metaphysical makeup.

Glaub heard footsteps approaching on the soft pebbles of the beach. "Did you bring me dinner, Charly?"

"No, sir."

He turned at the sound of Captain Shaw's voice. "Excuse me, Captain Shaw. I thought you were my servant."

The Captain came to a stop next to him, staring out over the water, his close-cropped hair moving slightly in the breeze. "Sir, may I speak informally?"

Glaub nodded. "Of course, Captain Shaw."

"I must be honest with you, regardless of the consequences."

Curious, Glaub motioned to him. "Please, walk with me."

They slowly made their way up the beach. Shaw was silent for the first few steps, then spoke quietly as he gazed out over the water. "When I joined the army of King Jolr, I was just a young man who thought I knew everything there was in this land. King Jolr was the only good king in the land and every other kingdom was the enemy." He glanced at Glaub. "Those are the thoughts of youth, when things are black and white. Over the past twenty-five years, I've seen three kings assume the throne of Uragon, and I've witnessed thousands of men die in useless battles between rulers who use those men without a thought."

Glaub said in a low voice, "You know, as counselor to King Jass, I could have you court-martialed for those words?"

Shaw laughed sardonically. "Yes, you could I guess," he turned to look directly at Glaub, "but we both know you won't do that."

Glaub held the man's gaze for a few steps, wondering what exactly he was trying to say. He calmly raised an eyebrow and asked, "Why is that?"

"Because, I know you are not just a counselor to the king."

Glaub was growing tired of this game, so he stopped, and so did Shaw. Turning to face the Captain, Glaub raised and dropped his arms in frustration. "Just come out with what you want to say, Captain."

Shaw surprised him when he went to one knee, looking up with calm eyes. "I want to serve you, Robe of the Oblate."

Honestly shocked, Glaub took a small step back. "Why do you say this?"

"Because I saw you disappear into thin air the other night, and then reappear, only to do it again with your servant. Only a Master of Numbers could do that."

Thoughts raced through Glaub's mind. How did this man know about Numbers or the Oblate? Was he in the employ of the Oblate, or even of the Black Robe himself?

"Tell me how you know these things, and do not lie, for I will know if you are duplicitous."

Shaw nodded, his face solemn. "My father was briefly a member of the Oblate before he died from a wasting disease. He tried to train me in mathematics but I had no aptitude for Numbers. What I do know is that my father spoke of the Oblate as the one true force for good in all the lands, and I am tired of serving petty kings."

Glaub sensed he was telling the truth as he knew it, although this truth was based on falsehoods. Glaub had witnessed the foundation of the Oblate by the Haissen thousands of years ago and had watched as the organization grew in power and influence across the kingdoms of the land. It had often done some good in preventing large-scale wars, but any good was usually done to protect their profits and power. The Robes had started to think of themselves as the true rulers of the lands, that they were more powerful than everyone and everything and therefore had the right of rule. He and his father had allowed the Oblate to continue to exist only because it was easier to keep an eye on them when they were organized.

Looking into Shaw's eyes, Glaub knew he couldn't destroy the good memory of this man's father, so he placed his open palm on Shaw's head. "I accept your service and place you in the true employ of the Oblate, but you must commit to one immutable tenet."

Shaw stared up at him in something close to awe. "Anything."

"You must never share any of this information with anyone, not your wife, your kids, your comrades, or your god upon forfeiture of your life. Do you so promise?"

"Yes, upon my life."

"Then rise." Glaub hated playing this game, but he had to do it to keep the Captain in line.

Shaw stood up and clasped Glaub's outstretched hand, his eyes showing complete devotion. "Thank you. Give me my first order."

"Your first order is to act like this didn't happen."

He saluted. "May I know our true mission?"

Glaub wondered just how much he should tell the Captain, and finally decided on the truth. "I am trying to find the Aleph Null."

"The Aleph Null, sir?"

"You don't know what that is, do you?"

"No, sir."

"The Aleph Null is a person who can control Black Numbers, a subset of regular Numbers."

Shaw was smart, uneducated though he was. "So, someone like you, then?"

Glaub nodded. "Yes, although the Aleph Null does not necessarily know how to handle that amount of power and may use it with malicious intent. I must find him and decide if he is worthy to have such power. Do you understand?"

Shaw nodded immediately but waited to speak, clearly expecting there to be more to the story.

"I must also deal with the Black Robe of the Oblate, who is powerful, but has the darkest mind I've ever encountered. He enjoys killing and torturing people and his ambition knows no bounds. I have been spying on him and suspect I will have to eventually kill him."

Shaw's face hardened. "If there is one kind of man I've grown to despise over the years, it is one who harms others just because he can. I will help you in any way I can."

Glaub smiled, relieved he had gotten the Captain's character correct. He was a good man. "I am glad we are as one with this." He turned his head to look back to camp. "We should return. If you need to speak with me about any of this, do so only when we are truly alone. My servant Charly knows some of our business, but not everything. So refrain from talking even with him."

Shaw agreed and they returned to the camp.

The night passed uneventfully and the next morning they got an early start toward Death Falls.

Chapter 33

The feast had included rich meats and succulent fruits, with ripe early-summer vegetables and soft breads accompanied by berry wine and sweet mead. After they had eaten their fill, the Zranh brought out simple musical instruments and everyone danced and sang, clapping their hands with laughter. Melinda was pulled into a dance by the young Gorepeth named Falweth, and she found herself laughing, too, as she twirled and hopped to the music. She thanked him for the dance and he bowed, his eyes twinkling with merriment. Melinda sat down to catch her breath and saw Pronni watching the young man. When she noticed Melinda observing her, she blushed and turned away.

A young Zranh girl held a reed cup out to Melinda. She accepted it and sipped, surprised to find it was crisp, white wine made from wild flowers. She nodded her thanks to the young girl, who smiled and returned to a spot across the dance circle. Melinda touched Eithes on the shoulder. "Why don't you go spend some time with that girl? She looks about your age."

Eithes leaned closer to Melinda, looking uncomfortable being around so many strangers.

Melinda knew the girl was growing too attached to her and it wasn't healthy, so she spoke more firmly. "Eithes, I want you to get to know these people. It is important for a future leader to interact with all Zranh. Now go."

Eithes' eyes hardened and she nodded as she stood. "Yes, Leillireph." She walked around the circle and Melinda watched her shyly approach the young Zranh girl. The girl smiled and slid over so Eithes could sit. Melinda felt a happy warmth when the girl pulled a flower from her hair and handed it to Eithes, who looked down at it briefly before hesitantly smiling back and putting it into her own hair.

Melinda stood and walked over to Eidle, who sat in a chair away from the dancing.

The old woman beamed as Melinda approached, indicating she should pull a chair over.

Dragging the chair next to Eidle, Melinda sat down with a sigh. "You have a wonderful clan, Eidle. I've not laughed this much in my entire life."

Eidle turned serious. "I sense the sadness inside of you. You have been through much sorrow in your life. I hope someday you find extended happiness."

Melinda looked to the floor, feeling a tear leak from her eye. She wiped it away and looked back up. "I do not foresee that happening any time soon."

"And why do you say that, Leillireph?"

For some reason, Melinda found herself wanting to share with the old woman. But she didn't know how to start.

Eidle sensed her reticence and placed her wrinkled hand on Melinda's cheek, smiling kindly to her. "Let's go to my chamber where we can talk privately." She pushed against the wooden arms of the chair, her arms shaking from the effort to stand.

Melinda handed her the cane sitting next to her then put out her arm for Eidle to hold with her free hand. They walked a few dozen paces into the cave and then Eidle turned to her right, where they entered a smaller cave, its floor covered in thick furs. Melinda helped her to sit on another chair and she sat on the floor at the woman's feet.

Eidle breathed hard and took some time until she could speak. "Thank you, Melinda. It is quieter back here and I was growing tired from the festivities."

Melinda pulled her knees to her chest and wrapped her arms around them. "Thank you for this celebration. It is nice to relax and let my Quadrant have some fun. I am almost sad we must leave in the morning." This was the second feast they had provided for her. Not planning to, they had stayed with Eidle's clan for seven days now and it was time for them to leave.

"I know, but that is the morning. We are here, now, and I want you to tell me why you are so melancholy."

Melinda felt the familiar wall she always put up when around other people, but it was like Eidle could see it, for the old woman gently placed her hand on Melinda's cheek and leaned down, her eyes moist. "It's alright. You can say anything you want to me and it will remain forever between us."

With those words, it was like a floodgate opened and tears burst from Melinda, running freely down her face as she cried, leaning her face against Eidle's hand. The woman caressed her hair and made soft sounds, comforting her. Melinda had not cried like this since she had been a little girl, and while a part of her was ashamed to show such emotion, another part of her didn't care.

Feeling exhausted, Melinda finally looked up at Eidle and wiped the tears from her face. "I've not done that in ages. I don't know why it happened now."

Eidle smiled kindly down at her. "One cannot hold emotions in all the time. Crying and laughing are two ways for the mind to remain healthy and strong. You need to do more of both, Leillireph."

Melinda nodded, wiping her sleeve across her runny nose as she sniffled.

"Please, tell me what is making you so feel so miserable."

Melinda thought of Crowdal, of the Zranh she considered family, of the responsibilities she carried as Leillireph. It was all too much and she felt the tears welling up again, but she pushed her emotions down. "I do not want to burden you with my problems."

"Nonsense. I am almost one hundred years old. I am quite able to share in your burdens."

Melinda nodded, wiping at her nose again. "I think I may love the Trith that accompanies the Aleph Null."

Eidle's eyes grew wide.

"But as you know, that relationship can't happen because I am Leillireph, the one who carries the pure blood of the First Mother. It is up to me to inject that blood back into the Zranh," she sobbed, "which means I must choose a Zranh as my mate so we can have children that will have the first blood."

Eidle looked away for a long moment, her eyes troubled. When she turned back, her eyes softened. "Melinda, your path will be made by you alone. Outside forces may cause you to divert at different points, and those diversions may turn out to be your true path, or they may lead you from it." She cupped Melinda's chin and leaned close. "You may have feelings for this Trith, and you may truly love him. But is that your true path, or is that a diversion? To know which is which is difficult, but you must choose wisely how to move forward with your life. When you come to those areas where your path splits, only you will know which way to turn."

Melinda felt her head spinning from the woman's words. What *was* her path? She desired Crowdal, and maybe she even loved him, but she had known him for barely a fortnight. Was that enough time to really know someone? Maybe he really was the diversion and her true path was with the Zranh. The choices she had made up to this point in her life, to become a healer, then to accept her place amongst the Zranh, were her path, weren't they? She had accepted that she was Zranh and that acceptance made her decision about Crowdal for her. She belonged with her people, and although she would help her friends without reservation, Crowdal would remain just one of those friends.

Melinda felt her tears dry up completely and she stood up, looking down at Eidle. "Thank you. I know what I must do now."

Eidle nodded sadly. "May your path be true, Leillireph."

Chapter 34

When he had seen it from the top of the hill earlier that morning, the forest had not looked very far away and Sid had estimated they would reach it by nightfall. But as they marched single-file through the tall green grass of the plain, they didn't seem to be getting much closer to the forest, even though this plain was small compared to the great plain they had spent more than a fortnight crossing on the way to the Srithian Wood.

The afternoon passed slowly but the walking was pleasant and easy. Agnes and Drax had gotten into a deep discussion about mathematics and theoretical equations, and Sid was impressed by their intelligence and ability. Where mathematics were easy for him and he could instantly extrapolate solutions from even the toughest problems, he had come to realize that most people could not do what he could. Agnes was brilliant, and while she had to more methodically work her way through complex equations, she rarely made mistakes. Listening to Drax query her, though, Sid realized that Drax put both of them to shame with not only his mathematical knowledge but his ability to look beyond standard mathematics and into nonfigurative theories that made even Sid's head spin.

As he walked, Sid let their discussion fade to the background and he looked up at the partly-cloudy sky, seeing blue for the first time in what felt like ages. The sun warmed him during the brief times it peeked through the quickly-moving clouds, and as much as he loved and missed the Wilder Hills, he would not miss the constant rainy days and nights.

Sid felt something crawling on him and he absently scratched at it as he thought of Melinda and wondered how she was. He missed her and hoped someday he would get to see her again. He felt the crawling sensation on his arm so he peeled back his sleeve to see a wood tick making its way up his forearm. He pinched it between two fingers but no matter how hard he squeezed, the tick wouldn't die, its legs moving back and forth frantically. He hated ticks more than any insect, often finding them with their heads buried in his skin, and their fat, blood-filled bodies sticking out. He remembered pulling one off himself when he was young and the head had broken off inside his skin. It had formed an open sore after he had scratched at it overnight and his father had to use a knife to cut the skin open and remove the blood-covered head. Ever since that day, Sid had been paranoid about getting ticks on him, always checking himself completely after playing in the woods and grassy areas around his house.

Sid threw the tick from him in disgust. So far this spring he had not had any on him, but now that the weather was turning warmer, he knew they would be out in full force. He felt something crawling on his neck and reached back to pull another tick from him. Sid threw it far away, and when he looked down to check himself, he was shocked to see his trousers were covered with them. He swore loudly and started to brush them off wildly.

Crowdal turned at the commotion. "Sid, what's wrong?"

"Ticks. They're everywhere."

Everyone looked down at themselves and were soon brushing at their arms and legs, though no one with the sense of desperate urgency about it as Sid.

Sid pulled up his shirt and saw at least ten ticks on his stomach. He yelped and started brushing them away, his voice rising in panic as he yelled out, "We must have walked into a nest of them! I've never seen this many!"

Agnes touched his arm. "Sid, calm down, they are just ticks, they won't hurt you."

Sid didn't really hear her though as he felt ticks crawling up his legs and near his privates and he quickly pulled down his trousers, frantically picking them off, not caring that he was naked. He looked up and saw that the forest was not far away, its ground covered with pine needles, so he began running with his trousers still around his legs. He bent down and pulled them up as he ran, yelling over his shoulder, "Quick, everyone to the forest!"

Sid ran for all he was worth and when he made it to the forest, he dropped his pack to the ground and quickly stripped off his clothes. As he dropped them to the ground, he saw hundreds of ticks crawling over them. He turned back and saw the rest of the group taking their time as they walked toward him; he couldn't understand how they could be so calm.

As he resumed picking the ticks from his skin, everyone else reached the forest and got undressed, even Agnes. The Haissen calmly watched everyone and Sid noticed that they didn't have even one tick on them.

Sid turned to Agnes. "Turn around, I'll pick them from your backside." She did as he asked and Sid saw dozens of ticks crawling on her back and in her hair. He got them all off, although some were already stuck into her skin. Luckily, they hadn't gotten fully set and came out relatively easy.

When he finished with Agnes, she turned him around and removed at least fifty ticks from his backside, then checked his head carefully.

They all stepped away from where they were standing, as the ground was crawling with the ticks they had removed.

Nik grinned. "At least they are not Yathen ticks. Those suckers grow as big as Crowdal's hand."

Sid felt his eyes roll back, dizzy from just the idea of ticks that big and he heard Agnes shush Nik. He pointed a shaking finger at the ground. "Can you create a fire equation and burn them?"

Agnes nodded and the ground soon burst into flame, the ticks sizzling and popping all over.

Sid turned to the pile of clothing and felt his skin crawling just looking at the tick-infested clothes. "Burn them, too."

Nik quickly stepped forward with his hands up. "Whoa, no you don't." He quickly picked his clothes up, backing away with them. "You're not burning my clothes." He began picking the ticks off, muttering something about wasting perfectly good clothes over a few stupid little ticks. Everyone else grabbed their clothing and began cleaning them of the insects.

Agnes turned Sid's chin so he would look at her. "Sid, listen to me; I'm not going to burn your clothes, alright? I'll pick them clean so you don't have to."

He felt his cheeks turn red in embarrassment and she came into full focus. "No, that's alright, I will do it. Sorry, I kind of lost it there."

She laughed lightly. "Hey, we all have our fears."

Sid nodded and picked up his clothes, holding them with two fingers as far away from him as he could. He flicked the ticks away from him until they were gone. Then he put his clothes back on, still feeling like ticks were crawling on him. After checking areas where he felt them crawling and finding no ticks, he finally ignored the phantom insects and picked up his pack, flicking a dozen ticks from it. Thankfully, it was tied tightly shut so they couldn't get inside.

Soon everyone was dressed and Crowdal looked carefully around. "It doesn't look like the ticks are in this pine forest, but keep an eye for them from now on. I don't mind them, but some of them carry disease and can make you sick."

Nik pointed into the forest and said melodramatically, "I don't know, Crowdal. I've heard there are ticks in there the size of a person."

Tulman pushed Nik, making him stumble forward. "Enough, Nik. The joke's over."

"Alright, alright. Can't a guy have a little fun?"

They all started forward into the forest and Sid found himself looking around for giant ticks, then chuckled at his own stupidity. He noticed pine trees everywhere and was sad that none of them were giant Miq trees.

The air grew damp and sunlight only occasionally filtered down through the branches, making the forest feel gloomy. There was no undergrowth and their footfalls were hushed on the soft, needle-covered ground.

The rest of the afternoon went by quickly and as dusk crept up on them, they set up camp in an area where a thin stream ran in a shallow gully, providing water for drinking and cooking.

Nik looked around as they set up their sleeping areas, then turned to Tulman while swinging his bow from his back. "I see deer tracks next to the water. I'm going to head upstream and see if I can get one."

Tulman nodded. "Good hunting."

Nik snuck up the edge of the stream, picking his steps carefully to be as quiet as possible and was soon out of view.

Sid watched him go, wishing he had his own bow so he could go with. Back in the Srithian Wood, Nik had offered him Richard's long bow after he had been killed, but the tension of the bow was too great for Sid to pull it back, so Nik had burned it with Richard's body.

Sid saw Crowdal talking with Writhgarth so he joined them.

Writhgarth raised his hand angrily. "I don't care if you can vouch for us, I've met a few Trith in my time as Captain of the Yisk Patrol and if they want to pick a fight with someone, nothing will stop them from doing so. I think if we walk into the Trith Nation with the Haissen, there will be no way to stop a deadly fight from erupting between them."

Crowdal acknowledged Sid, then turned back to Writhgarth. "I guess you are probably right. I don't exactly have much standing with the Trith anymore and there is probably no scenario where the Trith would pass up a contest of swords with the legendary Haissen; and knowing the Haissen like I do, it will be a blood bath."

Writhgarth glanced at Sid, "What do you think?"

"I don't know. Maybe we can ask the Haissen to stay hidden in the forest so the Trith don't kill them?"

Crowdal grimaced. "It is not the Haissen I'm worried about getting killed. I don't want my family and friends to be killed by them."

Sid's eyes widened. "I didn't think of it that way."

"I've faced a few Haissen and know I got lucky each time. If the Haissen fight as a Murder, I can't imagine how much death would result before it was over. The question really is, will the Haissen leave your side, Sid? They are pretty committed to your safety."

Agnes joined them, overhearing the conversation from where she had been sitting. "The Haissan that journeyed with me is named Saleth. She may be able to answer that question."

Crowdal cocked his head. "She? The Haissen are male and female?"

Agnes laughed lightly. "Of course, how do you think they procreate?"

Crowdal's cheeks reddened. "I guess I never thought of them in that way. Alright, call her over."

Agnes turned and motioned to a Haissan standing not far away and it glided over, stopping next to Agnes.

"Saleth, we have a question for you."

She hissed, "Yes?"

"As you know, we will soon approach the Trith Nation. They are a race that believes everything can be settled with a sword and we are concerned that if you and your fellow Haissen enter their nation with us, they will be unable to stop themselves from challenging you to battle. We don't want that to happen."

Since it wasn't a question, Saleth didn't respond, so Sid asked, "Would you and your Haissen consider staying hidden in the forest while we spend time with the Trith?"

Saleth remained silent for some time, then said, "No. We committed ourselves to your safety, and entering the Trith Nation is not safe. We will not leave your side."

"What if I told you I would be safe and I ordered you to remain behind?"

Saleth looked directly at him. "Then you would be ordering us to break our oath. It would remain broken forever."

Sid looked at Agnes, then Crowdal and Writhgarth. "What should we do?"

Crowdal turned to Saleth. "What if just one or two of you came with, while the others waited far enough away to avoid a major fight? Would that keep your oath intact?"

Saleth nodded immediately.

Crowdal smiled. "Good, then if you all agree, let's proceed with this plan."

Sid turned to Saleth. "Can you please choose two Haissen who will join us when we get closer to the Trith Nation? I would like to have this all set before we get there."

Saleth tilted her head and turned away without a word, gliding over to a Haissan who was standing on the edge of the camp and whispered to it. The other Haissan nodded slightly.

And that was it.

Sid turned back. "Well, let's hope that just two Haissen will not tempt the Trith into violence."

Crowdal and Writhgarth didn't look entirely convinced, but it was the best plan they had if they wanted to give Sid a chance to figure out what he needed from the Trith.

Crowdal's stomach rumbled loudly. "I think it's time to get some food in my belly."

Writhgarth snorted. "When is it ever *not* the time for that with you?"

They built a fire and as darkness descended, Nik entered the camp with a small doe hanging around his shoulders.

Tulman actually smiled and took the deer from him. "Nice hunting, Nik. Fresh meat will be a nice change after having nothing but that stinking dried meat for so long."

Nik smiled. "Let's get some steaks over the fire, then."

They both began to butcher the deer, skinning it quickly and then cutting thick steaks and putting them on sticks over the fire. Writhgarth cut out the heart and liver and threw them into a pot of water, adding in some herbs and wild tubers he had dug up during the journey, to make a soup.

Sid sat next to Crowdal, putting his hands closer to the fire to warm them. "How long do you think till we get to your home?"

Crowdal shrugged. "It is called a Circle, actually, and I would say no more than two days."

"A Circle?"

Crowdal nodded, "The Trith Nation encompasses all Trith. Individual Trith encampments or villages are called Circles."

"I thought a Circle was the ring for young Trith to battle in?"

"A Circle means many things to us."

Sid pushed a stick into the fire until it started to burn, then twirled it in a small circle. "It feels like we've been traveling forever, doesn't it?"

Crowdal nodded as he stared into the flames.

Sid continued, "It's hard to believe the things we've been through. I often think how strange it is that just this past winter I was living with my father in a tiny, three-room house in the woods outside of Orm-Mina with no idea of the vast lands around me. Now we are just a few days away from your Circle in the Trith Nation on what seems like the other side of the world." Sid glanced at Crowdal. "Are you nervous about seeing your family and friends again?"

Crowdal turned to him and his eyes looked troubled. "A little, I guess. I certainly didn't think I would be coming back home so soon, and to be honest, I am not sure if I will be accepted back."

Sid put his hand on Crowdal's knee. "Well, at least you are returning with friends who will support you no matter what."

Crowdal was quiet for a long time, then he glanced down at Sid, looking uneasy. "Thank you, Sid. That means a lot to me."

Chapter 35

The forest was quiet as Tris studied the area where Obsidian had taken him away from his Hunters and small party. There were tracks on the ground that looked to be many days old, so he glanced up at Obsidian as she stood silently off to the side. "How long did you have me in your lair?"

She shrugged.

"I asked, how long?"

"I don't see the sun or moon while in my burrow. Four days, maybe as many as six."

Tris seethed, knowing Sid was that much farther ahead of them now. And who knew where his Hunters had gone. His anger faded as he looked at Obsidian's beautiful face, then down at her stiff nipples pushing against the fabric of her cloak. He found himself gazing at her for a long time, wanting her here and now. Then he shook his head to clear the thoughts away and had to physically stop himself from stepping closer to her. He wasn't sure why they had such a strong sexual connection. Was it a mutual connection, or was it something she innately possessed and was doing to him?

Tris hated to waste more time, but he needed to get a handle on the sexual bondage he felt when around her. He studied Obsidian's physical makeup, using his power of Numbers to see how her supernatural structure compared to his own. He formed the Numbers into equations and they melted into her body, pulsing with a sexual power that made it difficult for him to concentrate. He pushed the sexual feelings away and concentrated on the math, creating new formulae to interact with the changes to his equations. Her metaphysical makeup wavered just on the edge of his understanding, but then it was as if chaos entered his mathematical structures, pulling the complex equations into base variables no matter how hard he focused on the math. Finally, Tris pulled back in frustration, although it was a frustration mixed with awe.

Obsidian was like no other being he had run across. She possessed some type of power of Numbers, though it seemed to be an innate part of her makeup. She repelled his mathematical inquiries while attracting them at the same time, the result a chaotic jumble of twisting power that made his equations burst apart before he could understand what she was made from. He was still no closer to understanding why he reacted to her in such a primal way and this made him uneasy. He could still use his Numbers to control her physically, which was something at least.

Tris looked up at her face and saw what might have been a smirk before her eyes narrowed slightly as she returned his gaze. He would have to keep a constant watch over her, to make sure he knew just who was controlling whom.

As if reacting to his thought, she turned and arched her breasts slightly, her nipples showing in profile as she gazed around the forest. His eyes were involuntarily drawn to her breasts and he had to force himself to look away and focus on determining where his party had gone. He concentrated on the tracks around him and picked out a set that only showed faintly, really more of a slight disturbance in the leaves, indicating it was likely made by one of the Hunters. He also saw heavier tracks, obviously left by his body guards and pack men, leading back the way they had come. It looked like his party had split up, with the Hunters pressing forward while the men returned to Reilen, probably assuming he had been killed.

Tris was glad the Hunters were so singular of purpose and still dedicated to him. He added a simple equation to the faint track that took in the dimensions of size and depth, then projected the equation outward, looking for exact matches in the makeup of the forest floor. The footprints of his Hunters almost glowed as they led to the west.

He started forward, hearing the light footsteps of Obsidian behind him, and followed the trail of his Hunters for the rest of the day and through the night, and by the next morning the tracks had gotten fresher and easier to follow.

With little warning, they came out of the Kuldragg Forest and looked out at green, rolling hills and deep valleys that stretched westward for as far as he could see. The glowing tracks led down and into the valley below where a river curved lazily in the center.

He descended the slope and stopped by the water's edge, seeing the remains of a camp with the ground torn up from what looked like a battle. He didn't see any bodies, though, so whoever had won had obviously cleaned up the camp.

It began to rain lightly, the raindrops cold and heavy. Tris pulled up his hood and suddenly felt exhaustion catching up to him after traveling day and night. He didn't want to sleep outside in the rain, yet he didn't want to waste what little reserves of energy he had left to create a portal equation, so he motioned Obsidian closer.

"Yes, Master."

"I do not wish to stay out in this rain. How far can you teleport us?" She looked as if she didn't understand his question, so Tris asked, "Can you return us to your cave from this distance and bring us back to this spot later?"

Her face filled with lust and she nodded immediately.

"Good, then let's go back for some rest. We will return here later in the day."

Obsidian opened her arms and he stepped into them. The air shimmered and went black, then they were back in the cave, her bed looking soft and inviting.

He walked over to the furs piled high, stripping off his clothes as he did so and fell onto them in exhaustion, pulling a thick and soft bear pelt over him.

Obsidian slid under the pelt and her naked body pressed against his, her breasts pushing against his side.

Tris was so tired he could barely think, but when her fingers closed around him, caressing him to hardness, he forgot all about his exhaustion.

When they finally finished, he fell asleep, completely drained in every way.

He awoke, feeling rested and hungry, and opened his eyes to see Obsidian staring at him from the same position she had been in when he had fallen asleep, her eyes inviting him to satisfy himself in carnal ways, but he ignored his sudden erection and slid from the bed.

"We must eat, then return to the valley as soon as possible."

Obsidian's eyes narrowed with anger, but she nodded and got out of the bed, her black and shiny body lithe and perfect. She put her arms over her head and stretched again, knowing the effect she had on him.

Tris tore his eyes away from her and forced himself to get dressed, pulling on his still damp coat. He heard a hiss from her but didn't turn to look, not trusting himself to deny her again. As he slid his arm through the sleeve, his shoulder quivered in pain, the wound from the Rissen blade still bothering him. He gritted his teeth and when he straightened out his arm the pain subsided. He felt Obsidian's arms slip around his waist and was about to object when the air shimmered and they appeared back in the valley.

It was still raining, so he grumpily pulled his hood up. He created the tracking equation but no tracks materialized. He cursed, realizing the heavy rain had erased the tracks so well that not even his equation could detect them. Looking at the valley stretching to the west, he thankfully realized there was no other way Sid could have gone. He got an idea and turned.

"Can you transport us to the other end of this valley?"

Obsidian shook her head. "No, I can only go where I have already been. I have never been here."

"But you can see the end of the valley in the distance."

"One mistake and we could reappear inside a hill."

Tris cursed again, but understood. It was almost identical to his use of the portal equation. If he tried to go somewhere he had never been, he couldn't anchor the equation to anything, creating the likelihood of emerging into solid rock or in a tree, or any other number of obstructions.

"Come on, let's get moving then."

He set off at a brisk pace, following the river down the valley. It really was quite beautiful, so different from where he grew up in Orm-Mina.

Obsidian followed him and he missed her calculating look as she reached out as if to swipe the back of his head with her talons, only to pull them back and fall into step behind him.

Chapter 36

A squirrel walked hesitantly down the side of a pine tree, moving in a stop-start motion, sniffing constantly and lifting its head as it studied Drax and the bread he held out.

Drax didn't even breathe as he waited, and then smiled when the squirrel closed the last little bit of distance and stopped by his hand. It put its little front paws onto his fingers and sniffed at the piece of bread in his palm. It crawled forward and quickly picked up the bread and started eating it, looking directly at him. It quickly finished and sniffed around his palm some more and not finding anything else, turned and scampered back up the tree to a branch. It turned and looked back down at Drax, waiting to see if he had any more food.

"Sorry, little buddy, that's all I can share."

The squirrel chattered at him and then ran further up the tree, disappearing around the other side of the trunk.

Drax turned from the tree to see Agnes watching him with a smile on her face.

"That was very sweet of you."

He shrugged and sat down by her. "Just a way to pass the time."

Her smile grew. "I think not. I have studied you and have come to believe that you are a kind and gentle man."

"Maybe at one time, but now I really don't know."

She edged closer to him and took his hand. "May I ask you a personal question?"

Drax heard her heart-rate quicken, but not from fear. She was genuinely interested in the question she was about to ask, so he shrugged again. "If you must."

"I get the feeling you were not always in possession of such…abilities. What happened?"

He slid his hand from hers, picked up a dried pine cone and began snapping the woody scales off, each cracking easily and giving off a spicy scent. He glanced sideways at her and said, "I trained for the last five years to be a Fahrin Druin."

Agnes's eyes grew large but she stayed quiet, so he continued.

"I didn't so much care about their philosophy," he gestured dismissively with his fingers, "that the Aleph Null was evil and what not. I really just wanted to study there and read everything I could get my hands on." His mouth turned up in a slight smile. "You see, I am smart. I don't say that to brag, I say it as fact. I not only understand everything I study, whether it is mathematics, chemistry, or languages; I remember every single thing I've ever done in my life – every word I've read, every problem I've solved, every breath I've taken, every single moment I've ever experienced. I never forget anything and I can recall everything with total clarity."

Agnes leaned forward and breathed out, "That's incredible."

Drax shook his head, "No, it's not. People always looked at me like I was a freak, at least until I learned to suppress my abilities and pretend I was like everyone else."

"I'm sorry, Drax."

He tilted his head down, tossed the remnant of the pine cone away and put his hands in his lap.

Agnes seemed lost in thought, and then she said quietly, "I don't understand how that relates to your physical abilities, though."

"It was my mind that drew me to the attention of someone very powerful. He changed my body and brain in ways that made me…more than human."

She pulled back, her eyes showing confusion and maybe a bit of fear. "A man changed you? What do you mean?"

"He made my body better in every way. I'm stronger and faster, I hear on different frequencies, I heal almost instantly – the list goes on. And the biggest change is…"

"What?"

Drax turned, looked directly into her eyes and whispered, "I am immune to any kind of mathematical attacks. Not even the Aleph Null can harm me."

"That is impossible. No one could have the amount of power required to do those things to you. The only one I can think of is the Aleph Null."

Drax waited for her to ask the question.

Agnes' face turned white. "Did Sid do this to you?"

He shook his head no.

"But, if not Sid, then who?"

Drax looked back at the ground and was quiet for a long time, uncertain if he should say more. He wasn't sure why he had even told her all of this in the first place. Maybe he was tired of being alone. Making a decision, he stood up and looked down at her. "I am sorry; I should not have said any of this. Please, just forget it." He turned and walked into the forest, needing to be alone.

He stepped over tree roots and around trees without paying attention to his surroundings until he was a great distance from the camp. He saw an large, old fallen tree and sat on it, dangling his legs and kicking his boots into the dirt. Why had he confided in Agnes? While he had mentioned some of his abilities to Sid after the incident with the Korpor, they had not discussed it further since then. He had finally started to feel like a part of the group, even if it was just the smallest of parts, and even the Vringe named Writhgarth had started talking to him. Now he would be back to being an outsider.

Drax brought forth the image of Walter and it appeared in his mind as clearly as if he were looking at him in the flesh. The image was of Walter the last time Drax had seen him in his small room, just as the Faouthger had summoned him. Walter had looked scared, although he had hidden it well. Maybe a part of him had known Drax would never return.

How he missed Walter, especially the way Walter treated him like a normal person despite knowing exactly how different he was, even back then. He wondered what Walter would think of him now.

Drax was so lost in thought that he didn't hear anyone approaching until it was too late and he was tackled to the ground. He looked up into an older woman's face, not moving because she held a knife to his neck. Behind her he counted at least eight more women holding long blades in each of their hands.

Drax could probably have thrown her off before she could slice his neck, but he could tell by the way they held themselves that they were warriors he shouldn't underestimate.

The woman leaned forward and whispered, "Are you the Aleph Null pretender?"

"Pretender? Interesting choice of words. No, I am not."

"Then who are you? And don't make a fuss or I will kill you."

"My name is Drax. I travel with the Aleph Null."

She pressed the knife into his skin a little more. "How many travel with the Aleph Null pretender?"

"Five travel with him, plus twelve Haissen."

Her eyes briefly widened, but that was the only indication she had been shocked by the mention of the Haissen. She leaned closer, her eyes hooded. "Has the Black Robe caught the Aleph Null pretender yet?"

Drax honestly had no idea what she was talking about and his look seemed to satisfy her.

She nodded. "Since you travel with the one we hunt, we cannot let you warn the Aleph Null pretender of our existence until we find the Black Robe again."

Drax heard her slow beating heart beat slightly faster, the only indication she was about to slice his throat, so he shoved her away so violently that the woman flew at least five paces before landing on her back, sliding another two paces before coming to a stop.

She instantly flipped to her feet, holding a knife in each hand as she and her fellow Hunters sprinted toward him.

Drax jumped to his feet and instead of running away, ran forward and leapt over them with a summersault, ultimately landing behind them.

They turned before he landed, and he was amazed by their reflexes. But they didn't advance. The older woman cocked her head and put her knives away as she slowly strode toward him with her hands up.

Drax heard the faintest of footsteps approaching from behind him and he spun around, slapping the knives from both hands of the woman who had appeared directly behind him as she sliced at him. He then spun to a second woman and chopped her wrists, causing her knives to plunge to the ground, both sticking deeply into the dirt from the power of his blows. A third woman was already slicing at him with the two knives she wielded. Drax saw the knives as if they were moving in slow motion, so he grabbed both of her hands and removed the knives with a twisting movement, and in a single fluid motion he spun around to hold them to her neck, crossed and ready to slice. The entire process from beginning to end had taken no more than three heartbeats and the older woman stopped mid-step, staring at him in awe.

Drax calmly said, "Now, if we could stop here for a few moments, maybe we can come to an agreement as to what should happen next. I don't want to kill any of you fine warriors, much less all of you."

The older woman nodded and made a small motion. Every one of the warriors put their knives smoothly away. She put her hands up. "We seem to have made a mistake. You may let Doris go, she will no longer try to kill you."

Drax removed the knives from Doris' neck. She turned and he smoothly spun the knives around, holding them out hilt first. She nodded to him, taking the knives and returning them to the sheaths on each side of her waist.

Drax stepped to the older warrior and asked, "Who are you?"

"We are the Hunters of Reil—" she paused, then said, "we are the Hunters."

Drax eyed her, interested as to why she stopped herself from saying, 'Reilen'. "I have read some texts on the Hunters of Reilen and everything I have read stated you are honorable and honest, yet you will not hesitate to kill when necessary. So tell me, if you are no longer going to try and kill me, but your intention is to kill the Aleph Null, what do we do now?"

"We are not tasked with killing the Aleph Null pretender."

"He is not a pretender; he truly is the Aleph Null. You stated that you were hunting him, why?"

"We are at the service of the Black Robe of the Oblate to help him locate the Aleph Null pre... the Aleph Null. What the Black Robe chooses to do with the Aleph Null has not been shared with us."

At the mention of the Black Robe, Drax narrowed his eyes. "I have never heard of the Hunters of Reilen serving anyone but the King of Reilen."

The warrior's face changed, showing the barest hint of fear. "This Black Robe is a powerful man who does what he wants without remorse."

Drax cocked his head to the side. "You seem to be someone who wouldn't take orders from one like that. Why do you serve him?"

"The Hunters served the King of Reilen for hundreds of years. But recently, the King of Reilen fell into thrall to this Black Robe and he ordered us to do what this Black Robe said."

"Why didn't you just kill this Black Robe if he is such a man?"

She blushed and her face turned even harder. "I tried. He is too powerful."

Drax considered all she had said, wondering just how they would resolve their differences. "May I ask your name?"

"I am Gee."

Drax tilted his head down slightly in greeting. "Gee, what if I told you that I am hunting this Black Robe and will kill him when I find him."

She responded without hesitation, "I would say that you will fail."

"That might not be as easy as he'd hope, for I have a secret weapon he does not know about."

"Which is?"

"His power of Numbers cannot harm me."

She studied him for a long moment. "If that is true, then we will help you in any way we can."

Drax held his arm out and Gee clasped it firmly. "Follow me back to camp and please don't make any sudden movements around the Haissen until I have a chance to explain things. They are committed to the Aleph Null."

Gee nodded and fell into step beside Drax, her eight Hunters following.

As they approached the camp, he raised his voice. "I enter the camp with some people who mean us no harm."

Three Haissen stepped closer to Sid, but that was the only indication they gave that they had heard Drax. He turned to Gee. "If you don't mind, can you ask your Hunters to stay outside of the camp while I bring you in?"

Gee gave the slightest motion and her eight Hunters stopped and stood at ease, although Drax suspected they were anything but.

Stepping into the camp, Drax saw everyone had turned to see who he had brought with him.

Sid and Crowdal strode forward to meet Drax. Sid's eyes widened a little when he saw Gee, obviously not expecting to see an older woman out here in the forest.

Drax and Gee stopped in front of them. "I would like to introduce you to Gee, leader of the Hunters of Reilen. Gee, this is Sid – the Aleph Null, and the Trith is Crowdal."

Sid didn't respond to Drax's introduction, but Crowdal whistled quietly, his eyebrows raised. He bowed at the waist as he towered over her. "I am honored to meet you, Gee. I have heard much of your famed Hunters. Your reputation is high amongst the Trith."

Gee's mouth turned up at one corner as she bowed back.

Drax said, "Gee and her eight Hunters have some information you may find useful. First, let me say they are no longer a threat to you, Sid."

Sid was looking at the eight Hunters standing just outside the camp, but at these words, he snapped his head toward Drax. "What do you mean, 'no longer' a threat?"

Gee turned to Sid. "The King of Reilen was put into some kind of thrall to the Black Robe and we were forced to assist him in hunting you, Aleph Null. But we now choose to join with you if you will help us to kill this Black Robe and restore the King's free will, and thereby our service to the throne."

Crowdal narrowed his eyes. "The Black Robe is hunting Sid again? How close is he?"

Gee looked up at him. "I do not know. We lost him in the Kuldragg forest when something attacked us. It killed four of my Hunters and took the Black Robe. We have seen no trace of him since then."

Crowdal looked at the eight other Hunters. "I am sorry for your loss. I honestly can't imagine anything being able to kill four of your Hunters. What was it?"

"One of my Hunters named Doris caught just a glimpse of it." She turned her head, "Doris, come here."

A young Hunter immediately entered the camp.

"Doris, please report what you saw kill our Hunters."

The Hunter's eyes tightened. "I was first upon the scene and saw a woman with shiny, black skin. Her hands had long talons that dripped with blood and gore. She took the Black Robe into her embrace, then the air shimmered and they were gone. The remains of our Hunters were scattered all over, torn to shreds and cast aside like so much garbage." Her fists were tightly clenched as she finished.

Gee nodded and Doris returned to her place outside of the camp.

Sid ground his teeth together, his mouth set hard. "Maybe we will be lucky and you forced the woman to take Tris away to finish killing him."

Gee shook her head slightly, "I do not think anything could kill the Black Robe that easily." She stared at Sid, a strange look on her face. "You are not what I expected, Aleph Null."

Sid grinned. "I seem to be told that a lot."

Crowdal put a large hand on Sid's shoulder. "Sid is one of the best men I've ever known. It only takes a few moments to know he is, as I'm sure you will find." He took his hand from Sid and extended it. "You are welcome in our camp, Hunters of Reilen."

Gee took his hand and shook it with stoic confidence, despite that her hand looked like a baby's compared to Crowdal's large one.

Sid gestured toward the eight Hunters. "Please, join us."

The eight women stayed where they were until Gee tilted her head and they immediately stepped forward and stood at attention behind her.

Drax sensed the tension and was beginning to think he had made a mistake in inviting the Hunters of Reilen to join with them.

Then Gee surprised him when she spoke directly to Sid, "You don't remember me, do you, Sidoro?"

Chapter 37

Sid looked closely at the Hunter named Gee. "You know me? I am sorry, I do not recognize you."

She nodded. "It doesn't surprise me. The last time you saw me you couldn't have been more than six years old, not long after your mother died."

"Six years old? I don't understand. Who are you?"

She reached out but quickly pulled her hand back, seeming uncomfortable. "Sidoro, I am your aunt. Your father is my younger brother."

Sid stepped back. "That's impossible. Father always said he didn't have any family."

Gee closed her eyes briefly, a look of pain crossing her face. When she reopened them, her face was hard again. "That is because I had no mathematical ability and the Oblate does not permit its members to have contact with any family who do not belong to the organization. I joined with the Reilen army and my skills soon landed me with the Hunters. Even though I hadn't been trained at an early age with the group like most of the Hunters, they saw my abilities and accepted me as one of their own. When I heard of your mother's death, I thought maybe I could reconnect with my brother in his time of sorrow. I was wrong."

Sid felt her pain and closed the distance between them until they were almost touching. He studied her face closely, wrinkling his brow as he tried to remember her. He was about to give up when a faint memory surfaced of a woman standing in their kitchen. He remembered sunlight hitting her face through the open door, of her looking larger than life as his father yelled at her to leave, one of the few times he had ever heard his father raise his voice. Was that memory of Gee? He couldn't be sure, but the way she stood in front of him now with a shaft of sunlight shining on her reminded him strongly of the woman in his memory. He leaned forward and put his arms around her, hugging her tightly. "Aunt Gee, I like the sound of that."

Gee remained stiff in his embrace at first, then warmly hugged him back, squeezing him so hard he could barely breathe.

"I have missed you so much, Sidoro. So many times I was traveling through the area around Orm-Mina and would stand in the woods watching you play for a few moments before moving on. I had never dreamed that you would turn out to be the Aleph Null, despite my brother's cruel intentions of bringing you into the Oblate. If your mother had lived, she would never have let Danicu do this to you."

Sid felt tears well up and fall down his cheeks. "Father had mother kidnapped and held prisoner for ten years."

Gee's eyes narrowed as she pulled away from him. "I am sorry,

Sidoro. He told me she had died in an accident. I always knew Danicu was treacherous, but I would never have thought he would harm his own wife. I will help you find and free her, I promise."

Sid shook his head. "She was brought by Tris, known to you as the Black Robe, to use as leverage against me when he tried to take my Black Numbers."

Gee looked around. "Where is she?"

Sid's voice cracked as a sob escaped. "She sacrificed her life to save me and give me a chance to fight Tris. I failed to kill him, but I won't fail next time."

Gee leaned forward and pulled Sid into her arms again. "I am so sorry, Sidoro. She was an amazing woman and someone I always admired." She leaned back so she could look into his eyes. "I promise you this. I will stand by your side no matter what happens and I will help you in any way I can to destroy this Black Robe."

Sid swallowed, then wiped the tears from his face. "Thank you, Gee."

"Please, call me Aunt Gee."

Sid couldn't help from grinning. "Do you think your Hunters would mind such informality?"

Gee turned to her eight Hunters and they all shook their heads, a few of them openly smiling. She turned back to him and said, "They don't seem to mind."

"Alright, Aunt Gee. Would you like some food and water? Nik over there makes these great hand-held bread meals that are amazing, although the bread is not very good because we got it from some people who attacked us a while back."

Gee nodded. "We would like that."

Nik stood, quickly took out the food and began slicing the bread, meats and cheese, assembling them together.

The Hunter named Doris knelt down by him, staring at the creation. "What is that?"

Nik grinned. "I haven't named it yet, but I'm going to get rich selling these in the bigger cities."

He offered one to her and she took it, turning it over in her hand. "How do you eat such a thing?"

Nik had finished making a second and put it to his mouth, taking a huge bite. Around the mouthful of food, he said, "Like this."

Doris looked up at Gee, who was smiling slightly. She tentatively put it to her mouth and took a small nibble, then took another much larger bite, nodding in appreciation.

Nik grinned as he swallowed. "See, I keep telling my friends that I'll get rich from these, but they don't seem to believe me." He bent down and started assembling more of them, handing them to the Hunters as he finished making each one.

The women sniffed the food, eyeing each other with embarrassment until Gee accepted one from Nik and immediately took a huge bite.

Nik smiled and pointed at her while looking at the other Hunters. "See, she likes it."

The Hunters all began eating, some raising their eyes in wonder, others showing distaste.

Writhgarth muttered something Sid couldn't hear as he grabbed a piece of meat and tore into it.

After the meal was done, Sid stood up. "I think we should get going. Crowdal said we are getting close to the Trith Nation and I'd like to get there as soon as possible."

Gee looked at him quizzically. "Why are you going to see the Trith?"

Sid felt himself flush and looked at Agnes and Crowdal, wondering if he should tell the Hunters why they were going there. Agnes shrugged, as did Crowdal, indicating it was up to him. He took a deep breath and said, "I lost my power of Numbers while fighting a giant monster that attacked us. I believe the Trith may have some information to help me get my Numbers back."

Gee stood and said, "Then, let's get going."

Sid was amazed by her calm yet tough demeanor. He got the feeling he was lucky she was now on his side. He wouldn't have wanted to face her if she wasn't.

They quickly packed and were soon continuing their trek through the Muldragg Forest.

Sid looked around in amazement. He had started his journey by himself this spring. Now it was early summer and he was on the other side of the land accompanied by all of these amazing people.

They walked in silence for the rest of the day and had an uneventful night. The next day was warm and sunny and they got an early start, setting out not long after sun up.

As the morning gave way to afternoon, Sid pushed a branch out of his way and looked up to see that the sun was high overhead. Realizing he was hungry, he opened his mouth to suggest a quick stop for food when the Haissen in front came to a quick halt and pulled out their swords.

Crowdal swore lightly.

Sid leaned so he could see around the Haissen and Crowdal and his mouth fell open as he slowly tilted his head back. In front of him stood twenty Trith, most of them as tall as Crowdal, towering over his group like adults standing over children. But where Crowdal was tall and thin, these Trith were tall, heavy and muscular, with arms as thick as Sid's whole body. Their faces were craggy and weather-worn, and all had long, bushy beards that hung to their chests. Around their shoulders were thick bear skins that were clasped at their chests with massive steel buckles. The swords they held were as long as an average human man was tall, the thick steel a smooth, bluish-grey that seemed to catch any light instead of reflect it.

The leader stepped forward without drawing his sword. He was older than the rest, his long hair a mixture of red and grey as it hung past his shoulders. His beard was the same as the others, but grew thickly and hung to his waist, braided tightly in a complex knot system. He crossed his arms, each covered with thick, black tattoos that seemed to move as if alive as his muscles flexed and rippled.

Crowdal stepped forward, looking the man directly in the eyes.

Sid looked from the older man to Crowdal and immediately saw a strong resemblance between them, specifically at the way their eyes flashed with the same kind of anger.

The leader spoke, his voice low and gravely, "You return; give me one reason I should not kill you."

Crowdal faced him, fearless and stoic. "You are welcome to try."

The Trith glared at him, his face rigid. "You tempt me," he clasped Crowdal around the back of neck with a hand, "but I think your mother may be upset if I returned with just your head."

Crowdal grinned. "Or maybe she would be happy if I returned with yours, father."

The Trith roared with a deep laughter. "It is good to see you, son."

Writhgarth quietly muttered, "Great, more Trith," under his breath.

Crowdal's father looked past Crowdal and he narrowed his eyes. "And who have you brought with you?"

"Father, these are my friends, and they are here with my promise of protection."

His father looked disdainfully at them. "You surround yourself with those that need your protection? You were to travel the land so you would accept your great heritage as a Trith."

Crowdal stared at him, unblinking. "I didn't mean that they are to be protected; I meant that I asked them not to harm you, the Trith."

The great Trith laughed at the joke, but then noticed Crowdal wasn't being flippant. He growled and drew his sword. "Is that so?" The nineteen other Trith stepped forward, raising their swords.

Crowdal sighed and put up his hand. "Father, may I introduce you to my friends?"

His father hesitated, eyes flashing with murderous intent.

Crowdal roared, "Father!"

His father turned his eyes away from the group and he raised his sword, rumbling, "No one raises their voice to me, not even my son."

Crowdal stood tall, his hands up. "Then listen to me before you attack."

"You have my attention."

Crowdal pointed behind him. "I want to introduce you to my *friends*," saying the last word in a louder voice. He pointed at Sid and

Agnes. "This is the Aleph Null and the Red Robe of the Oblate. They have a power of Numbers beyond anything ever seen in the land." He then pointed, "And this is Writhgarth, Captain of the Yisk City Patrol. This is Tulman, captain of a mercenary team, which includes Nik, the best archer I've ever seen. Behind him is Drax, he is…well let's just say I would not go against him in a fight if I had anything to say about it."

His father growled, "So far, I'm not impressed."

Crowdal continued, "In the rear are the Hunters of Reilen."

At this, his father raised his eyes just the smallest amount, for even the Trith had heard of them.

Crowdal turned back to his father. "And those who wear the robes," he paused, then whispered, "They are all Haissen."

At this, his father actually took a step back, his mouth hanging open, and a murmur of disbelief rose from the Trith behind him. He stared hard at the Haissen and with obvious effort he tore his gaze away from them to look hard at Crowdal. "That is impossible. The Trith have sought the Haissen for thousands of years to no avail. I do not believe you."

Sid held his breath as Saleth stepped forward and stopped next to Crowdal and his father. She slowly pushed her hood back, revealing her white alien face and hissed, "We are real, and we serve the Aleph Null as well as Crowdal. They are the only two beings in the land who we bow down to. For more than two thousand years, the Haissen have never been defeated in combat, including scores of Trith who found us and died by our swords." She motioned toward Crowdal, "That is until we met this Trith, who recently defeated three Haissen in a battle to the death. We will follow him anywhere he leads us."

Crowdal's father turned his head to look at Crowdal, his eyes wide with awe.

The area became silent as everyone waited for the great Trith leader to respond. The giant looked again at the Haissen, then to the Hunters of Reilen, and let his gaze rest on Sid for a brief moment. Then he threw his head back and laughed deeply, slapping Crowdal's shoulder with a huge hand. "Well, son, let's not keep your mother waiting." He turned to his Trith, "Put those swords away. Keol, go on ahead and warn the Circle that we approach with strangers. If anyone raises a sword to any member of this group, they will answer directly to me."

Keol nodded and disappeared into the trees.

Crowdal turned and formally said, "Everyone, I would like you to meet my father, Uuthdal, King of the Trith Nation."

Sid stared at Crowdal in wonder.

His best friend was a prince

Chapter 38

As Melinda pushed the pine branch away from her face, she caught a glimpse of movement in the distance. She immediately stopped, as did the two Quadrants who surrounded her. She spied the short, brown fur of a doe as it stepped around a tree, her nose high as she nibbled the leaves from a bush. Melinda motioned with her eyes and Pronni shifted into the Raith world. Melinda watched the deer disappear from view and then Pronni reappeared next to her carrying the dead deer, already gutted.

Smiling, Melinda said, "Let's stop here for a rest."

Pronni handed the deer to Nren who took the carcass and started cutting into it immediately. He was joined by a young member of the second Quadrant, who had been assigned by Eidle to protect her, and they made quick work of the process, piling up the raw meat.

Melinda saw a rock not far away and wearily made her way over and sat down on the warm stone. It had been a long journey so far and she hadn't slept much the previous night of the celebration, speaking with Eidle until late into the evening.

Eithes sat on the ground next to the rock, ever by her side.

Melinda smiled. "Eithes, I prefer to be alone for a few moments. Please go help prepare the meat."

The young woman nodded and left her without a word, rejoining the others.

Melinda watched them work for a while, enjoying how easily they all seemed to get along despite being of different clans. She closed her eyes, feeling the slight breeze ruffling her hair. She crossed her legs and sat straight, breathing deeply and slowly. A Ripper bird gurgled in the tree behind her and as she concentrated, she could hear the soft burbling from three young Rippers in a nest high up in the tree. To her left, Melinda heard two squirrels chasing each other across the ground and then up and around a tree, chattering as they went.

It was so peaceful that she wished they could stay and relax here for the rest of the day. Maybe a part of her didn't want to see Crowdal and Sid again, that maybe it would just be easier not to. Her heart beat quicker at the thought of Crowdal, though. He was a Trith, a giant that stood more than twice her own height, but she often found herself fantasizing of what it would be like to be intimate with him. She flushed at the thought of what the size of him must be in that area she had not yet seen. Heat filled her, but unlike the heat of the Raith world, it was concentrated between her legs. She forced herself to think of other things and eventually she felt her heart rate return to normal.

She was being stupid. Sex was sex and that would not interfere with what she wanted in life. She was Zranh and in the end, she wanted to be only with the Zranh.

She would see if Sid needed her help, and if not, she would part ways and return to her people, the people she loved.

The Trith were not far away now, no more than a day or two of travel, and this would all be over soon no matter what happened.

Falweth brought over a sizzling cut of deer meat on a pine branch, handing it to her with a grin.

"First steak goes to you."

"Thank you. It smells delicious."

He was about to leave when she put her hand on his arm. "Falweth, may I speak with you?"

"Of course."

Melinda nodded for him to sit next to her on the rock. "Do you have anyone special in your life?"

He cocked his head. "You mean, am I betrothed?"

She nodded.

"No, although there is someone I have my eye on."

"May I ask who?"

Falweth grinned and tilted his head toward the fire. "Your Gorepeth is quite special."

Melinda smiled. "When we finish with this mission, I would be happy to see you and Pronni get married."

Falweth put up his hands. "Hold on, I said I liked her. I am not looking for marriage yet."

"I know, but I would like to bring our two clans together as one, and while I can do that officially as Leillireph, a marriage between members of our clans would be a sturdy bridge to link us together."

Falweth studied her, suddenly serious. He surprised her when he nodded assent. "I will think about asking her, but I can't say if she will agree even if I do." He glanced over at Pronni as she turned a stick with a hunk of meat on it. "She is strong and independent," he grinned, "maybe she will ask me, instead."

Melinda smiled. "Maybe she will. Thank you for discussing this with me."

He shrugged. "Is there anything else?"

"No, that's all. Go enjoy some food. We'll leave as soon as we finish eating."

Falweth returned to the fire and Melinda closed her eyes again. She had hated to ask that of Falweth, but as Leillireph it was her responsibility to do what was best for the Zranh.

Melinda finished the deer meat and felt herself start to doze when the sound of tearing flesh and a long gurgling scream brought her fully awake in an instant. She jumped to her feet and turned to see two Zranh falling to the ground, their bodies torn and bloody.

The area was empty of Zranh, so Melinda instantly shifted to the first frequency of the Raith world. She immediately saw a woman with skin so black that she looked like a statue, her arms spread wide, her sharp, claw-like talons extended and dripping with blood.

Around the woman stood the rest of her Zranh, knives out and circling her for the kill.

Then the woman disappeared.

One of the Zranh, a young man with long brown hair, who always wore a kind smile, screamed as his stomach was ripped open, his intestines spilling out to the ground with a wet splash. He looked down in confusion before falling to his side.

Melinda gasped and instantly shifted to the third frequency, stopping time completely. As she completed the transition, she saw the woman with the shiny black skin frozen, hunched over the body of the young Zranh, his bloody liver in her hand.

Melinda started forward, a murderous rage boiling inside her, then she gasped and halted, her mouth hanging open in disbelief as the woman slowly turned her head and looked directly at her, snarling in surprise, showing a mouth full of sharp teeth.

Chapter 39

Sid followed Crowdal and the six Haissen that led them toward
the Trith Circle. He studied Crowdal's back and saw how straight and
stiffly he walked, as if he were being led to his own hanging. Sid had tried
to talk to him as his father led them back to the camp, but Crowdal's face
was set hard, his eyes seeming to not see anyone. Crowdal was no longer
the fun-loving, easy-talking friend Sid had always known. It was as if he
had morphed into someone else in the blink of an eye.

Agnes squeezed Sid's hand and leaned in to whisper, "Give him
some time. This is probably the toughest thing he has ever done."

Sid glanced at her. "What do you mean? He's just going back to see
his family and friends."

"Tell me, if you were walking toward your home right now to
confront your father after all you found out he has done, including
having your mother kidnapped *and* giving his approval to have the
Korpor *Ring* you, would you be yourself right now?"

Sid swallowed and looked down, feeling ashamed for not seeing
what his friend was going through. "You are right. It's just so hard seeing
Crowdal like this and not being able to help him."

Agnes squeezed his hand again. "I know. All we can do is be there if
he does need us and until that time, let's remember that we need to try
and figure out what the Black Manuscript meant by *Trith* and *Circle*."

Sid had been so concerned for his friend that he had briefly
forgotten exactly why they were here. "You are right, thank you for
reminding me. I am putting Crowdal through this because I asked him to
take me here. The least I can do is make the most of it."

Up ahead, the trees began to thin out and he could hear the noises
of a large permanent camp. The sounds of men yelling orders, the ring of
steel on steel, and the laughter of children all mixed together as they came
out of the tree line and into the Trith Circle, which was at least as large as
the town of Oiro, if not bigger, with a wide main street that ran to the
center of the Circle.

Sid realized that the Trith called their towns Circles because the
buildings were built so closely together they formed a wall that ran in a
circle around the camp, with guards posted along the rooftops, spaced
every few hundred paces. As they progressed toward the center, he
noticed the homes and buildings of the Trith were built in concentric
rings, and the closer they got to the center of the Circle, the more
colossal the buildings became, although even the most basic of the outer-
ring homes were at least three-times the height of any house he had seen,
even in the great city of Yisk. They were built from rough timbers, but
were well-constructed and strong, obviously to withstand the extreme
weather and elements this far north. The doors were tall and wide, at least

four-times his own height.

These were the houses of the Trith.

Sid smiled, remembering waking up in the room in Yisk and seeing the bed next to him completely crushed and collapsed to the floor, Crowdal stretched out and snoring on top of it, his body almost as long as the room. Being a giant was difficult in the cities made for regular-sized folk. Sid felt angry all over again as he thought of the hatred he had seen in people's faces as they glared at Crowdal in Yisk just because he was a Trith. He could definitely see why they lived in such a remote place.

Sid turned to Writhgarth and whispered, "Why do they build their towns in a circle like this?"

Writhgarth spoke softly out of the corner of his mouth, "It is a war strategy. If a large army attacks, there is only one road into the center of town. All of the side streets move in circles, randomly intersecting with avenues that allow access to the next ring. The Trith would bottleneck any army that attacked. And if the attacking army tried to burn down the town, they would fail because the fires would burn in a circle. But only a few homes at a time would burn because of the wide spaces between rings and water trenches between every fifth house."

Sid whistled as he nodded to Writhgarth and looked up at a building at least five times taller than any he had ever seen.

Behind Sid, Nik was talking to Doris. "I wonder if I could sell my handbreads to these Trith while we are here."

Sid turned in time to see Doris punch Nik's shoulder as she said, "Handbreads? You are calling them handbreads? Why would you choose that stupid name?"

Nik rubbed his shoulder. "First of all, ouch. Second of all, my last name happens to be Handbread. What's wrong with naming them after myself?"

She glared at him, thinking he was joking, but then she saw he was being serious. "Your last name is really Handbread?"

"No. It's Smyth. But I happen to like the name 'handbreads' for my concoctions."

Doris grinned, "Well, at least it's a name. I'm surprised you were even able to come up with that."

Sid turned to face forward, grinning. He had noticed that Nik and Doris had become fast friends, spending all of their down time together. They seemed to have been made for each other.

They entered a large center square, which looked strange inside of the Circle. Crowdal turned to face them and motioned at a Trith. "Follow Kulweg, he will take you to a building where you can rest and eat. I have to go with my father for some family business."

Sid stepped up to Crowdal. "Do you want me to go with you?"

Crowdal's eyes softened as he put a hand down to his shoulder. "Thank you, Sid, but this is something I must do alone." He addressed the whole group, "Do not leave the building until I return." Without another word, he turned and followed his father around a corner.

The Trith named Kulweg motioned contemptuously, "Follow me." He led them down a street to their left and after a few dozen steps he turned to open the door of a non-descript building, signaling them to enter.

Six Haissen led the way and Sid noticed Kulweg giving them a covetous look, his eyes shining with violent desire.

Sid entered the building, followed by the rest of his friends and the remaining Haissen. He looked around in awe. The room was at least a hundred paces across with a thick, wood-beamed ceiling that came to a peak far above. The floor was made from rough wood and along the edges of the room, dozens of animal pelts were laid out on the floor for sleeping, ranging from bear to deer and animals he couldn't begin to recognize.

Kulweg indicated a door in the far wall. "Through there are facilities for shitting and pissing. We'll bring food later." He glared down at the Haissen, then turned his head slowly away from them to look at the rest of the group and said in a voice laced with the threat of violence, "Do not even think of trying to leave this building." He grinned as he glanced at the Haissen. "If you do, the penalty is death." He hesitated, looking like he was hoping a Haissan would step through the door in front of him. When no one moved, he snorted in annoyance and exited the building without a backward glance.

Sid followed Agnes to a spot along the wall and sat down next to her on a thick bear pelt.

Agnes stretched her back, then turned her neck in a circle, the cracking muted in such a large room. She sighed and said, "We may have a long wait. We should get some rest while we can."

Sid nodded and turned to look at the closed door, wondering how Crowdal was doing.

Chapter 40

Glaub looked up at Death Falls in awe, even though he had seen them many times before. At least a thousand feet above him, the outlet from the Bertol Sea reached the continental plate, separating the northern from southern hemispheres and falling in a series of water falls, each a hundred or more feet high. The final fall splashed into a basin that then flowed south into the Paigonian Sea.

A trail led up the side of the continental fault only a hundred paces from the falls, wet from the constant spray and slippery from algae and moss. It was a shortcut to the top that only the most desperate or foolhardy of people used. Most people traveled the five leagues to the west where the continental plates met in a gentler fashion, the road wider and only moderately steep. But Glaub didn't want to waste two full days of travel on the detour.

Charly gazed up at the trail that hugged the side of the cliff and whistled, although Glaub could barely hear it over the roar of the falls. He yelled out, "How are we supposed to make it up that trail?"

Glaub cupped his ear and yelled, "What?"

"I said, how are we going to get up that thing?"

Glaub motioned his men to come as close as possible so he could be heard by them all. "Alright, here's what we need to do. Go single file and hug the wall as closely as you can. Watch each step and test the slipperiness of the rock before you place your full weight on it."

Captain Shaw leaned forward and yelled, "What about the horses and mules? I don't know if they will make it?"

Glaub reached into his pack and pulled out a sack and dropped it to the ground. "I've led horses up many times before. Take five pieces of leather each from that sack. Tie one over your horse's eyes so they don't get frightened, then tie the others securely around the hooves to give your horse better traction on the stone. We will lead them up the path instead of riding them, and if we are careful, we should all make it up without incident."

Shaw nodded and passed the orders to his men. They all did as told and the horses settled down a little, although a few of them moved their heads up and down while stamping their front feet. But the soldiers were all experienced horsemen and were able to eventually calm the huge animals.

Glaub raised his hand, then lowered it, leading the way with his horse behind him. He walked it along the side of the tumbling white water of the basin where a path about two paces wide led toward the cliff. He glanced into the basin and saw thousands of huge golden fish jumping from the surface of the turbulent water.

They soon made it to the first cliff, where a waterfall crashed to their right. The trail led away from it, leading up at a twenty-degree angle. Glaub followed the trail with his eyes and saw it make a sharp switchback after about a hundred feet back toward the waterfall. That was the difficult spot, he remembered, as it turned at a sharp angle that slanted away from the cliff until it flattened out again at an easy ten-degree angle, leading to the top of the first waterfall. Taking a deep breath, he stroked his horse's muzzle a few times, then started up the trail, staying as close to the cliff wall as he could. His horse balked when it started up the incline and Glaub had to pull hard to get it moving.

The rock was damp and slippery, but he made it to the switchback and craned his head up and to the right, not remembering the turn being quite so steep. One slip and he and his horse would tumble right off the trail and fall to the ground far below. He looked back and saw everyone lined up behind him, so he pulled his horse forward. Even covered with leather, the horse's hooves struck the stone hard as it slipped and scrambled up and around the turn.

Glaub kept a tight hold on the reins, pulling for everything he was worth to keep the horse moving. At the very top of the turn, his left foot slipped out from under him and he went down hard to his right knee, cracking it against the stone. Pain flared up, but he instantly pushed himself back to both feet and pulled until the horse climbed up the final part of the turn and was on the standard incline again. They were both gasping for air as he patted its nose.

He continued up the incline and soon arrived at a wide area at the top of the first waterfall where another large basin collected the water from the next waterfall that crashed down into it. The next part of the trail led around the basin and up to their left. He waited here until Charly arrived, followed by each of the soldiers, last of which was Captain Shaw.

He shouted, "Great job, everyone. Only four more to go, but luckily the rest are not nearly as difficult."

They made it to the top of each set of waterfalls without any problems or losses, and as Glaub stepped to the top of the final waterfall, he let go of his tension, slumping his shoulders in exhaustion as he pulled his horse to the flat area along the waterway that led to the Bertol Sea about a half-league away.

Charly soon arrived and sank to the ground, kissing it over and over. He looked up at Glaub with a grin. "You know, it would have been easier if you would have just transported us up here."

Glaub shrugged. "It builds character doing things the hard way."

"Character? I am perfectly fine not having any of that."

Glaub smiled as he took out his water skin and took a long drink, followed by another, smacking his lips when he was done.

Another of the soldiers crested the trail and pulled his horse to safety, and as the next soldier appeared, he grinned at his friend, but the grin fell away as his horse stumbled and started scrambling, but in its panic it moved in the wrong direction. The soldier turned and pulled as hard as he could to keep the horse from the edge, but he was no match for the weight and power of the beast as it teetered on the brink, then toppled over the edge. The soldier did not have time to let go of the reins and was pulled over the edge with it.

Glaub ran over, peered carefully over the side and smiled. The soldier and horse had fallen into the deep water and miraculously, they had both survived and were swimming toward the edge of the basin. Then Glaub's smile faded as they were caught in a strong current that pulled them in a circle back out to the center of the basin, from which they got caught in the main current that rushed over the edge of the waterfall. The soldier dropped the reins and swam against the water flow for all he was worth, but it didn't matter as he was sucked over the edge of the waterfall with his horse.

The rest of the soldiers had arrived at the top and Captain Shaw rushed to his side. "What happened?"

Glaub looked over at him. "One of the soldiers, I think his name was Eric, went over the edge trying to save his frightened horse. They survived the fall into the basin but got sucked over the next waterfall."

Captain Shaw grimaced, then nodded. "I guess we are lucky to have only lost one."

Glaub made a decision and shook his head. "I am going back down to see if I can help him."

"That is too dangerous."

"No, it is my responsibility."

Captain Shaw pulled away. "Then let me go instead."

"No, you stay here and help set up a quick camp to let everyone rest; this is my responsibility."

He turned to go when Shaw grabbed his arm, his eyes shining with respect. "Be safe, sir."

Glaub nodded and started back down the steep path. He considered teleporting to the bottom, but he didn't want to miss Eric if he was struggling in one of the other basins. While it was much easier without leading a horse, it was just as dangerous trying to keep his feet from slipping, especially at the switchback. But he managed, and soon made it to the next basin. He scanned the water but saw no sign of Eric or the horse, so he started down the next trail. At the switchback, his right foot slipped out and he landed on his butt, sliding out of control toward the edge, and falling over the hundred-foot drop.

The ground rushed up to him and he calmly created the portal equation and fell into it. He couldn't stop the momentum of his fall and knew he would exit the portal at the same speed, so he did the calculations to have the portal open into the water of the bottom basin, then opened it. He hit the water hard and looked up through the crystal clear, swirling water as he kicked to the surface, his clothes making it difficult to move. He was about to create another portal and swim through it when his head broke the surface and he took a deep breath.

Glaub wiped water from his eyes and saw he was in the middle of the basin, so he turned toward the shore and swam strongly against the current. As he went, he felt his hands brushing against the bodies of countless fish, and one actually jumped and landed on his head. He closed his eyes and swam until his hand struck the rock of the basin edge. He was exhausted and struggled to pull himself up when a hand clasped around his arm and he looked into the smiling eyes of Eric, who hauled him up the rock to the ground.

Glaub lay on his back, gasping as he tried to get as much air into his lungs as he could.

"What happened, sir? I thought you were safe at the top?"

Glaub opened an eye and nodded as he sat up. "I saw you make it to the basin and then go over the waterfall. I had to come look for you."

Eric just stared at him for a few moments, then whispered, "You came back for me?"

"Of course I did."

The soldier bowed his head solemnly. "Thank you, sir. But you should not have risked your life for me. I am just a soldier."

Glaub rested his hand on Eric's arm. "I do not believe anyone is 'just' a soldier. No man's life is worth more than another's." He looked around and saw the horse shivering not far away and stood up. "Shall we try this climb again?"

Eric grinned. "Second time is the charm, right?"

They coaxed the horse up the trails of each waterfall without incident and at the very top, they made sure to keep control of the horse until it was on the flat ground with the others.

Everyone cheered when they arrived, clapping Eric on the back and shaking Glaub's hand.

Captain Shaw had a look of almost worship on his face as he nodded to Glaub.

Glaub felt his legs quivering from fatigue and he almost collapsed to the ground, accepting some food and wine from Charly. He knew the Captain and the men would follow him anywhere without question now and he felt the weight of that responsibility press down hard on him. He would do everything he could to keep them safe and ensure he earned such devotion.

Glaub looked up and saw the sun high overhead. It had taken most of the morning just to get to the top, but he decided to start off right away and travel toward the shores of the Bertol Sea to put as much distance as they could from Death Falls. He quickly changed into dry clothes, feeling warm again after the freezing waters of the falls. No one argued at his plan to leave right away, not even the horses, and they started off at a slow trot. By the time the sun approached the western horizon, they had been traveling up the coast of the Bertol Sea for some time. The air was warm and the setting sun was hot on their backs when he called a halt for the night.

They set up a quick camp on the beach. The sea was perfectly calm, barely a ripple to be seen as the setting sun made the water glow a deep orange. Three of the soldiers caught some fish and they ate well as darkness descended on the camp.

It was a beautiful night as the stars appeared overhead. Glaub lay back on his blanket with his arms folded behind his head and stared at the twinkling lights that filled the entire sky, when he felt the communication open between him and the Black Robe.

"*Yes, Black Robe? How may I be of service?*"

The Black Robe's voice dripped with barely-controlled contempt and boredom as he said, "*I doubt you can be of service, fatty. But on the outside chance you can help, I decided to let you give me a report.*"

Glaub thought he caught the sound of a groan of pleasure and wondered just what the Black Robe was doing. "*Yes, Black Robe. We ascended Death Falls and are now camped on the coast of the Bertol Sea. We have had no sign of the Aleph Null.*"

The Black Robe sighed. "*I told you he was already in the Muldragg Forest, likely heading for the Trith Nation. So quit wasting time camping along the sea and head inland to the southern area of the Muldragg Forest, then turn due north. Even someone like you should be able to do that, no?*"

Suppressing his anger, Glaub acted like he was frightened. "*Yes, Black Robe. We will do that tomorrow.*"

"*No! You will start right now. I don't care if it is night.*"

"*Of course. Yes. We will leave immediately, Bla—*" Tris disassembled the communication equation before Glaub could finish, so he closed it on his end, as well, and opened his eyes. He wondered if it was even worth pretending to be a Blue Robe anymore.

As he reviewed the information he had secretly acquired during their conversation, he supposed even that little bit of extra information was still worth it. He saw that the Black Robe was in Muldragg Forest, about a day north of the Trith Nation, and he was apparently having intimate relations with a woman, or man; he had no idea of the Black Robe's sexual orientation, and he honestly didn't care. What it did mean, was the Black Robe was distracted but still closing in on the Aleph Null, if the Aleph Null was really at the Trith Nation, that was.

He could no longer waste time traveling at such a slow pace if he wanted to get to the Aleph Null before the Black Robe. Even if he kept his identity from the Black Robe, it didn't mean he had to keep his soldiers with him. It was time he went out on his own.

He stood up and called his men to join him. They all stepped over, some rubbing sleep from their eyes, asking what was going on.

Glaub raised his arm for silence. "Gentlemen, I am sorry, but things have changed and I must leave you now and continue on my own. You can backtrack and take the long way around Death Falls and return to Urgaer."

Captain Shaw stepped forward. "I will not leave your side, sir."

Charly cocked his head sideways as he looked at Glaub. "Me, neither."

Glaub put up a hand, "Now wait a moment, this is not…" but Eric stepped closer and said, "I am also not going anywhere, sir." He turned to the rest of the soldiers, "How about it, men?"

The rest of the soldiers all said they were staying, some whooping and cheering Glaub's name.

Eric turned back to Glaub. "You are stuck with us, sir."

Glaub turned in a circle and saw smiles and nods from the soldiers. He felt unworthy of their dedication and loyalty, which he would test with what he next had to say.

"Thank you, men. I can't tell you how much this means to me. But I must be honest with you and give you a choice based on the truth. You see, I am not just the counselor to King Jass."

Eric turned in a circle with his arms out. "I think we all know that already, sir. No counselor to the King would risk his life for common soldiers."

The men nodded, all talking at once.

Glaub held up his hand for silence. He looked at each man. "What I have to tell you I have not told more than a handful of people in my life. I must request a promise from each of you that you will not repeat any of this to anyone outside of this group; not to your wives, lovers, parents, or other soldiers." He pointed to Eric on his right and he promised, followed by each man until the last, which was Captain Shaw who said, "You know I do."

Glaub smiled to the Captain, then lifted his chin. "Thank you, everyone." He paused for several moments before continuing in a deep voice, "Gentlemen, I am immortal and have been alive since before the time man conquered this land."

The men looked at him like he was crazy, glancing at each other and rolling their eyes, some of them openly grinning and shaking their heads at his tale.

Glaub held his hand up, palm out. "Let me finish before you decide I am crazy. You see, I was already old when I met a man named Juor two thousand years ago. He was just a common man with an uncommon ability to lead others, and I was with him when he raised an army of men to conquer the wild lands of the west and proclaim himself King of a new kingdom he named Uragon."

Some of the soldiers began shifting their feet, so he quickly continued, "You may be wondering just how crazy I am. Well, to alleviate your concerns, I will tell you my biggest secret: I am a master of

Numbers."

Some of the men who had been smiling at his story, not believing any of it, gasped loudly when he said that. For even common soldiers had been children once and remembered being told the tale of the Korpor to scare them, of how it searched for children with a power sometimes referred to as Numbers, although it was just a word in the story that most did not understand.

Glaub now had their attention and said, "Let me demonstrate." He created a simple light equation and added a factor of a hundred to it, activating it with a gesture of his hand. The entire beach lit up almost as brightly as if it were daylight.

The men all cried out, shielding their eyes as they looked around in wonder.

He added a variable for the color yellow and activated it around him, making his entire body glow.

It was enough for the simple soldiers, and as one, they turned to him and dropped to their knees, except for Charly and Captain Shaw.

"Please, stand and promise me you will never fall to your knees to me again – I am not your master." He deactivated the light equation, returning the beach to the semi-darkness of the soft flames of the fire pit.

The soldiers tentatively stood, though many had fear in their eyes.

"Please, do not fear me. I promised myself long ago to never harm an innocent person. You have nothing to fear from me."

The men relaxed a little more, some even managing to smile slightly.

Glaub nodded. "Now, you have a right to know my true plans. I am going to travel to the heart of the Trith Nation in search of a young man who has a power of Numbers similar to mine. I must find him and judge him to see if his character warrants his having such powers. For you see, power like this can corrupt, and it takes a strong person to resist using it for wicked reasons."

Eric raised his hand. "Excuse me, sir. How will you know if this person is good or evil?"

"By his actions, Eric, as well as by the friends he keeps. Which brings me to the reason I didn't want you men to travel with me. There is another who commands an impressive control of Numbers, who has a vile and dark mind to go with it. I must destroy him, but even I may not be able to keep you all safe during that confrontation. I consider you all my friends and want no harm to befall you."

Captain Shaw pointed at the men. "Sir, we are used to risking our lives. A little danger will not deter us, and to be called friends instead of soldiers is more reason than any of us has ever had before to risk our lives."

The men all nodded, their faces showing pride.

Glaub felt a sense of relief knowing he wouldn't be traveling alone. It was not that he was afraid; he was just tired of his solitary life, and the past fortnight of traveling with these men had shown him how much he missed being around people who accepted him for who he was. He put his hands together, palm to palm and lowered his head to touch them with his chin, "Thank you, every one of you. Now, get some sleep. We will leave in the morning."

The men cheered as one and then turned away to return to their bedrolls.

Charly leaned in and whispered, "Nice speech."

Glaub looked at him. "It wasn't meant to be a speech. I truly wanted these men to decide their futures as men, not as soldiers. Now get some sleep. We start early in the morning."

Charly studied him for a moment, then nodded and laid down on his blanket not far away.

Glaub turned to the Captain. "You get some sleep, too, Captain. Tomorrow will a busy day."

Shaw nodded and turned away, leaving Glaub alone.

He sat down and put his back against a large boulder and tilted his head back to stare up at the stars again, wondering if he was doing the right thing allowing his men to accompany him.

Chapter 41

Melinda froze mid-step when the black-skinned woman turned to look at her, still holding the liver of the Zranh she had just murdered. What she saw was impossible for her to comprehend, of movement inside the third frequency, where everything was supposed to be still.

The woman turned and stood straight as she stared at Melinda with pure black eyes, cocking her head slightly in her own surprise. She wore a cloak that was open at the front, showing her naked body.

Melinda hardened her voice. "Who are you?"

"I am Obsidian. How do you move like me?"

Melinda stepped closer, holding her hands on the hilts of her knives. "I am Zranh."

The woman narrowed her eyes. "The Zranh are like children; they do not move like me."

Melinda took another step. "They are my children and you just murdered three of them. For that, I will kill you."

Obsidian dropped the liver to the ground and spread her arms wide, her talons wickedly gleaming in the light. "You are free to try."

Drawing her knives, Melinda leapt forward, swiping one knife across the woman's face while plunging the other into her heart, but the woman disappeared before Melinda connected, throwing her off balance. She stumbled to one knee and turned her head left and right, quickly looking for the woman who, impossibly, had vanished while in the third frequency of the Raith world.

Melinda prowled around the area but found no tracks indicating where the woman had gone. The trees grew thickly, making it difficult to see any real distance in any direction. Just as Melinda was about to turn, she felt the barest whisper of moving air against her neck and dove forward, rolling and coming to her feet, spinning with her knives held defensively to block the swiping claws of the woman, the sound of them sliding along the steel loud in the stillness of the Raith world.

Obsidian's eyes widened with fury when Melinda spun and tried to sweep her legs out from under her. She was able to mostly avoid Melinda's attempt but still stumbled back, off balance.

Melinda leapt forward and spun in the opposite direction mid-jump, both knives swinging in a hissing arc and slicing into the woman's stomach with two parallel cuts.

Obsidian stumbled back again, astonished by the ferocity of Melinda's attack. She looked down at the blood spurting out of the cuts, then back up to Melinda, her black eyes opened wide. Then she disappeared.

Melinda stayed in her fighting stance, looking around her to make sure the woman didn't reappear and attack from a different direction.

After a few long moments, Melinda stood up straight, dropping her arms to her side but not putting her knives away.

She had hopefully wounded the woman enough to drive her away for good, although she doubted she would be that lucky. This changed things for the Zranh. Her people had always been hunters, moving about unseen and holding the advantage in every situation. It had never occurred to her that there might be an alpha hunter who could do everything the Zranh could do and more. She would have to cycle between the frequencies more often now to try and avoid being caught off guard.

She approached the three dead Zranh, her heart heavy at seeing Nren and Oeth lying dead on the ground along with Fiejweth, the younger brother of Falweth. Three more Zranh who would not get the chance to live their lives and grow old, all because of her.

Melinda did her best to make the bodies presentable, cleaning the blood from their faces and covering their grisly wounds with blankets. She bowed her head and closed her eyes in a moment of silence before she released the heat and shifted to the first frequency where the rest of the Zranh currently were. They quickly turned toward her as she stood.

Pronni stepped forward, her knives still in her hands. "Leillireph, did you kill the black-skinned woman?"

Shaking her head, Melinda wiped her blood-covered hands on a small piece of cloth. "No, she got away. I wounded her, but did not kill her."

Falweth knelt by his dead brother and caressed his cheek.

Melinda put a hand on his shoulder. "I am sorry I was unable to save him."

Falweth pulled the blanket up, covering his brother's face and turned to look up at her. "He was Zranh and died like a Zranh. He will be honored by all."

"He will be, I promise." Melinda turned to Pronni. "Let's bury our dead. We don't want to start a funeral pyre in these thick woods."

The young Gorepeth briskly nodded and without a word, she took a small hand shovel from her pack and started digging. She was joined by Trombey, one of the members of Falweth's Quadrant, and they soon dug a hole large enough for all three fallen warriors. Sweating, they climbed from it and the others lowered the bodies down, carefully placing them on top of each other in positions of respect, arms folded and eyes open.

Melinda spoke in a clear voice. "Rest now, Fiejweth, Nren, and Oeth. Your battles are over. We honor you for who you were; we honor you for who you are; we honor you as Zranh." She picked up Pronni's shovel and filled in the hole, as was her responsibility as Leillireph and leader of the Zranh. She was sweating by the time she placed the last bit of dirt on the mound and stepped back. The rest of the Zranh sprinkled pine needles over the grave so it blended in with the rest of the forest floor.

Melinda handed the shovel to Pronni, then shifted to the third frequency of the Raith world to ensure they were alone and safe before shifting back. No one even knew she had been gone. Motioning with her hand for the six remaining Zranh to step closer, she explained what had happened when she had fought the woman named Obsidian. When she got to the part where the woman had disappeared while in the third frequency, Falweth and Pronni both hissed, "Mithenzz."

Melinda turned to them. "You know this woman?"

Falweth glanced at Pronni before saying, "Yes, Leillireph."

"Who is she?"

"Mithenzz is the one who lives in darkness, the evil in the woods," he paused briefly before quietly saying, "and the only thing all Zranh fear."

Melinda pulled on her pack, and adjusting the straps, coldly said, "Well, I do not fear her."

The Zranh nodded, respect and awe showing on their faces.

Turning to the southwest, Melinda stared resolutely into the trees and said, "Let's get this journey over with." She started forward and Pronni quickly jogged forward so she could get in front of her. Eithes strode by Melinda's side, looking fearless.

As she walked, Melinda thought of the Mithenzz named Obsidian and visualized her body lying on the ground with two knives buried in her heart.

Chapter 42

The door to the house in front of Crowdal opened and a woman hobbled out, staring at him as he and his father approached, the breeze ruffling her shoulder-length hair. Her face was set in a hard expression, her lips pressed firmly together with eyes squinting against the sun.

As Crowdal got closer he noticed grey streaks in her black hair, mainly around her temples. Her shoulder drooped sharply to the left, her arm quivering as she supported herself on a cane. When he had left the Circle two years ago, his mother had seemed young and full of vitality, but now she seemed frail and defeated, something he had never expected to see in his mother. He stopped in front of her, not sure what he should do. The silence stretched out until she smiled and held out a shaking hand. Crowdal took it and stepped into her embrace, feeling her thin body and worrying he would harm her.

"Oh stop hugging me like you think you will break me, Crowdal."

Crowdal chuckled and tears streamed down his face as he squeezed her, though he still didn't squeeze too hard.

She let the cane drop as she wrapped her other arm around him, tapping his back as she cried into his shoulder. Finally, she pushed him back and looked into his eyes, smiling. "It is good to see you, son. I began to wonder if I would ever see you again."

Uuthdal stepped forward and spoke gruffly, although his eyes were warm as he said, "Stop mothering the boy, Veronnu, and let's get inside before you catch a sickness."

Veronnu rolled her eyes, "Oh shush." She took Crowdal's hand in hers and Uuthdal placed the cane into her other hand. She led Crowdal into the house, limping as she took small shuffling steps.

Crowdal looked back at his father with an unspoken question, but Uuthdal shook his head that it wasn't the right time. Crowdal turned back toward his mother and as he stepped over the threshold of his home for the first time in two years, the smell of the house hit him, exactly the same as he remembered: cooking stew, freshly baked bread, and the everyday smells of his family. He almost felt like he was a child again, coming home from sword practice, hungry and thirsty and being handed a hunk of still steaming bread fresh from the oven, his mother smiling down at him.

His mother led him to the kitchen and let go of his hand. "Sit." She put on a thick mitten and opened the door to the oven to take out a loaf of bread, its crust browned perfectly. With a shaking hand, she slowly set it onto the countertop, grabbing the edge to balance herself.

Crowdal started to stand but she waved him back down. "I am not completely useless yet."

Uuthdal left them in the kitchen, and as he turned away, Crowdal saw his father's face strained with grief.

Veronnu grabbed a big knife and cut into the loaf of bread, her shaking hands causing the steaming hot slice to be jagged and uneven as it fell to the table. She picked it up and put it onto a small wooden plate, then put a large pat of butter on it and handed the plate to Crowdal.

Crowdal accepted the plate and his mouth watered at seeing the butter melting in a pool in the center of the bread. He set the plate down and looked at her. "Mother, what happened?"

Veronnu sat down and motioned at the bread. "Eat first, while it is hot."

"But mother…"

"I said eat!"

Crowdal couldn't help but smile. She still had the fire inside of her that he remembered. He took a large bite of the bread and closed his eyes as the hot liquid butter filled his mouth. He chewed and swallowed and quickly finished off the slice. He smiled at his mother. "I haven't had fresh bread in a long time. You haven't forgotten how much I love it, have you?"

She smiled, her eyes twinkling with humor. "I have never known anyone who loves bread more than you, Crowdal."

He placed his hand over hers and leaned forward, "Mother, what happened to you? You were healthy when I left two years ago."

Veronnu shrugged. "It is the sickness that catches so many of us. I feel it inside, eating away at me."

"But there must be something that can be done."

Shaking her head, Veronnu caressed Crowdal's cheek with her free hand. "No, son, there is nothing. The healers give me only a fortnight to live, maybe less."

Tears welled up in Crowdal's eyes and he tilted his face to push it against her hand. He felt like someone had filled his veins with cold water, numbness overtaking him. It couldn't be true. His mother had been the epitome of health when he had left the Circle, strong and fit as any Trith. She was only 49 years old and had always been his pillar of strength. His father was almost 60 and still as strong as one half his age, but would he be next to get the sickness?

Crowdal sat back in his chair feeling the true presence of mortality for the first time in his life. He had accidentally killed his best friend two years ago, and since then had killed many, while watching still more friends die. But death had always been a distant concept, something that happened to others, maybe even to him. But knowing his mother would die in just a matter of days drove the dagger of mortality deep into his heart.

Veronnu saw his pain and sat back, her eyes flashing. "Don't you dare feel sorry for me or for yourself. This is life and with life comes death. It is a certainty we all must face." Her eyes softened. "Crowdal, I do not want you to be sad. You came back to me before I take my final journey and that is a gift to us both. Let's not waste that gift on sorrow. We need to laugh and feel joy at the time we get to spend together now, for that is a gift that not everyone gets in this world."

Crowdal wiped the tears from his eyes and nodded, knowing she was right.

"Good. Now, how about another slice of bread?"

"Sure, but let me cut it."

"Nonsense. You sit there." She got up from her chair and yelled into the other room, "Uuthdal, quit hiding in there and join us."

The scrape of a chair sounded in the other room and heavy footsteps approached, then Uuthdal's massive frame filled the doorway.

"Don't just stand there, sit down."

Uuthdal looked at Crowdal, then stepped into the kitchen and sat down, the chair creaking from his weight. "So, what have you ladies been talking about in here?"

Crowdal felt himself smile at the familiar quip his father had often used when he caught Crowdal and Veronnu talking in the kitchen.

Veronnu put down a plate of roughly sliced bread and smacked Uuthdal on the shoulder. "Quit saying that. Crowdal is a man now."

Uuthdal glanced at Crowdal and nodded. "Aye, that I know. From all accounts, he leads a group that includes a Murder of Haissen."

Veronnu whipped her head around to stare at Crowdal. Her voice came out in a whisper of fear, "Haissen? They really exist?"

Crowdal nodded. "Yes. Although they really follow my friend Sid, who is the Aleph Null. They do what I say but only at the request of Sid."

Her eyes grew even larger. "You travel with the Aleph Null?"

It was Crowdal's turn to be surprised. "You have heard of the Aleph Null?"

"Of course I have. We Trith are one of the oldest races in this land. We have gathered many tales during our travels. One of the oldest is about the one who can control great powers – one called the Aleph Null."

"Why had I never heard that story?"

Veronnu shrugged. "It isn't a common one. Or maybe you heard it but weren't paying attention. Do you really travel with the Aleph Null?"

"Yes, I do. Sid is in the holding room right now."

Uuthdal grabbed a piece of bread, spread some butter on it and said, "Crowdal also travels with the infamous Hunters of Reilen, a Vringe, some mercenaries, and one man who even I think is dangerous just by looking at him. Our boy seems to have gotten mixed up in something big."

Crowdal glanced at his father. "That is actually why I am back here." He took a deep breath and held it before continuing, "The Aleph Null needs your help."

Veronnu looked at him with a puzzled expression. "Our help? What could he possibly need from the Trith?"

"I think he needs to be the one to explain it to you both."

His mother looked at Uuthdal and even though they didn't speak, they seemed to come to a mutual decision. His mother nodded, "Get my cane and let's go see your friends."

Crowdal stood up and handed her the cane. "I can bring them here – you don't have to walk that far."

"Nonsense. The exercise will do me good. Plus, I want to see these Haissen in person. It isn't every day that I get to meet walking legends."

Uuthdal folded the slice of bread and stuffed it into his mouth as he stood up, wiping his hands on his trousers.

Veronnu slapped his hand. "Stop that and use a towel."

Uuthdal nodded without arguing as he reached for a towel.

Crowdal grinned.

The real leader of the Trith Nation was his mother.

Veronnu motioned Uuthdal to leave, saying, "Gather the Council and meet us at the holding room right away."

Uuthdal nodded and left.

A cold sweat built on Crowdal's forehead and he wiped it away with the back of his hand. The Trith Council was made up of seven Trith – three men and four women, and was led by his mother and father, the king and queen. The rank of king and queen in the Trith Nation was nothing like that of the human kingdoms; it was more of a title based on history, for Uuthdal and Veronnu were from the two oldest families in the Trith Nation and therefore had the rank, it had nothing to do with their being married. Everything depended on the Trith Council hearing what Sid had to say and whether or not they would allow him to do what needed to be done.

He put his arm out to his mother, who took it as they exited the house. The nineteen Trith who had met them in the woods were waiting outside. Some looked at Crowdal with open disdain, and Crowdal recognized them all, having grown up with them. He grinned when he saw Juldall, who smiled back at him. Crowdal put out his hand and they shook hands vigorously. "It is good to see you, Juldall."

"You too, Crowdal. How long has it been? Three years?"

"Two, but who's counting? How is your sister doing?"

He grinned. "Rielissa is still pining away for her lost Trith prince."

Crowdal felt a thrill go through him. He had hated leaving Rielissa. They had been good friends since they had been kids and she had been the only real friend he had other than Dwimdal, who he had killed during their Circle ceremony. He forced himself to look unaffected by what Juldall had said. "Maybe I'll stop by and say hi to her."

"You had better. If you don't, she will hunt you down to the ends of the land."

Veronnu barked out, "Enough talking."

Juldall stood up straight and at attention.

Crowdal apologized to his mother for keeping her and slowly led her down the street, making sure to keep her steady and stopping often to let her rest. The streets filled with Trith as they walked, everyone coming out to see the prodigal prince. Some were whispering about him, but he ignored them all and they reached the building where his friends were being kept as the sun hung low in the west, casting a deep orange glow about the area.

The Trith guarding the door opened it and stepped to the side so they could enter, followed by the nineteen special guards.

Sid jumped to his feet and jogged over to Crowdal, his face looking worried. Agnes was right behind him, and soon the entire group stood in front of Crowdal and his mother. Before he could introduce her to Sid, there was a commotion and his father led five older Trith into the room, most looking angry at being taken from whatever they had been doing.

Crowdal sighed.

This was not going to be easy.

Chapter 43

Blood flowed from the deep slices in Obsidian's stomach and she hissed in pain as Tris pushed a clean cloth against her wounds, trying unsuccessfully to stop the blood from seeping out of the deep cuts. She would bleed out if he didn't stop the bleeding so he took a deep breath and sent his Numbers into her wounds, calculating the way the tissue was parted, where the muscle could be reconnected, how the blood vessels could be repaired – creating equations of such complexity that he needed to spend extra time to verify their accuracy. When he was sure he had taken into account every aspect of the wounds, he started connecting the equations to the tissue, one at a time, and where he did, the tissue fused together until it was whole again, as strong as it had been before. Sweat ran down his temples by the time he completed the equations, fusing the top-most layer of skin last.

Tris sat back and wiped sweat from his forehead with his sleeve. He had done something similar to his own body after he had been so badly wounded in the Srithian Wood, but he had days to work on himself then and since he innately felt the damage inside of himself, it was easier to repair the tissue.

Obsidian sat up hesitantly, feeling the smooth skin of her stomach with her hands and looking at Tris in astonishment. There were not even any scars left, so complete were his mathematical equations.

He put his head tiredly against the wall. "So tell me what happened."

She stepped over to him and knelt between his legs, looking into his eyes with lust, whispering, "Let me thank you, first." She caressed him through his trousers and he felt himself harden despite his exhaustion, something she so easily did to him.

He put his hand down to push her away but pulled it back quickly when she hissed at him, her eyes widening slightly in anger. "Now, now my pet. No need to get cross with me. We will have our fun soon. First, you will answer my questions."

Obsidian sat back on her heels and finally nodded.

"Good girl. So please explain how you got such wounds. The last thing I remember was falling asleep here, then being awakened by your hisses of pain. Where did you go?"

Her look turned cold and dangerous. "Just before we returned back here, I smelled Zranh in the air. So I returned to the forest after you fell asleep to hunt them. I hate the Zranh more than anyone and kill them when I can."

Tris motioned to her stomach, "How did one of them manage to wound you?"

"The Zranh normally move about in the space where humans can't go, but I can go where even the Zranh can't, which allows me to kill them unseen." She hesitated as her face twisted in fury. "But there was a woman moving through my space, something I have never seen before. She was Zranh, but somehow not Zranh. We fought and she was extremely fast with her knives, attacking me with a fury unlike anything I've witnessed. I barely escaped back here."

Tris had read about the elusive Zranh in the Oblate library and had found it hard to believe they could move through different planes of existence. But the author of the book claimed to have captured one and tortured her for her secrets. There were two frequencies the Zranh could move through, which allowed them to move faster than everything around them. There was a brief mention of the Leillireph, a Zranh who could move through a third frequency and stop time completely, but it seemed from the writings to be a myth.

He looked hard at Obsidian. From her report, it seemed this Leillireph existed and was someone very dangerous, indeed. "What did this Zranh-who-was-not-a-Zranh look like?"

Obsidian described the woman. Tris was dismayed that he didn't recognize her as anyone he knew. "Do you think you will be able to sense this woman if we get close to her again?"

Obsidian nodded. "I would smell her from many leagues away."

"Good." He looked down at her breasts. "Now, for that thank you."

Her eyes grew lidded and she eagerly crept forward. He was soon moaning in ecstasy. Sometime later, how much time he didn't know, they finished, sweaty and out of breath.

Tris slid from the bed and got dressed. He looked down at her naked body. "Put your robe on and let's get back to the forest."

Obsidian lazily got out of the bed, looking less-than-enthused to be leaving.

Tris glared at her and she moved faster, soon enveloping him in her arms.

They appeared in the Muldragg Forest and Tris looked around at the wet ground. It must have recently rained. Gods, he hated the rain. The mosquitos were thick in the damp air, buzzing around him, many landing on his skin and sinking their proboscises into him, searching for blood. He created a simple array around himself to keep them from biting him, then killed any remaining on his skin. Obsidian didn't seem to be bothered by them as she gazed around the area, her eyes narrowed.

"Do you sense the woman?"

Obsidian slowly shook her head, no.

"Good, then let's go. We have some time to make up." He started heading southwest. The forest had been getting thicker and denser, the further into it they traveled.

He considered his pathetic Blue Robes, not for the first time irritated by them. But they had been somewhat successful in gathering small forces to help with his plan, so they weren't a complete waste.

The female Blue Robe from Paigon was currently on the south coast of the Bertol Sea with a medium-sized army of one thousand Paigonian soldiers she had acquired from the King of Paigon with the promise of enough gold to run his kingdom for ten years.

Tris smiled when he remembered her fearful request for the gold from the Oblate. He had agreed, as the Oblate had more gold than all of the kingdoms of the land combined, but he had enjoyed making her almost beg for his forgiveness for promising so much to the king. Unfortunately, the army moved slowly, barely covering a dozen leagues a day. It would take them another few days to reach the Trith Nation.

The ugly woman from Yathen had only gathered a force of three hundred men and were just approaching Death Falls. Even though they still had farther to go than the Paigonian army, they moved a little quicker and should reach the Trith Nation around the same time.

The oldest male Blue Robe from Tauben had not been able to secure any type of force from the king, so Tris had used the communication equation to burst the two main blood vessels in his head, killing him instantly. Tris had no use for weak people.

The last Blue Robe was the fat one. He had secured a small expeditionary force and was moving the quickest of them all, already heading toward the Trith Nation and probably not too far south of his own location in the Muldragg Forest. But the kid was weak and had no backbone, so Tris didn't expect much help from that group. At the very least, they might provide some backup if needed. The fact that he didn't expect any of his armies to survive against the Trith didn't bother him. He wasn't looking to defeat the Trith, he just wanted to create some chaos so he could capture Sid.

He still had his contacts in each kingdom, ranging from high-level councilors, to the king of Reilen. Unfortunately, Reilen too far away to be of much help with his plan.

Up ahead, Obsidian halted and lowered to a crouch while staring to her left. Tris increased the solidity of the array around him and stepped up to her. "What is it?"

She didn't answer at first as she stared, every muscle tensed.

"I said, what is the problem?"

Obsidian slowly turned to look at him, her eyes the last to shift to him. "I do not know. I have never sensed this creature before."

"Tell me what you sense."

"It is large and moves almost silently as it hunts what we hunt."

Tris motioned his head in the direction they were traveling. "Go, tell me what you find, but do not attack or kill whatever is out there. Report back what you find."

She disappeared without a word and almost instantly reappeared. "Well?"

"It is a creature with white fur that hurts me when I look at it. I wish to kill it."

A thrill ran through Tris. "How far away is it?"

Before she could answer, Obsidian glanced behind Tris and cried out, disappearing instantly.

Tris smiled as he turned. "Hello, my pet. Why have you been ignoring me?"

The Korpor stepped from around a large tree and faced him, its hideous faced twisted in a grimace.

Chapter 44

When Sid heard the door open, he turned his head expecting to see just Crowdal, but when he saw him accompanied by an older female Trith, he could immediately tell it was his mother. She had the same kind eyes as his, eyes that also held a deep strength. She looked physically ill and weak, but still projected a sense of power that couldn't be ignored.

Nineteen more Trith entered, the elite guards of Uuthdal, who took up protective positions around her and Crowdal.

Sid jumped to his feet and ran over to Crowdal, followed quickly by everyone from his own group. The Haissen stood calmly by, but Sid knew they would instantly spring into action if anyone threatened him.

Before he could say anything, there was a commotion behind Crowdal and six more Trith barged into the room, led by Uuthdal, most of them looking angry.

Crowdal looked behind him and when he turned back to Sid, he had a pained look on his face.

He looked up at his friend and said, "Crowdal, what's going on?"

"Sid, I would like to introduce you to the Trith Council, and specifically, to my mother, Veronnu."

The older woman stepped forward, looking hard at Sid. "So, you are the Aleph Null."

Sid shook his head. "I was, but am no longer."

Angry muttering arose from the Council behind Veronnu, but she put her hand up and they all instantly quieted. "It appears you have a long story to tell us, but before you do, please introduce me to your group."

Sid turned and introduced everyone. When he got to the Haissen, the Trith in the room tensed, their hands tightening on their sword hilts.

Veronnu stepped toward the Haissen. She was almost twice their height, making it look like a mother approaching children. "So, you are the famous Haissen. Please remove your hoods."

The Haissen all slid back their hoods, revealing their pure white faces.

The tension amongst the Trith became so thick that Sid thought the slightest movement by the Haissen might lead to an all-out battle between the two races. But Veronnu spoke coldly to her Trith without looking at them, "If even one of you removes your sword, you will be executed."

One of the Council members stepped forward, a thin and ancient-looking man. "You do not have that authority."

Veronnu turned to him. "You are right, I do not." She pointed at the Haissen next to her. "But their swords do."

Kulweg, the massively-built Trith who had guided Sid and the group to this building stepped forward, his face flushed and his eyes glinting. "I do not fear these *Haissen*." He almost spat out their name.

Uuthdal glanced at Veronnu. "We will not be able to keep this situation contained forever. There isn't a Trith in this Circle who will be able to control their pride and avoid a fight with the Haissen. It could quickly get out of control and these are our guests."

Veronnu shook her head. "No, Uuthdal, that is a bad idea."

Uuthdal looked at Crowdal. "You brought them into our Circle knowing every Trith would want to challenge the infamous Haissen. This is the only way."

Crowdal nodded acceptance. "But only one challenge, and not to the death."

Kulweg smirked. "I can't promise that."

Sid tugged on Crowdal's shirt. "What's happening?"

"I'm sorry, Sid. We wanted to leave the Haissen far outside of the Circle to avoid this, but we didn't get the chance. If we don't allow one formal challenge, there will be chaos and bloodshed before the night ends." He turned away from Sid and approached the Haissen, speaking softly to them.

They nodded slightly.

Crowdal turned to face the Trith. "Your challenge has been accepted. Who do you choose as challenger, father?"

Kulweg stiffened with rage at the insult, but Uuthdal pointed to Kulweg, bringing a cruel smile to the Trith's face.

Veronnu grunted. "So be it. Everyone, to the arena."

Sid followed Crowdal through the door and down the street to a large, open area. In the middle was a circle approximately forty paces across, surrounded by a border of rocks. Dozens of tall, unlit torches surrounded the circle, and since the sun had set, the Trith guards quickly lit them, illuminating the area with flickering, orange light.

Kulweg stripped off his tunic and dropped it, along with his scabbard, to the ground, holding his giant sword in one hand, flexing his massive muscles and smiling harshly in anticipation of the challenge.

Trith came from all parts of the Circle and crowded around the arena, anticipation thick in the air for the fight to come. They had all heard of the Haissen, the one race who were rumored to be as good with a blade as the Trith, and not one of them would miss the first chronicled fight in known history between the two races.

Uuthdal stepped forward. "Who do you challenge, Kulweg?"

"I want their best, whoever he is."

A Haissan stepped forward and Sid recognized her as Saleth.

The king asked, "What is your name?"

"Saleth."

Kulweg turned to Crowdal and asked, "Is he their best?"

Crowdal shook his head. "You can't rate her as the best because every Haissan is at the same elite level of skill with the blade."

Not understanding what Crowdal was saying, Kulweg spat on the ground. "I won't fight a female. I said I want their best."

Crowdal sighed, then raised his voice to be heard over the muttering of the Trith surrounding the circle. "Like the Trith, the Haissen males and females are no different in skill-level or ability."

Uuthdal raised an arm for silence. "Saleth, do you accept the challenge?"

She nodded without emotion.

"There are two rules. You will not use any kill-strikes and you will not maim or seriously injure your opponent. This is an honorable fight. If you are forced out of the circle, you forfeit. If you are disarmed, you forfeit. If you choose to admit defeat, you must drop your sword or step from the circle." He turned to look at each Trith. "After this challenge, no matter who wins, there will be no further actions taken against the Haissen. No challenges. No illegal fights. No retribution." At their silence, he bellowed, "Do you understand?"

The Trith all yelled out, "Yes."

Uuthdal motioned for Saleth to enter the circle.

She stepped over the stones and waited calmly, neither withdrawing her sword nor removing her robe. She did not even acknowledge Kulweg, causing him to growl as he glared down at her.

Uuthdal motioned with an arm and a loud gong rang out.

Kulweg roared as he charged Saleth, his great sword held high, the steel a dark blue as it caught the light of the torches. He was so large that, to Sid, it looked like he could just raise his foot and crush Saleth. He brought the sword down in a mighty blow but it struck the ground as Saleth stepped to the side, still not drawing her sword.

Kulweg roared again and swung his sword in a backward arc, the steel whistling through the air as it moved with speed and deadly accuracy.

Saleth jumped clear over the sword and landed lightly on her feet. Kulweg lost his balance, having expected to cut her in half, and had to put a hand to the ground to stop himself from falling over.

Uuthdal called a halt to the fight and roared, "I said no killing blows. This is your one and only warning, Kulweg."

Kulweg slowly pushed himself upright, glaring at the Haissan before nodding to his king. He calmed himself and stood tall, holding his sword in the Gaiken position.

Saleth smoothly slid her curved sword from its scabbard and faced Kulweg with an almost supernatural calm.

Kulweg slowly approached her and when he was within striking distance he lunged forward, raising his sword slightly and striking down with speed instead of power.

Saleth deflected the blow, connecting with his sword at an angle that allowed her to push and slide her sword along the edge of his, then lift it to block another quick strike from the left. Her sword was half the length of Kulweg's, the steel thinner and lighter, so she could use incredible speed and calculated angles to avoid direct impacts that might break her blade.

Kulweg knew he had the advantage of steel strength as well as reach and he used both to his benefit, leading with strikes that kept him just out of her range. He grinned, flexing his chest and arm muscles in the firelight, showing off. He performed complicated maneuvers, flicking his sword in different directions with the confidence that comes from someone who has trained with a sword his whole life.

They moved about the circle, Kulweg always attacking. As yet, Saleth had not tried to strike at him, and to the Trith who watched the match, it looked like she was overmatched and always on the defense.

Sid looked briefly at the Trith around the circle and saw that many of them were openly contemptuous, obviously expecting a much grander display of swordsmanship from the legendary Haissen.

Then Crowdal called out, "Saleth, you've played with him long enough. Just finish this fight."

The Trith around him growled in anger at the insult, and when Uuthdal glared at him, Crowdal shrugged.

Kulweg roared with fury at Crowdal's remark and attacked Saleth relentlessly, his sword a blur as he struck at her with every move he had. She blocked and ducked and swayed in a dance of movement that was beautiful and deadly.

Then she started moving directly toward Kulweg while blocking his blows, surprising him with her fearlessness. It was almost impossible to both defend and move forward, but she was doing it.

Saleth started forcing him back a step at a time and before anyone knew it, she became the aggressor as she flicked her sword at him, forcing him to block her strikes.

Kulweg ground his jaw as he tried to reclaim his advantage, but when he attempted to strike back at her he sliced his arm, the cut shallow but leaking blood. He roared and kicked out at her but Saleth smoothly pivoted away from the kick, slicing into his shin at the same time with such precision that it parted his leather boots but just touched the skin underneath, causing the barest hint of blood to show.

Kulweg ignored the cut and jabbed at her with his long sword, hitting nothing but air as she ducked and spun, slicing across his stomach, again leaving just the barest scratch.

Uuthdal leaned over and whispered to Crowdal from the corner of his mouth, "Did she intend a killing blow with that one? Do I need to stop this?"

Crowdal whispered back, "No, she intended only to scratch him."

Uuthdal turned to him, looking stunned, "Such precision is impossible during a match such as this."

"Nothing is impossible when it comes to the Haissen." Crowdal motioned with his head toward the fight, "She will end the fight now."

Kulweg backed up as Saleth relentlessly attacked him, not able to stop his retreat until he was forced to the edge of the circle, his back heel touching one of the stones. He had nowhere to go and tried to block her sword strikes but couldn't stop them all, looking like he was flailing his sword at a swarm of bees. Then he stumbled back and fell out of the circle, landing on his back, the Trith that surrounded the circle jumping quickly out of the way.

Saleth stood just inside of the circle, her sword in her scabbard, her body perfectly motionless as if she had been standing still the whole time instead of fighting a Trith twice her size.

Every Trith around the circle was stunned into silence, staring back and forth between Saleth and Kulweg on the ground.

Sid looked at Uuthdal and saw the king staring open-mouthed at Kulweg and the Haissan who had bested him. Then he shouted, "The challenge is complete and the Haissan is the victor."

Angry yells and curses erupted around them, the Trith jostling each other, some with their swords out as they eyed Saleth in the circle.

Uuthdal roared, his face red with anger, "Put your swords away or face my wrath. Stand down, now!"

The Trith angrily put their swords away and quieted down.

Kulweg pushed himself to his feet, his face red with anger and shame. He raised his sword and Uuthdal yelled to him, "Put your sword away, Kulweg. The challenge is complete and you lost."

But Kulweg didn't hear him as he glared at Saleth. Then he leapt into the ring with a roar, his sword held high and descending in a violent strike meant to cut her in two.

Saleth waited until his descending sword was an arm-length from her head, then she lunged forward in a blur underneath the blow, then leapt up, drawing her sword and slicing across his stomach in one impossibly fast movement while spinning out of his way. She landed with one leg bent forward, her head down, her sword out, dripping thick blood onto the dry dirt.

Blood sprayed out, covering Saleth completely as Kulweg landed hard on the ground. He looked down at his stomach, which was now sliced open from side to side. His intestines slid out and fell to the ground. He quickly dropped his sword and tried to pull them back up, covered with dirt and grit though they were. Kulweg grunted as his strength gave out and he collapsed to his knees, looking confused, his eyes wide and leaking tears. Then the great Trith fell forward to the dirt, his intestines crushing underneath him. A cloud of dust rose around his now still body before settling back onto him.

Saleth flicked the blood from her sword then returned it smoothly to her scabbard while standing up straight. Her entire front was covered with blood, her white face now completely red with thick gore.

The entire circle was silent, everyone in shock.

Sid heard Crowdal whisper to his father and the king nodded, his eyes never leaving Kulweg's body.

The king stepped forward into the circle and raised his voice, "Kulweg has dishonored us all and has paid with his life." He turned and glared at every Trith. "There will be no retribution against any Haissan or member of their group. I will personally deal with anyone who disobeys this command. Do I make myself clear?" When no one responded, he bellowed, "Do I make myself clear?"

A chorus of affirmations rang out and Uuthdal turned to Saleth. "You fought honorably and fairly. Your reputation is well-deserved."

Saleth nodded and hissed, "Thank you, King Uuthdal."

The king offered his hand and Saleth shook it. He then turned, "Now, let's have a feast."

One of the nineteen guards asked, "What about Kulweg?"

Uuthdal glanced down at the body. "Throw him into the refuse pit. He will not be honored by fire."

The Trith nodded, his eyes hard as he motioned for another to help him carry the body away.

The king rejoined Sid and his group. "You are now free to move about our Circle at will. Now come, we will eat and drink and tomorrow we will discuss your reason for being here, Aleph Null." He turned and started across the street.

Veronnu grimaced at Crowdal and whispered, "Stay together and keep a watchful eye. Kulweg was well-respected and had many friends."

Crowdal nodded. "I am sorry it had to end like this. We do not want any more bloodshed."

"You may not have a choice in the matter. Now, let's eat and you can tell me where you have been these past two years." She took his arm and they started down the street.

Crowdal turned to look back at Sid and the rest of the group and softly said, "Stay close to me, everyone."

Sid took Agnes' hand and followed, glancing at the two Trith who picked up Kulweg and carried his body away, thick blood dripping behind them as they walked, leaving a red trail in the dirt.

He hoped this would be the only death while they were here.

Chapter 45

Drax stood up from the ring of people and Trith around the fire and touched Sid's shoulder. "I am going for a walk."

Sid looked at him and whispered, "Be careful."

Nodding, Drax left the light of the fire and headed up the dirt street. The night was dark and the torches were few, creating many stretches of deep shadow along the street. He passed many dark side streets, but with his enhanced vision he could see almost as clearly as if it were day. He needed some time alone to think, to figure out his future because he wasn't really sure why he was staying with the Aleph Null. He now knew that Sid wasn't dangerous, even if he did get his power of Numbers back, so there was no reason to stick around. Sid was well-protected by his friends and didn't need Drax's help. No matter how hard he tried to act normal, Drax knew he would never be accepted by this group as a true friend.

Perhaps it was time to move on and hunt the Black Robe named Tris, who had stolen the Black Numbers. He had hoped that this Tris would show himself to Sid, but so far there had been no indication he was close by.

Drax closed his eyes as he walked and calculated the odds of finding the Black Robe based on all the factors he knew. No matter how many times he ran through all of the scenarios, the odds still tilted in his favor if he stayed with the Aleph Null. Sighing, Drax knew he would have to stay for a while longer.

He opened his eyes and in the distance saw a quick and furtive movement as someone ducked behind a corner of a building. He hadn't been able to see who it was, so he slowed down as he approached the corner. He listened carefully and heard the breathing and heartbeat of someone who was anxious and frightened.

Stopping a few paces from the corner, he spoke softly, "I know you are around the corner. Please show yourself."

The breathing and heart rate quickened.

When no one stepped forward, Drax spoke with a sharper tone, "Leave the darkness and step out here where I may see you."

Drax heard a whimper, then an exhalation of breath and tentative movement. He put his hand to his knife handle but relaxed when a young Trith stepped around the corner. The Trith couldn't be more than Drax's own age and though he towered above him, he was still a couple hand-spans shorter than Crowdal because of a severely hunched back that sloped sharply to the left. Drax tilted his head up and saw his face was also severely deformed.

One of the Trith's eyes was scarred over with puckered skin, and his mouth couldn't fully close because the lips were permanently crooked, the top of his right lip split and pulled up and away from over-sized upper teeth. Drool ran down his chin and the Trith quickly wiped it away with a cloth.

Drax smiled. "What may I do for you, kind sir?"

The Trith looked down at him, astonishment on his face that he was being spoken to with kindness. He moved his lips but only an unintelligible sound came out.

Drax tilted his head. "You can't speak, can you?"

The Trith shook his head no, his good eye glistening with sadness.

Suspecting he knew the answer to his next question, Drax asked, "Why do you hide way out here instead of joining the feast?"

The Trith tried to shrug but his left shoulder wouldn't move, making the effort seem more like a spasm.

Drax felt a deep melancholy fill him at what this young Trith must endure on a daily basis. He had seen a boy back in the Fahrin Druin school who had a cleft palate, his upper lip almost non-existent. He had been ridiculed mercilessly by the other boys until one day he had just disappeared.

Drax smiled again at the Trith and indicated the darkness, "You prefer the darkness, don't you?"

The Trith nodded slowly and made the same sound.

Drax stepped closer and the Trith turned and ran back into the darkness around the corner, whimpering.

"It's alright, I won't harm you, master Trith." He stepped slowly around the corner and the Trith ran back a few more steps and turned to look over his good shoulder with fearful eyes.

Putting up his hands, Drax calmly said, "It's alright. I am a friend." He took a step forward and the Trith didn't run, so he kept taking one slow step at a time until he was behind him, then he sat down, cross-legged, in the dirt and smiled, motioning the Trith to join him.

The Trith turned with jerky movements and looked down at him as if he thought it was a trick.

Drax shook his head. "I won't harm you or ridicule you. I just want to be your friend."

The Trith regarded Drax for many moments, then glanced back into the darkness, then back at Drax until he seemed to make a decision and awkwardly lowered himself to the ground, his legs straight out, his shoulder hunched far down to the left. A tear fell down the Trith's cheek and he wiped it quickly away with the same cloth he used to wipe his drool.

Drax smiled again. "Can you read and write?"

The Trith nodded eagerly.

Drax saw a stick on the ground and leaned over to grab it, causing the Trith to cringe back. He stopped and put up his other hand, "It's alright, I am just going to use this stick to write with."

The Trith eyed it warily before leaning forward again.

Drax slowly picked up the stick and brushed the dirt in-between them until it was smooth, then wrote his name to the side so they both could read it. "My name is Drax. What is your name?"

Drax held the stick out and the Trith tentatively took it with a three-fingered hand that curled permanently inward. But with practiced ease, he gripped the stick and wrote smoothly in the dirt, indicating a high intelligence existed inside his broken body.

Drax tilted his head and read, "Calix," and smiled. "Hey, our names are very similar, aren't they? I'm Drax and you are Calix."

Calix grinned, though it was difficult with his deformed mouth, and nodded enthusiastically. He bent forward and wiped the dirt and wrote, "It is good to meet you, Drax."

Drax laughed with genuine humor. "I am glad to meet you, too, Calix."

Calix's split upper lip stretched even further upward over his large upper teeth, but the smile disappeared and he leaned forward to wipe the dirt away, then wrote, "Why are you being nice to me?"

Drax was silent for a few moments, then said, "Because, I see a good person and would consider it an honor if you would be my friend."

Calix stared at Drax, his lip quivering and his eye moist. Then he took Drax's hand and just held it for a few moments. He finally let it go and bent down to wipe the dirt and wrote, "I am your friend, Drax."

The simple gesture filled Drax with a comfort he had not felt since he had left Walter, and without thinking, he reached out and took Calix's hand back into his. "Do you mind if I hold your hand for a while? It has been so long since I've felt the touch of another in friendship."

Calix studied him for a moment, then squeezed his hand and smiled his awkward smile.

Drax squeezed his hand in return, "Thank you."

They sat like this for some time until Drax let go of Calix's hand and asked, "Do you have family here?"

Shaking his head, Calix wrote, "I am alone."

Drax reached up and put a hand to Calix's shoulder and said, "Then we are alike that way, too, for my mother and father no longer walk this land."

Calix made that strange sound again, although Drax could hear sadness and pain in it. Calix was about to write in the dirt again when Drax heard approaching footsteps coming from both directions. He glanced to his left and right and saw two Trith approaching from each direction.

Calix heard them too and looked up in alarm as the four Trith stopped a pace away, blocking both directions.

The tallest and most muscular Trith stepped forward and crossed his arms, smirking down at them sitting next to each other. "It looks like clubfoot Calix has found a little friend." He glanced at his associates and pointed down, "And a human, too; he can't find a Trith to be his friend so he has to resort to playing with a puny human."

The other Trith laughed and one of them kicked dirt at Drax and Calix. Drax closed his eyes in time, but Calix had been too slow and the dirt hit him square in the face. He spat it awkwardly out of his mouth and wiped at his good eye.

Drax looked up from where he sat. "I don't think Calix wants you here. Why don't you leave him be?"

The leader looked down at him and scowled. "How dare you talk directly to me? Your friends may be protected at the feast, but that doesn't mean you are way out here."

Drax figured the Trith was no more than twenty years old, but age didn't excuse bad manners. He pointed into the darkness, "Go on home and work on your manners."

The Trith's face turned red and his eyes narrowed in anger. He pulled out his sword and held it up. "I am going to kill you, human. And after I kill you, I will finally end Calix's miserable life."

One of the other Trith put his hand on the leader's arm and spoke, worry in his voice, "Don't, Uethgar, we are forbidden from harming the humans on order of the king."

Uethgar shook his friend's hand off. "The king is getting soft. He should not have thrown Kulweg's body into the pit after that Haissan cut him down. He should have ordered a full attack on the intruders."

His friends didn't look convinced, and backed away a step.

Drax motioned his head at the other Trith, "Listen to your friends, Uethgar, they are right."

It was as if something inside of Uethgar snapped, for he roared and swung his sword down onto Drax. But like always, Drax saw it moving as if in slow motion and calmly rolled to the side. When the sword struck the ground, he leapt to his feet, grabbed Uethgar's thumb and bent it backward until the sword slipped from his grip and fell to the dirt. He then released the thumb and spun around and swept Uethgar's legs out from under him, sending him to the ground with a heavy thud.

With a scream, Uethgar yelled out to his friends, "Kill him!"

But his friends only stared at Drax in wonder and a little fear, backing up a few steps with their arms up.

Uethgar climbed to his feet and rushed Drax, attempting to get him into a bear hug so he could crush his spine.

Drax slid feet-first between Uethgar's legs and as the Trith stumbled forward, Drax leapt in a backward summersault back over Uethgar's head, grabbing his neck as he did and letting his momentum pull the Trith face-forward to the ground. Drax slid around onto Uethgar's back and interlocked his arms around the Trith's thick neck, slowly increasing the pressure until he passed out.

Drax sat cross-legged on Uethgar's back and looked at the other three Trith.

One of them glanced down at Uethgar. "You killed him."

"No, I just put him into a deep sleep." He grabbed Uethgar's hair and pulled his head back. Uethgar snorted, then began snoring, and Drax gently laid his head back down. "See? Just sleeping. Now, why don't you three apologize to Calix for your bad manners, then carry your friend back home and put him to bed."

The three Trith looked at each other, then offered their hands to Calix, saying they were sorry. Calix shook each hand, his eyes wide with wonder.

Drax stood and stepped closer to Calix as the three Trith picked up Uethgar and carried him into the darkness.

Calix watched them until they were out of sight, then got to his feet and bent low to hug Drax, making his strange sounds, only this time the sounds carried feelings of gratitude. Finally, Calix straightened up and looked down with tears in his good eye.

Drax said, "You are very welcome," and then motioned to the ground, "now, let's continue our conversation, shall we?"

Calix grinned and sat back down and picked up the stick. He smoothed out the dirt and wrote, "Tell me about you."

Drax smiled. "I don't think you will believe me."

He then told Calix his entire life story.

Chapter 46

Tris stepped up to the Korpor and caressed the smooth grey skin of its face. *"I am glad to see you, but am quite irritated with you. Why did you not answer my repeated communication attempts?"*

"I am sorry, Master. I thought the Aleph Null had been killed and I fled to the forest, unsure what to do for the first time in my life."

Tris cocked his head. *"I forgive you, but you will never ignore me again, will you?"*

The Korpor lowered its head. *"No, Master."*

"Good, we have that out of the way. Now tell me, why did you think the Aleph Null was dead?"

"Our connection from the Proofing and the Ringing was severed. I could not sense the Aleph Null."

Tris studied the Korpor. *"You say the link was severed? Is it still gone?"*

"Yes, Master."

"Then why do you now track the Aleph Null?"

"Because I found him by accident in the Kuldragg Forest and was shocked that he still lived."

"You found him? Then why isn't he with you now?"

The Korpor glared at Tris, its eyes suddenly blazing with fury. *"A man who is not a man fought me and took the Aleph Null from me."*

Tris laughed, *"A man fought you? Please, you expect me to believe that a man bested you?"*

"He was faster and stronger than me, and my gaze did him no harm."

Tris thought for a few moments about who the man could be. Another variable had been added that he had not planned for. No matter, he would deal with this man when the time came. *"Do you have anything else to report?"*

The Korpor nodded. *"The Aleph Null travels with the Trith and Vringe, like before. But he also travels with the Haissen."*

Tris had been looking off into the trees but whipped his head around at this information. *"The Haissen now serve Sid? Impossible!"*

"It is true, Master."

Tris cursed and stomped a few paces away, his face twisted in fury. He turned to the Korpor. *"Are there any other surprises?"*

The Korpor shrugged. *"A small band of female humans joined up with him a short while back. That is all."*

Tris gritted his teeth. *"Do they wear grey clothing?"*

The Korpor nodded.

Tris swore again. He couldn't believe his Hunters of Reilen betrayed him to join with Sid. He would reserve a special pain for them when he caught them. *"How far away are they now?"*

"They are at the Trith Nation. I followed them and got as close as I could but

had to back off when the Trith patrols almost discovered me. They are a half-day to the southwest. I was biding my time until I could find a way to get him, for even if he is no longer the Aleph Null, I still want him."

Tris' eyes widened. *"What do you mean 'even if he is no longer the Aleph Null'?"*

The Korpor seemed uncomfortable. *"I no longer sense the Numbers inside of him. He seems like any normal human now."*

Tris took a step back, stunned by this information. Sid had lost his power of Numbers? How could that have happened? He looked up at the Korpor and snarled, *"Are you sure he no longer has the power of Numbers? There is no way you could be mistaken?"*

"He is free from the Numbers. I am positive."

Tris paced around the area, his hands clasped behind his back. The only reason he could think of for Sid losing his Numbers was that the giant creature that had hunted Sid had somehow taken them, as it seemed linked to the power of Black Numbers. But then why didn't it kill Sid?

Or maybe it had something to do with the obelisk. It was said to be the source of the Black Numbers. Maybe it somehow stripped Sid of his Numbers. But Tris didn't sense anything from the obelisk when he had gone back to the clearing.

Tris wanted to scream, hating not knowing what was going on. If this were true, then there was really no reason for him to hunt Sid any longer, as he was useless.

Or was he useless? Why were the Haissen and Hunters of Reilen serving Sid if his power of Numbers were gone? Unless, yes...unless he found some way that he could get them back. If that were the case, maybe the Haissen and Hunters were protecting him until he could regain his Numbers.

Maybe there was hope still for Tris to get the secrets of the Black Numbers. He could capture Sid as planned, which would be easy now that Sid didn't have his Numbers, and take him back to Obsidian's cave where he could not escape and wouldn't need to be guarded.

Whereas before, in the Srithian Wood, Tris had made the mistake of thinking all he needed to do was rip the Black Numbers from Sid's mind, this time he would slowly delve through Sid's mind, as there was a chance his secrets to the Black Numbers were a part of his metaphysical makeup. If that turned out to not be the case, then Tris would consider helping Sid get his Numbers back, but only long enough for Tris to examine the entire Black Numbers schema intact inside Sid to see how it was structured. Then, once he was sure he had what he needed, Tris would rid himself of Sid once and for all.

Now that he had control of the Korpor again, Tris could use its location to travel instantly via the portal equation to where it was, which made things so much easier now.

Tris felt confident this was a good plan. He turned back to the

Korpor. "*I need you to pinpoint Sid's exact location within the Trith Circle. I will stay away with my companion, who is very important to me, as I need her abilities for what is to come, until you can send me his exact coordinates.*"

The Korpor stared at him, then said, "*It will be very difficult for me to enter the Trith Circle.*"

"*I do not care how difficult it will be, just do it, and do not fail me. When you locate Sid, notify me immediately and I will order my armies to attack the Trith to create a diversion.*"

The Korpor nodded and faded away into the forest.

Tris called out, "Obsidian, you may come out now."

She appeared next to him, looking around uncertainly.

Tris patted her arm. "You need not fear my pet Korpor."

Obsidian looked at him. "I do not like that creature."

"Well, it won't bother you while I am around. We are close to our quarry, but things have changed slightly. The Korpor will track down the Aleph Null's exact location and send it to me so I can transport us directly there."

"I can do this for us. Why don't we kill the Korpor? That would be much more fun."

Tris smiled. "You will not harm it. I still need its special set of skills. Speaking of skills, I am feeling in need of yours. Let's go back to our chamber."

Obsidian instantly sidled up to him and wrapped him in her arms. They appeared in her chamber and as she dropped down to her knees, he sent out a command to the Korpor, "*Make sure you tell me if anything changes with Sid.*"

The voice of the Korpor filled his mind as Obsidian enveloped him with her mouth, "*Yes, Master.*"

Chapter 47

With practiced ease, Glaub created the portal equation. It swirled in front of the soldiers as he turned to them. "Let me ensure this exits where I want it to, then I'll come back."

The soldiers eyed the swirling colors with fear and anxiety.

Glaub stepped through the portal and appeared in a square in the forest paved with stones. He looked around and saw a water well in the center. This stone square was all that was left of the foundation of a house he and his father had built here in the Muldragg Forest. There was a similar foundation in the Kuldragg Forest where he and his father had also lived for a long time many years ago. He had not visited that one since he had gone out on his own.

Glaub bent down and ran his fingers along the stone he was standing on and still felt the power of Black Numbers deep within it, pulsing with energy. He had chosen this location to arrive via his portal because he knew the trees of the forest would not have reclaimed it, making it safe to exit the portal without worrying about stepping into a tree.

If he remembered right, the Trith Nation was only a day or two southeast of here. He'd considered opening his portal directly in the Trith holding building, a place he had visited long ago, but he didn't think it was advisable knowing the Trith's penchant for instant violence against intruders. So the stone foundation was as close as he could safely get to the Trith Circle while keeping his men safe. He surveyed the area and didn't sense anyone, so he stepped back through the portal and reappeared back at the camp. A few of the soldiers swore when he reappeared, startled even though they knew he was coming back.

Charly stepped forward. "Everything alright?"

Nodding, Glaub glanced at each of the men. "Are you sure you want to do this? You can still choose to return to Urgaer. I honestly will not mind." When none of the men spoke, Glaub pointed at the portal. "Lead your horses through one at a time and when you arrive, keep walking forward to give the next man room. If you are ready, then I will lead, followed by Charly, then each of you in our standard marching order."

Everyone nodded with serious expressions on their faces.

Glaub led his horse through and arrived at the foundation, quickly leading his horse into the woods.

Charly arrived with his horse, followed by each of the men and their horses. Captain Shaw was the last to arrive and when his horse cleared the portal, Glaub casually dismantled the equation and the swirling air popped and disappeared.

Glaub pointed to the southwest. "We will head out in that direction. The Trith Nation should only be a couple days away. We will make camp some distance from the Trith until I figure out what I need to do regarding the Aleph Null."

The trees grew too thickly together to ride so they had to lead their horses through the forest, picking their way carefully over fallen trees and into and out of shallow gullies. Even when the ground was level, they had to lead the horses around tree after tree, unable to travel in a straight line. By nightfall they had only traveled a league and were all tired. They set up camp in a small clearing and set two rotating guards.

The next morning, as they sat around the fire, one of the guards suddenly yelled out in alarm. Swords were pulled and defensive positions taken as the soldiers prepared for a possible attack.

Glaub turned to see a beautiful woman standing at the edge of their camp. She was surrounded by five very capable-looking young men and women, and by her side stood a girl of no more than twelve or thirteen years of age.

He motioned for his soldiers to stand down as he approached the strange people. Then, with a start, he realized he was looking at Zranh. He had come across the race ages ago and had spent an entire summer with them. During that time, he had learned that their mythical reputation as assassins was incorrect and unwarranted. In fact, they had been a warm and friendly people once he had been accepted into their camp. But he had not run across them in a thousand years or more.

Glaub stopped a pace from the Zranh and bowed deeply with his hand over his heart. The Zranh didn't respond as they studied him with hard eyes. He straightened up and looked directly at the beautiful woman who was obviously the leader. "I am honored to meet the Zranh again. You are welcome in our camp."

The woman's eyes widened a little at the mention of their race and a small smile creased her mouth. "We have been watching you and your men. What is your purpose here?"

Glaub knew that Zranh respected honesty and privacy above all else, so he said, "We search for the Aleph Null."

The woman's eyes grew wider, showing she knew about the Aleph Null, which was an interesting development. Whether they meant the Aleph Null harm or not was the question, so he asked, "You know of the Aleph Null, it seems. Do you intend him harm? Because if you do, then we may have a problem."

She studied him intently for long moments, then seemed to come to a decision. Her posture relaxed a little, "We are friends of the Aleph Null. It seems that your intent is not to harm him either, is that correct?"

"Yes, it is."

She stepped forward with her hand out, "My name is Melinda, and this is my Quadrant."

Glaub shook her hand firmly. "My name is Glaub," he pointed behind him, "and these are my friends, but don't let their appearance worry you."

Melinda smiled, and he thought she was the most beautiful woman he had ever met.

He held his hand wide, "Please, join us for a while."

Melinda stepped forward, her Zranh never leaving her side.

Glaub motioned for her to sit by the fire and he sat across from her. "So tell me how the Zranh and Aleph Null know of each other?"

She was silent for a while, as if deciding how much to tell him. Finally, she put her hands out to warm them over the fire and said, "I have known Sid, that's the Aleph Null's name, for some time now. I traveled with him and our friends from Yisk up through the great plains. We were pursued by some very," she paused briefly before saying, "unpleasant people. We got split up early this spring and I'm trying to catch up with them again."

Glaub was intrigued even more. One of his goals was to try and get a sense of the Aleph Null's character, and this first indication was positive, so he raised an eyebrow as he looked at her and said, "He must be a virtuous person for the Zranh to count him as a friend."

Melinda nodded as she rubbed her hands together. "He is one of the best people I've ever known."

"I've yet to make his acquaintance."

She studied him intently. "Why are you interested in Sid, then?"

Glaub sensed no duplicity in her, so he asked, "Have you ever heard of the Oblate?"

She nodded, her eyes narrowing.

"I was temporarily a Blue Robe and…"

Melinda jumped to her feet, her blades out, glinting in the light as she glared across the fire at him.

He put up his hands, "Please, let me finish. I am no longer a part of the Oblate, and I only was before so I could gather intelligence on the rumors I had been hearing about the new Aleph Null. Believe me when I tell you that I plan no harm to Sid if he truly is the honorable person you say he is."

Melinda slowly sat back down, her knives no longer in her hands. "You are going to judge him?"

He nodded, "In a way, yes."

"Why do you believe you must do this?"

Glaub took a deep breath and exhaled slowly. It seemed he was telling a lot of people lately who he secretly was, and he was not sure why he kept doing it. He considered Melinda for a few moments, then decided to tell her the whole truth even though he had just met her. "Because I am like him."

Melinda cocked her head. "What do you mean?"

"I am an Aleph Null, too."

She laughed, and when he didn't join in with her, she stopped, her face showing disbelief. Finally, she said, "That is impossible. Sid is *the* Aleph Null. There can't be more than one."

"Why do you say that? Why must there be only one Aleph Null?"

"Because, well, I just assumed the Aleph Null was a singular name for a specific person only."

Glaub smiled. "I can see why you might assume that."

Melinda regarded him with some fear. She put her hands back toward the fire. "From what Sid said, the Oblate has been searching for thousands of years for the Aleph Null. How did they not know you were an Aleph Null when you were in their very organization?"

"Because I chose to hide my identity."

Melinda's eyes narrowed. "I know from experience that the Oblate has spies everywhere and the new Black Robe is exceptionally powerful and cruel. How could you just walk into the center of the Oblate and become a Blue Robe without being caught?"

Glaub shrugged. "The members of the Oblate are nothing but children playing politics, and the new Black Robe is nothing more than a teenager who has some small power of Numbers. He is no threat to me."

Melinda smirked. "You are awfully sure of yourself for someone not much older than Sid."

This time, Glaub laughed with genuine humor. He put up his hand when she grew angry. "I'm sorry, I am not laughing at you."

Not looking mollified, Melinda said, "Then why are you laughing like an idiot?"

His laughter trailed away, though he couldn't wipe the smile away as he said, "When you said I was not much older than Sid, I couldn't help but laugh. You see, I was already old when the kingdoms of this land were born."

Melinda looked at him like he was insane.

"It's alright if you don't believe me. Although I should mention that except for my friends here, you are the first person I've confided that truth to in hundreds of years."

"And why did you do this?"

Glaub instantly felt the humor of the situation disappear, the familiar emptiness returning to dwell inside of him. He felt tired as he put his own hands out to the fire. "Maybe I am a good judge of character. Or maybe I am just tired of hiding from everyone."

Melinda was quiet for a long time as she stared into the flames beneath her hands. No one spoke in the camp; it was as if everyone held their breath. Finally, Melinda looked up and whispered, "I believe you."

They sat without speaking, warming their hands over the fire, when Glaub glanced at her. "You know, even though we've just met, strangely, I feel like I've known you for a long time already."

She looked confused, her eyebrows lowered and her forehead creased as she studied him.

"What's wrong?"

Melinda lowered her eyes. "Nothing is wrong. It's just that I have a sudden and strange feeling that I know you, too. I can't explain it."

Glaub shook his head, trying to clear his thoughts. Something had happened between him and this strange woman he had only just met, but it seemed natural, as if he had been meant to meet her. He heard someone cough behind him, which brought him back to the here-and-now. He smiled. "We appear to have the same destination; would you care to travel with us?"

Melinda hesitated only briefly before nodding.

"Good. Are you and your Quadrant hungry? We have plenty of food."

"We accept your hospitality. Thank you." She motioned her fellow Zranh to sit around the fire. The young girl stepped over to her, gazed around at the rough-looking men and pushed closer against Melinda.

Glaub noticed and moved around the fire until he was closer and winked at her. "You don't have to worry about them. They look mean but are all pretty good guys. In fact, my friend Charly over there, the one with only one hand, is probably more scared of you than you are of him."

The girl looked over at Charly and giggled softly. "Why does he only have one hand?"

Melinda hushed her, "Eithes, that isn't polite."

Glaub leaned in and whispered conspiratorially, "He got clumsy one day and a horse stepped on it."

Eithes made a face. "That's disgusting."

"He doesn't have many friends. Would you consider going over and saying hi to him?"

She hesitated and looked up at Melinda, who nodded, so she stood up and shyly approached Charly.

Glaub watched as she tugged hesitantly on his shirt. Charly turned his head and smiled when he saw her. She said something and he nodded, pointing down at the bedroll he was trying to tie with his one hand. Eithes bent down and put her finger against the string and Charly deftly used his fingers to carefully loop it into a knot, then used his teeth and fingers to pull it tight beneath her finger. He said something and Eithes giggled. Charly stood up and walked to the next bedroll and she helped him roll it up, laughing at something else he said.

Glaub turned back to see Melinda smiling openly as she watched. "Thank you. You are very perceptive and kind."

"Charly is a good guy and makes friends very easily."

Melinda pointed at one of a couple dozen small birds that were sizzling on sticks over the fire. "Do you mind?"

"By all means, please."

She motioned for her Zranh to take one each, which they did, quickly tearing pieces of meat off and popping them into their mouths, blowing air with their mouths open to cool the hot meat before chewing it. After a while, Melinda turned to Glaub. "So if you are an Aleph Null, and have been alive for so many years, why do you care about Sid being an Aleph Null?"

"Because, my father has…I mean, *had* been vigilant over the past few thousand years to ensure no new Aleph Null were born. He feared what such a person with the power of Black Numbers might do to the peoples of the lands."

Melinda said, "*Had* been?"

Glaub looked down briefly, "He recently passed away."

"I am sorry. I also just lost my grandmother. It is not easy to lose someone so close, is it?"

He looked up at her and grimaced. "No, it isn't. I am sorry for your loss."

They sat in silence for a few moments, then Melinda asked, "What are your plans for Sid once you meet him?"

"To be honest, my original plan was to judge him – to send my Numbers into him to verify his character. I will still do it, but I think he will be worthy to have the power of Black Numbers without using them to harm others."

Melinda turned to him. "And what would you do if you found him to be unworthy of such power?"

Glaub hesitated, then sighed. "To be honest, I had always left such things to my father. But I guess I would have to strip him of his Numbers."

Melinda gasped. "You could do such a thing?"

He nodded. "It is better than what my father would have done. He would have ended Sid's life without hesitating."

"Why would your father have done such a thing?"

Glaub stared hard into her eyes. "Because, when he was young, he fell victim to his own power and almost destroyed the entire land and everyone who lived in it. He barely came to his senses in time and every day after, he vowed that no other person would gain such power."

Melinda asked, "What about you?"

"I proved to my father that I would never harm another with my power of Numbers, and I never broke that promise."

Eric stopped by Glaub. "Sir, we are ready to depart at your word."

Glaub glanced at him. "Thank you, Eric."

He stood up, as did Melinda.

"I look forward to continuing this conversation, Melinda."

"We will stay in the woods and warn you if we see any threats."

"Thank you. Will I see you when we stop for the night?"

Melinda nodded and disappeared in front of him, her Zranh following suit almost immediately.

Glaub blinked several times, whistling under his breath. He had witnessed the Zranh perform this feat long ago, but had forgotten just how amazing they were. He heard Charly calling Eithes' name and turned to see Charly spinning slowly in a circle as he looked for her.

He called his name and Charly looked up, worry in his eyes.

"Charly, she joined her fellow Zranh but will return this evening."

Charly looked at him, confused, so Glaub motioned him over. "Charly, do you know what a Zranh is?"

His friend shook his head, no.

Glaub called his men over, and when they were all gathered, addressed them. "Gentlemen, those people we just met are the Zranh."

A few of the men gulped loudly as they looked fearfully around.

"They are our friends, so let's treat them as such."

Charly spoke, "How did they disappear like that? Can they do what you do?"

"No, Charly. The Zranh have the ability to move through differing states of time, so to speak. They can enter a frequency of time so we appear to them to be barely moving."

Captain Shaw nodded. "I have heard old tales that they are assassins who are never seen, but I never thought they truly existed."

Glaub stood. "Those tales are not true. Yes, they move unseen, but they won't harm us unless we give them reason to. Believe me when I say that if they wanted us dead, you would never know what happened."

His men looked around the area.

"You won't see them, so stop looking for them. Now, let's get going."

The men quickly finished preparing to leave and were soon moving through the forest.

As Glaub walked, he wondered at the strange forces at work around this new Aleph Null.

Chapter 48

Trith were certainly a dedicated race, Sid thought, shielding his eyes against the rising sun as he peered through the window at the dozen or more Trith training in the large square across from their building. They practiced all manner of fighting techniques, from hand-to-hand combat, to sword and knife fighting. He had awakened to the sounds of steel-on-steel impacts well before the sky had begun to lighten and had tried unsuccessfully to go back to sleep until he realized he might as well get up.

He turned and saw that Agnes still slept soundly, her brown hair stuck up at odd angles, yet she still looked beautiful to him. Across the large room were the Hunters of Reilen. They had set up a separate sleeping area away from everyone, although they were starting to be more friendly as of late, especially Doris and Gee. Doris had begun sleeping with Nik at night, the sounds of their energetic lovemaking last night causing Tulman, Writhgarth and Gee to yell out in unison for them to be quiet. Nik and Doris had giggled under their bear pelt, but had been relatively quiet after that. The low moans from Doris had caused Agnes to crawl on top of Sid, though, and they had proceeded to make love, too. It was at this point that Tulman and Writhgarth had both muttered something unintelligible and left the building, followed by Gee.

Sid smiled at the memory and saw Gee approaching him from across the room.

She smiled as she came to a stop next to him. "It seems you had some fun last night."

Sid blushed as he nodded.

"Don't feel embarrassed. Sex is good for the body and mind."

Sid turned away, uncomfortable talking about this with his aunt. He spoke while looking out the window, "What are your plans for today?"

She stepped up to the window and looked out. "I don't know. Maybe I can talk the Trith into letting me train with them."

Sid glanced at her. "You would go against a Trith, even if it is just practice?"

Gee smiled. "Of course. It would be good to see how they fight. Maybe I'll learn a few things."

He grunted as he looked back out the window, "I could think of better ways to learn than going against one of them. They are so different from Crowdal in every way."

"Your friend Crowdal is definitely unique. I've met a few Trith in my life and never have I met one as gentle and kind as him."

Sid nodded. "This has become especially apparent after coming here. He really is out of place here and I feel bad I asked him to bring me here."

Gee turned away from the Trith outside. "What is it you hope to find here?"

"That's the thing, I have no idea. The Black Manuscript didn't give any details."

Curious, Gee asked, "What exactly does the manuscript say?"

"*Trith, Circle, Zranh, Raith,* and *Death.*"

Gee was quiet as she thought about what he said, then she asked, "What if it doesn't mean anything specific?"

"What do you mean?"

"Just that: what if it was something as simple as directions for where you had to go, but when you got there, maybe it would just work itself out?"

Sid considered this idea and it made a certain kind of sense. He had been wracking his brain over those five words for the past few fortnights without getting any closer to knowing what they meant. Now he was with the Trith in their city, which they called a Circle. Two of the hints had to do with being where he was right now. Maybe things *would* be revealed to him. He shrugged, "Maybe you are right, Aunt Gee. Thanks for talking it through with me. I don't want to keep you from your practice, though. Why don't you go on out? I'll be fine."

Gee smiled and hugged him briefly, then turned and left the building.

He looked out the window and watched her walk fearlessly up to the Trith. She said something and they laughed at her. She said something else and they turned angry, then one of the Trith rudely gestured for her to enter the training square.

"What's going on?"

Sid turned to see Tulman standing behind him.

"Gee has asked the Trith to let her train with them. They don't seem too happy with her request."

Tulman's eyes glinted and he turned away, heading for the door, speaking as he went, "Come on, let's go watch."

He held the door open and Sid quickly followed him outside. Two Haissen joined him and had, in fact, never left his side since they had entered the Trith Circle. They quickly crossed the street to the training square, where Gee stood calmly in the center waiting for a Trith to join her.

The Trith argued amongst themselves before one of them pulled his tunic over his head and tossed it to the ground as he marched over to Gee. He stood more than twice her height, contracting his chest muscles repeatedly as he stared down contemptuously at her. Each of his arms were almost twice as thick as Gee's whole body, his biceps bulging like two boulders.

Sid turned to Tulman, "What is she doing? She's going to get killed."

But Tulman just smiled as he stared at her, his eyes glinting with what looked like pride. "I think you underestimate her like the Trith do. Size does not matter; fighting style does." He pointed, "See how the Trith flexes his muscles? He is trying to intimidate her and show off to his friends at the same time. He has no idea who he faces."

Sid looked up at Tulman. "What do you mean? Do you know Gee?" He nodded, "Aye, I do."

Before Sid could ask anything more, the Trith bellowed and charged Gee. She stood perfectly still, looking relaxed as the giant ran at her.

The Trith swung a massive fist at her but she ducked just enough for it to miss, then danced to the left, still keeping her hands at her side.

The Trith swung another fist at her and it was obvious that the idea of practice fighting was much different for the Trith than for other races, for if his fist had connected, Gee would have likely been killed.

She moved quickly around the circle, getting close enough to lure multiple punches out of the Trith and soon he was sweating and breathing hard as he expended energy chasing her. He finally stopped and yelled angrily, "Stand and fight you cow…," but before he could finish the sentence, Gee ran forward so quickly that even from this distance, Sid barely saw her move. She jumped up at the last moment and punched the Trith with a speed and strength Sid couldn't believe, crushing his nose with a spray of blood.

Gee dropped lightly to the ground and casually stepped back a few paces as the Trith roared in pain, putting his hands to his bloodied nose. Then he screamed with rage, dropped his hands and charged her with murder in his eyes.

Gee dodged to the side and as the Trith tried to change direction, she juked in the other direction and ran around him, then leapt on his back, scrambled up the Trith's spine and viciously clapped her open palms against his ears with a loud smack. The Trith roared again and raised his hands to his ears. When he did, Gee wrapped her arms around his corded neck and locked them together, squeezing with all her strength.

The Trith was dazed by the combination of the strike to his nose and crack to his ears and couldn't react in time to stop her from putting him in the choke hold. He struggled, but with no real purpose, his eyes looking glassy and blank until he eventually sank to one knee, then to the other. His face turned bright red and his eyes bulged, then he fell face-first to the dirt. Gee released her hold just before he hit the ground and leapt from his back to land lightly on her feet. She turned to face the Trith along the edges, breathing only slightly harder than usual.

The area was silent for a long time before an older Trith approached Gee and stopped in front of her. They stared at each other for many moments, then he held his hand out as he glanced down at the Trith lying unconscious in the dirt. "I have been the hand-to-hand trainer here for three decades and I have never seen such fighting skill. Like most of us,

Oleg thought himself unbeatable. You have taught him, and us, a very important and necessary lesson. We cannot rely only on our superior strength and size." He turned to the other Trith. "I want each and every one of you to remember this fight and never forget that you *can* be defeated. We have only trained against each other for too long and that weakens us as fighters." He pointed to Gee, "This Hunter of Reilen has shown us that we do have weaknesses and we must thank her for that."

The Trith were silent for a few moments, then they all turned to her and half-bowed, although some still showed anger.

The trainer turned fully to Gee. "We honor you and thank you for this lesson."

Gee bowed to him. "Thank you…"

"Pughall."

Gee smiled, "Thank you, Pughall. You honor an old woman like me."

Pughall laughed, deep and loud. "Old lady…right. You and your Hunters are welcome to train with us any time."

Gee bowed again, "We will take you up on that." She turned and approached Sid and Tulman. As she did, the trainer bellowed out, "Alright, Julwedell and Ruodal, front and center."

Sid looked over his aunt's shoulder as two Trith began circling each other with arms out while the trainer dragged the unconscious Trith out of the circle. He looked back to his aunt as she came to a stop and said, "That was amazing, Aunt Gee."

She smiled at him and as she turned her head to Tulman, she blushed slightly, forgetting Sid was even there.

Sid looked back and forth between them then backed away. He heard Tulman say something softly to her, but didn't hear what was said as he quickly made his way down the street to look for Crowdal. There was a history between Gee and Tulman he felt he had no right to be a part of.

Sid found himself walking without really paying attention until he realized he was lost. He was about to turn around, when he saw Crowdal open the door of a grand home guarded by many Trith and step down to the street. He didn't see Sid at first, looking lost in thought.

Sid ran forward and yelled his name, but was stopped by the guards.

Crowdal looked up and smiled tiredly when he saw it was Sid, waving the guards back.

Sid stepped forward and said, "How are you doing? I've not seen you since early last evening."

"I'm sorry I have not been able to spend much time with you, Sid."

"Is everything alright?"

Crowdal shook his head sadly. "No, it is not. My mother took a turn for the worse last night."

Sid had no idea Crowdal's mother was that ill. "I'm so sorry,

Crowdal. Is there anything I can do?"

"Actually, I was just on my way to get you. My mother has asked to speak with you."

"Me? Why me?"

His friend smiled through his pain. "Because I told her all about you and that you traveled here to try and get your Numbers back. She wants to hear your whole story in the hope she may be able to help."

Sid realized his mouth was hanging open, so he snapped it closed. "Thank you. I would be honored to meet with your mother, but I don't want to tire her out or cause any problems."

"She asked for you, Sid."

"Alright, when does she want to see me?"

Crowdal motioned to the building he had just exited, "Right now, actually. Follow me, and don't make any quick movements. The Trith Council is with her inside and are on edge with her failing health. They don't want you in there, but she overrode them."

Sid widened his eyes. "She can do that?"

Crowdal genuinely smiled this time. "Sid, my mother is the true ruler of the entire Trith Nation. Her word is law."

Sid gulped and felt himself start to tremble when Crowdal put a hand on his shoulder and leaned down. "Sid, it will be alright. Just be yourself and tell the truth. Speak only to my mother and ignore the rest of the Council."

Sid nodded and followed Crowdal to the tall door. A guard opened it and bowed his head to Crowdal as they passed through. The inside of the house was open and airy, filled with sunlight beaming through two large windows. A bed had been made up by the windows, which was surrounded by seven Trith, with Uuthdal at the head, holding the hand of Crowdal's mother, who was propped up with many pillows.

She saw him as she looked between two of the Trith and smiled, motioning him to come closer with a shaking hand.

Sid stepped closer to the bed, but the Trith were blocking him from getting through, making him feel like a child trying to get past a group of adults. Then Sid heard her speak sharply, "Move out of the way and let my guest through."

The two Trith in front of him looked back to Veronnu then down to Sid in surprise and irritation, shifting to the side begrudgingly.

Sid stepped up to the bed, but his head barely reached the platform. Then Crowdal was next to him with a chair, motioning Sid to climb up. Sid had to jump to get enough leverage to pull himself up onto it. When he turned to sit, he was eye-level with Veronnu.

She smiled at him and said with a shaky voice, "Thank you for coming to see me, Sidoro."

He smiled shyly, shifting to get comfortable. "Thank you, Queen Veronnu."

She made a tsk-tsk sound, then said, "You must just call me Veronnu."

An angry murmur rose behind Sid and she glared at the Trith behind him. Sid glanced behind him as she said, "You will be quiet or I will ask you all to leave."

The Trith quickly quieted down, though a few still gave Sid venomous looks.

Veronnu nodded, "Now, Sidoro, please tell me why you are here."

Sid felt himself relax a little, and at a nod from Crowdal, told her his whole story. At the part where Crowdal saved his life from the roadside criminals outside of Oiro, Uuthdal grinned at his son and said, "You always did like to play with your opponents, son."

Crowdal grinned back at his father, and Sid saw Veronnu's eyes sparkling with love for her husband and son.

When Sid got to the moment when they met Boren and Athgar in the woods, Veronnu looked troubled. She turned to one of the Council members, "Has there been any word about them?"

An older female Trith with white hair and a wrinkled face shook her head. "We have heard nothing in almost a year."

Veronnu cursed, and Crowdal leaned down, explaining to Sid in a soft voice, "Athgar and Boren were members of the Council. Per tradition, Trith often go on journeys in search of a sword event that defines their lives. But they should have returned by now, so something bad may have happened to them."

Veronnu nodded agreement with Crowdal, then asked Sid to continue with his account.

Sid quickly described their capture by the Masteen, the death of his grandmother and their escape with the help of Agnes. Veronnu's eyes hardened at the cruelty of Mrs. Wessmank's death but didn't interrupt.

Sid briefly talked about their journey across the great plains and climbing the shaft up the cliff, and even one of the Council members drew in a breath at his description of the climb. At this, Crowdal turned to the Trith and grinned, "Nothing like doing a few thousand pullups in the morning."

They chuckled behind Sid and he waited a few moments before he continued. When he described the battle in the Srithian Wood between Crowdal and the Masteen Vorn Maghuur, Uuthdal stared at Crowdal in awe, and the Council members murmured in appreciation.

Uuthdal put his hand on Crowdal's shoulder and said, "First you defeat three Haissen, and then the Masteen Vorn Maghuur himself? I wouldn't believe it was true if anyone but the Aleph Null had said it." He turned to Sid to explain. "The Masteen has almost mythical stature among the Trith, and he has killed a score of Trith who have sought him out for their personal sword event. Only one Trith ever came close to defeating him. Her partner witnessed the fight and reported that although she cut the Masteen's face very badly, she eventually lost her life to him, too." He turned to look at Crowdal again. "Son, your four sword events will go into our lore as the greatest set of events of all time."

The Council members all enthusiastically agreed.

Uuthdal beamed with pride, then leaned forward until he was almost touching Crowdal's forehead with his own, his eyes damp. "I am proud of you, son."

Crowdal's own eyes grew damp and he lowered his head once. "Thank you, father. But what Sid has accomplished surpasses anything I have done." He turned to Sid. "Complete the story of the Srithian Wood."

Sid took a deep breath and told of his battle against the Black Robe, the Korpor, and how his mother sacrificed her life to give him the power of Blood Numbers to defeat his enemies. At this, Veronnu put her hand over his. "I am sorry, Sidoro. Your mother sounds like she was a woman of greatness and dedication, someone I would have been honored to meet."

Sid wiped his wet cheek and nodded, then continued his story with his battle against the Unnamed One and how he cast it into the unknown dimension inside the obelisk, but it ripped his power of Numbers from his mind at the very moment it disappeared into the obelisk. He finished by repeating the five words from the Black Manuscript.

Veronnu and Uuthdal both glanced at each other before turning to Sid in amazement. Veronnu turned to Crowdal and whispered, "Is this all true?"

"Every word, mother. Sid didn't even tell you how he fulfilled a two-thousand-year-old Haissen prophecy and healed their race from a sickness that had been killing them for generations."

The king and queen again looked at Sid, then both bowed their heads slightly. "We are honored that our son Crowdal travels with you and calls you a friend, Aleph Null."

Sid didn't feel like he deserved their admiration and respect and Crowdal nudged him, so he quickly said, "The honor is mine." Then he added, "I could have died many times over had it not been for your son; I owe him my life and consider him my best friend."

Their faces filled with pride as they looked at Crowdal.

Crowdal put his hand on Sid's shoulder again. "Do any of you know what those five words Sid read in the Black Manuscript might mean?"

Veronnu was quiet as she gazed at the ceiling in thought. Then she put her shaking hand out for Uuthdal. "Would you get the history book?"

Uuthdal immediately left and thumped up the stairs. Sid could hear his heavy footsteps on the floor above, then he came back down the stairs and entered the room with a thick, leather-bound book, handing it to Veronnu.

She flipped through the old and cracked pages, scanning down them with a shaky finger before moving on to the next. Finally, she found what she was looking for and looked up at Sid. "We have had a few prognosticators in the many thousands of years we have been here in this forest, and we wrote down the projections that came from their trances. I have read these many times in my life, but have found them more interesting the older I've gotten. As you spoke, I remembered there was one of them I hadn't ever understood before, but now it may actually make sense."

She lowered her eyes to the book and read, "The silent, ill-formed one living in darkness shall see the thread that leads from the numberless one; this ill-formed one will lead him to the one who goes where the ones who move inside our world cannot go."

She looked up at Sid, her eyes wide. "A Trith lives among us named Calix who is…ill-formed. He may be the one you seek. As for the rest, I still do not understand it."

Sid felt excitement race through him and Veronnu saw it. "What is it, Sidoro?"

He smiled. "The thread refers to the stream of power that connects me to the obelisk. I think it is made from Numbers and it exits my head here," he touched the back of his head. "It always leads in the same direction, toward the Srithian Wood."

Crowdal spoke up now, excited. "And the ones who move inside our world must be the Zranh. Melinda!" he exclaimed.

Sid grinned and slapped Crowdal's arm in his excitement.

Veronnu smiled at their obvious friendship. She motioned at one of the Council members. "Go and fetch Calix and bring him here."

Sid heard footsteps and a door open and close.

Veronnu suddenly lay back against her pillows and closed her eyes, looking exhausted.

Uuthdal leaned forward and took her hand in his. "You need to rest now."

She opened her eyes a crack and smiled weakly. "I will be able to sleep the long sleep soon enough. Do not rush me."

Uuthdal chuckled, "I wouldn't dream of it, woman."

With a small smile, Veronnu turned to Crowdal. "Tell me, son. Are you happy with your life now?"

Crowdal took her other hand and spoke softly, "Yes, mother. I have finally found my place in this world."

She whispered, "I am so glad."

Sid felt tears falling down his cheeks again and he really wanted to let the three of them have some private time, but as he started to slide off the chair, Veronnu shook her head. "Please stay. You are family now."

Uuthdal drew in a sharp breath, as did Crowdal and the Council members behind him.

Sid wasn't sure why the reaction was so strong. Then Veronnu turned to the Council members. "Yes, I said it and meant it. From this moment forward, Sidoro is of my family, with all the rights and privileges that go with that."

Sid glanced at Crowdal in confusion, but his friend shook his head for Sid to remain silent.

The door opened behind him and Sid turned to see a Trith approach with his head bowed down, his shoulder leaning to the left. Then from behind him stepped Drax, who glared aggressively at Sid.

Veronnu motioned them forward and smiled. "Ah, Calix. It is good to see you."

Calix lifted his head and tried to smile, and Sid's eyes widened at seeing the deformed mouth and eye pulling the skin of his face in unnatural directions.

Veronnu leaned a little to look at Drax. "And why are you here? I didn't request you."

The Trith Council member who had fetched them apologized, "He would not leave Calix's side, even when I threatened him. I figured it was more important to get Calix here as soon as possible. Would you like us to detain him now?"

Veronnu studied Drax carefully, then shook her head. "That will not be necessary. He is protecting Calix, something none of you have ever tried doing. What is your name?"

"It is Drax, Queen Veronnu."

"You are welcome here, Drax. We will not harm Calix. In fact, Calix may be the only person who can help Sidoro."

Calix suddenly turned to look at Sid, his eye widening as he looked at the back of Sid's head. He then turned to look at something.

Sid smiled at him. "You see the thread that leads from my head and out through that wall, don't you?"

Calix turned his eye back to Sid and stared at him for many moments before nodding and making a strange noise with his mouth.

Drax stepped closer. "He said, 'Yes, Aleph Null'."

Veronnu looked at him in amazement. "You can understand Calix?"

Drax smiled. "I have spent the whole night talking with him and have come to understand that he speaks a complex and full language he has created. Since he can only make a few sounds, he uses them in intricate combinations along with emotion, tone, volume, and cadence. Calix is a genius and none of you have ever bothered to know that about him."

Calix smiled his strange smile and reached out to take Drax's hand.

Veronnu looked between the two of them, then chuckled. "I always suspected there was more to Calix than met the eye. Calix, please accept my sincere apology."

Calix made another set of sounds and Drax said, "He thanks you, Queen Veronnu."

Sid had watched all of this, feeling like he was missing a huge chunk of information.

Calix looked down to him and made a long series of noises.

Drax said, "He sees Numbers inside of you but they are like the dead that waver between this world and the spaces inside this world."

Sid stopped breathing. This was almost exactly what the Myrss had told him. He whispered, "Can you help me bring them back to life?"

Calix made a quick noise.

Drax smiled. "He says, 'maybe'."

Sid stood on the chair and faced Calix. "Thank you, Calix. I am in your debt."

Calix tried to grin, then slapped him on the shoulder playfully, which accidentally sent Sid tumbling from the chair. He made a strange noise and awkwardly bent down to help him up.

Sid laughed. "I'm alright."

Crowdal smiled down to Sid and spoke over his shoulder, "Mother, thank you for your help in figuring out it was Calix who we were searching for; we couldn't have done it without you."

When there was no reply, Crowdal looked back toward his mother and his smile faded when he saw her staring vacantly up at the ceiling, unmoving but with a small smile frozen on her face.

Chapter 49

Crowdal sat in the shade of the building across the street from the house he had grown up in, where his mother's prepared body now lay in repose. It had been the hardest two days of his life since she had died. He picked up a small dusty rock and absently stroked it with his thumb as he turned it in his hand and gazed up at the perfectly clear-blue sky. He still couldn't believe his mother was gone. One minute she had been full of life and the next she was dead.

Just like that.

Tears started to flow down his cheeks as an image of her from when he had been a little boy filled his mind. It had been a warm and sunny summer day, just like it was right now, and he had come into the house after playing with his best friends Rielissa and Dwimdal all morning, it being one of the few days off from sword practice that Trith children got each summer. His mother was in the kitchen baking bread and he stopped to peer over the counter as she pulled a tray of steaming loaves from the oven. As she placed them in front of him, his eyes had grown wide at the wonderful smell wafting toward him. His mother had smiled, and grabbing a knife, she had cut a thick slice, the loaf wiggling back and forth as she cut it because it was still so hot. She placed it on a plate with a thick dollop of butter in the middle and handed it to him with a wink, saying, "Don't tell your father or he will demand a hot slice right from the oven, too."

Wiping at his tears, Crowdal chuckled and cried at the same time as he remembered how he had kept that promise to his mother thinking at the time she had been serious. The chuckle faded away and he whipped the rock across the street in anger. Why did she have to die? He thought of Sid and cursed his friend for losing his power of Numbers, knowing he could have probably saved his mother with his mathematical powers. But as quickly as that thought came, he shook his head at his selfishness. It wasn't Sid's fault. It wasn't anyone's fault, just stupid fucking Fate that his mother had caught the wasting disease. He smiled at just thinking that curse word and the wallop he would have gotten from his mother if she had ever heard him use it.

Hearing footsteps, he turned his head and saw his friends coming down the street toward him, Sid and Agnes in the lead, followed by Writhgarth, Tulman, Nik, the Hunters of Reilen, and Drax and Calix. The Haissen strode a few paces behind everyone and Crowdal had to grin at the effort it must have taken Sid to get them to stay even that short distance back. He knew the Haissen might be a distraction – it was just like Sid to think of Crowdal first.

They came to a stop a pace away and Sid approached Crowdal alone, kneeling by him. He was silent for a moment and then softly asked,

"How are you holding up?"

Fresh tears fell down Crowdal's face and he had to struggle to keep his lips from trembling. Finally, he managed to say, "It's tough, Sid. So much tougher than I could have imagined."

Sid stood and leaned in to hug him. Crowdal hesitated at first, but then returned his friend's hug.

"I know it is, Crowdal, and you will hurt every day after this. But believe me when I say that the hurt is not a bad thing. It is all I have left of my mother and I will never let that pain go."

Crowdal nodded, the tears flowing freely now. "Thank you, Sid." He pulled back and wiped at his eyes and saw that Sid was openly crying, as well. Crowdal chuckled and when Sid looked at him questioningly, he shrugged and said, "I was just picturing your mom and my mom talking to each other in the afterworld, shaking their heads at their sons sitting here crying together."

Sid wiped his tears away and laughed, "I bet they are."

Crowdal squeezed Sid's shoulder and stood up, towering over his friend. "I suppose we should get inside before my father comes out looking for me." He turned to his friends. "Thank you all for coming like this. I really appreciate it."

Writhgarth stepped forward and held his hand out.

Crowdal bent low to grasp it and Writhgarth squeezed it hard.

"You are my friend, Crowdal. There is nowhere else I would want to be."

Tears started to fall again and Crowdal quickly wiped them away. "Thank you, Writhgarth." He looked up and nodded to everyone. "Now, let's get this over with." He turned and strode across the street. As he approached the door, the two Trith guards opened it for him with a solemn nod of their heads. Crowdal stepped through and into his house, stopping in the entryway to take a deep breath when he saw his mother resting on a raised platform in the middle of the main room, his father standing stoically next to her and talking to one of the Council members. When he saw Crowdal, he said something and the Council member glanced at Crowdal and nodded, before making his way further into the room to join the other fifteen or so high-ranking Trith who had gathered.

Crowdal took a deep breath, then walked over to his father and held out his hand, "Father."

Uuthdal glanced at his outstretched hand, then stepped forward and wrapped him in a tight bear hug, slapping his back hard, then put his mouth to Crowdal's ear and whispered, "Propriety be damned. This is my house and I loved your mother more than anything in this world and I know you felt the same about her."

Crowdal nodded and hugged his father back, holding him for a long time before they separated. They stood, almost touching noses, hands resting on one another's necks. Then Crowdal released his father and looked down at his mother. She looked completely at peace and very beautiful. Her hair was combed and she was still smiling, looking for all the world like she was just sleeping. He reached down and caressed her cheek, the skin soft but cold, then leaned down and whispered, "I love you, mother." He studied her face for a long time, committing every detail to memory, then caressed her cheek one final time before straightening up and nodding to his father, who made a signal with his hand.

Four of the Council members came forward, lifted the platform that his mother rested on and waited for Crowdal and his father to lead the way out of the house, then followed behind with his mother.

Crowdal stepped onto the street and blinked his eyes a number of times in the bright sun, then he and his father turned and walked side-by-side down the street until they reached the massive, unlit funeral pyre in the center square where every single Trith in the Circle gathered, all standing tall and wearing full battle gear.

As Crowdal and his father approached, every Trith turned and bowed low, staying in that position.

They stopped at the funeral pyre and turned to let the pall bearers set the platform down. Uuthdal then went to the front and Crowdal stepped to the rear and at a nod, Crowdal slipped his arms under his mother's legs and his father did the same under her shoulders and head. They both lifted as one, carefully climbed up the steps to the platform on top of the pyre and carefully laid her down, positioning her arms over her chest.

Crowdal stepped back but Uuthdal stayed with his head bowed as he stared at his wife. Crowdal waited patiently until his father lifted his head and, with a face streaked with tears, motioned for Crowdal to descend.

His father stayed at the top of the pyre and turned to address the assembled Trith, raising his voice to reach them all. "Veronnu, Queen of the Trith Nation, wife to Uuthdal, mother to Crowdal, and beloved to you all, we give you back to the great Trith Nation in the afterworld. May you look down upon us and guide us as you've always done." He then began to sing, his voice low but powerful, the words felt more than heard.

> *When this life ends and your sword is put away*
> *And battles once remembered fade from our memory*
> *The life we once loved begins again on a breeze*
> *That whispers your name in the first breath of spring*

Uuthdal's voice faded away and he stared up at the sky for a long time. Then he descended the steps and took the burning torch from its holder and set it to the flammable kindling at the base of the pyre.

The flames burned low at first, but then grew and spread quickly until Crowdal and everyone had to take a number of steps back from the raging inferno.

Crowdal watched the flames catch on his mother's clothing and he wanted to rush up there to pull her to safety, but he soon couldn't see her through the twisting fire and he knew she was truly gone. He stood by his father and they watched through the afternoon until the pyre finally collapsed upon itself and burned down to hot coals.

The sun was almost setting when Crowdal looked away from the coals and was startled to see Sid and his friends still standing behind him, along with the thousands of Trith. Everyone had been silent the whole time, a true testament to their respect for his mother.

Uuthdal lifted his head also and said in a loud voice, "Everyone…to the feast."

The Trith all raised their swords to the sky and shouted out, "Veronnu…Veronnu…Veronnu." Then they saluted Uuthdal and Crowdal before turning as one and marching out of the square.

Crowdal walked over to Sid and the group, feeling exhausted and not wanting to join in with the feast that was tradition after a major funeral. He tried to make things less dark by saying, "So, that was fun."

Writhgarth chuckled and said, "Trith," under his breath, as he had done many times before. But this time the word was tinged with respect and honor for his friend.

Sid looked up at Crowdal, "Should we go back to our sleeping quarters now?"

"No way. You are not only my guests, but my friends. And you are not going to make me go to this thing alone." He lifted his arm, "Come on, let's get drunk."

Uuthdal walked up and said, "Aye, I second that."

Crowdal smiled at his father, wondering if he would, indeed, actually get drunk tonight. He never had been much of a drinker, despite the reputation of the Trith and their almost legendary thirst for ale. As the king of the Trith, he took the responsibilities of ruling seriously and only drank on occasion.

His father clapped a hand on Crowdal's shoulder and they all started toward the celebration area where Trith were already laughing and toasting with full tankards of beer, while off to the side a pit the length of the square was covered with coals, the smell of cooking meat making even Crowdal's mouth water. He knew that underneath those coals there were probably three hundred deer that had been slowly cooking since that morning.

A full tankard of ale was slapped into his hand by his old friend Juldall, one of the few friends he had growing up.

Juldall raised his own tankard and clinked it to Crowdal's, "To your mother, Veronnu."

Crowdal nodded and took a deep pull from the ale. It was cold and refreshing, although true to Trith fashion, it tasted terrible. "Thank you,

Juldall. I'd like you to meet my friends." He proceeded to introduce him to Sid and everyone in the group, and Juldall greeted them all with a smile and handshake.

Crowdal took another sip of his ale, then heard a quiet voice behind him say, "I am so sorry for your loss, Crowdal."

He turned and looked into Rielissa's eyes and found he couldn't speak. He hadn't realized just how much he had missed her until he looked at her now. She was about two hand-spans shorter than he was, and while some considered her ordinary-looking, he thought she was beautiful and always had been. She gave off a sense of strength and independence that Crowdal had always admired.

"So, are you just going to stand there and stare at me all night like an idiot?"

Crowdal grinned and it was as if the two years they had been apart melted instantly away. He reached out and ruffled her hair, "Hey there, runt."

She knocked his hand away but her eyes danced with merriment as she said, "Stop that. You know I hate it when you do that!"

Crowdal dropped his hand and when he didn't move, she said, "Idiot. Fine, I'll hug *you*, then."

She stepped forward, wrapped her arms around his waist and squeezed him tightly with her head against his chest.

He was startled at first, but then returned her hug, resting his chin on the top of her head. "It's good to see you, Rielissa. It has been too long."

Rielissa pulled her head back and looked up at him, tears in her eyes. "I am sorry we are reuniting under these circumstances."

Pushing a strand of hair from her left eye, Crowdal nodded. "I still can't believe she is no longer here. It doesn't seem possible."

A tear ran down Rielissa's cheek and without thinking, Crowdal leaned down and kissed her. She was surprised at first, but then returned his kiss with warmth and love until they pulled apart and stared into each other's eyes. Then Crowdal remembered his friends and turned his head to see them standing a few paces away but no longer looking at him, giving him his privacy. He grinned at Rielissa, "Come on, I want you to meet my friends." He took her hand and led her over to them and they must have heard him, for they turned to face him.

"Everyone, this is one of my oldest friends, Rielissa."

She punched his arm, "Hey, I'm younger than you!"

Crowdal grinned. "This is Sid and Agnes. And this guy is Writhgarth – don't let his gruffness fool you, he is as good a person you will ever meet." He went on to introduce everyone else and they fell into easy conversation as the night went on. Juldall joined them, followed by a few other Trith and Crowdal felt his sorrow dissipate as he laughed and talked. He also wasn't unhappy when he felt Rielissa take his hand at some point, and held it until late in the night when the celebration began breaking up. Sid and Agnes finally stood and said they were going to bed, and were quickly followed by everyone else in the group.

When they were finally alone, Rielissa leaned in to kiss Crowdal and he didn't hold back for the first time in his life. When they finally broke the kiss, she leaned back and said, "Wow. Why didn't you ever do that in all the years we had the chance?"

Looking deep into her eyes, Crowdal thought about it for a long time, then said, "Because, I never knew just what you meant to me until I saw you tonight."

Rielissa kissed him again, then stood and pulled him to his feet. "Come on." She led him into the darkness and when they arrived at her house, she pulled him through the door without pausing.

The rest of the night was filled with ecstasy, love and joy, and Crowdal never thought once of Melinda.

Chapter 50

It was mid-day, two days after the Queen of the Trith had been cremated, when Saleth heard a commotion at the main entrance to the Trith Circle. Shortly after, a high-pitched whistle reached her, rising and falling like the song of a whale, a sound that she knew only the Haissen could make and hear. She sprinted down the street, the other eleven Haissen right behind her. Up ahead she saw two dozen Trith yelling and jostling each other with swords out, facing the forest.

She smoothly slid to a stop, dust rising around her as the remaining Haissen halted behind her. The Trith didn't see her yet and she was prepared to cut them all down if need be to get through, but Crowdal came running up the street followed by the Aleph Null and the Red Robe. They stopped next to her and Crowdal shouted for the Trith to stand down. When they didn't respond, he stepped forward and pulled one back. When they recognized him, they all quieted down and stepped back to let him through.

As the Trith parted, Saleth saw three Haissen calmly standing at the edge of the forest.

When the three saw her, they stepped forward and bowed.

Saleth approached them and bowed in return, saying, "Who are you?"

A male stepped forward. "We are from Haisissei."

She showed no emotion, although she was as surprised as a Haissan could be by the news. No Haissan had returned to their homeland of Haisissei, a huge island off the north coast of the Srithian Wood, in the more than two thousand years since they had left it in search of the Aleph Null. As far as she knew, the Island had been uninhabited that entire time. She asked, "Haisissei has Haissen again?"

"The island has never been without Haissen."

This news actually caused her to blink.

The male Haissan nodded. "I apologize for shocking you like that, but we on the island recently felt our Sickness disappear. Our prophecy has come to pass and we are now free of all obligations with this land. All remaining Haissen are ordered to return to Haisissei immediately."

Saleth tilted her head. "Twelve of us are all that remain of the Haissen on the mainland."

"Then you twelve will return with us now."

Saleth turned and glided over to her eleven Haissen and spoke to them in their language, "We have been ordered to return to Haisissei. You will all go."

They all bowed in acknowledgement.

Saleth was silent for a moment, then said, "But, I will stay with the Aleph Null."

Tierre stepped forward. "I will stay, too. The Aleph Null's mother honored me in the Haissen library after I showed her how to get her Numbers back. I will now serve the Aleph Null until he gets his Numbers back."

Saleth motioned the remaining ten Haissen and they immediately joined the three Haissen at the edge of the forest. They spoke quietly with each other, then the leader nodded to her and Tierre and they all turned and faded into the forest.

Saleth and Tierre approach the Aleph Null, who looked confused. "The Haissen have been called back home. Tierre and I will remain with you, Aleph Null."

He looked at her, then Tierre, then quickly into the forest before turning back to her and saying, "Thank you for choosing to stay, but I do not want to keep you from returning home. As far as I am concerned, you owe no debt to me."

Crowdal called out his assurance to the Trith guards that everything was under control and they should return to their stations.

Saleth caught Tierre's glance and nodded slightly in return. The humans and Trith were noisy and unclean, but the Aleph Null had fulfilled the prophecy and she had sworn an oath to protect him. "We will stay with you, Aleph Null."

She stepped close to the Aleph Null and Tierre shadowed his other side as they returned to the center of the Trith Circle.

But as she walked, a big part of her ached to return to Haisissei with the others.

Perhaps someday she would see her homeland again.

Chapter 51

Sid returned with Crowdal, Agnes and the two Haissen to the building they inhabited in the center of the Trith Circle. A part of him was sad to see the ten other Haissen leave, but another part of him was happy for them to be able to return to their homeland. He had never known they had a home, but why wouldn't they? They had to have come from somewhere. He looked at the one called Saleth. "Where is your homeland, if you don't mind my asking?"

She didn't respond right away, and Sid apologized, thinking he had asked a question he shouldn't have. But then she called Drax over and asked him for his map. He returned to his sleeping area and pulled a folded piece of parchment from a pocket in his pack and returned, handing it to her.

Saleth unfolded it on the floor and pointed at the Srithian Wood in the northeast corner of the continent. "This is where the Haissen made landfall when we first came to this land." She moved her white finger out into the emptiness of the Sein Ocean and drew an imaginary outline of a large island, saying, "This is Haisissei, the homeland of the Haissen."

Crowdal, Agnes and Drax crowded around and Drax whistled softly, "I don't think anyone has ever known of the island's existence; not even Baldrick."

Saleth glanced at him. "It is no secret. No one has ever asked us about it."

Sid asked, "Who is Baldrick?"

Drax looked uncomfortable and stayed quiet.

"That's alright, you don't have to say."

He shook his head. "No, I should have told you about him sooner. I guess the timing was just never right." He took a few breaths, then continued, "Baldrick was the original master of Black Numbers."

Sid felt like a hammer had hit him in the head. He had heard a brief reference to an ancient master of Numbers when he had been in the Srithian Wood, but had forgotten about it in the chaos that had followed. His face must have shown his astonishment, for Drax nodded. "Yes, you are not the first Aleph Null."

Sid shook his head, "That is impossible. The Oblate has been searching for the Aleph Null for more than two thousand years and had never found evidence of one with such power of Numbers until me."

Drax tilted his head as he looked at him. "That is because Baldrick pre-dated the Oblate, so he was able to keep himself hidden from them."

Sid said, "Wait a moment. You know what happened to him, then?"

Drax looked directly into Sid's eyes. "I do know. He died right in front of me not long before you and I met."

The room was completely silent, then Sid asked, "He lived all these years? How did he die?"

"He was dying of a disease not even he could arrest with his powers. So he brought me to his secret home and used up every bit of his power of Black Numbers to make me what I am now."

Sid whispered, "What are you?"

Drax stood, looking down at him. "He made me into someone who can kill the wielder of Black Numbers. He made me what I am so that I would kill you."

The Haissen immediately stepped in front of Sid, and Crowdal pulled out his sword, the steel hissing as it came out of the scabbard.

Drax put up his hands. "Please, I will not harm Sid. While it was my mission, I have since come to learn Sid is not a threat to the land."

Sid stood up. "So this Aleph Null named Baldrick made you an Aleph Null?"

"No. I have no power of Numbers. He converted the structure of my body with the Black Numbers, making me invulnerable to any attack by the Aleph Null. He also modified my body in other ways, making me faster, stronger, and healthier in every way." He pulled out his knife and when a Haissan stepped closer he held it up, "Easy, I mean him no harm. I am just going to perform a demonstration of what I've been talking about."

The Haissen nodded for him to continue.

Drax held the knife against his arm and slowly dragged it across the skin, parting it neatly. Blood welled up briefly, then stopped. The skin knit back together smoothly and quickly until just the blood remained on his skin, which he wiped off with the edge of his tunic to reveal a thin scar.

Crowdal whistled. "We Trith are similarly blessed with quick healing, but it is not nearly that fast. A cut like that would take a couple of days to fully heal for us."

Agnes touched the spot where the cut had been. "That is amazing."

Drax shrugged. "Unfortunately, all of these modifications have had a side effect."

Sid looked up from his arm. "What kind of side effect?"

"I am no longer fully human, and as you know, that makes it hard to fit in with others, as they can sense my differences and it frightens them. So I am always alone now. Or at least I was, until I met Calix."

Sid looked down. It wasn't that he and the others had purposely excluded him, it just seemed easier to not try and force friendship on him when he didn't seem to want it. He took Drax's hand. "I am sorry; I honestly didn't think you wanted to be friendly with us. I would have tried harder had I known."

Crowdal and Agnes echoed his sentiment.

Drax shrugged, "That is in the past. I want you all to know that while I may still act differently, it is not my intent to be distant; it is just who I am now. But most importantly, I will help you with your search for your Numbers."

There was a soft knock on the door and it opened to reveal Calix standing there.

Sid motioned with his hand, "Come on in, Calix. You don't need to knock."

Calix stepped over the threshold and approached them all in the middle of the room, his face brightening when he saw Drax. He made a few gargling type noises and Drax smiled.

"Calix says he has thought more about the Aleph Null's Numbers and has realized he made a mistake."

Calix made more sounds, the volume rising and falling in complex movements, almost like a song.

Drax continued, "He says that while he can help you resurrect your Numbers, we must first find the Leillireph."

Sid had no idea what he meant and asked, "What is a Leillireph?"

"Not what, but who. She is the mother of all Zranh."

Sid turned to Crowdal. "Maybe once we find Melinda, she will know more about this."

Crowdal dipped his head in sorrow. "If we ever find her. She is supposed to be in the Branstall Wood until autumn, but it is already almost mid-summer. We may not make it back by autumn, even if we left right now. And the Zranh who took her said that after autumn passed, they would leave for the west and we would never find them again."

His face showed he was conflicted, his lips pinched together, his forehead thick with creases. "I need to stay and meet with my father and the Council a few more times, then I will hopefully be able to leave. All of this will likely take another fortnight. I am sorry, Sid. I could not get out of it even if I wanted to."

Sid touched Crowdal's arm. "Please don't worry about me. We will stay until you are ready to leave."

Crowdal grimaced. "There is one more important thing."

"What?"

Crowdal was as serious as he had ever been. "My mother officially made you a part of our family. That was not a simple statement. My mother was being her usual crafty self."

Sid narrowed his eyes. "What did she do?"

"You are now in line for the throne of the Trith Nation, and that means you are bound to Trith laws." He sighed. "Sid, you and I must fight for the title of King of the Trith."

Sid felt his skin turn cold. "But, your father is the king."

Crowdal shook his head. "He is indeed king. But he will not rule forever, and when it comes time for him to either step down or he passes away, then one of us will become the king."

Sid cried out in frustration and anger, "But why would your mother do this to us? She knows we are friends, not to mention that the Trith would never accept me as their king."

Crowdal smiled. "That is her shrewdness coming through. For my father likely still has many years left. That leaves us free to continue our journey, and if we are successful, then the Trith will have either their greatest warrior or the Aleph Null as king. She felt the Trith would be stronger either way."

Sid sat down hard. "But one of us would likely die in such a fight, yes?"

Crowdal smiled again. "No, Sid. The fight is not specified to be to the death. I could shove you lightly to the ground, and if you chose not to get up, then you would forfeit the fight."

Sid felt relief fill him and he let out a big breath. "Thank the gods." He looked up at Crowdal and grinned. "Hey, what if I wanted the kingship?"

Crowdal grinned back. "I would say, be my guest."

Chapter 52

Tris had been waiting for the past half day for all three Blue Robes to open the communication equation and give him an update on their location. It was already approaching evening, and he grew restless now that he was so close to capturing Sid again. He waited though, knowing the Blue Robes would contact him soon, and he had no problem passing the time with Obsidian.

The woman Blue Robe from Paigon was the first to reach out to him and he activated the equation on his side just as he climaxed inside of Obsidian. He groaned as he asked, "*Where is your army now?*"

Her voice was bitter in his head, "*Is this a bad time?*"

Tris waited for his orgasm to subside, letting her hear his groans of pleasure. He couldn't even remember her name and the sex they had in his Oblate chamber had not even been any good, so her jealousy was irritating. "*If I activate the communication equation on my side, it is because I wish to speak with you. Do not dare to presume that you have any say in the matter.*"

The Blue Robe sighed, which was a mistake. Tris added a few variables to the communication equation he had implanted in her brain and made it pulse against the nerves deep within. Her immediate cries of pain made him smile and he let her suffer for a number of moments before deactivating the pain part of the equation. He snarled at her, "*If you ever sigh in exasperation at me again, I will make you suffer like you've never suffered before, and then I will end your miserable life.*"

Her voice was weak and still echoed with pain as she said, "*I am sorry, Black Robe.*"

Tris got out of the bed and pushed Obsidian's hand away from his arm, ignoring her hiss, and walked around the room naked as he spoke, "*Now, where are you and your army?*"

"*My Captain says we are about a half day from the Trith city. We should reach it by nightfall. What do you want us to do?*"

Tris had been irritated by the slow progress the army had made, but now that they were almost in position, he grew excited. "*Do not attack until I order you to.*"

"*Yes, Black Robe.*"

"*I will be in contact with you again shortly.*"

He deactivated the communication equation before she could say anything more and activated the equation with the ugly Blue Robe from Yathen, not wishing to wait any longer for her to contact him. "*Where are you now?*"

She immediately responded in a professional voice, "*We are camped a short distance from the Trith Circle.*"

Tris nodded, secretly impressed that she knew the correct term for the Trith city. "*Good, remain there until I give the order to attack. When I do, you will give no quarter to the Trith, do you understand?"*

"*I do, Black Robe. I will not fail you.*"

Tris closed the equation and activated the one for the fat Blue Robe with the small expeditionary force. "*Report.*"

The Blue Robe responded quickly, "*We are in position, Black Robe.*"

"*I don't think your pathetic force will do much good in the main attack, so I wish you to hang back and watch for the Aleph Null in case he tries to escape. You will notify me if you see him.*"

"*Yes, Black Robe.*"

Tris closed the equation and turned to Obsidian. "Rise, my beauty, for it is time for us to go hunting."

Chapter 53

The communication ended and Glaub closed it on his side as usual so the Black Robe would not be able to snoop further into his mind. He sighed deeply, rubbing his temples. It had taken all of his willpower not to kill the Black Robe right then. In fact, he wasn't sure he shouldn't just kill him now – he certainly deserved to die. But Glaub had never summarily murdered anyone in his thousands of years of existence, and he wasn't about to start now. Despite Melinda's assurance that the Aleph Null was no threat, he could not be entirely sure of the Aleph Null's plans and maybe letting the Black Robe kill Sid was what was supposed to happen. The one thing he would not do was let his men get too close to the violence that was to come.

The darkness of twilight settled on their camp as he accepted a cup of hot tea from Charly. They were deep in the forest, about a half day to the northwest of the Trith Circle, and with the two armies to the south and east of the Circle, the odds were that the Aleph Null would try and escape in their direction.

Glaub whistled for Melinda and before he finished, she appeared next to him in the darkness. He smiled, genuinely happy to see her. They had spent the past few evenings talking late into the night and had formed a real friendship, maybe even something more. He sensed from her that she also felt something for him, although as yet neither had acted on their feelings. His heart beat quicker as he looked at her beautiful face. "I have some information."

Melinda sat down, folding her legs smoothly. "What have you learned?"

"The Black Robe has two armies approaching the Trith Circle from the south and east and they will likely attack tonight."

Her eyes grew wide and her lips almost disappeared at this information. "Then we need to go to Sid now and warn him."

"I am not sure that is the best thing. The Trith are a violent and proud race. Going into the heart of their Circle is risky."

She looked at him with hard eyes, "I will not be seen."

"And how would you get Sid away? And if you did, would that be the right move? I wonder if it might just be safest for him to remain with the Trith."

She thought for a few moments, then shrugged. "Maybe, but I need to at least warn Crowdal about the impending attacks."

Glaub thought about it and deep down he knew she was right, they couldn't just sit idly by waiting to see what happened and risking letting innocent people die. He had traveled all the way here in disguise to find out more about the Aleph Null and what the Black Robe's plans were, and he now knew the Black Robe was planning to have thousands of people killed for the sole reason of creating a diversion so he could capture the Aleph Null. Glaub had been to the Trith Circle a number of times in his history and knew the place well, so he nodded to Melinda and stood up. "Alright, I agree. I can take us there right now if you like."

Melinda breathed out and stood also. "I just told my people to wait here. I'd better go alone, though, as I can move while in the Raith world and get there quicker."

Glaub smiled, amazed again by her abilities. He motioned Captain Shaw over and told him to wait here also. Then he created the portal equation.

Melinda eyed the swirling darkness in front of her with distrust. "What is that?"

"It is a portal that will take us instantly to the holding building within the Trith Circle. I do not know where the Aleph Null is located, but when I was last there, I was put in this building. It is where the Trith keep all visitors and is as good a starting place as any. This way, you will not need to tire yourself out. Also, I need to meet the Aleph Null."

Melinda stepped through the portal without warning, and he stared briefly at the empty space where she had just been, amazed again by her fearless nature, then he quickly followed her.

He stepped into the center of the huge Trith room he had remembered being in so long ago. Melinda was already running toward a group of people, including two humans, a Vringe, two Trith and two Haissen, shouting, "Sid, Crowdal!"

Suddenly an older woman in grey was next to him holding a wicked blade to his throat. She leaned in and whispered, "Do not move."

Chapter 54

The Korpor knelt in the shadows of three tall pine trees on the perimeter of the Trith settlement and studied the activity going on around it. It wasn't a human city like the Korpor had often seen. For one, it didn't have walls around the center. Instead, the huge buildings of the Trith were built back-to-back in a circle around the city, effectively standing as a wall. They had cleared the trees for dozens of paces between the forest and the constructions, making it easy for the Trith to guard themselves. The only real way to enter the city was along the heavily-guarded main entrances from the east and west.

Opening its eyes wide to let as much light into them as it could in this deep part of the night, the Korpor spotted Trith sentries spaced every thirty paces on top of the buildings for as far as it could see, all armed with great longbows.

The Trith sentry directly in front of the Korpor moved her head in a wide sweep at a regular interval, looking right and left as she searched her field of view. The Korpor knelt perfectly still as it studied her movements, then, as she had her head turned completely to the left, the Korpor sprinted across the space as fast as it could and reached the dark base of the building before the sentry had even begun turning her head back in the opposite direction.

Looking up the wall of the building, the Korpor saw it was built from thick logs with no windows on the outward-facing side. It moved to the left three paces and reached high, slowly sank its claws into the crease between logs and pulled itself up by one arm. It then repeated the procedure with its other paw, moving up silently and slowly until it was just below the roofline where it stopped and hung, listening to the movements of the sentry. It could hear the creak of thick leathers as she turned her head and when the leather stopped creaking, the Korpor pulled itself quickly up the rest of the way and sprinted across the roof to a large chimney, putting its back to it.

No alarm was raised, so the Korpor sprinted confidently to the other side of the roof and lay flat at the edge, looking down. The street below it ran in a circular route and another set of buildings were built opposite, though these were a little shorter than the outer-wall building it was on. It studied the roof across from it and saw no sentries, so it leapt across the wide gap, landing lightly in a crouch. It sprinted across this roof and stopped in the deep shadows of another chimney.

It sniffed the air, searching for the scent of the Aleph Null. Luckily it was a relatively warm night and the Trith were not burning fires, so it didn't have to try and filter any scents through thick smoke. The Korpor turned its head as it inhaled the air and to its right it caught the faint, but specific, smell of the Aleph Null.

The Korper glided from chimney to chimney on each building, moving slowly in the shadows, jumping to the buildings across each street as it worked its way to the center of the city. It made a final leap to the roof of a large building and its gill-like nostrils flared widely as it inhaled deeply and shuddered at the intoxicating scent of the Aleph Null in the room directly below it.

The Korpor spoke to the Black Robe in its mind, "*I have located the Aleph Null.*"

The Black Robe replied instantly, "*Send me the coordinates.*"

It concentrated and the Black Robe said, "*Excellent. Just sit tight, my pet.*"

The communication ended without another word so the Korpor crouched down and waited in the darkness, saliva dripping from its mouth as it fought back its desire to smash through the roof and take the Aleph Null.

Chapter 55

Sid turned when he heard his and Crowdal's names being called and even though he recognized Melinda's voice, he froze. His brain couldn't process that it was Melinda running across the torch-lit room toward them.

They had all still been awake, discussing the events of the day. Crowdal turned at the voice and grinned so broadly that Sid thought his face would never be able to return to normal again. Crowdal took three steps and picked her up, spinning her around as he hugged her.

She wrapped her arms around his neck and laughed as pure a laugh as Sid had heard before. He found himself grinning as he ran over to them, followed closely by everyone from their original group.

"Put me down, Crowdal, I'm getting dizzy," laughed Melinda.

Crowdal set her gently down and stepped back, his smile still splitting his face wide.

Melinda gazed up at him for many moments, then turned and quickly wrapped Sid in a hug. He squeezed her hard, not believing she was really here.

She let him go and pushed him back to look at him. "You look good." Tousling his hair, she playfully said, "But you need a haircut."

Sid grinned, "It feels like forever since we've seen you."

She nodded, "I know, but we are back together now and that's all that matters." She turned and quickly hugged Writhgarth. "It's good to see you, Writhgarth."

He rigidly hugged her but his eyes were wet with barely controlled tears, "Aye, that it is, lass."

Nik stepped forward and slugged her shoulder softly, grinning. "You haven't been off getting rich from my idea for handbreads, have you?"

Melinda laughed and winked at him, "Don't worry, your secret is safe with me. Wait, you are calling them 'handbreads' now?"

Nik stepped back in mock anger, "I happen to think it's a catchy name."

Tulman nudged Nik out of the way and held his hand out to Melinda, which she shook professionally.

Agnes held back, since they hadn't really had the chance to get to know each other very well, but Melinda gave her a quick hug. "It's good to see you, Agnes." She put her mouth to Agnes' ear and whispered something Sid couldn't hear and Agnes turned her head and blushed, nodding as she quickly looked at Sid, then away just as fast.

Melinda beamed as she stepped back.

Crowdal spread his hands, "How did you find us? We were just trying to figure out how we were going to search for you and then you just appeared here. Speaking of which, how *did* you get in here?"

Melinda grew serious. "That is a long story and one we don't have time for right now. Glaub and I came to warn you."

Crowdal raised an eyebrow, "Glaub?"

Turning, Melinda saw Gee holding a knife to Glaub's neck across the room and called out, "Whoever you are, let him go, he's my friend."

Gee turned her eyes to Sid and he nodded. She removed the knife from Glaub's neck and stepped back.

The man Melinda had called Glaub rubbed the spot on his neck where Gee had held her knife and turned to bow slightly to the woman. "You are very good at what you do."

Gee nodded and replied, "Thank you."

Glaub smiled at her, then walked up to the group, stopping by Melinda's side.

Melinda turned to the group and said, "I would like you to meet Glaub," she glanced at him and he nodded, so she continued, "he is an Aleph Null."

Sid inhaled sharply and whipped his head around to look at Glaub, then at Melinda.

"Yes, Sid. He is like you, although *much, much* older."

Glaub looked at Melinda, "You didn't have to add that extra 'much' in there."

Melinda grinned with the familiarity of a friend, which Sid found interesting.

Glaub turned serious as he extended his hand to Sid, "Well met, Aleph Null. It is a pleasure to finally meet you."

Sid shook his hand, staring at him with his mouth hanging open. He finally got his wits about him and shut his mouth, then felt a nudge of pressure against his mind, which it didn't seem he could do anything about.

Glaub's eyes narrowed as he studied him, then he turned to Melinda. "You did not tell me he'd had his Numbers nullified." When Melinda looked at Glaub with questioning eyes, he turned back to Sid. "You just recently had your power of Numbers nullified, didn't you?"

Sid could only nod, unable to find any words. Who was this man? How could he tell his Numbers were gone? Could there really be another Aleph Null? All these questions sluggishly moved through his thoughts until he forced his mouth to work, saying, "Yes. It happened after Melinda was taken from us."

Melinda asked, "What happened, Sid?"

Sid briefly relayed the events that had taken place in the Srithian Wood and as he did, Glaub's face paled. Sid asked him, "You know what the Unnamed One was, don't you?"

Swallowing, his eyes glinting with respect, Glaub nodded. "First of all, my condolences for the loss of your mother and friends, as well as your power of Numbers. I recently lost my father, also." He seemed to not want to continue but then he squared his shoulders and said, "It was my father who created the Unnamed One many millennia ago. He subsequently imprisoned it in a Black Numbers array that was supposed to be unbreakable. How it was released, I do not know. But the fact that you imprisoned it in the inner space of the obelisk is simply astounding."

Drax stepped closer and cut into the conversation. "I am sorry to interrupt, but are you Baldrick's son?"

Raising his eyes, Glaub said, "I am. And who are you?"

Drax put his hands together, palm to palm, raising them to his chin. "My name is Drax, and I was with your father when he died. He was a great man."

Glaub stopped breathing as he stared at Drax in shock. "Why were you with him?"

"Baldrick was very sick, something that not even he, with his mastery of Black Numbers, could cure. He was aware of the birth of a new Aleph Null, as well as another who had stolen the power of Black Numbers. Because he didn't have the strength to physically search for and kill them, he used the last of his power of Black Numbers to remake my body to provide me with the abilities to perform these tasks for him."

The room was silent as everyone watched the two. Sid wasn't sure what would happen and was relieved when Glaub relaxed and held his hand out to Drax, saying, "I know my father well and that sounds just like something he would do. Thank you for being there with him at the end; I wish it had been me."

Glaub turned to Sid. "I have performed a quick scan of your mind." At Sid's look of anger, he said, "I am sorry for the transgression – believe me when I say I regret having to do it. I am happy to find that you harbor no malicious intent, nor are you power hungry. In combination with Melinda's testimony, as well as the friends you keep, I have decided that you are free to keep the power of Black Numbers if you get them back." He looked intensely at Sid and lowered his voice, "But I will keep an occasional eye on you just to be sure."

Crowdal stepped behind Sid, towering over them both. "What gives you the right to judge Sid?"

Looking up at Crowdal, he said, "I have the right because my father almost destroyed the entire land before he got control of the overwhelming lure of Black Numbers. He almost let them consume him, so he knew first-hand just what such power can do to the one who wields it. He and I vowed to never let that happen again."

"And what gives you, personally, that right?"

Glaub shrugged, "I guess because I have never used my power of Black Numbers to harm another in my many thousands of years of life."

This seemed to satisfy Crowdal, although he still didn't appear to fully believe that Glaub was that old.

Sid wasn't sure either. "Melinda, do you believe Glaub is who he says he is?"

She immediately nodded. "I do, Sid."

"Then that is good enough for me. You mentioned that you had to warn us about something?"

Melinda took in a sharp breath. "I can't believe I forgot." She motioned for Glaub, "He knows more than I do. Glaub, please tell them."

Glaub regarded Sid and then tilted his head to look up at Crowdal. "The Black Robe has gathered two armies that are camped close by here and he plans to use them to attack the Trith Circle. I believe it is all just so he can create confusion and chaos and in the middle of it, drive Sid into the forest where he can be captured."

Crowdal cocked his head as he looked down at Glaub. "How do you know all of this?"

"Last year, I felt there was a great power about to be released in the land. I knew the Oblate would likely be involved, so I went undercover within their organization as a simple Blue Robe to see if I could find out if another Aleph Null had truly been found. You must understand that there had not been another Aleph Null since my father and I were born. A couple of fortnights ago, the Black Robe killed all but four Blue Robes. He sent us to gather as many forces as we could from our posts in the great kingdoms. So when he implanted a communication equation in my head to keep tabs on me, I reversed it to listen in on his thoughts. Sid, he wants your secrets to Black Numbers and is willing to kill thousands to get them." Glaub glanced at Crowdal, then back to Sid. "He has about 1500 soldiers in the darkness of the forest ready to attack as I speak."

Crowdal nodded, his face grim. "I must go warn the Council. Thank you." He sprinted to the door and burst through it without slowing down.

Sid glanced at Melinda and Glaub. "How much time do you think we have?"

Before Glaub could speak, a horn blew, followed by another, then another.

Glaub glanced at the door, his face looking bleak. "I think we just ran out of time."

Chapter 56

T he horns blew with ferocity as Crowdal sprinted down the torch-lit street. Trith emerged from every building, running to their assigned areas. Crowdal knew from experience how hard the Trith trained for just such a situation. More than two-thousand Trith lived in the Circle and half of them would gather at the two entrances, while the other half would gather in fighting units throughout the city, ready to address any specific threats. The Trith Circle had not been attacked in millennia, but that didn't stop them from having drills every day. He noted grimly that many Trith were smiling openly in anticipation of a battle and he scowled at their love for violence.

Crowdal arrived at the Council chamber and pushed through the elite nineteen guards who stood outside of the Council building, most of them not even noticing him as they eyed the area around them, hands gripping their sword hilts tightly.

Bursting through the door, he dodged a courier, who sprinted by him out the door and slowed to a brisk walk as he approached the table where the Council members stood looking down at a map of the Circle. One of the older Trith named Fofre looked up and motioned him to join them. "Crowdal, it is good to have you here."

At the mention of his name, Uuthdal looked quickly up from the map and nodded to him. "Crowdal, good timing. We must determine the attack points and…"

Crowdal interrupted him. "I have some vital information about the attack."

His father closed his mouth mid-word and angrily motioned for him to speak, obviously not liking being interrupted, not even by his son.

"I have learned who is attacking and why."

At these words, the room became instantly quiet, for the Trith were, above all else, warriors and knew the importance of good intelligence.

Crowdal pointed at the map, "There are two small armies here and here. Although they only total about 1500, they are accompanied by the Black Robe of the Oblate, a man I have faced before." He looked at each Council member before continuing, "He is not a man to be taken lightly, wielding a power of Numbers equal to the Aleph Null. I've seen him do things you would not believe. So I think our priority is finding and killing him without mercy." Crowdal described Tris, ending with, "We have some powerful people in my group, but I need them to protect the Aleph Null, since his own power of Numbers is temporarily absent."

Uuthdal nodded briskly. "We will handle the armies and this Numbers man. They will be no match against us."

Crowdal shook his head in frustration. "Do not underestimate this man. Kill him quickly if you find him." But Uuthdal didn't acknowledge what he said, already pointing to areas on the map and issuing orders. Crowdal stood still for a moment, then sighed, knowing his warnings had fallen on deaf ears. At least he had performed his duty and warned them.

Crowdal left the room, which went unnoticed by all assembled there, and sprinted back toward the holding building. As he ran, he already heard the sounds of battle in the distance: steel striking steel, terrible screams of agony, chaotic shouting. A part of him felt the pull of battle but he pushed those thoughts away.

Rielissa charged around a corner in front of him and he yelled out her name.

She slid to a halt, turned her head and trotted over to him.

"Crowdal, we are being attacked."

"I know and it is because of my friends and I."

Rielissa knew his whole story and shook her head. "It's not your fault, but I really need to get to my post at the east entrance."

Crowdal felt an icy fear move through him and he shook his head. "They will be alright without you. Come with me instead."

She hesitated. "No, I must report to my post."

Crowdal grabbed her hand. "Listen to me. The Black Robe is out there and he has the power to kill with just a thought. I could use you as extra protection for the Aleph Null now that there are only two Haissen left to help guard him."

Rielissa still looked torn, so Crowdal stood straight and said, "As the heir to the throne, I release you from your post duty."

This official release was enough for her to finally nod. "Alright, lead on."

Crowdal turned and ran down the street, Rielissa right behind him, and they quickly arrived back at the building.

***

Sid rushed over as Crowdal and Rielissa closed the door. "What should we do, Crowdal? Should we stay here or try and escape the Circle?"

Crowdal put his hand on Sid's shoulder as they walked over to the rest of the group. "We definitely can't escape into the forest, that is exactly what Tris wants us to do."

Sid looked up, "So we fight?"

"No, we stay right here. There are two thousand Trith between us and the Black Robe and his armies. This is the safest place and is easier to defend if need be. Rielissa will help us."

Melinda nodded in agreement, then turned to Glaub. "Can you return to our camp and tell my Zranh to stay hidden? I do not want them to enter this battle."

Glaub took a step forward and disappeared, causing everyone but Melinda to step back in surprise.

Sid stared in awe at the spot where Glaub had just been. He had seen Tris do this, but it still amazed him. Before he could say anything, Glaub stepped into the same space, this time accompanied by a girl.

Glaub raised his hands, "I am sorry, Melinda. Eithes would not take no for an answer."

The girl ran over to Melinda, who hugged her briefly before pushing her away, concern in her eyes. "Eithes, it is not safe here. You must let Glaub take you back."

Eithes shook her head emphatically. "I will not leave you and you can't make me."

Melinda grimaced. "That is something I most certainly can do." She looked at the girl and then Melinda's eyes softened and she smiled. "But I won't because I am actually glad to have you by my side again." She turned Eithes to face everyone. "I would like you all to meet Eithes." She then introduced Eithes to everyone, ending with Crowdal.

Eithes gazed up at Crowdal in awe, a small smile on her lips. She didn't even come up to his waist.

The sounds of battle grew closer and Crowdal ran to the door and opened it just a little to peer outside, then pulled it open wide with a curse and drew his sword as he ran out.

Rielissa looked torn as she pulled her sword out, like she wanted to follow Crowdal but knew she needed to stay and help protect everyone in the room.

Melinda suddenly disappeared from in front of Sid. One moment she was there and the next she wasn't. He stumbled back in disbelief, then felt a hand on his arm and turned to look at Glaub.

As if he could read Sid's mind, Glaub said, "She is Zranh. She is Leillireph."

Sid stepped back. "Did you just say Melinda is the Leillireph?"

"Yes, she is."

Sid looked over at Calix and he nodded solemnly. Sid turned back to Glaub, "I was told by Calix over there that the Leillireph was key to my regaining my power of Numbers. I can't believe it is Melinda. What does Leillireph mean, exactly?"

"She is the reborn mother of the Zranh who has the power to stop time completely. Her power frightens me more than any I've ever come across before."

Stunned to the core, Sid raised a shaking hand to push his long hair from his eyes. Melinda was able to stop time? How could that be? Before he could say anything, Melinda reappeared, her clothing soaked in blood, her hair wild and wet with gore.

Then Crowdal burst through the door, his sword also dripping blood. He pulled the door shut and placed a thick bar across it.

Sid stepped to Crowdal's back. "Crowdal, what's going on?"

Crowdal didn't respond, staring vacantly at the door, then he slowly turned, his face ashen and his eyes wide with shock.

Melinda spoke for him. "The army has broken through the perimeter." Her voice cracked as she said, "Much of the Trith force at the east gate has been incinerated by the Black Robe. There is nothing left but smoking bodies."

Rielissa gasped before raising her lip in a snarl.

Crowdal walked over to his friends like a broken man, but his eyes glinted with barely-controlled fury as he growled, "I am going to kill Tris if it is the last thing I do."

Rielissa stepped close to him and said, "If I don't kill him first."

Glaub turned Melinda toward him. "What happened to you? Are you injured?"

Melinda quickly checked herself over. "No, I am fine. I killed a hundred men of the advancing army and would have killed them all but…she attacked me again."

Sid asked, "Who do you mean?"

Melinda turned, her face pinched with anger. "It is a woman with shiny, black skin who attacked my Zranh in the forest. She can enter the third frequency of the Raith world like me, and then go even further."

At everyone's blank looks, she waved her hand. "Forget all that for now. Just know that she can move unseen and she is deadly."

Melinda's image seemed to flicker, and if Sid had not been looking right at her he would not have seen it.

Melinda noticed his look. "I am entering the Raith world constantly to ensure she is not here."

Crowdal finally came to his senses and looked at Glaub. "Could you get everyone out of here?"

Glaub nodded that he could, but said, "We must be careful, as that is exactly what the Black Robe wants us to do."

"How far can you take them? Could it be someplace Tris wouldn't know of?"

Glaub's eyes brightened. "Yes, of course. I could take us to Urgaer, or even to my father's secret home."

Drax smiled slightly at the mention of the last place.

Sid turned to Crowdal, "Wouldn't you come with us?"

With sad eyes, Crowdal said, "I must stay here and help defend my people." He glanced at the door, "In fact, I really need to get out there now."

Calix stepped forward and touched his arm, making soft sounds.

Drax spoke, "He says you are not meant for this fight. Your place is here with the Aleph Null."

Crowdal glared at Calix, but as he did, Calix put his hands to each side of Crowdal's head and closed his eyes. A few moments passed and then Crowdal's glare faded away and he slumped his shoulders. "I understand. Thank you, Calix."

Calix made more soft sounds and Drax said, "He says he is sorry."

Melinda looked as if she wanted to take Crowdal's hand, but instead she turned to Glaub. "If you do this, I must stay here and return to my Quadrants, then return to my people."

Sid had been silent, but at this he spoke up. "Melinda, I haven't been able to tell you yet, but for me to get my power of Numbers back, I need you."

She looked at him questioningly. "Me? Why?"

Sid pointed at Calix. "Calix can see things and knows much, and he says the key to getting my Numbers back is the Leillireph. And that is you, right?"

Melinda glanced at Calix, then back to Sid. "I am Leillireph, yes. But what do you need from me?"

Sid shrugged. "I do not know. We haven't had a chance to really figure it out yet."

The roar of hundreds of approaching men could be heard, screaming and yelling as they fought more Trith. Then there was a whoosh of fire and more screams, making Crowdal's and Rielissa's faces turn red with anger. Crowdal cut in, "We need to get out of here, now."

Glaub nodded, but before he could act, a woman with pure black skin appeared a few paces away. She opened her arms and Tris stepped from her embrace.

Melinda instantly disappeared as did the woman with shiny black skin, leaving Tris, who smiled at Sid and said, "So, we meet again, old friend."

Sid reached for his Numbers but found nothing. He screamed in frustration inside his mind at not having them to kill Tris.

Then Glaub stepped in front of him and faced Tris, saying, "I cannot let you harm the Aleph Null."

Tris' eyes widened. "Is that so, fatty? Do you really think you can stop me?"

Glaub shrugged. "I am not going to stop you. Unfortunately, you have forced me to do the one thing I do not want to do."

With a mocking voice, Tris asked, "And what might that be, oh great Blue Robe?"

Glaub looked genuinely sad as he said, "I am going to have to kill you."

Tris grinned, and as he did, he waved a hand at the Hunters of Reilen, who had quietly crept up behind him with knives out, and they started screaming in agony. Then their screams ended just as quickly and they looked around in wonder.

Tris glared at Glaub, "How dare you cancel my equation?"

Glaub walked forward, and as he did, Tris' eyes grew wide as he started sliding backward across the floor with each step that Glaub took.

Tris grimaced and his eyes narrowed as he concentrated, but he only managed to slow down his slide for a few moments before Glaub flicked his finger and he flew backward and struck the wall hard, his arms and legs splayed wide against the wood. He struggled but could not move, and for the first time his face showed real fear.

Glaub slowly walked toward him, his own face showing anguish. "I do not wish to do this and it makes me unhappy that you have forced me to."

Tris strained but was held fast.

As Glaub walked, he moved his hands casually left and right as if he were swatting mosquitoes out of the way. "Your simple equations are of no use against me, so please halt your attacks."

Tris closed his eyes and concentrated. The air pressure of the room grew until Sid's eardrums felt like they were going to burst.

Glaub stumbled briefly but quickly got his balance and then the pressure was gone. He stared at Tris with incredulity. "You were really going to destroy the whole building and everyone in it? You are truly beyond saving."

Tris' eyes grew even wider and he gasped, "How did you disassemble that set of equations? I created them to be constantly changing. There is no way anyone could have taken them apart." He cried out, "Who are you?"

Glaub stopped in front of him and studied him briefly. "I am the son of Baldrick, the first of the Black Numbers masters. Your mastery of Numbers is strong for one so young, but you do not control the Black Numbers." Glaub concentrated and Tris cried out in agony, then screamed in frustration, tears running down his face.

"I have removed the schema of Black Numbers that you stole from Sid."

Tris screamed out, "No!"

"I will save them for when Sid is ready for them. I am sorry for what I am about to do."

Tris stopped screaming and glared at him, his face wet with tears.

Then he grinned.

Sid started to yell out when he saw the woman with black skin appear behind Glaub, but he stopped when Melinda's bloody and torn body flickered into view on the floor.

Chapter 57

When Melinda saw Obsidian appear in the room with the Black Robe, she immediately jumped to the third frequency of the Raith world, hoping to get the smallest advantage on her, but as Melinda transitioned, the woman instantly appeared along with her. Everyone else in the room remained rooted to their spots, frozen in time.

Melinda pulled out her two knives and crouched down in a fighting stance, snarling, "Let's finish this once and for all, Obsidian."

Obsidian removed her cloak, revealing her fully naked body, and even though she was a woman, Melinda felt a sexual stirring in her core as she gazed at Obsidian's beautiful breasts and hairless sex between her legs. When she looked up, Obsidian smiled as if she knew the sexual thoughts going through Melinda's head. She sensually arched her back, thrust her breasts out and practically cooed, "Or we could skip the fight and do something more mutually fulfilling."

Melinda was confused by the feelings coursing through her as she stared at the woman's erect nipples. While she had always appreciated the beauty in women, and had on occasion wondered what it might be like to be physical with one, she had never really given it much more than a passing thought. Yet now she couldn't seem to get her mind to work through the powerfully sexual sensations that settled over her.

Obsidian hooded her eyes and licked her lips, swaying her hips provocatively as she slowly walked toward Melinda.

The sexual desire grew in her, her own sex growing damp. Through the sexual fog that threatened to overwhelm her, Melinda smiled and lowered her knives.

Obsidian touched her own nipple and said in a husky voice, "You will feel pleasure like you've never felt before, Zranh mother." She was only a couple paces from Melinda now as she absently clicked the talons of her other hand together.

Melinda let her take another step then leapt forward, slicing down with both blades at her stomach. It caught Obsidian by surprise and she jumped back at the last moment, looking down at the two cuts in her shiny black stomach. Unfortunately, Obsidian had been able to get just far enough back that Melinda's blades didn't bite very deeply, but the sexual fog had lifted immediately and Melinda felt clear-headed again.

Obsidian growled and dropped into a crouch, her arms out and talons spread wide as she moved slowly to the left of Melinda.

Cursing herself for not getting in a killing blow, Melinda held her left blade out with her right blade down to her side as she moved to the right, trying to lure the woman into a bad angle. But Obsidian was too smart and kept herself facing Melinda.

Melinda motioned with her left blade, "It looks like I cut in exactly the same spots that I did before. I bet it hurts."

Obsidian didn't take the bait and look down at her stomach, instead she smiled maliciously as she clicked her talons together, the sound loud in the total silence of the third frequency of the Raith world. "I will carve you much deeper than that, and you will know exactly what the pain feels like."

Melinda saw that Obsidian was getting close to Glaub as they moved about the room, so she switched directions and as she did, she leapt forward with a battle scream, her left blade slicing downward across the woman's breasts while she stabbed to the kidney with her right blade. But Obsidian disappeared before she could connect.

Landing on the floor, Melinda immediately rolled forward with the momentum, feeling the burn of her side being sliced open. She came out of the roll in a crouch, scanning the room.

Obsidian was gone again and Melinda knew she could not stay still for even a moment, so she sprinted across the room, turning directions constantly, and as she did, she felt quick disturbances in the air and more cuts to her body as Obsidian appeared in quick flashes for just long enough to rake her talons out at Melinda, then disappearing before Melinda could slash at her in return.

Knowing it wouldn't work to try and match her blow for blow, Melinda slid to a stop not far from the door to the outside and stayed perfectly still, her head down, holding her knives at her sides. She slowed her breathing and closed her eyes to concentrate on the stillness of the Raith world where not even the air moved. She listened with all of her senses, searching for any kind of sound or change in air pressure or movement.

It was so quiet she could hear the blood flowing in her own veins, the sound soothing. Then she felt the slightest movement of air in front of her and sprang forward, while slicing upward with her blades. She felt the soft resistance of parting flesh and heard a soft intake of breath from Obsidian. Melinda opened her eyes just in time to see descending talons strike her face, slicing deeply into her cheek as she tried to pull away. Pain assailed her and she cried out involuntarily as she fell to the floor.

Obsidian stumbled back, holding her hand to two deep cuts in her side.

Melinda felt blood spraying from her cheek and she frantically reached up to push her hand against the cuts but her fingers slipped inside of the deep gouges instead.

Obsidian growled in anger and agony and she disappeared.

Melinda could not hold onto the third frequency and felt herself shift out of the Raith world, too.

The room burst into motion and no one saw her lying by the door. She lifted her head and saw Glaub advance on the Black Robe, who suddenly flew back against the wall.

Melinda put a hand to her cheek and felt her vision waver at all the blood. She got a bad feeling when she didn't see Obsidian anywhere. She reached deeply inside her energy reserves and forced herself to enter the first frequency of the Raith world, but failed to fully transition.

Closing her eyes, she pushed the pain away enough to try again. The warmth filled her until she was able to just slip into the first frequency, and as she did, the pain from her wounds expanded to unbearable levels, but she refused to let herself cry out.

Movement caught her eye and she saw Obsidian taking small steps toward Glaub's back as she held her bleeding side.

Suppressing another cry of pain, Melinda forced herself to her knees, and then to her feet. She pulled out her small boot knife and stumbled forward as quietly as she could behind Obsidian, but her foot scraped the floor and the woman turned just as Melinda lunged forward with her blade.

Obsidian caught her wrist and plunged her other talons deep into Melinda's stomach.

It felt like her insides had burst into flames and this time she couldn't stop herself from crying out.

Obsidian pulled her talons out of Melinda's stomach with a sickening squish of blood and as she did, Melinda used the last of her strength to wrench her hand free from the woman's grasp and ram her small knife into the shiny black skin of Obsidian's side.

As the blood pumped out of Melinda, she put a hand over the hole in her stomach and felt her strength fully give out, and through teary eyes, she saw Obsidian stumble back and disappear.

Then Melinda felt her vision quickly fade and she collapsed to the floor and saw nothing more.

Chapter 58

Sid was the first to see Melinda laying on the floor, her face pumping vast amounts of blood from frighteningly deep gashes. Her robe was sliced open in at least a dozen places, showing more cuts, and she laid in a pool of her own blood.

The woman with black skin was bleeding from deep wounds herself, but she had enough strength to plunge her talons into Glaub's back before Sid could warn him.

Glaub arched at an impossible angle as the woman twisted her arm viciously and then yanked her hand from his back with a spray of thick blood.

Sid screamed out as Glaub crumpled to the floor next to Melinda. He ran forward, pulling out his Rissen blade as he did, intending to kill the woman. His two Haissen were by his side as he heard Crowdal cry out for him to stop, but he was beyond listening, only wanting to kill.

But Tris was free from whatever Glaub had used to hold him and suddenly Sid and his Haissen hit an invisible wall and found themselves unable to move.

Tris glanced around the room and Sid heard cries of alarm from his friends. He was able to turn his eyes enough to see them all frozen like he was. Then, to Sid's surprise, he saw Drax sprinting forward at an incredible speed, completely unaffected by the arrays that Tris had created.

Sid turned his eyes forward as Tris concentrated on Drax, but no matter what he seemed to try, Drax kept coming. Tris looked confused but didn't waste any more attacks as he turned back to face Sid. His old friend's eyes blazed with barely controlled insanity, his lip raised in a snarl. Sid knew he was truly in the presence of evil.

Tris looked to his left and narrowed his eyes at Drax who was almost upon them, and turned to the obsidian-colored woman. "It's time for us to go now."

The woman quickly wrapped Sid and Tris in her bloody embrace.

Sid saw the air turn black around him and then a strange sense of movement caused him to feel dizzy. The air and dizziness quickly cleared though and as the woman stepped back, he found himself standing in a cave lit with flickering candles.

Tris leaned close to Sid, his eyes glinting with barely suppressed violence. "Welcome to your final resting place, Sid." He smiled, although it made Sid shiver, then he slowly kissed Sid's cheek and whispered in his ear, "You will not leave here alive."

***

The Korpor, hunkered down on the roof of the building where the Aleph Null was located, had waited for instructions from the Black Robe when he had arrived inside the building with the black-skinned woman. But when no communication came, it had crept down the wall at the back of building and quietly opened the door. Before it could enter, though, it sensed the Black Robe disappear with the Aleph Null.

In shock at being left behind, it didn't hear the eight Trith come around the corner of the building until they gave a war cry and charged. It quickly turned to face the threat, opening its eyes wide.

The Trith cried out in pain from its gaze but charged it with shouts of fury, their swords out and already bloody from battle.

The Korpor howled in frustration, then quickly scaled the building and ran for its life, jumping from building to building.

Chapter 59

Crowdal, suddenly free from whatever had been holding him immobile, cried out as Sid, Tris, and the strange woman disappeared from the room.

Drax arrived at the spot where Sid had just been a fraction of a moment too late.

Crowdal ran to Melinda and slid on his knees to a stop next to her. Tears ran down his face and he gently reached out and turned her over onto her back.

Her face was flayed open from four cuts across her cheek, and in her stomach was a gaping hole the size of a fist. He pulled off his shirt and tore it apart, pressing one clean piece of cloth against her cheek to try and stop the bleeding, while rolling up another and pushing it into her stomach wound.

Melinda's breathing became more shallow as he quickly examined the other wounds on her body and though they bled freely, they did not seem to be as deep as the ones on her face or stomach.

He bent low and whispered, "Don't you dare leave this world yet, Melinda." Tears flowed freely as he lightly kissed her lips. He heard the rest of the group surround him, and then Gee knelt next to them.

"I can try to help her."

Crowdal looked at her through his tears. "Please, do everything you can." He glanced over to the man named Glaub and saw him laying immobile on the floor, so he yelled out, "Drax, Calix, see if you can do anything for Glaub."

They both turned and flinched when they saw Glaub with a hole in his back and stepped quickly over to him.

Gee called out, "Doris, bring the medical kit."

Doris ran to their area of the room and dug quickly through her pack, pulling out a fairly thick, wooden box and returning swiftly to hand it to Gee.

Opening the box, Gee spoke as she removed a bottle of liquid, a bundle of clean cloths and a sewing kit. "We need to stop the bleeding in her stomach first." She pulled her knife out of its sheath and sliced Melinda's shirt away to get better access to the wound in her stomach. Gee carefully pulled out the red, blood-soaked cloth Crowdal had stuffed into the hole and studied the jagged, deep wound that pulsed thick blood with every beat of Melinda's heart. She opened the bottle and poured a liberal amount of pure alcohol into the hole, causing Melinda to arch her back in pain. "Crowdal, hold her down."

Crowdal immediately placed his hands against Melinda's shoulders.

"I need to look as deeply as I can into the wound. Hold her tight." Gee carefully peeled the cut flesh back and patted at the blood as she peered closely into the wound. "It looks like no organs were damaged, but I need to sew her shut in stages, as there are cut blood vessels that will make her bleed to death if I don't reattach them. Doris, thread me a needle."

Doris handed her the needle and thread and Gee started sewing.

Crowdal had no idea how she could see what she was doing through all the blood, but she worked quickly and with sure movements.

Crowdal leaned down and whispered into Melinda's ear, "Keep fighting."

After a long, tense time of working, Gee dabbed at the wound and no new blood welled out. She sat back with a sigh. "I think I got all of the vessels done." She turned to Doris. "Get another needle and thread and sew this closed while I work on her face."

Gee shifted so she could pull the dark, red cloth away from Melinda's cheek. As she did, Doris knelt on the other side of Melinda and began to expertly sew the stomach wound closed.

Gee opened the bottle of alcohol again and poured the clear liquid onto the four slices on Melinda's face. Melinda moaned but didn't wake up.

Gee then held a fresh cloth against the wounds for long moments, the fabric turning bright red. She pulled it away and pressed another against the cuts, then pulled it away as well, but the cuts still bled freely. Grimacing, she leaned forward with the needle and thread she had used on the stomach wound, speaking at the same time, "I need to sew these closed too, they are very deep." She looked up at Crowdal, then motioned Writhgarth over. "I want both of you to hold her still. She cannot move at all during this procedure."

Both Crowdal and Writhgarth grimly nodded in understanding placing their hands against Melinda's arms and body.

Gee leaned forward and peeled the first slice wide open. Melinda groaned again and involuntarily tried to move away, but Crowdal and Writhgarth held her firmly. Gee dabbed at the inside of the cut and saw what she needed to do in the brief time before the blood filled it up again. She began sewing the cut with very small stitches.

Crowdal watched her, having never seen something like this done before, asking, "What are you trying to do?"

Gee spoke without looking up or stopping, "The cuts go all the way into the cheekbone and I am trying to close them while leaving as minimal scarring as I can. Now please stop speaking."

Crowdal watched her work in amazement, her fingers moving quickly and steadily.

Gee repeated the work on each of the slices on Melinda's face, then stitched up the lesser cuts on her body. The sun was rising by the time she finished, cutting the last of the thread and sitting back, stretching her back, loud popping sounds filling the room. She sighed, "I think she may live, although she has lost a tremendous amount of blood. It ultimately comes down to her. We shouldn't move her for at least a fortnight, though, to give the wounds time to heal. Bring me a few furs so we can keep her warm."

Nik and Tulman quickly retrieved thick furs, placing two on top of each other on the floor.

Gee motioned at Crowdal and Writhgarth, "Alright, very carefully, I want you to gently lift her just enough to slid her onto the furs. On my count of three; one, two, three."

They smoothly slid her over, eliciting only the smallest of groans from Melinda. Gee placed a thick bear fur over her.

Crowdal caressed her forehead, then looked up, "Thank you, Gee."

The older woman nodded and stood up, cracking her back again before turning to one of her Hunters. "Layli, do you have a report on what is happening outside."

Layli stood straight. "Once the Numbers man disappeared, the Trith quickly destroyed the human invaders. It appears the Trith lost at least five hundred, most from the fire of the Numbers man. Every single human has been killed."

Gee nodded. "Thank you. Crowdal, if you need to go speak with your people, I will ensure Melinda is well-cared-for."

Crowdal glanced up at her, his face twisted with conflicting responsibilities but then he nodded and caressed Melinda's forehead once more before standing. "Thank you. I do need to go." He turned to the two Haissen. "Stay on alert until we know the threat is fully over."

They both nodded.

Crowdal turned and saw Rielissa standing not far away, looking uncomfortable. He crossed to her and took her hand. "Would you stay here and help watch over everyone?"

She leaned forward to kiss his cheek, saying, "Go and don't worry, I will do my best to ensure your friends' safety."

Crowdal nodded and left the building, feeling numb and broken. Sid was taken by the Black Robe, Melinda was badly injured, Glaub was likely dead, and more than five hundred Trith had perished. A part of him felt dead inside and a blackness filled his heart as he made his way to the Council chamber. The blood pumped quickly through him and he clenched his jaw tightly as he thought of the Black Robe and his black-skinned woman.

For the first time, he welcomed the rage that boiled inside of him.

He welcomed his heritage.

He was a Trith.

Chapter 60

In the deepest recesses of his consciousness, a spark flared to life, the barest glint of light and heat that indicated self. The spark flickered weakly, seeming to fade and waver on the edge of nothingness. Then it stabilized and expanded slightly, pulsing in time to something As it did, it grew larger and gave off real heat.

Heat that filled him.

Him.

The flame spread and glowed brighter and with it came pain – pain like nothing he had ever felt, but he embraced it, for if there was pain, there was also life. The pain pointed him to an area of blackness that sucked at his life force, pulling it into a swirling emptiness he knew would lead to ultimate nothingness.

He floated, unsure what he needed to do, or even who he was.

He drifted toward the swirling vortex of nothingness and in a panic he felt the tactile presence of something deep within and instinctively grasped at it. As he touched it, it solidified into a number. He pulled it close and realized it was real, that he could move it, touch it, feel it.

Number.

Numbers.

His Numbers.

Full consciousness slammed into him, hurting him, but he laughed and cried as he remembered his name.

Glaub.

He was Glaub, and he was mortally wounded.

Glaub reached for the Black Numbers that always existed inside of him and they were there for him. He pulled them and they responded to his touch instantly. He looked at the swirling blackness of the vortex and created an equation of Black Numbers that was the antithesis of the nothingness and flung it into the vortex. The equation attached to the swirling walls and where it did, the swirling nothingness stopped so suddenly that the rest of the vortex backed up and overflowed into space. The equation he attached to it began to devour what was left of the vortex until there was not enough left to sustain the structure and it imploded with a simple swish.

The threat of death was gone, but the pain still radiated out and filled him.

He reached out with his mind and examined the damage to his body, seeing it seemed to be localized in his back, spine, and stomach. He created equations of such complexity that even he struggled to proof them. He concentrated with singular purpose until he knew they were correct, then attached the equations to his broken body one at a time and in the proper order. How long it took, he had no way of knowing, but as he worked, the pain lessened.

Then he was finished.

Glaub opened his eyes to see the strange man named Drax kneeling by his side. Moving his eyes to the other side, he saw the malformed Trith named Calix, and when they made eye contact, Calix tried to smile, and while his mouth was incapable of smiling, his one good eye twinkled with intelligence.

Drax wiped a cool damp piece of cloth against Glaub's forehead and said, "You are seriously injured. Lie still."

Glaub sent his thoughts into his body to ensure he had healed every piece of damaged tissue, then smiled and struggled to a sitting position.

Drax started to place a hand against Glaub's chest to hold him down, but he stopped in astonishment. "Your spine was severed and your lung was deflated and shredded. You should not be able to move, much less be alive."

Glaub folded his legs underneath him and carefully stretched his back. It cracked loudly and he felt some pain, but the spine had settled into its place, whole and strong. He looked at Drax and grimaced as he said, "Now that hurt."

Calix made a series of sounds and Drax nodded before turning to Glaub, saying, "He says he sees no damage inside of you anymore."

"He is right. I have the ability to heal myself, although I must confess: I almost lost the battle this time. The nothingness had a hold on me for the first time in my life and I was barely able to push it away." He looked around and saw Melinda lying under a bear pelt not far away. "Is she alright?"

Drax glanced over at her with worry in his eyes. "I do not know. Gee has done all she can for her. Whether she will make it through is unknown."

Glaub closed his eyes and sent his thoughts into Melinda's body and was momentarily aghast at the amount of damage inside of her, amazed she was still alive. He was drawn to the stomach wound and realized she would not survive from it even though the woman named Gee had done amazingly complex work to repair it. Her lung was torn, and the damage was just too great for normal medicine to repair. He examined the variables of the wound and placed them into a set of mathematical equations that interconnected. He double-checked them then lowered the set into the wound. The equations folded into the lung and surrounding flesh, tendrils of Numbers and variables worming their way into the deepest nerves and fibers of the wound until Glaub was ready and activated the set of equations as one. Heat flared out and the sounds of flesh knitting together filled the air for long moments until the final layer of skin folded down and sealed itself. As it did, Melinda's heartbeat slowed down and her breathing became smoother.

Glaub slumped in exhaustion. Even for him, such an expenditure of energy took a lot out of him, especially after he had just returned from certain death himself. He pushed the fatigue away and sent his Numbers into her cheek wounds, which were thankfully less severe and easier to repair. By the time he finished, he lay back and closed his eyes with a smile. "Melinda will be alright. But now, I must sleep."

* * *

Crowdal and Rielissa entered the building where his friends were and Crowdal immediately strode to Melinda's side, hoping she was still alive but fearing the truth. The young Zranh named Eithes sat by her side, holding her hand. As he knelt and touched Melinda's forehead, he could tell that, miraculously, she breathed easily and her cheeks were rosy and looked healthy where there had been deep gashes.

Drax came over and knelt by him and before Crowdal could ask, Drax said, "Glaub healed her. She will make a full recovery."

Crowdal released a breath he hadn't even realized he had been holding and a sob of joy escaped him as he leaned down to kiss her cheek. He looked up through teary eyes and asked, "How is Glaub?"

Drax glanced over at his sleeping form and said, "He is going to be alright, too. I have never seen so much power in my whole life, not even in Baldrick. Glaub was as close to death as one can get before passing into the afterworld, yet he had the strength to come back from the edge of death and heal himself completely."

Crowdal looked over at Glaub. "Can we trust a man with that much power?"

Drax was silent for a long time, then said, "Yes, I believe we can."

Crowdal felt ready to collapse from his own exhaustion, so he stood and yawned before thanking Drax. He strode a few paces away to stand by Rielissa and called everyone over to join him.

Writhgarth, Tulman, Nik, The Hunters of Reilen, Drax and Calix, and even the Zranh girl, Eithes, approached.

Writhgarth looked sadly at Crowdal and Rielissa and said, "I am sorry to hear of the horrific losses your people suffered."

Crowdal pushed hair from his face and said, "Thank you, Writhgarth. It was the worst attack in the history of the Trith Nation. We lost one thousand and seventeen Trith last night, including Rielissa's brother Juldall and four of the Council members. But we are Trith and we will recover. The events here will never be forgotten."

Writhgarth spat into a small ceramic cup. "And we lost Sid to the Black Robe."

Crowdal ground his jaws together and nodded. "That brings me to why I called you over." He looked at each of them and hardened his voice, "We are going to get Sid back, and we are going to kill that Black Robe son of a bitch once and for all."

Epilogue

In the deepest part of the Muldragg forest, far from the Trith Circle and the stinking remains of the decimated armies, the Korpor stopped, leaning on a nearby tree to get its breath. It had run through the night after barely escaping from the bloody battles with its life.

The Korpor snarled as it thought of the Black Robe's final treachery. He had left the Korpor to its fate as it was chased out of the Circle by the Trith, chortling at the Korpor when it had contacted him asking for extraction.

It could clearly remember the Black Robe speaking in its mind, his voice dripping with contempt, "*I am sure you have the ability to escape, my pet. Unless you are that useless, in which case, goodbye and good riddance.*"

The Korpor raked its claws across the tree trunk, gouging deeply into it as it snarled again with fury.

The Black Robe had captured the Aleph Null and the Korpor was no longer of any use to him. Straightening its shoulders, the Korpor raised its face and roared into the sky, lowering its head as it ran out of breath.

It narrowed its eyes and a vicious smile spread across its face.

So be it.

The Korpor would take back the Aleph Null.

Then it would tear apart the Black Robe and eat his heart.

So absorbed in its plans for revenge, the Korpor didn't notice the eight Myrss perfectly camouflaged in the brush not far away. They remained silent as the Korpor turned and made its way deeper into the forest.

Then, as one, they started following the Korpor.

THE END

Thank you for reading
Broken Numbers: The Aleph Null Chronicles: Book Three.

If you purchased this book from a website, I would greatly appreciate an honest review. Reviews are one of best ways you can help an author.

Look for the conclusion to the Aleph Null Chronicles in
Beyond Numbers: The Aleph Null Chronicles: Book Four.

About the Author

Dean Frank Lappi was born in Virginia, Minnesota in 1968, a place that is part of the well-known Iron Range, where most of the iron ore in the USA is found.

In 1996 he graduated with a Master of Arts degree in English and has worked in a number of industries since then as an Information Developer and Web Content Manager.

He is married to the talented Erica Anderson, his amazing Editor and Muse.

Dean is very active on **Twitter** (@DeanLappi)
and
Facebook (https://www.facebook.com/author.dean.lappi)

www.ingramcontent.com/pod-product-compliance
Lightning Source LLC
Chambersburg PA
CBHW030648260626
47157CB00007B/2540